NIGHT BIRD CALLING

NIGHT BIRD CALLING

CATHY GOHLKE

THORNDIKE PRESS
A part of Gale, a Cengage Company

Copyright © 2020 by Cathy Gohlke.
Scripture quotations are taken from the *Holy Bible,* King James Version.
Thorndike Press, a part of Gale, a Cengage Company.

Thorndike Press® Large Print Christian Romance.
The text of this Large Print edition is unabridged.
Other aspects of the book may vary from the original edition.
Set in 16 pt. Plantin.

LIBRARY OF CONGRESS CIP DATA ON FILE.
CATALOGUING IN PUBLICATION FOR THIS BOOK
IS AVAILABLE FROM THE LIBRARY OF CONGRESS.

ISBN-13: 979-8-8857-8356-9 (hardcover alk. paper)

Published in 2022 by arrangement with Tyndale House Publishers, Inc.

Printed in Mexico
Print Number : 1   Print Year : 2023

For Jesse Stephen Gardiner
Whose name aptly means
Gift and Crown
You are joy, adventure, and discovery
to me, Beloved Grandson
All my love, forever

ACKNOWLEDGMENTS

Night Bird Calling is a book that has long lived in my heart. It could not have been written without the generosity, help, and insights of others.

My deepest gratitude to

My brother, Dan Lounsbury, who introduced me to the names "No Creek" and "Saints Delight," bestowed upon me North Carolina histories of Wilkes and Surry Counties — the early homes of our maternal grandparents — and supplied me with numerous histories, articles, and links to obscure details of North Carolina history from the mountains to the Outer Banks. Thank you for your early read and insights into this manuscript. I love that we share a love for all things quirky and Southern. Special thanks to Dan and his dear wife, Randi, who allowed me to spend long and lovely writing days on their porch and for keeping me supplied with sweet tea and good fellowship.

Those dear ones, some who've gone before

7

and some who still walk with me, who helped me through a horrific time in my own life — a time that was not wasted, but that helped make me who I am and that I pray God uses through the pages of this book to bless others in need with the help He has given me.

Oswald and Biddy (born Gertrude Hobbs) Chambers. Biddy's shorthand transcription and publication of her late husband's talks and writings have impacted the world as one of the most widely read devotionals in the Christian world for over eighty years — long after his (and now her) death. Excerpts from daily devotions found in Chambers's *My Utmost for His Highest* help make this story a compass to the heart of our Lord. Even now, all these years after they were written, Chambers's words daily convict and inspire me.

Biographies of Oswald and Biddy were so helpful in better understanding their lives, their timelines, and their inspiring commitment to Christ. Special thanks to Michelle Ule, author of *Mrs. Oswald Chambers,* and to David McCasland, author of *Oswald Chambers: Abandoned to God,* for their detailed writings.

Natasha Kern, dear friend, sister in Christ, and agent extraordinaire, who always knows that there is more to the story than I can begin to explain, and for encouraging me on that writing journey of discovery.

Stephanie Broene and Sarah Rische, amazing Tyndale editors. I love that each of you sees so clearly the holes in my stories that I do not see and helps me find a way to bring to the page all that is in my heart. Yours is a gift — rare and sweet.

To all of my Tyndale team — Elizabeth Jackson (acquisitions editor), Andrea Garcia (marketing manager), Lindsey Bergsma (designer), Katie Dodillet — thank you for all you do to bring my stories to readers. You bless me each and every day.

Robert Whitlow, wonderful author and attorney-at-law, for generously helping me understand the legal ramifications of trusts and the importance of the recording of deeds, and for brainstorming possibilities to escape "deep legal waters" in this work of fiction. I'm so grateful. Any misunderstandings or mistakes are mine.

My dear mother, Bernice Lemons, who gave me insights and family stories from the South that spanned years before and during WWII. Some of those memories are fictionalized in this book.

Etta Idol, dear friend of my mother's and of mine, who shared rich memories of growing up in Wilkes County, North Carolina. Parts of Garden's Gate were inspired by your lovely childhood home.

Terri Gillespie, dear and wise friend, amazing author, and the one I always go to with questions of Jewish life and culture. We have walked many literary miles together, including the pages of this book. Thank you for your early read and thoughtful insights.

Carrie Turansky, wonderful author, whose precious friendship and encouragement never wavers. You've shown me so much of the love of Christ. I hope I've shared some of that in this book. Thank you for your early read and insights for this manuscript.

Stephanie Green, dear and brilliant friend, for your early read of this manuscript and for giving me your insights into the times and people of this story. I value your thoughts and sisterhood in Christ.

Vanessa Miller Pierce, generous and best-selling author, for your early read of this manuscript and wise insights. Thank you for opening my eyes to things I hadn't seen.

My family — husband, son, daughter and son-in-law, grandchildren, sister, brothers, nieces and nephews, all the greats and all those we claim by marriage — life is more precious because of you. Thank you for praying for my writing and for all your encouragement.

In appreciation and memory of my maternal grandparents, whose lives, stories, and times pepper the pages of this book. You gave me so much, and though you no longer walk this earth, you continue to inspire me by your love and examples through precious memories.

I will always appreciate the words of my uncle Wilbur Goforth, who helped me see that service for the Lord and His people happens both inside and outside the church. When torn between two career paths for the second half of my life's journey, he reminded me that a sure way to know I am working in the will of God is to ask, "Do I have joy? Is this yoke easy? Is this burden light?" The answer is yes — writing gives me great joy. This yoke fits securely but does not chafe. This burden is true but shines as light in my heart!

Beyond all measure I thank my heavenly Father and Lord Jesus Christ for gifts of hope, life, love, family, and unmerited salvation. Life is precious because of Your love and constant, tender care. Life is joyful in Your presence. May this book become an instrument of hope and healing that points only to You, for You are the hope we crave, and You are the healing and salvation we so desperately need.

CHAPTER ONE

Philadelphia, Pennsylvania
May 1941

My mother was a beautiful woman, a magnificent and generous woman who loved music and poetry and literature and gardens. She loved to dance, though she only ever did so in the privacy of her room, with me. Her smile, though rare in her last months, brightened the sun. She was a devoted wife and loving mother, however ill-used by her husband. If anyone says differently, they're a liar or misled by my father.

Mama loved lilacs and roses and the call of the whip-poor-will to keep her company in the dead of night — a memory she treasured from her childhood. She once told me that God in His heaven must think we mortals cannot sustain the wonder of such heady fragrance for long; that's why lilacs bloom only in spring and for so short a time. It's the reason roses must have two seasons to spread their blessed gifts. It's why whip-poor-wills

13

don't sing all year long in the North Carolina mountain air.

The fragrance of those flowers filled her room as she squeezed my hand for the last time and closed her eyes.

I didn't want her to go, and yet begging her to stay would have been selfish. At long last she had a chance to be free. Of course she should take it.

Mama left me with two directives: One, to take care of myself, no matter the cost to my reputation. Two, when I found myself brave enough, I was to hand deliver a ruby ring to her aunt Hyacinth in No Creek, North Carolina — a ruby ring that Mama said she'd taken when she ran off to marry my father. She didn't explain why she'd taken the ring or what she meant by taking care of myself heedless of my reputation, but she made me swear to do both and to never tell my father or my husband. I swore, for she was dying, though I had no idea how I'd ever fulfill such vows.

Gerald no more let me out of his sight than my father had allowed my mother from his.

I'd sewn the ring and Grandaunt Hyacinth's address into the lining of my purse so I'd have them with me always and out of my husband's sight. Gerald was known to rifle through my closet and chest of drawers in search of my diary or some stray clue to my faithlessness, suspicious of my every move as

14

he was. I never gave him cause, but his constant surveillance and recriminations made me feel as if I'd done something soiled and dirty, and that made me jumpy. How soiled and dirty can a woman get going to the market or the library or to church?

It was much the way Mama had lived and I'd been raised, only I'd truly believed that marriage to Gerald, a man ten years my senior who'd seemed so godly and smitten with me, might be different. He might love me, might be glad to share a new life. Seven years had taught me otherwise. Year-round, no matter the heat of summer, I wore long sleeves to cover the evidence of my husband's displeasure and disappointment — the results of his bursts of anger, which were inevitably my fault.

At least now Mama was free of my father and free of worry for me. The temptation to join such freedom was compelling, like the feeling you get when standing too close to the ledge of a high building or leaning beyond a sharp cliff that hangs over the sea. It pulls and pulls. One small step is all it would take. The thing that held me back was not fear of death or even eternity in my condemned state, but fear that I might not be successful, and then I would be forever at Gerald's mercy, as Mama had been at the mercy of my father — mercy, where there is none.

■ ■ ■ ■

Dusk had fallen by the time I'd hung the last dripping tea towel over the rod to dry. Out the church kitchen window I saw that the parking lot sat empty, except for the five elders' cars that stood as soldiers in a row.

At least Gerald wasn't waiting on me.

I wrapped the last slice of Sarah's applesauce cake — her parting gift for Mama's funeral luncheon, made the morning Mama passed.

I wasn't hungry — couldn't eat — but was tempted to light the stove and make a cup of tea, to sit down and savor Sarah's last bit of cake alone in the dark, to remember her and hope she thought of me. *Sarah, how I miss you now!*

Sarah was Mama's longtime housemaid, there before I was born, and the only real friend my father had allowed her. It was as if he didn't see her because she was colored, as if he couldn't imagine Sarah would have a thought or a voice or influence Mama's life in any way. Sarah endured more of my father's tirades than any woman should, all for the sake of loving and caring for Mama to the bitter end.

But the day Mama breathed her last, Sarah vowed she'd not live another night under the same roof with "that man." She'd baked the

16

cake, packed her bag, and left to buy a bus ticket to join her son in Chicago, even before they carried Mama's body out the door.

Her leaving had been a jolt nearly as hard as Mama's death, like earth shifting beneath my feet with nothing but air to grab hold of. Sarah'd been my friend, too — confidante and comfort to me all my growing-up years. Ever present in my parents' kitchen, caring and tender, her warm brown arms held me through crisis after crisis. She'd been a tower of refuge and strength. I wondered what we'd given her. I hoped it was something.

Both women gone in a day. I had to find a way to get on.

I tucked the wrapped cake in my purse and snapped it shut.

Funeral luncheons at our church lasted for hours and always took their toll on emotions stretched taut, on toes and arches crammed into Sunday heels, but at last I was done. As long as I'd thought of it as *a* funeral luncheon and not *my mother's* funeral luncheon, I could keep my frozen smile in place, set one foot in front of the other as a good elder's wife should.

Deliberately, I untied my apron and hung it on the hook in the church pantry, flicked off the light switch, and locked the kitchen door. Somehow, those little finalities and the enormity of the dark and empty community room opened the floodgates I'd kept shut. I

17

closed my eyes, leaned against the locked door, and let the tears course over my cheeks. There was no one to hear or see.

Except for the elders' meeting going on upstairs, the church was deserted. Gerald would expect me to wait for him in the car. But it was cold and I had no key to start the engine or heater. Neither Gerald nor my father believed in women driving automobiles, so why would I need a key?

The thought of going home with Gerald after this horrendous day made my stomach swell into my throat. There'd be no end of ridicule about the tears I'd choked back during the service. I could hear him now: *"We're not to sorrow as others who have no hope. Your lack of faith and self-control sets a poor example. The wife of an elder should mark a standard, behave above reproach."*

If only the elders' meeting could go on long and distract him. They were discussing the church's position in light of Great Britain's pleas to our government for help in its fight against Germany. *Should the church publicly state its disapproval of America providing Britain with implements of war? Should the women of the church be allowed to contribute to the "Bundles for Britain" — contributions of clothing, knit items, medical supplies, staples and cash for the hospitals and families that had been bombed out? Would that be helping the*

18

poor or risk appearing that the church approved of war efforts and therefore of war? Gerald held strong views that as followers of Christ, we were not to enter into the activities of the world, regardless of the war's moral implications or the needs of others. If the meeting didn't go according to his liking, there would be the devil to pay at home.

Just a moment in a quiet place. Alone. That was all I wanted. *The sanctuary.* Not that I believed God would listen if I prayed there or anywhere. I loved Him, longed for Him to love me, but knew that He could not. I was too sinful, beyond loving. That message came repeatedly through Gerald's and Father's disapproval. But just now, for only a moment to be quiet, to be still and alone — surely God would grant me that. I climbed the stairs and slipped into the dusky sanctuary, taking a seat halfway up the aisle nearest a window.

I lay down on the pew, closed my eyes, and pulled my feet into a fetal curl. Just for a moment.

The steady drone of voices coming from the back of the church woke me — that, and the light that poured from the vestibule into the darkened sanctuary. I squinted, was about to sit up, when I recognized the two voices. I lay back down, in the shadows.

"God's been merciful to free you, Brother Shepherd." Gerald's smirk came through loud and clear.

"Marriage is for life. I endured till death parted us." Was that a smile in my father's voice?

"And now it's done."

"Yes," Father sighed, "now it's done. And life goes on."

"Cleanly, I suppose. You're lucky."

"Blessed."

"And your debts?" Gerald asked. "You'll inherit Rosemary's property."

"Apparently not. At least not what I'd imagined and she'd led me to believe." I heard my father's exasperation. "It was not in Rosemary's name as we'd both supposed."

"You're sure?"

"I spoke with her aunt, though I'll have someone investigate to make certain."

"Well, now. That is a disappointment. It would have been a nice reward, paid those embarrassing debts."

"You needn't concern yourself. There are other means."

"Still, based on what I saw as a member of the family, I can't help but wonder if more than God helped Rosemary's end along."

"That's scandalous. Don't repeat it."

"I wouldn't want to, of course. . . ." My husband hesitated. "But I might need incentive." There was a long moment of silence while his words sank in.

"What do you want, Gerald?"

"I don't need money. Nothing so coarse." Gerald waited another long moment. "The thing is, your daughter's not . . . stable. I believe you'll agree."

"Lilliana's emotional like her mother."

"An emotionally unstable young woman in my estimation. She's also physically healthy and liable to live a long while."

"As I said, marriage is for life. The elders would never agree to divorce, if that's what you're getting at."

"Yes, marriage is for life. Unless . . . it's not." My husband's measured words sent chills up my spine.

"The church permits one cause for divorce. You have no case."

"Not adultery . . . but instability, leading to insanity, is cause for divorce by Pennsylvania law."

"Not by the laws of God or the church."

"Not unless the insanity might lead to adultery or justifiably strong suspicion of adultery."

"You're reaching."

"I need witnesses. It would be best to have her institutionalized — avoid scandal and guarantee me appropriate sympathy. The kind of sympathy I saw exhibited for you today."

"You'll never find 'witnesses' to such a lie. Lilliana's well-thought-of, well-liked. And she's already gone to the police about your . . . heavy hand. No one would believe it."

"That was unfortunate and might be a stumbling block, unless someone else brings the allegation of her instability and the suspicion of promiscuity. Someone who's known her a long time. Someone respected in the community who can testify in court and intimate the possibility of more than indiscreet behavior."

I heard the pew creak as my father sank into it. "She's my daughter. You can't be serious."

"Never more. I have friends in high places who are willing to be influenced for you or against."

"This is blackmail. You can't force me, and you can't prove anything. I may have been firm with Rosemary — she tried my patience — but I didn't kill her."

"Reputations are easier to ruin than incarcerations are to achieve, I grant. You value your eldership, your standing in the church and in the community. I imagine you're counting on both in plotting your future. I've noticed your roving eye."

"Pastor Harding severely reprimanded Lilliana for airing your dirty laundry before unbelievers. That's precisely what you'd be doing based on lies."

"I should never have married a child."

"She'd turned sixteen when the agreement

was made. Seventeen when you married. That may be child enough, but you wanted her then and I agreed. You can't plead that she's a child now."

"I won't need to, not if I produce witnesses to testify against her."

"There's another woman. Is that it?"

Gerald hesitated. "The point is, I'm still a young enough man and I don't want to wait until your daughter dies an old woman to get on with my life, any more than you wanted to wait for Rosemary's demise. I need the church's blessing to remarry. Anything less is untenable."

A minute passed. No more. "Let me think about it . . . if there is a way to proceed."

"Lilliana's grief for her mother weighs her down unnaturally. Now is convenient — and timely. Don't wait too long."

Tense and barely breathing, I willed my father to take up for me, say how ludicrous, how unfair this scheme was, but there was no more. Finally footsteps echoed down the aisle and through the doorway. The vestibule light disappeared, and the outer church door closed. The engines of two cars started; then came the sound of gravel spewing as they pulled from the parking lot.

I lay in the hard pew a long time, fearing to get up and find a way home and fearing not to.

■ ■ ■ ■

When at last I walked out of the church and into the empty parking lot, I stood beneath a streetlamp. Barely shielded by shrubbery, I counted the money in my purse. One dollar and fifty-eight cents left over from the purchase of groceries. Eighty dollars given into my keeping that day by a well-to-do parishioner as a donation toward my mother's funeral — which I was instructed to give to my father. I'd not been entrusted with so much money in my life — not in my father's house and certainly not in my husband's.

It was pitch-black beyond the streetlamp — a mile and a half to Gerald and home. But I dared not go home. There was no way to pretend I hadn't heard; one look at my face and Gerald would know that I'd discovered his plans. What he might do, I could imagine.

I couldn't take sanctuary in my father's house or in the house of any one of the church members. It wouldn't be fair to draw anyone else into the mess of my marriage — the stink of my "dirty laundry" — and whom dared I trust? Who wouldn't be afraid of the disapproval or discipline of the church elders or even of their own husbands?

When I'd run to my father for help four months after I'd married, he'd shaken his head and expressed disappointment in me.

"Perfect love casts out fear, Lilliana. Your fear of Gerald proves that you lack love for him — and worse, for God. God is love, and without love, without forgiveness in your heart, you cannot hope your Father in heaven will forgive you."

The time Gerald had beaten me black-and-blue and I'd run to the police, they'd told me, "All men knock their wives around a little from time to time. Don't worry. Go home. He'll settle down." My husband had threatened to kill me if I ever told another soul about his outbursts — kill me and then himself.

No, I couldn't go home.

In the opposite direction lay the center of the city and the Philadelphia train station. Eighty dollars. I wondered how far it could send me.

There was only one person, other than Sarah, whom my mother had trusted with the secret shame of her marriage — the year I was five and we ran away together. I fingered the lining of my purse and the shape of Grandaunt Hyacinth's ruby ring . . . a sort of secret friend, a talisman of comfort. Thinking of it so had seemed silly and perhaps childish at the time of my mother's directive — as if I'd ever have an opportunity to deliver it. Now it was a lifeline . . . I hoped.

CHAPTER TWO

No Creek, North Carolina

Eleven-year-old Celia Percy tore a muslin square from her petticoat. Her mama would be fit to be tied at such loss and utter destruction, but how else was she to pretend she had a pocket-handkerchief like the girls in Edith Nesbit's book, *The Railway Children*? She needed to make sure that the owner of the Southern Railway, who surely rode the train to its end each night, glimpsed her waving madly as the whistle pierced its way up the mountain — although not so much that he stop the train, at least not yet. Not until the day she could truly save the train and every passenger from sure and certain death. Then, and only then, could she beg him for help to free her daddy from jail, just as Roberta had begged the railway owner for help for her own dear father. Tonight was practice.

Celia perched herself at the far end of the No Creek platform, then decided it might be best to wave from farther up the hill since she didn't really want the train to stop. She wasn't quite sure she wished her daddy returned home just yet. Even with the shame of it all, life was a sight easier with him gone, though she daren't say that to her mama. Celia wished, more than anything, that she could leave her life and step into a story — a new world, just for a time.

It was dusk, and Celia knew the chances of anyone seeing her ran slim to none, which suited her just fine for this practice race. She waited until the train crested the hill before stretching her arm to the sky and waving with all her might. She expected the train to zoom on by; then she'd run like the wind, chasing it, just like in the book. Hardly anybody got on or off in No Creek, and if there was no one with a ticket and no one standing on the platform, the train never bothered to slow.

So she waved her heart right through her arm and out the pocket-handkerchief. A woman pressed her face against the glass and peered out the train window toward her. Tentatively, the woman raised her hand in return, much to Celia's surprise.

The train slowed, spluttering and choking. Celia stopped waving. Realizing she might be the cause of the slowing train, she began waving both arms, running full tilt down the hill and screaming, "Go on! Don't stop! I didn't mean it!"

The train stopped dead and a passenger,

helped by a porter, stepped down the stairs, right onto the platform — the young woman who'd returned Celia's wave.

The woman must not realize she was in No Creek. This was something Celia could do to help. "You don't mean to get off here, lady!" she yelled. "You want to get back on the train — now! Quick! Go on!" Celia raced on, fearful that the train would pull away before the woman realized her mistake.

The woman evidently heard her and glanced, worriedly, back toward the train. Celia reached the far end of the platform just as the conductor hopped aboard.

"No, wait!" Celia panted, still running, still waving the woman onto the train and begging the train to hold. But neither happened. By the time Celia, doubled over with a stitch in her side, reached the woman, the train door had closed. The engine gave a lurch and pulled away. "This is No Creek, ma'am! You don't mean to get off here!"

"What's the matter with No Creek?"

"Nothin's wrong with No Creek!" Celia huffed indignantly, still unable to catch her breath.

"Then why mustn't I come here?" The woman tilted and pulled back her head. She had skin like cream. Her hair, wound up in a loose knot, was the color of chestnuts full ripe, and her eyes the color of the Blue Ridge come dark — just the skin and eyes Celia had always dreamed of having. But her own pale skin freckled mightily in the sun and she couldn't deny the brown eyes and silk brown hair of her family.

Celia stopped short. She recognized that quizzical lift of one eyebrow. Of course. Why hadn't she thought of this before? "You're Miz Hyacinth's guest, ain't you?"

"Aren't you," the woman responded as if correcting grammar came automatically with speech.

"Yes, you are." Celia was sure of it. Only a teacher or a teacher's kin would talk like that to a total stranger.

"How did you know?"

Celia couldn't believe the woman was serious. As if anyone new came to No Creek. As if anyone passing through might care about Celia's grammar or dress like city folk — other than a woman of Miz Hyacinth's caliber. "Mama said to keep an eye out for you. Miz Hyacinth told her she expects you any day."

"She did? She's expecting me?" The woman sounded relieved, then alarmed, all in one breath — a curious thing and one Celia would have to think on later. The woman seemed to catch herself and extended her gloved hand. "I'm . . . pleased to meet you."

Celia remembered her manners and extended her own hand. "Pleased to meet you, ma'am. I'm Celia Percy, only daughter of

Gladys and Fillmore Percy, sister to Chester."

The woman smiled, pressing her lips together. Celia nodded, thinking "pleased to meet you" was no kind of name, and why did the woman not say?

Celia's mama had told her that Miz Hyacinth's own mama had been Miz Rose and that her sister had been Miz Camellia. Miz Camellia's daughter, the niece Miz Hyacinth had raised and who'd run off, was Rosemary. A flower or flowerlike name, a name that rang with music, was only fitting for the Belvidere women. Celia loved words and had been guessing all afternoon what this new person's name might be, sure and certain that if she was kin, she, too, would have a flower name. And now, not to know after meeting her — well, that was exasperating. But her mother had told her not to ask questions if she met Miz Hyacinth's guest.

Celia's breath came a bit steadier. She was glad to be the welcoming committee for such an important person. The lady looked suddenly pale as a ghost but like she'd stepped out of a New York magazine, dark tweed suit with black hat and gloves and all — only tired and rumpled from traveling.

"Well, I'm glad to meet you, too, Celia Percy. How do you know Hyacinth Belvidere?"

"Everybody in two counties knows Miz

Hyacinth."

"Oh. Who were you waving to just now?"

"The owner of the railway line."

"He was on the train? I didn't see him. I thought I was one of the last ones off."

"Most likely. Not many stops left before the train finishes up in North Wilkesboro." The woman blinked as if she didn't quite understand, but Celia, knowing time was of the essence, rushed on. "Dark falls fast and when it does, it's pitch-black here. You want to get on up to Miz Hyacinth's. Not much moon tonight."

"Yes, thank you. It's been so long since I was here, I'm not sure I know my way. Could you direct me?"

"Sure! It's on my way home." It wasn't, but if they hurried, Celia hoped snooty Janice Richards might see them pass by from her front window, or Ida Mae, postmistress and proprietress of the general store, might not have locked up. She'd see and tell. Either would get the word out in a flash and raise Celia's status in the community watch. "Don't you have a bag? A trunk? Miz Hyacinth figured you'd stay awhile."

"No, I — I didn't bring my things. Perhaps later." The woman sounded uncertain.

There was something curious about that but pleasing. Celia liked to travel light through life, too. Carrying stories in the head didn't take much luggage but they were powerful company.

"I don't want to frighten her, coming in so late in the dark."

"She'll never know."

"You said she was expecting me." The woman's anxiety pricked Celia.

"She is." Celia walked ahead, trusting her to follow. "But dark is dark."

The lady didn't appear to understand that either, but Celia knew they'd best get on with it. "If the road gets wiggly in those high-heeled shoes, you can take them off. Nobody'll see now."

Halfway up the dirt road the woman asked, "Do you know the rail line owner, that you were waving to him?"

"Never met him." Celia wasn't certain she wanted to confide in a stranger. But the woman was, after all, kin or friend to Miz Hyacinth, and Miz Hyacinth was true as blue. "I was practicing, you see, building my reputation." She could feel the woman's stare in the gloaming. "You ever read *The Railway Children*?"

"By Edith Nesbit — yes, of course!" The woman's voice brightened.

Celia drew a breath. Here was someone who loved books, just like Miz Hyacinth, just like Celia herself; she could hear it in the lift of the woman's voice. *A kindred spirit, surely.* "Remember how the kids waved every day to the train — and the man, the rich man who owned the rail line, waved back?"

"I do."

"If they hadn't done that, they'd never have made acquaintance of such an important person, and if they hadn't done *that*, he never would have gotten to know them before they saved the train. And if they hadn't saved the train and all those people on it from sure and certain death, then he wouldn't have been forever grateful and helped to get their daddy, innocent as a spring colt, out of prison."

"I'm sorry. I don't understand the connection."

"It's plain as day." Celia didn't mean to be impertinent, but surely the woman understood English. "A person's got to start somewhere."

"Are you saying that your father is in prison?"

"I am," Celia said matter-of-factly, glad that was now out in the open. She hated the truth of it, but the need to confess her family shame worried her at every turn. She figured it best to get it out and over with first thing. Being the daughter of a convict had its drawbacks.

"So you hope that the railway owner will help to prove his innocence and have him exonerated?"

"I'm not exactly sure. I mean, I want him to spring Daddy — I do — but maybe not just yet. Maybe let him set there in the

33

jailhouse long enough to think things through. I reckon he ain't entirely innocent," Celia conceded. "He was caught running 'shine into Winston-Salem."

"Your father makes moonshine?"

"Not 'makes it.' Runs it in his horse and wagon for them that do — and was never caught, not once, until he borrowed Cletus Everett's new car and sped like a demon with his tail on fire clear into the next county. He was half-lit and never drove a car so far or so fast before. Made himself noticed, so the sheriff stopped him. Took our horse and wagon to pay part of the fine. The rest comes out in jail time, I reckon." Celia sighed. "It's not so romantic to be doing time for something wicked you *did* do as for something you never did — like in the book. But knowing the line owner might come in handy one day, just the same."

"Just the same." The woman repeated the words, though Celia wasn't sure she sounded entirely sympathetic.

CHAPTER THREE

By the time we neared Garden's Gate, Grand-aunt Hyacinth's home, the moon, slim as it was, had climbed over treetops and hillsides, a silver crescent giving little light to our path. Still, I imagined the picket-fenced garden, fragrant with lilacs even in the night air, and the large and rambling house — white with four three-story columns across the front porch. It was the grandest house in No Creek — the only grand house, or had been when I was a child.

Someplace off to my left, a night bird called a song I remembered from long ago, stirring memories of Mama and her love of whip-poor-wills in late spring on the mountain. They reminded her of something — something I couldn't quite remember in the moment. The night sky overhead, splattered with a million stars, stole my breath. I wondered if Mama knew I was here, if she smiled down on me for doing her bidding, or if she sympathized with my uncertainty.

35

I remembered asking her once why the town was called No Creek — a funny name for any town. I could still hear her delighted laugh and lapse into her Southern drawl, the one my father had so tried to rid her of:

"Darlin', don't you know — big creeks, little creeks, fast creeks, slow creeks run like a widow's tears through the foothills of western North Carolina. Peppered along each of those creeks are white clapboard churches named for the creeks by which they reside, the perfect place for summer baptisms: Fleetwood Creek Church, Spring Creek Baptist Church, Harmony Creek Church, Watauga Creek Church, even Lost Creek Baptist Church. Shady Grove Baptist has no creek. One of our great-great-great Belvideres who founded the town settled there purely for the view of the mountain and dug a well, then built a church on down the road in that wonderful shady grove. Ever after they've gone over the hill to the nearest lake for baptisms."

"Mama," I whispered. "I miss you so."

We walked slower now. I couldn't see anything but the faintest silhouettes, could only trust that Celia Percy knew the way to the front door. A gate swung open on creaking hinges. The familiar shadowed outline of the great house loomed comfortingly ahead, but not a light shone through door or window. It couldn't be past eight o'clock.

"Watch the step — up one, two. . . . Here's the porch," Celia whispered.

"It's so dark. Do you think she's home?" *Where will I go if she's not here?*

"Oh, she's home. Mama brought her supper by early on. Miz Hyacinth don't need the light, so she don't waste it. Sits mostly in the dark. Likely she's gone on to bed."

Why would she sit in the dark? Has she grown eccentric in her old age? She must be nearing seventy by now. My heart pounded. *Dare I just walk in and make myself at home?*

As if able to read my thoughts, Celia assured, "She'd want you to go on in and take your rest. You'll see her in the morning."

"I haven't even told her I was coming. I didn't know until — until yesterday."

"Must have been a presentment. Your room's big, near big as our cabin. Flowered wallpaper, and all to yourself. You don't have to share with nobody, if you can imagine such a thing. I hardly can."

"I don't understand —"

"She's been looking forward — had Mama come up here yesterday noon and clean her guest room special, top to bottom."

"She did?"

"I said so. Second door on the left, top of the stairs. Miz Hyacinth has electric — there's a switch inside the door — and indoor plumbing. You won't even need the outhouse." With that, Celia tripped down the steps. "See you tomorrow!" A moment later hinges on the gate creaked open again, and Celia was gone in the fading light — a pale and brown-eyed will-o'-the-wisp in golden-brown pixie cut.

"Thank you, Celia Percy!" I called softly, but there was no answer.

I stood, unnerved and undecided. Here at last — a place from which I'd carried precious childhood memories of time with Mama and the woman who'd loved us both, just as we were. But Father had found us, even then, way out here. *Will he think to look for me here now? Will he send Gerald?*

I shivered in the cool air that blew down the mountain, bringing me back to the moment. *There's nothing for it but to go forward. Whoever Aunt Hyacinth is now, I'll deal with tomorrow. It can't be worse than what I left.*

I tried the door. Unlocked — something no one in Philadelphia would think of doing. For better or for worse, I stepped through, flicked the light switch on the wall, and closed the door behind me.

Morning light swam through white organza curtains — curtains whose ruffles stood to bright attention as if they'd been starched and ironed only moments ago. I blinked and closed my eyes again, claiming my bearings in the large and sunny room, recapping the long and weary days before: Mama's slow decline and death, her funeral, Gerald and Father's conniving in the darkened church, hours of walking in the dark to the Philadelphia station and a night and a day of train travel, arriving to an apparently abandoned house — a house young Celia Percy vowed was not empty but waiting for me.

I hadn't tried any of the other doors in the upstairs hallway the night before, except the open bathroom. I hadn't explored the downstairs. I didn't want to pry — didn't think it right to traipse through Aunt Hyacinth's great house. It was enough and more that she'd expected me, planned and had someone prepare a room for me. I couldn't imagine how that was, or why, but I'd gratefully sunk into the freshly made bed. Just before my eyes closed, I'd wondered if I was actually the guest she was expecting or if there was someone else. I'd been too tired to entertain that thought long.

A floorboard creaked behind my head. I rolled over to see a bed pillow hovering scant inches above my face. I gasped, rolling in the opposite direction, off the bed and onto the floor. The pillow jumped and lunged toward the bed with force, its holder tumbling onto the mattress — a squat figure sprawled across pillows and bedclothes.

"Aunt Hyacinth?" I spluttered.

"Lilliana? Lilliana Grace? Is that you?" she mumbled into the pillow slip.

"Yes — yes, I'm here." I spoke from my crouch against the wall.

"Oh, child, I thought you were an intruder!"

"You were going to smother me?" My voice rose with each syllable. Still, I pulled myself up from the floor and tried to lift Aunt Hyacinth from the bed onto which she'd fallen.

"Oh, my dear," Aunt Hyacinth groaned as I righted her. "You simply can't be too careful — a woman living alone."

I don't think you and your pillow are good protection, never mind the unlocked front door!

"I'm sorry I frightened you, my dear. This is not the welcome I intended. I'm really very glad you've come."

"Thank you, Aunt Hyacinth." Though I felt little conviction in that moment. "I don't know how you knew I'd come, but I promise not to stay a moment longer than necessary."

"But you must. You must stay forever!"

I didn't know what to say to that, and Aunt Hyacinth wasn't really looking at me, after all.

"Well, now that you're here and we've settled that neither of us has ill intent —" Aunt Hyacinth spoke with a twinkle in her voice — "what do you say we get some breakfast?"

"That sounds wonderful." I hadn't eaten

anything but the slice of Sarah's applesauce cake since the funeral luncheon two days before. The rumbles in my stomach gave fair warning.

"Do you see my cane, my dear? By the door, perhaps? I may have left it there."

A long white stick leaned against the door-jamb. *She's blind. She can't see a thing.*

"Is it there?"

"Yes — yes, I'll get it." Celia's words came back to me — *"Dark is dark."* Had Mama known Aunt Hyacinth lost her sight? Were they in touch at all over the years? I wished I could ask Mama — so many things. I placed the cane into my grandaunt's hands.

"There, that's better. My old friend." Aunt Hyacinth smiled, patting the cane, and the bells came back into her voice — bells I remembered from long ago. "I'll see you downstairs in a few minutes. Perhaps we can find something together. I believe Gladys Percy brought some eggs by yesterday and a loaf of bread. Do you like to cook?"

"Yes, I do."

"That's grand. We'll make some French toast. I have a bit of maple syrup tucked back from before these Depression days. It's ancient, don't you know! We'll make a party. There may even be some raspberries."

"I'll be down to help as soon as I'm washed and dressed, Aunt Hyacinth."

41

"You found the washroom down the hallway?"

"I did, thank you."

"Excellent." Aunt Hyacinth stopped by the door. "I'm really very glad you've come, Lilliana. You know, I loved your dear mother with all of my heart. I want to hear everything . . . when you're ready."

The sudden lump in my throat swelled and I couldn't speak, so I nodded, though I realized too late Aunt Hyacinth didn't see.

CHAPTER FOUR

Aunt Hyacinth, I was very soon convinced, saw all things clearly with her heart and her years of memory.

"Raspberries are just outside the door. Olney Tate planted canes close to the house years ago so I could step outside in my nightdress of a morning and gather to my heart's content. A party is not a party without berries."

That was the second, or maybe the tenth, thing that gave me pause. I knew there would be no berries yet — not till summer — but I dutifully stepped outside the door into the May morning chill. I wished I could conjure berries for Aunt Hyacinth.

My lungs filled with the fresh morning air and scent of flowers; my ears filled with the chirping of chickadees and Carolina wrens nesting amid the bounty of blossoming fruit trees — a regular symphony — and I drank in the blue of the mountain before me. It was a slice of heaven, just as I'd remembered —

not a fantasy of childhood at all. Only now the tangled raspberry canes showed few blossoms rambling beyond their path, and the orchard's carpet was strewn with fallen and broken limbs. As for the house, it was still as big and imposing as ever. But layers of old paint peeled from the clapboarding three stories high, from the sashes around windows, and from every step.

Aunt Hyacinth's mind is going. Her money's evidently gone, and she's blind but still doing her very best. I have no money to offer to help her or pay for my keep. How can I come here and add to her troubles? The weight of that knowledge was lifted only by a thought. *Can I be a help to her in some way?* I summoned my spirits as best I could and stepped inside. "I'm sorry, Aunt; the berries aren't quite ripe yet."

Aunt Hyacinth stared at me — or in the direction of my voice — as if I'd lost my mind. "Of course they're not. It's only May, child!"

"Then, what — ?"

"The berries in the pantry outside the door." Aunt Hyacinth clapped a hand to her forehead. "You wouldn't know about that, would you? Land sakes, where's my mind? Once we're past freezing, I have Gladys bring things up from the root cellar a little at a time to leave in the pantry so I can get them.

44

Those old cellar steps are more than I can manage anymore."

I laughed self-consciously, more relieved that her mind had not gone than that there were berries.

But Aunt Hyacinth laughed fully, the laughter of bluebells and church bells, and shooed me out the back door once more, urging me to check the door to a narrow pantry on the far right of the porch. The jar of red raspberries was just where she'd said it would be, along with canned jewels of bright-orange carrots, green snap beans, scarlet tomatoes, and deep-purple blackberries, the lid of each jar marked with a raised letter for its contents. I'd forgotten the beauty of Aunt Hyacinth's rows upon rows of homegrown fruits and vegetables, the glory of her garden. But who kept her summer garden now, or were these from the garden of another? Who canned these treasures? Surely she could not.

The smell of freshly ground coffee filled my nostrils when I opened the kitchen door. Aunt Hyacinth had the cast-iron skillet heated, butter bubbling, and was just lifting thick slices of white bread from egg batter and plopping them in. Not seeing didn't stop her from cooking; that was clear.

I opened the jar of berries, drained the juice to save, and spilled them in a little cut-glass dish I found in the cupboard.

"Carry the tray and this cloth into the front

parlor directly down the hallway there, won't you, dear? I love the morning sun in that room. It warms my bones." Aunt Hyacinth had brought out a tarnished silver coffee service and her very best china and bid me spread the damask cloth across the tea table. "We might as well do this right." She smiled, delighted as a child at Christmas.

We'd barely settled in the large and brightly lit room when Aunt Hyacinth reached for my hand — so like Mama. I clasped her frail hand in response, and Aunt Hyacinth prayed with the awe of a penitent approaching Mount Sinai. "Dear Lord, we rejoice in this beautiful day that You've made! Thank You! Thank You for the morning sun, for the birds that sing, for the love of family and the treasure of Lilliana that You've brought me. We sorrow for the reason, Lord, for the loss of my beloved Rosemary, of Lilliana's precious mama. Comfort us, Father; help us to balm one another's hurts even as we joy in our Rosemary's homecoming. Lead us through this day. Make us a blessing to one another and to all who cross our threshold. Thank You for this food and for bodies and minds to enjoy it. In Jesus' name, and for Your glory, amen."

I hadn't even told Aunt Hyacinth yet that Mama had died, but it didn't seem to keep her from knowing, and how that knowing came about worried me. Still, tears I didn't want to shed threatened. "The funeral was day before yesterday."

"I thought it might have been." Aunt Hyacinth spoke quietly, reverently, stray tears on her own cheeks.

How was it that she could glory in bounty one minute and sorrow in depths the next? How did a person traverse the mountaintops and dip to the valleys and soar up again so smoothly — all the while convinced she could approach the throne of God and be assured of His love? For surely she was. I heard it in her voice.

"Will you pour for us, Lilliana?"

"Of course." I held the tarnished pot as steady as I could. The coffee service, the grand piano on the far side of the room, the spacious fireplace and faded but fine appointments of the room were like stepping into old-world grace. "Thank you for taking me in last night. For everything, Aunt Hyacinth. This meal is wonderful."

"Stop thanking me at every turn, Niece. This is your home now, for as long as you want it. After I'm gone, it will be yours entirely."

"Aunt Hyacinth, that's not why I came. I came because . . ." I didn't know how to continue, how much to say.

"Because you had no other choice. You'd nowhere else to go."

I shifted in my seat, ashamed of my need,

ashamed of my transparency, confused by what she seemed to know without a word from me.

"It's all right. I understand, better than you know. I know that your father did not treat your mother well, that she died of a weary and broken heart. I know that he long ago forced her to will everything to him and to exclude you from that will with the promise that he'd care for you and protect you if anything ever happened to her."

"Did Mama write that to you?"

"She told me when you were both here, but she didn't need to. I haven't heard from your mama since the day your father took you both away. I suspected that was what he was after when she ran off with him as a girl, but hoped I was wrong." Aunt Hyacinth set down her bone china cup, sloshing just a little of the coffee as the saucer found its nesting place. "She wrote me a couple of years after their marriage, asking about Garden's Gate — if I'd made a will. She encouraged me to do so and to make her — or better yet, her husband — beneficiary and executor so that nothing would be left to the state but 'kept in the family.' I knew then."

"I don't know anything about that."

"He vowed that she and their children would share legally in everything. She wanted to believe him, but I knew it was a lie. Everything that man did was a lie. From the moment he proposed to the day he buried my Rosemary."

It was a hard conversation. He was my father, after all, and though I knew he was willing to sell me to "insanity" to cover his tracks and save his reputation, that he'd as much as sold me to Gerald as a young bride for whatever favor it bought him in the church, it felt all skewed that I wouldn't take up for him, that I couldn't. *Honor your father and mother* resounded through my brain.

"Your mama, God rest her weary soul, knew the truth, too. Not that she'd admit it at first, mind you, but she came to it later. He was a slick one, a smooth one, a charming sort, and he wanted her money — or what he believed was her money. He'd convinced her she was not smart enough to manage her affairs — that she needed him to handle everything." Aunt Hyacinth huffed. "Rosemary was a brilliant girl, a brilliant woman. He knocked the confidence straight out of her like straw stuffing."

I held my breath. She could be talking about me — about Gerald and my lack of stuffing. That she'd known Mama when she was more than a frail woman intrigued me, excited me. It also reminded me that I had a ring to deliver.

"Not getting me to affirm his lawyer's 'encouragements' was surely a disappointment, but I suppose he believed I'd seen the light and acquiesced. In any case, he wanted the recognition your mother's beauty brought him. I imagine Rosemary just hoped she'd outlive him to make things right . . . for you."

The stone walls in my stomach shifted and crumbled. Here was the first person I might count as an ally, even if it was too late for Mama. "He doesn't know I'm here — neither him nor . . . anybody."

"You mean your husband?"

I swallowed. "You know I'm married." Would this be it? Would she send me away — back to my rightful place?

"I felt the groove on your ring finger when you placed your hand in mine just now. You must have taken it off recently." She sighed. "It's what men like your father do — marry their daughters off young. What sort of man is your husband? A good man?"

Aunt Hyacinth's deductions made my head swim. It was good I hadn't lied to her — or "neglected" to tell her I was married, though I'd considered it. I'd become very good at pretending, at lying to cover up for Gerald's outbursts and for his sometimes-antisocial behavior — or more difficult still, at pretending everything was all right when he fawned charm. But I meant to start fresh now, whatever I did. In barely a whisper, I forced the truth between my lips. "No. No, he's not." Silence spread between us, the half-eaten toast and coffee growing cold. "He

50

doesn't know I'm here. I ran away — from Gerald and from my father."

Aunt Hyacinth drew a deep breath as if she'd been waiting for me to speak. "Good. I'm glad you did. They won't hear it from me."

It was like being handed a pardon — the worst of sinners and I was pardoned. "Why? Why will you help me?"

"Because it's right. Because I loved your mother. Because I love you for your own sake, Lilliana. I would have taken you both in years ago, if only Rosemary had been able to leave your father. You know he telephoned the day she died."

"Father?" And then I remembered the conversation in the church sanctuary — Father saying something about calling Mama's aunt and his debts.

"He said he knew I would want to know and that he would be needing to sell the house — my house — to pay for Rosemary's final expenses."

"What? That's not true. He has enough for that, or at least I think he does, and people in the church are helping him." I felt my face warm. I'd taken that eighty dollars donated by one of the wealthier members and used it to buy my train tickets. And yet I knew that hadn't been the only donation.

"I told him as much — that he should be able to pay his own wife's expenses. He said I should know that Rosemary had willed everything to him, and of course that included Garden's Gate. He thought I should know before he sent a lawyer and agent to sell." Aunt Hyacinth shook her head. "He so generously offered me a month to move."

"You willed Mama your home?"

"I never married. You may not know that. I raised your mama when her mother — my sister, Camellia — died."

"Mama told me. She always thought of you as her mother."

"Rosemary was a daughter to me, all I ever loved as my own in this world, and she came to me as a very little girl. She barely remembered her own mama."

"I remember the summer Mama brought me here."

"Do you? I didn't know if you could; it was so long ago and you were such a tyke."

"Those were the best days of my life, of my childhood. Until he came."

"He came and terrified your mama into going."

"He wanted to leave me here."

"It was all I could do not to keep you. I feared what your life would be with him, but I knew your mama needed you as much as you needed her. I knew that you were all that made her life worth living once she was under that man's spell."

"Why didn't she stay or come back here —

to you, to Garden's Gate?" I asked questions I'd pondered over and over for Mama — and for me.

"She was afraid. She was so very afraid of him. He vowed he'd hunt her down and get her back, no matter where she went, and that he'd go to court to claim desertion and prove her an unfit mother."

"Could he have done that?"

"It's a man's world, Lilliana, don't you know?"

I did know, had every reason to know. "Then he will come. If Garden's Gate is his, he'll sell it. He won't care that he turns you out, Aunt Hyacinth — or me."

"Come here? Oh, I don't think he'll be coming here."

"But you said he —"

"He was right that I'd willed my home to Rosemary. She was to inherit it after I pass, not before. Somehow he'd gotten it in his head that I'd put the property in her name already. There is a grave plot in the church-yard in her name; that's all. A place where I'm to be buried. I put it in Rosemary's name believing she could handle the details when the time comes, that she'd outlive me. That's what he inherits — little good it will do him. Though I'm sorry about that now. Unless he allows me to purchase it from him, it will mean I won't be buried next to my family." Aunt Hyacinth sighed. "I'm no fool. I won't sign over my home — my family's home for five generations — until I draw my last breath."

"And then he'll take it. Take it and sell it."

"No, he won't. I talked with my lawyer the moment I hung up the phone. I've made a new will. Garden's Gate will be yours when my time comes."

"But you hardly know me!"

"I hope we'll change that. And even if we don't, there's no one else I'd want to have it. You are bone of my bone and flesh of my flesh, Lilliana Grace. Your grandmother and I grew up in this house. Our father was a child in this house, along with his older brother and sister. The Belvideres have owned this land since No Creek was founded before the Revolution. I'd like it to stay in the family, of course. Our family has lived here long years. I hope you will — if you want."

I didn't know what to say. It was an extravagant gift, but too much, too soon, and how could I commit to such a life? How could I know what my future might bring — other than threats from Gerald and Father?

"If you choose to sell Garden's Gate after I'm gone, I trust you to sell it for a fair price and a good reason, an amazing future — nothing less. Certainly not for a man who treats you poorly. I love my past, but I love your future more." Aunt Hyacinth spoke in my direction.

I wanted — desperately needed — help and sanctuary, at least temporarily. But would I be able to stay? *What if Gerald comes for me? And if Garden's Gate becomes mine, couldn't he take it? Sell it?* Whether or not he could, did I want to commit to a life in No Creek, North Carolina? Did I want to commit to anyone ever again?

"What do we need to do to make certain they don't find you? Have you asked yourself that?"

It took me a moment to register Aunt Hyacinth's question. But I'd thought of little else during the long hours of my train ride. "I took off my ring. I threw it in the first trash bin I came to." I realized too late that perhaps I should have sold it, plain gold band that it was, but I'd just wanted to get rid of it — a shackle on my finger. "I thought of changing my name. But I can't do that legally, not without leaving a trace."

"No, I suppose not. But it's a good idea, before either of them think to come here or to telephone here again. It's one thing for me to say you're not here, but our telephone operator is chatty and all too willing to share gossip she shouldn't."

"He — Gerald — wants to divorce me."

"That's good, isn't it? You'd be free of him." Aunt Hyacinth's face gained color.

"He wants to do it by having me committed to an institution — declaring me unstable

55

and insane, then fabricating a story that the instability made me promiscuous. That gets his divorce within the state of Pennsylvania and his freedom and sympathy within the church."

"That's ludicrous!"

"He's convinced Father to back him up — to make it seem that my grief for Mama is excessive and unnatural and sent me over the edge. I think he's willing to pay people to stand as 'witnesses' for — for whatever he says."

Aunt Hyacinth didn't say anything for a time. I wondered if she believed me. Why should she? It was all so outlandish. "I overheard them. They didn't know I was listening. Gerald threatened to expose Father's treatment of Mama and, I think, some of his past behavior toward other women."

"Stirring the pot."

Try as I might, I couldn't keep my voice steady. "I don't want to be locked up for the rest of my life, and I can't keep on there. That's why I left as I did — not a scrap of luggage, nothing but my purse — and your ring. Thank heaven I'd sewn it into the lining or it would still be in Philadelphia. Oh, I must give it to you — I promised Mama."

"Lilliana!" Aunt Hyacinth's voice trailed my exit.

But it was a good excuse to dash up the wide staircase, gaining time to pull my heaves into deep breaths. I sat on the edge of the poster bed, taking time to calm my nerves, to blow my nose. The shame of my desperation, of my father and husband counting me as nothing but a burden to be gotten rid of, overwhelmed my heart.

Aunt Hyacinth must have thought me crazy, but I couldn't help that. It was best to get everything out in the open and know just where I stood with her — what she believed. I couldn't bear to trust her and find myself betrayed into Gerald's or Father's hands.

Pulling the ring from the lining of my purse at last, I straightened my skirt — much the worse for wear these last three days — and made my way downstairs. Aunt Hyacinth still sat by the window. If I didn't know she was blind, I'd have thought she was watching the cardinal outside her window peck at the seed she must have spread across the wide sill. She didn't turn her head as I entered the room — not until I slipped the ruby ring into the palm of her hand. Her quick intake of breath told me she recognized it.

"Henry's ring. I never thought to see this again." She fingered it lovingly, caressing the intricate setting. "Until your father telephoned, I didn't know if I'd ever see *you* again. Not that he suggested you'd come. I just knew from the way he talked that you had no home with him, and I wanted to be ready — in case."

"Thank you. Thank you. Mama said she took the ring from you." I couldn't imagine my mother stealing, and yet hadn't I just used money that wasn't mine to escape my husband?

Aunt Hyacinth shook her head. "I gave it to her. She didn't want to take it, knowing what it meant to me. But she needed 'portable wealth' — something valuable that's small and can be hidden. I wanted her to have some small security — some means of escaping your father if she ever needed to. If I'd given her cash, he would too easily have found it."

"I never saw the ring until Mama told me to dig it from the lining of her robe. She must have kept it near her always." *Like I did, in my purse.*

"I'm glad. I'm glad if it gave her comfort. I'm only sorry now that she didn't sell it to get away from him."

"Father bullied her — all my life he bullied us both. I thought marriage would be a way to escape him, but it didn't work like that."

"I'm so sorry that it didn't." Aunt Hyacinth slipped the ring on her finger. The combination of small diamonds and cut rubies sparkled in the morning sun. I wondered if she could see it at all. "You could have sold this and run far away. I love this ring, but it was gone for me. I would never have known."

"It wasn't mine, and Mama made me

promise to return it to you . . . when I could."

"She knew you would — that you'd come — that you'd need to come." Aunt Hyacinth smiled. "That was her way to protect you, to give you an opportunity — a possibility, even though she couldn't allow herself that gift."

That hadn't occurred to me. I'd sometimes blamed Mama for not loving me enough — wished she would have taken me away, taken us both away from the horror we lived. But I knew, too, that she'd done her best to stand between Father and me when he grew angry. She'd been helpless to prevent my marriage — helpless in so many ways. Yet she'd given me Aunt Hyacinth's ring to return, and her address, thereby opening a window for sanctuary. *Oh, Mama! You loved me even more than I knew.*

"We must think of a new name for you before your father or husband telephone or send someone looking for you. I haven't told anyone that I was expecting my grandniece or why — only that I was expecting a relative. I didn't know how things might play out, if you'd really come or how soon."

"A girl named Celia Percy was at the platform when I arrived and showed me the way here."

"Oh, dear. Did you tell her who you were? Your relation to me?"

I tried to remember. I'd been so weary and so relieved to have a guide through the dark.

"No, I was conscious not to give my name. I didn't know if you'd let me stay and I didn't want to leave a trail for Gerald or Father to follow. I don't think I said that I'm your niece — or you're my aunt — but she said you were expecting me or someone."

"It's good you didn't give your name. Celia's a dear, but whatever you said will likely be all over town by now."

The lump in my stomach settled into a deadweight.

"Well, it can't be helped. Did you say where you were from? That you're married?"

"No, I didn't."

"All right, then, we're going to begin as if Celia heard nothing or as if she got it wrong. Your name is Grace — that's true, your middle name — and you are, after all, a Belvidere by blood. We'll let it be thought you're a distant cousin come to live with me as a companion in my old age. That's plausible and will do for now. We'll let them assume that you're a maiden cousin looking for a place."

I nodded, feeling the sting and reality of part of that and the relief that perhaps if I could earn my keep, I really could stay without becoming a burden. "I can be that companion to you, Aunt Hyacinth. I can keep house and cook."

"We'll work it out. It just might be a new beginning for both of us — though we must be careful not to exclude Gladys Percy, Celia's mother. She's been helping me with groceries and food, even a little cleaning and cooking now and again. I've needed the help, and she's needed the work."

"Celia said her father's in jail for running moonshine."

"Yes — he's not been much account, but it's not fair to judge. There's no legitimate work in No Creek — not since this ugly Depression began. The few businesses that were here closed early on, except for the general store. So many folks have moved down into the cities, hoping for factory or mill work. Times are lifting, or so I'm told, but there's still nothing here. Men are desperate for employment of any kind — anything that will put meat on the table and shoes on their children's feet. Moonshine is the only income too many have, though few would admit to making or running it." Aunt Hyacinth shifted in her chair. "No, I want to employ Gladys and her children as much as I can. Thanks to Papa's Belvidere legacy and my savings over the years, that's still possible. Gladys is raising those children — remarkable children, really — on her own in a bleak little cabin half a mile away. But I know there are other things that need doing around here that she doesn't tell me — probably doesn't want to hurt my feelings or take advantage. Now that you're here, we'll think on that."

CHAPTER FIVE

Celia thought it great good fortune that the roguishly handsome Reverend Willard happened along with Miz Hyacinth's mail from the post office just as she and Chester stepped through the front gate to deliver a dinner basket. *Roguish* was a new word for Celia and she figured that, what with his shining brown eyes, the dimple in his chin, and all that thick wavy hair, it fit Reverend Willard to a T, despite him being the preacher. If he wasn't so old — probably nearly thirty — she might have turned sweet on him herself.

Her mother had told her to slip in the back door and set the basket on the kitchen table, call out to Miz Hyacinth that it was there, and leave without pestering, but the reverend's presence all but guaranteed a front door entrance and a sit-down welcome.

Celia'd spent most of the night staring into the open beams of the ceiling in the cabin room she shared with Chester and their mother — ruminating over the mysterious stranger. *Ruminating* was another new word for Celia, one she'd recently added to her Eagle tablet of Amazing New Words and had written between the lines of the newsprint wallpaper above her bunk. She'd been glad to think on it.

Where had the woman come from, and how was she Miz Hyacinth's long-lost kin that nobody'd ever heard of? It was something how she knew about *The Railway Children* and the sophisticated way she hadn't blinked an eye at Celia's portrayal of Roberta. Celia'd imagined all sorts of tragic romances and interesting background stories for the woman in tweed — the woman with no name, at least not any she'd given.

"You're guessing, Celia," Chester had said when she'd told him that. "You're just makin' stuff up in that ole head of yours and it's likely to get us both in trouble."

"You didn't see her, Chester," Celia had scolded. "You have no idea what a perfect mystery woman she is. Where'd she come from in the dead of night? Why didn't she have a trunk or a case of any kind? Why didn't she give her name when I gave mine? How is it that she's turned out like a New York fashion plate?"

"I wouldn't give you my name. I wouldn't give you the time of day if you didn't beat it out of me. And you just read about that 'fashion plate' business in Pearl Mae's Hol-

63

lywood magazine. I saw it on the counter in the store, so stop throwin' around big words."

Celia gave up after that. There was no sense wasting her breath. You couldn't convince eight-year-old brothers of anything. They thought they knew it all.

But today all that would change. Today, because the Reverend Jesse Willard was there, Miz Hyacinth was bound to introduce her guest in the grandeur of her parlor, and the mystery of the woman in tweed would be solved. The promise of a solved mystery thrilled Celia — Nancy Drew at heart — but there was something to be said for not knowing, for imagining and investigating and drawing her own conclusions. After all, this was the first mystery the town had encountered since the day the German Jewish Dr. Vishnevsky had set his foreign feet on No Creek soil.

"Celia and Chester, good morning!" Reverend Willard always sounded like he was surprised and glad to see them, though he saw them near every day.

"Morning, Reverend."

"Looks like you have something good to eat there."

"Mama sent fried chicken and corn bread and a mess o' greens for Miz Hyacinth and her guest. Did you know she has a guest arrived in the dead of night last night? Did you know I met her at the train and helped her

64

find Garden's Gate?"

"So Ida Mae told me when I picked up mail this morning. I'm glad you were the welcoming committee. You surely did us all proud."

Celia couldn't help but lift her chin at that and cast a meaningful glance Chester's way.

"Shall we knock and go in together?"

"Sure, Reverend. That'll be swell."

Reverend Willard smiled as if he knew some secret joke, but knocked just the same, turned the knob, and called out, "Miz Hyacinth? Are you home for company? It's Reverend Willard and the Percy children, come bearing gifts."

Of course she was home. Miz Hyacinth never left her house, what with her blindness and all. It was just the reverend's polite way of letting her know he was coming in so's she'd know who it was and wouldn't bother herself about answering the door.

"Come in! Come in! It's a party!" Miz Hyacinth called from the front parlor, clapping. "I want you to meet Grace!"

Grace? Grace isn't a flower name. Grace doesn't sound like bells or rain dancing or anything in particular. The weight of disappointment that settled onto Celia's shoulders was not helped by Chester's plucky grin.

But Reverend Willard doffed his hat and picked up a smile that Celia had rarely seen — a light-dancing-in-the-eyes kind of smile that brought out the dimples lining his

65

cheeks. "Good morning. I'm pleased to meet you, Grace. I'm Jesse — Jesse Willard. Welcome to No Creek!" He said it with more enthusiasm than the enthusiastic preacher was known for, and that made Celia take notice.

But the woman in tweed — still in tweed — barely smiled. Miss Grace looked about as relaxed as a cat strung out on a clothesline. "How do you do, Reverend Willard? A — Hyacinth — has told me about you and the Percy children. Celia and I met last night."

Reverend Willard smiled from ear to ear and couldn't seem to stop. Celia wondered if he was as mesmerized by Miss Grace's Blue Ridge eyes and peaches and cream skin as she was. "I hope it was a good telling. We're a pretty tame lot around here but always glad to welcome newcomers."

"Grace has come to help me, Reverend. She's going to live here at Garden's Gate as my companion."

"Why, that's wonderful! Our community is twice blessed."

"I note the family resemblance," Celia said, her head cocked to one side, the basket still on her arm. "Got the same eyes as you, Miz Hyacinth."

"My Grace is a Belvidere through and through." Miz Hyacinth looked directly toward Celia's voice, her sightless blue eyes dulled, but a firm set to her mouth.

66

"Close family, then." Celia nodded, that part of the mystery solved.

"I'm so very glad for you, Miz Hyacinth! There's nothing like family, and I for one feel a lot better knowing someone's staying here in the house with you."

Celia knew Reverend Willard meant it. He'd spoken often to her mama over his concern for Miz Hyacinth living alone in her big ole house.

Miss Grace smiled, still nervous, Celia noted.

"As do I, Reverend Willard. As do I," Miz Hyacinth affirmed. "Now, all of you, won't you sit down and take tea? Grace, would you mind putting the kettle on? The reverend and I share a pot of tea whenever he comes to call — one of my greatest pleasures."

"Of course." With that, Grace Belvidere disappeared into the kitchen with the speed of a servant, Celia hot on her heels.

"Mama sent me up with this basket for your supper, Miss Grace. Miz Hyacinth's partial to Mama's fried chicken and corn bread. She said the greens'll act as a spring tonic, and there's some peppermint leaves in a napkin from Granny Chree for tea, ought to settle Miz Hyacinth's tummy."

"That's so kind of your mother! And who is Granny Chree?"

"Granny's an old midwife and herbwoman. You'll get to know her, in time, but not easy.

67

She don't take to strangers. Comes and goes in the half-light. Goes way back with Miz Hyacinth — from the time she was a young'un. They trade herbs and tonics and such."

"This is so generous of your mother and Granny Chree. Please thank them for us, won't you?" And then she hesitated. "I believe Hyacinth will want to send your mother something for her trouble and expense. I'm just not sure . . ."

"Mama says it's a glad-you're-here-and-welcome gift. The chicken was one of Miz Hyacinth's half strays anyway. . . . Will you be cooking for Miz Hyacinth now? Doing her laundry and such?"

Miss Grace hesitated. "I don't know, truly. We haven't talked through our arrangements yet. Has your mother been doing those things for her?"

"Yes, ma'am. She has." Celia knew it wasn't her place to say and her mother would likely twist her ear if she knew, but it was too important to the welfare of the Percy family not to speak up. "I believe she'd like as not to continue."

"I feel certain A— certain Hyacinth would like that as well, and I know I surely would. There's a great deal I need to learn."

"Don't you know how to cook?"

The woman smiled. "I know how to cook some things, but I'm sure your mother is more accomplished in that arena."

Arena. Celia simply thrilled to the sound of new words. "Are you a teacher, like Miz Hyacinth?"

"No, no, I'm not so accomplished as that, either. But I do love to read. I sensed last night that you do, too."

"Yes, ma'am. More than anything. Least I did before the school closed its library — collecting all the books before the school year ends and all. Well, I like reading at least as much as private investigating."

"Private investigating?"

"You know, detective work. I listen to *Dick Tracy* on the radio whenever I come by here or if I can get Ida Mae to tune in down to the store. I'm getting very good at deductions."

"I see."

"For instance, Miz Hyacinth made it clear from the set of her mouth that I'm not to ask too many questions about you, like, are you married and where'd you come from and why'd you come in the dead of night and exactly how are you kin to Miz Hyacinth and why don't you have a flower name?"

Miss Grace nearly dropped the teapot lid. "Well, there's not much mystery about me, but I believe Hyacinth is encouraging good manners. Asking too many personal questions isn't polite."

"Hmm. Reckon that could be. Mama says

I'm not much accomplished in that arena."

Miss Grace smiled as she set the pot and cups and saucers on a tray, but Celia noticed that her fingers trembled and that a finger on her left hand bore the slightest indentation from a ring gone missing. It was one more thing to note in her investigation.

The Reverend Jesse Willard prized the hours spent in Miz Hyacinth's company, and today he'd brought a gift he knew she'd treasure. It was all he could do to sit patiently through the tea that the lovely Grace served — a woman he was certain would be even more lovely if only she'd smile and relieve the furrow between her brows.

By the time Celia and Chester drank their tea and ate half the pumpkin bread Ida Mae had sent with him to welcome Miz Hyacinth's guest, the fidgets had taken hold of his fingers. He was that eager to share the letter he carried in his pocket. "Ida Mae sent me up with mail for you."

Miz Hyacinth brightened. "A letter? From over the pond?"

"From over the pond, indeed!" he crowed. "Miz Biddy."

"Biddy Chambers, my old friend in England," Miz Hyacinth explained to Grace. "We met the year I went with your mama — she was fifteen then and just blossoming — and a cousin to New York City — October

70

1908, the beginning of a beautiful tour to see the fall colors and traipse the steps of New England's literary greats. Oh, how your mama loved New England! Biddy was working as a stenographer in the city. I met her in a café over tea and we girls hit it off right away.

"Of course, she was already in love with her Oswald and headed back to England the next month, but we became fast friends. I'd hoped your mama and I could join her in England after Papa died. But by then, everything in Biddy's life and mine had changed." Hyacinth's voice trailed off a bit, but Jesse determined to keep the mood light and the memories happy this day.

"Grace, do you know Chambers's writing?" Jesse hoped the letters of Biddy and the writings of Oswald would be a love they'd all share.

"No, I'm sorry; I don't." But she didn't sound sorry, just distant.

"We must rectify that, my dear," Miz Hyacinth insisted. "You'll love his book and Biddy through it just as we do."

"That was so long ago — 1908. How is it you know them, Reverend Willard?"

Hyacinth laughed — the recovered sound of bells lovely as ever, Jesse thought. "You'd best explain, Reverend. While I can't see you now, I don't believe you've aged quite so much as that these past two years."

71

"I met Oswald Chambers through his writings, while in seminary. A professor guided me to them through previously published papers and the devotional that Mrs. Chambers compiled after her husband's death."

"*My Utmost for His Highest* — writings that came to the world because of Biddy's indefatigable shorthand, I might add," Hyacinth inserted proudly, on behalf of her friend. "If not for her faithful recordings and transcription, they would never have seen the light of day."

"The world — all of us — would be poorer without them," Jesse affirmed. "Which brings me to Biddy's letter and today's reading. She has quite a bit of war news in this one, I'm afraid. Are you ready, my friend? Which first?"

Hyacinth settled back into her chair. "The reading; then I'll savor whatever Biddy writes for the rest of the day."

Jesse pulled a well-worn book from Hyacinth's nearest bookcase and thumbed to the bookmark. "We don't follow the days, just keep reading each time I'm able to come visit. Today's reading is from May 6.

" 'Stand fast therefore in the liberty wherewith Christ hath made us free.' " Galatians 5:1.

"A spiritually minded man will never come to you with the demand — 'Believe this and that'; but with the demand that you square your life with the standards of Jesus. We are not asked to believe the Bible, but to believe the One Whom the Bible reveals. . . ."

Those words meant the world to Jesse. He could not count the times in life that thought gave him peace, the days it drove him and his questions to Jesus. He wondered if Miz Hyacinth and Grace felt the joy and relief he did in that reminder, if it set their hearts free and their faith firm. He hoped so.

Chapter Six

I'd only sat to be polite. But now I was riveted to the reading. I'd been raised in a church that virtually demanded we see as the leaders saw, claiming we were unable to understand the Bible for ourselves. Gerald, my father, and the elders said we were to follow their teachings because they possessed the mind of Christ. Oswald Chambers's words would be heresy to them. I pulled my mind back to Reverend Willard's reading.

"Always keep your life measured by the standards of Jesus. Bow your neck to His yoke alone, and to no other yoke whatever; and be careful to see that you never bind a yoke on others that is not placed by Jesus Christ. It takes God a long time to get us out of the way of thinking that unless everyone sees as we do, they must be wrong. That is never God's view. There is only one liberty, the liberty of Jesus at work in our conscience enabling us to do what is right."

"Don't get impatient, remember how God dealt with you — with patience and with gentleness."

I had given myself to Jesus — thrown my heart and soul into His hands at a young age, loving Him and wanting more than anything to be yoked to Him, to be loved by Him. But somewhere along the line, Pastor Harding, my father, the other elders, and Gerald had all stepped in between Jesus and me, judging and condemning not only my actions, but my motives, my heart's desires, suspicious of my very thoughts until I didn't know who I was or even what I thought independently of them. In time, I'd taken those judgments as crushing judgments from God . . . for didn't Pastor Harding say he was shepherd of the flock? He was, in fact, considered by our church God's mouthpiece in the earth and I was to be subject, surrendered to his authority. I'd grown convinced that if they could not love me, neither could God.

Involuntarily, I shuddered. There was nothing patient or gentle in the ways they had dealt with me. Now, to hear that Jesus looked at us differently, perhaps could look at me differently than they did . . . it seemed impossible. Was this truth or heresy?

"Grace? Grace?" Aunt Hyacinth was speaking.

"I'm sorry; what did you say?"

"Did you enjoy the reading, my dear?"

"Yes," I stammered. "Very much." But Reverend Willard's expression turned quizzical, as if I'd sung out of tune. I felt as if the room closed in, sucking air from my lungs. "Please excuse me while you read your letter. I'll take the tea things away. Would you like another cup, Reverend Willard?"

"No thank you, Grace. I'm fine." He looked disappointed.

"There's no hurry with those dishes. You're welcome to stay and listen, my dear. I'm sure Biddy will have news of the war in Britain. They've suffered terrible bombing."

"Yes, I've read about that. Thank you, but I think I'd like to get these done." Before I'd lifted the tray, Reverend Willard stood and took it from me.

"Allow me to carry those for you."

"Really, there's no need."

"Then grant me the blessing."

I didn't know how to respond to that, so simply walked ahead of him into the kitchen and tied an apron around my waist, not turning when I heard the tray set down on the table.

"I hope we'll see you in church Sunday."

"Oh, I don't think so." Nothing could be further from my hopes. I'd come to escape the church — and God if need be — not to find Him confronting and condemning me again. "I'll stay here with Hyacinth and keep

76

her company."

"I think Miz Hyacinth would love to come to church. She's refused offers to help her get there for fear of burdening others — and I can't help but believe from a little damaged pride. But I can tell she's missed it. It's a short walk, and now that the weather is warmer, it would do her good to get out — as long as she has a strong arm to lean on and eyes to guide her."

I felt the high-ceilinged walls closing in again. "We haven't talked about it. There's so much to work out. I've only just arrived, you know."

He backed off then. "My apologies. I don't mean to push. I'm just so happy you're here — for Miz Hyacinth's sake. She's needed someone for a long while, but not given in to saying so. I'm surprised she has now, but I believe it's just in time. I've been concerned for her."

I turned to face him now. There was nothing else to do without displaying abject rudeness. "And you've apparently been a very good friend to her. Thank you for that."

He smiled that unnerving, disarming smile again. "I'm entirely the beneficiary. Miz Hyacinth has been a great friend and confidante to me. She's a wise and godly woman."

I nodded, doing my best to look everywhere but into his eyes, brown with flecks of amber light and a ring of green outside the pupil, a perfect brightness against his dark hair. For the first time I noticed the ticking of the grandfather clock in the hallway. "Well, I'd like to get on with these dishes, and I think Hyacinth is eager for her letter."

"Yes, of course. It was grand to make your acquaintance, Grace, and I hope you'll reconsider that invitation to church." He reached his hand for mine and held it a moment too long.

CHAPTER SEVEN

As she plunked into the pew, Celia squirmed in her itchy Sunday dress — too tight by half — and squeezed a finger between her chin and the elastic strap that secured the bonnet her mother insisted she wear. Her Sunday shoes were an inch too tight and the rough pine pew made her backside go numb. Slouching was impossible. *Constructive — or is it constrictive?* Celia couldn't remember which *amazing new word* it was, but one of those captured just how she felt. How Chester sat bolt upright and still on the other side of their mother in his green woolen sweater and too-short, strangling tie was beyond her.

She hoped Reverend Willard wouldn't get revved up this week and go on and on as he did when filled with the Spirit. Why, just last summer Wanda Whitcomb had claimed she was slain of the Spirit during one of his "magnificent sermons" — though Celia wondered if she wasn't just trying to catch the reverend's eye the way she fell. It wasn't that his sermons weren't interesting or entertaining or downright inspiring. It was just that a body could only sit still in such discomfort for so long.

But all that flew from Celia's head when her ears caught the tap, tap of Miz Hyacinth's cane coming down the aisle — a tap, tap that had not been heard inside Shady Grove Baptist for a good two years. Celia jumped up to catch a glimpse and wave to Miss Grace, who had a hold on Miz Hyacinth's arm, steering her to the pew across the aisle and up one.

"Celia," her mother hissed, "sit down."

Celia sat, but the arrival of Miz Hyacinth in church after two years' absence, and of Miss Grace — the woman in tweed, still in tweed — captured her attention for the entire service.

CHAPTER EIGHT

If I'd had my way, I'd never have set foot in that church or any other — never again. It was all I could do not to break down for the weariness of it all. The mental conflict, the flashing memories, the certainty that rejection would be repeated at every turn built anxiety and anguish in my chest. I feared it might explode any moment. But Aunt Hyacinth had been determined. It was her heart's desire to go — and evidently had been for a long time. She'd just refused to ask anyone to help her.

"But now you're here, Lilliana. You're here and it makes perfect sense that if you're working as my companion, you would take me — you would insist on taking me. And to tell the truth, I need to go."

I'd never been able to deny my mother anything, and this dear woman had raised Mama, offered her balm and home. Now she freely offered me the same — with so few questions asked. I could not deny her, but I could not shake feelings of condemnation from the church — any church.

If these people knew me — knew that I'd run away from my husband and father, knew that I wasn't really the "Miss Grace Belvidere" that Reverend Willard introduced to the congregation — they would surely be shocked.

I felt like that woman from Hawthorne's novel who wore the scarlet *A* on her chest. Not that I'd committed adultery — but I'd run away and let them believe a lie about me. *What will happen if they learn the truth — when they learn it? If Gerald or Father show up, looking for me? What will that mean, not only for me but for Aunt Hyacinth?* I turned away when the woman across the aisle smiled and nodded a greeting. I dared not get close to anyone. Let them think me a snob. *Please, God, if You have any mercy, let them not think of me at all.*

After service, before I could get Aunt Hyacinth to her feet and out the door, a woman nearly six feet tall and rail thin plowed her way through the congregants to push her hand into mine.

"Welcome to No Creek, Miss Belvidere. We're mighty glad to have you. I'm Mrs. Mae — call me Ida Mae, everyone does — postmistress and proprietress of the general store, also local midwife on occasion. If I can be of service to you or Miz Hyacinth, you just let me know. I know everyone and everything in the area. You have a question, you ask me. Isn't that right, Miz Hyacinth? I hope you told her."

"Yes, I've told her all about you, Ida Mae; you may depend on it." Aunt Hyacinth smiled innocently and gave my hand a conspiratorial squeeze.

"Thank you, Mrs. Mae — Ida Mae. I appreciate that. Right now, I believe I need to get Hyacinth home. It's been a long morning for her."

"Well, of course it has, bless her heart. Miz Hyacinth, you know we're mighty glad you came to church after all this time." Ida Mae raised her voice as if Aunt Hyacinth were not only blind but beyond deaf. "We've missed you, and I'm sure the good Lord is pleased to see you've returned to the fold."

It sounded like a backhanded welcome. I might not take up for myself, but I was ready to give Ida Mae a short retort on Aunt Hyacinth's behalf when Reverend Willard intervened.

"Two Belvidere women. We are blessed. Thank you, Grace, for bringing our dear friend, and thank you for joining us today. You ladies made the sun come out."

Ida Mae straightened. "Just as I said, Reverend Willard."

83

Reverend Willard winked at me.

Furiously, I blushed — I know I did for the heat that came up my neck. "Hyacinth, we need to get you home."

"I am feeling a little weary, but, Reverend Willard, I must thank you for that sermon. It was one I needed to hear just now."

"You take care, Miz Hyacinth. I'll be up to see you this week as usual. You'll be ready for me?"

"Of course we will." Aunt Hyacinth's smile rang through her vocal cords.

I steered Aunt Hyacinth carefully down the aisle, though one and another of the congregants wanted to stop and speak with her, to welcome her back and say how they'd missed her. At the door, though the reverend was already deep into another conversation, he looked up at me, tipped his head, and mouthed, *"Thank you!"*

I was glad to be holding on to Aunt Hyacinth, for I might have stumbled if not. I wasn't used to being appreciated or thanked or even noticed, and it felt foreign, odd, something I didn't know what to do with. But as Aunt Hyacinth and I walked slowly home, arm in arm, it felt warming, just the same.

CHAPTER NINE

Celia wasn't sure what set the fire beneath Miz Hyacinth — unless it was Miss Grace's arrival — but she was game for the flurry of activity at Garden's Gate. She just hated having to go weed garden and haul water for the widow Cramer half the day now that school was out and miss all the excitement. But whatever she missed by day she could hear about in the general store each afternoon. All she needed to do was stop in on her way home and offer to sweep the floor for a peppermint stick or a pickle. She'd hear the local gossip in five minutes.

Today Ida Mae was "confiding" in Joe Earl, which was rich indeed, because Joe wouldn't remember a word of it past five thirty when the Whistle Stop Bar & Grill opened for drinks down the other side of the train platform.

"I heard she's called Gladys Percy in to clean that big house from attic to cellar — paying her top dollar — and hired Olney Tate to rake up that entire yard and trim up and plow a garden space, late as it is to get started. She's depending on her 'companion' to oversee the entire operation. I just hope that woman isn't spending every last dime Miz Hyacinth's saved for her old age. That would be a crime. Miz Hyacinth'll need that money."

Celia kept sweeping, kept her ears sharp, all the while wondering, if sixtysomething wasn't Miz Hyacinth's old age, when that would be.

"It's not respectable, having that colored man working there all hours with those women alone in the house. I heard he's even brought his nephew up from Georgia to help out." Ida Mae leaned conspiratorially close to Joe. "You just tell me what some fifteen-year-old colored boy is doing leaving home and coming to the foothills of North Carolina. You reckon he was run out of town for something sinister?" She shook her head but kept on. Joe Earl never got a word in edgewise. "I don't know what No Creek is coming to. Two strangers in as many weeks. And what do we know of Grace Belvidere? I never heard tell of any such relative until —"

Just then the bell jingled over the store door and in walked Miss Grace.

"Good afternoon, Ida Mae, Celia." Miss Grace half smiled, nodding, but kept her face all business. She didn't speak to Joe Earl but pulled her eyes away the minute she saw him. She must not have met him before.

"Why, Grace, a pleasure to see you!" Ida Mae crooned as if she'd not just been talking behind her back thirty miles an hour. "How can I help you today? There's no mail for Miz Hyacinth."

"No, she's not expecting any just now. I've come to see about paint."

"Paint."

"Yes, something in a cream or pale yellow that will catch the light for the interior of the house, and white, for the outside."

"Miz Hyacinth wants paint now?" Ida Mae's voice held all the surprise of a snow-storm in June and just a tad of judgment. "She'll never be able to see it, you know."

"No, but she wants the house brought back to its glory, just the same, and I'm here to see it done as she wishes."

Celia grinned to see Miss Grace lift her chin and stand up to Ida Mae.

"We'll have to order it from Elkin — maybe even Winston-Salem," Ida Mae observed as if that was a big to-do.

"She expects that. When do you think it might be delivered?"

"If I place an order today, maybe by the end of the week, if they have it in stock. How much do you want?"

"Olney Tate recommends five gallons for the interior, for now. For the outside, he thinks we should order fifteen gallons and see how we go. We can order more later if need be."

"Olney Tate, is it? I heard he was doing some work on the grounds. Does Miz Hyacinth think it's wise to have him working inside the house?"

"Wise? Olney and his nephew are excellent workers. They've already done wonders with the garden and fencing."

"But you and Gladys Percy and Miz Hyacinth herself — all women alone in the house with him. I'm surprised Miz Hyacinth hasn't given that more thought. You know, near every week I have one or two men comin' in here, lookin' for work — drifters, but still, at least they're white." She leaned over the counter, past Joe Earl, pretending to whisper, but in a voice loud enough to be heard at the door. "It isn't seemly."

Celia couldn't see Miss Grace's face from where she was, but she saw her back straighten and heard the steel come into her voice. "I'm sure Hyacinth knows what she's doing. And I believe the Tates have been her longtime friends — for generations, as I understand it."

Now Ida Mae bristled and stood to her full height. Celia's breath caught, watching two she-cats size one another up.

"By the way —" Miss Grace turned, giving the store a glance, and smiled, obviously try-

88

ing to mend fences — "do you have any wallpaper sample books I might look through? Something we might order from?"

Joe Earl chuckled.

"What's so funny about that, Joe?" Ida Mae cut him short.

"This is No Creek, ma'am," he addressed Miss Grace. "Not much call for wallpaper round here. Most of us paper with the latest Sears and Roebuck or old pages of the *Journal-Patriot* or —"

"That's enough, Joe Earl. You'll have Grace thinking we're all backwoods here. But it's true; we don't carry wallpaper samples in the store. You'll likely have to go into Winston-Salem for that or call on the telephone and ask to have samples sent out on the train. Want me to ask the paint supplier for you?"

"No thank you. I think a trip into the city might be what's needed. Do you have a timetable for the train?"

Ida Mae handed one over. Celia figured it was the first one she'd doled out in years. "I'll put the paint order on Miz Hyacinth's bill."

"Thank you, Ida Mae. We'll settle up at the end of the month."

And then she was gone.

"Celia Percy, aren't you done sweeping yet?" Ida Mae snapped.

Celia swept faster, knowing Ida Mae needed to take it out on somebody. "Almost! Just a little more over in the corner."

"Be smart about it." And then Ida Mae's voice lowered to Joe Earl. "Did you hear that? Spending money like rainwater. 'A trip to the city might be just what's needed,' " she mocked. "Plunked it right on Miz Hyacinth's bill. 'We'll settle up.' Like it's her money."

"Might be. Miz Hyacinth's got no other kin, far as I know."

"None but Rosemary, who ran off as a girl. Though I heard she's up and died not but a couple weeks ago. And didn't she have a daughter?"

"Rosemary died? Where'd you hear that?"

Ida Mae rose to her full height with self-importance. "Never you mind. Just heard it, is all."

But Celia knew. Ida Mae's first daughter, Ophelia, worked at the switchboard that served all of No Creek and Ridgemont and Trent, down the road. What information Ida Mae didn't catch on the street, in the church, or at the general store, she learned from Ophelia's "tele-Mama."

Celia finished sweeping and tucked the broom in the corner. So taken with this new information was she that she nearly forgot her peppermint stick.

On the way home she muddled over all she'd heard. *Miz Hyacinth's bringing Garden's Gate back to its former glory. Does she mean to sell? Who'd buy in these times? Does she*

90

think she's going to live a long while, maybe even regain her eyesight, that she wants everything fixed up so? Or is Miss Grace goading her on, thinking she'll inherit it all, like Ida Mae said? That didn't ring true. Miss Grace didn't seem the greedy type. But just what type was she? *Must not have a penny to her name. She's still wearin' that tweed skirt, though it looks like Miz Hyacinth's too-big sweater on top now.*

Celia's mama had often said you can't count too much on family; they're like to let you down. And how was Miss Grace actually related to Miz Hyacinth, after all? And what about Rosemary dying? Celia had heard of Rosemary — a pretty woman a few years older than Celia's mama whose running off had near broke Miz Hyacinth's heart, long before Celia was born. The story went that Miz Hyacinth raised Rosemary like her own child after Camellia — Rosemary's mama, Miz Hyacinth's sister — and her husband died in a car accident. So how was it that Miss Grace showed up within days of Miz Rosemary's demise? *Demise* was a new word for Celia's growing list, one she'd found in the obituaries, and she favored using it. There was more to this mystery all the time, which suited Celia just fine.

CHAPTER TEN

I fumed on my way up the road to Garden's Gate. The nerve of that woman, implying impropriety on Olney Tate's part and lack of discernment on Aunt Hyacinth's! Olney and his nephew had proven the picture of deference and decorum to the point that it made me nervous and rather chagrined at my own consciousness of the color of their skin — especially since I'd grown up with Sarah, nearly a second mother to me.

I slowed my steps. But was I any better than Ida Mae? Was I mad because she'd dared to question Olney Tate or because she'd dared to question me? Why was it so hard to discern my own motives?

I'd never considered such distinct racial lines drawn in Philadelphia, supposedly "the city of brotherly love," though I'd known few people outside my white church — which taught that people of color were marked for Ham's punishment, the son of Noah who'd mocked his father's nakedness. My church taught that slavery had been the consequence for that sin. It never sounded right to me, never sounded like something God would do.

No longer under my father's or Gerald's thumb, I vowed in that moment to better notice, to think for myself, and to respect all good people — colored or white. I needed to be part of a better way, not part of the same old problem.

What struck me more than the color of his skin was the hunger and wonder in the eyes of Olney's nephew, Marshall Raymond, as he took in Aunt Hyacinth's library for the first time.

"All those books!" Marshall had whistled, slipping his hat from his head with the reverence one might offer in a great cathedral. "Never in my life did I think I'd see so many books in one place." He'd stood in the middle of the grand room and turned slowly, taking in every floor-to-ceiling shelf.

His wonder made Aunt Hyacinth smile. "The Belvidere library began with volumes brought from across the sea — years before the Revolution. Each generation has added to this largesse. I did all I could, until I could no longer see to read — or write to order. I miss that."

It was certainly an impressive room and an even more impressive collection.

"One day it will be yours, Grace. You'll keep the tradition alive, I hope."

I smiled and squeezed her arm affectionately. It seemed there was nothing more exciting to Aunt Hyacinth than to think of bequeathing all those books and Garden's Gate to me.

I already loved Garden's Gate. I loved its library. I couldn't help but be moved — and terrified. To be given such a gift . . . the knowledge of such a hope for my future thrilled me beyond belief.

But I knew that the moment Gerald found me and learned of this gift, it would disappear. He'd sell off every book, every antique, every family memento and the house and grounds before finding a way to rid himself of me.

No, I wouldn't say it in front of Marshall, but Aunt Hyacinth couldn't make me her heir and hope to keep anything in the family. And it would all come out when the legal process began. I knew that much. I wouldn't be able to forge my name on a deed and have it stick. There was no Grace Belvidere, and Lilliana Grace Swope was nothing and nobody, especially to my husband. *Aunt Hyacinth, you must simply live forever and let us enjoy this life together!*

I'd never known such freedom or been given such responsibility as Aunt Hyacinth gave me. She trusted me implicitly with work and decorating choices and with her money. I second-guessed myself time and again and in the end quizzed Aunt Hyacinth and asked Gladys Percy each time I saw her what she thought about this color or that fabric from Aunt Hyacinth's storehouse of old decorating fabrics.

More and more Gladys became a trusted friend. Aunt Hyacinth increased her hours at Garden's Gate, relieving me to work full-time on the redecorating and coordinating with Olney Tate about work on the grounds and the painting of the house.

I only wished I could tell Gladys my real name, confide in her at least that I was Aunt Hyacinth's grandniece and that my mama was Rosemary. The terrible ache of losing Mama and Sarah in one day was still so raw. I'd told Aunt Hyacinth about Sarah, and she seemed to truly understand. Still, I needed more, to share my grief beyond. It was such an overwhelming part of me. But trusting — confiding in anyone else — felt all too risky.

CHAPTER ELEVEN

It was Wednesday, time for Jesse's next visit with Miz Hyacinth. There was no new letter from across the pond, but they could have tea and some of Gladys's pecan cookies and play Miz Hyacinth's Victrola — maybe the Caruso records she was partial to. Perhaps he'd play the piano for her before he read today's devotional from *My Utmost for His Highest.* It was the weekday and visit that he looked forward to most. He hurried up the hill toward Garden's Gate.

For the four years of his pastoring, Jesse had been besought with casseroles and Sunday dinners and strong suggestions that any one of the fair daughters among the congregation might make him a fine wife. For those four years he'd managed to carefully dodge overt offers and still maintain the goodwill of the congregation. Not once had he been tempted or interested, not even when Joe Earl had slipped a little 'shine in the clogging party punch after a community working to

96

raise Grady Wilson's barn and Grady had all but shoved his youngest daughter into Jesse's arms.

It wasn't that the maiden ladies of No Creek were ugly — far from it. But Jesse had been sent away to finish school and college and then on to seminary in Kentucky. He'd encountered the world and books and new ideas about old thoughts. He'd learned to read music and to play the piano, though the church in No Creek had none. Now he longed for music, for art and literature and a companion to share the love of those things. He'd met no one in No Creek who might fill that longing or share those passions of a winter's evening by the fire.

Jesse had grown up dancing and still tapped his toes as readily as anyone when Joe Earl picked up a fiddle. He could clog with the best — fancy or Appalachian flat-footed — though even clogging was frowned upon by Baptist pastors and forbidden by his professors in seminary.

Truth be told, he wouldn't mind dancing arm in arm with a woman — the waltz, or even a foxtrot, though a minister of the gospel in the Baptist church dare not say such a thing. But would it be so bad if you were married to the woman? He could imagine that it would not, not if you did it in the privacy of your home and it didn't get back to the congregation.

But Jesse had found no such soul mate in No Creek. Miz Hyacinth, though a kindred spirit, was more the grandmother he'd always imagined, always wished for — and for that relationship, he was thankful.

He'd all but given up thinking he'd find a woman in No Creek who would make his pulse race and his head spin, a woman with whom he could share the music that gave him joy, the books that perplexed and inspired his mind, a woman who might fill the empty places in his heart. Now someone made to order from his imagination had appeared, and he could think of little else. Dancing seemed more appealing than it had in years.

He'd just opened the front door and was about to call out his usual greeting when he heard Miz Hyacinth's raised voice.

"I told you she's not here. Yes, she stopped to tell me of her mother's death — a death that apparently was helped along by her father's mistreatment. But she's gone now, terrified you would track her down, thanks to your hateful ways. You call yourself a man of God, a pillar and elder of the church, and yet you have violated our Lord's own commandment to love your wife. So heed His warning: 'But whoso shall offend one of these little ones which believe in me, it were better for him that a millstone were hanged about his neck, and that he were drowned in the depth of the sea!'

"You've grievously offended your own wife, caused my Lilliana to stumble, to believe God doesn't love her. You well know what the Bible says about those who oppress. You had a wife of the finest caliber, a jewel in any man's crown, and you mistreated her. The rose of our family, and you crushed her. It's no wonder she ran away.

"What? . . . If she'd asked me, yes, I would have helped her, but she did not, and she's gone. I'll thank you to never call me again. Even though she has not publicly called you out for your wickedness, remember that I have no such hesitancy should I ever hear that you have tormented her further."

The telephone receiver slammed into its cradle. It evidently missed the spot, for Jesse heard her wriggling the receiver to fit its nest.

Jesse had never heard Miz Hyacinth so worked up, and though he knew he shouldn't have listened, he couldn't imagine whom she was talking about. To his knowledge the only strangers who'd come to No Creek within the last several months were Grace and Marshall, Olney Tate's nephew.

But he couldn't stand in the doorway and he couldn't back out without Miz Hyacinth hearing him. So he called out, more quietly than usual, "Miz Hyacinth! It's Reverend Willard. Are you ready for company?"

She didn't answer, so he closed the door and walked into the front parlor, where his friend sat, trembling.

"Miz Hyacinth, how can I help you?" He knelt before her, taking her hands in both of his.

She shook her head, choking back sobs. He'd never seen her this way. Not before her stroke or even after, when blindness and the county had forced her to retire, intending to incorporate No Creek's two-room school-house into the larger school system to save county funds.

"Oh, Reverend, I've never complained to the Lord about my blindness, never taken it as anything but His will for these years of my life. But I'm complaining now. I'm angry and resentful of this old body that can't do a thing for someone I love dearly, someone who needs protection and care."

It wasn't the first time in his pastoring that Jesse had no words. How does a man answer for almighty God when he doesn't know His mind and can't fathom His ways? When he doesn't even know the circumstances of a person and is reluctant to pry? But there was power in prayer; that he did know. And that he could do.

"Father in heaven, holy above all, Creator and Sovereign, faithful and wise and true, we come to You now with the heartache and sorrow, the fear and longing, even the anger of my friend, Sister Hyacinth. We're beyond knowing what to do or even how to release that anger born of fear for her loved one. Protect that dear one, Lord. Lead her to safe haven and thwart those who would practice evil against her. Give my dear friend peace, Lord, in knowing You are at the helm of this ship and that You will steer this loved one safely to port. May Your will be done. May we be instruments in Your hands for peace and blessing and to help those in need. Through Jesus Christ our Lord, amen."

"Amen," Miz Hyacinth whispered at last. It took long minutes while Jesse knelt, stroking her hands until she breathed more evenly, before she squeezed his hands in thanksgiving and her old smile returned, if weary and crooked.

He stood, pressing a kiss against her weathered cheek. "How about I make us some tea?" Tea and time to sit with a friend were the answers for many of life's ills and grievous moments. Miz Hyacinth had taught him that, and Jesse had grown convinced of it.

Miz Hyacinth nodded, still unable to speak.

Jesse was glad to busy himself in Miz Hyacinth's big kitchen. Even for its cavernous size, the kitchen had always seemed a homey place, if not as well-kept and clean as it might have been in recent years. But now the kitchen sparkled. The windows sparkled, and there was genuine crystal sitting on the counter, catching the afternoon sun and sparkling, too.

It looked as if all the cupboards had been emptied and scrubbed, the shelves lined with fresh paper and the task of returning things to their places interrupted. The work of Gladys Percy and Grace Belvidere, he was sure of it. But where were those women? Miz Hyacinth had lived alone for years, but he didn't like to think of her alone now, not today of all days.

While waiting for the kettle to boil, he stared out the window. There, in the far end of the garden, he glimpsed a dark-blue shape with a gray topknot, bent over, intent on something in the soil. *Granny Chree.* He smiled and raised his hand in greeting, hoping to beckon her to the kitchen. He hadn't seen or spoken with the old woman in months. He'd like to now, like to ask her wisdom and remedy for her old friend and charge, Miz Hyacinth, but he couldn't leave Miz Hyacinth alone to go out to her. Just as quickly as he thought these things, Granny Chree disappeared, likely into the woods beyond, but reinforcing his belief that she wasn't quite of this earth. *Another time, Granny. Another time.*

Jesse stirred the tea in a pot he found on the counter and poured a pitcher of cream he found sitting in the icebox. Miz Hyacinth didn't usually take sugar, but he placed the bowl on the tray anyway. A little something extra seemed needed now. That was the kind of advice he was sure Granny Chree might give.

Ten minutes later he poured tea for his friend, stirred in sugar and cream, and handed her the cup and saucer. Her hands had stopped trembling.

"What you must think of me, Reverend," Miz Hyacinth lamented.

"Highly, as I ever thought. It only concerns me that someone could have grieved you so. I know you're a good judge of character. Perhaps your counsel will stand the man in good stead."

"I'm not sure it was counsel so much as threat."

"There is that. Where is Grace?"

Miz Hyacinth's color rose and her hand almost dropped her teacup. "She took the train to do a bit of shopping for us."

"She'll be back tonight?"

"Yes. Why?" Miz Hyacinth sounded nervous — threatened, even. It wasn't like her.

"I'm just glad she'll be here with you. It seems timely — providential, surely — that she's come now. I think she's done you a world of good. You seem more chipper than I can remember — well, generally." He tried to infuse a smile into his voice. "And Garden's Gate looks better than I've seen it since I was a boy."

Miz Hyacinth gave a half smile, though genuine. "That's my intention. I want it

103

perfect — perfect as it can be for Grace." She leaned forward. "I'm hoping she'll stay on, you know. I'm hoping she'll stay forever, even after I'm gone. But she'll have things to work out. She'll need all the friends and help possible. Will you be a friend to her, Reverend Willard?"

"You know you can count on me. I'd like to see her stay. I'd like that very much."

Miz Hyacinth sat back, apparently relieved. "Now, about our devotional. What does our friend say today?"

He ignored the marker in their book and flipped to March 30 — a passage he knew well and needed himself today. It was too easy to tell God what was needed, rather than to worship Him and leave the workings of another's life to Him.

" 'And He . . . wondered that there was no intercessor.' " — Isaiah 59:16.

"Worship and intercession must go together, the one is impossible without the other. Intercession means that we rouse ourselves up to get the mind of Christ about the one for whom we pray. Too often instead of worshipping God, we construct statements as to how prayer works. Are we worshipping or are we in dispute with God — 'I don't see how You are going to do it.' This is a sure sign we are not worshipping. When we lose sight of God we become hard and dogmatic. We hurl our petitions at God's throne and dictate to Him as to what we wish Him to do. . . .

"Be the one who worships God and who lives in holy relationship to Him. Get into the real work of intercession, and remember it is a work that taxes every power; but a work which has no snare."

"Yes!" Miz Hyacinth reached for Jesse's hand. He grasped hers warmly, firmly, understanding all that words could not convey.

CHAPTER TWELVE

I'd never so enjoyed the wonder of shopping and never gleaned such headache from the responsibility of shopping for another — or for me. Wrestling two large wallpaper sample books and several brown paper packages of clothing purchases, I boarded the afternoon train in Winston-Salem and settled back in the seat. No Creek's platform stop was hours away but would come soon enough.

Closing my eyes and wriggling my toes in my new and practical shoes felt pure luxury. They were a worthy first purchase, and I felt beyond grateful to shed those Sunday pumps. I just might never wear them again. The extravagance and rebellion of such a thought made me catch my breath.

Germany and Russia and the United States may be shouting at one another. Half a dozen countries may be at all-out war, and the US might be fearful of changing forever, but for this day, for this moment, I, Lilliana Grace Shepherd Swope, one of a long line of Belvidere women, am wearing new shoes, riding alone on a train, and I am free.

A new skirt and two blouses, a pair of slacks, stockings, and a summer dress appropriate for No Creek Sundays were tucked in the parcels beside me. At last I could retire my dark tweed suit, at least for the time being, and wear a pair of women's slacks — forbidden all my life by my father, Gerald, and the church in Philadelphia. I'd felt guilty just trying them on, uncertain if I should. Then I remembered how practical and modern Gladys looked in her homemade slacks and blouse to work in the yard and around the house. I gave my guilty conscience a shake and plunked down cash.

A nightgown and slippers, needed underthings, and a few toiletries rounded out my purchases and wardrobe. There was even enough left over to buy flannel and a length of wool to make baby clothes for the Bundles for Britain — thanks to the generosity of Aunt Hyacinth, who'd insisted on paying me a stipend for work as her companion.

As if any of it was work. Being with someone who loved me — someone who'd loved and cared for my mother, someone Mama had loved and trusted before her life became all I'd ever known — was a new sensation, a delight I could barely comprehend. And the house itself, set against the mountain range and surrounded by flowers and an abundance of graceful, old trees, took my breath away and filled me with a sense of tranquility, of peace. It seemed wrong to feel so happy, but happiness was addictive in a way I hadn't known.

When I ran away from Gerald and Father and Philadelphia, it had been without a plan. Part of me felt like a dirty thief in the night. Part of me felt like an unruly child run amok. I knew that one day I'd have to return, that one day I must go home and face the music.

I'd even tried to convince myself that given time, perhaps Gerald would come to miss me and regret his plans. Perhaps if I grew stronger, more confident, more womanly, he'd care for me as he'd said he did before we married. Perhaps he'd treat me better. I'd told myself that I just needed a little time to find a way to not be afraid of him, to learn to love him again. He was my husband, after all. Surely that was possible.

But after less than a week in No Creek, after going to sleep each night and waking each morning without fear of being slapped or pushed or kicked or ridiculed or shamed, without walking each day on eggshells with nerves stretched so taut I could barely breathe, I'd known I would never go back. Even if it meant running for the rest of my life or being shunned forever.

If only I could have God's forgiveness, His love and approval, life would be complete.

But I knew that wasn't possible. God was too holy to look at sinners and smile — and I was chief among sinners, "a snake in the grass," as my father had once labeled me. That message resounded through all my growing years and was reinforced in my married years. It ran like Aunt Hyacinth's Victrola recordings in my head.

Aunt Hyacinth spoke again and again about the all-absorbing, ever-forgiving, never-ending love of God. She shared every day about her friend Biddy Chambers and her joy in living in relationship with and for the glory of God, as Oswald Chambers, Biddy's husband, had done in his too-short life.

But I knew those things didn't apply to me. Aunt Hyacinth would understand that, too, if she knew the anger and fear and even hatred I felt toward Father and Gerald. I was soiled and shamed, as if I'd actually pulled a trigger on one or both of them. And I'd thought about it. Once I'd contemplated lacing Gerald's tea with sedatives to calm him down, or worse, rat poison. I'd even bought the sedatives. I never bought the poison. I didn't want to kill him. I just wanted the pain to stop.

So all those gifts — happiness, new clothes, and sensible shoes — felt like a mixture of pleasures only God could give and surely take away. I knew I'd one day be called to account for each one, in no way able to justify or explain my enjoyment of them. The conflict wearied my soul. But just for now, I forced those pounding thoughts aside, sank into my seat, wriggled my toes in new shoes, and enjoyed my stolen pleasures.

CHAPTER THIRTEEN

Celia was surprised to see Reverend Willard at the train platform of an evening. He wouldn't be going anywhere now. It was near dusk and the last train of the day. Who could he be waiting for?

It wouldn't do to practice her Roberta run in front of the reverend. He'd smile and think it silly, though he wouldn't say. So Celia ducked just out of sight, but close enough to watch.

The train jerked to a stop. Off stepped Miss Grace, so loaded down with brown paper packages tied up in string that the conductor had to help her down the steps, handing her more and a couple of big books besides. How she expected to tote that lot up the hill to Garden's Gate, Celia couldn't imagine.

But the reverend stepped right up, grinning as if he'd been waiting for her all day and had nothing better to do in life than heft those big books and parcels.

Miss Grace protested, Celia could see, but

not enough to speak on. Celia followed at a discreet distance, not wanting to be thought spying, but close enough to eavesdrop. Accomplishing both things at once just wasn't working, so she settled for interpreting from afar their facial expressions when turned toward one another, taking special note of the way they gestured and walked or didn't walk on. All she could tell was that Reverend Willard was serious and sober and worried over something, if Celia was any judge of character — and she knew she was.

And it appeared that whatever he'd said made Miss Grace turn perturbed, maybe even frightened, stressed in her cat-strung-on-a-clothesline kind of way, and then beaten down. She'd looked so happy when she'd stepped off the train. What could Reverend Willard have said to her? It wasn't like the reverend to bring folks to their knees except for prayer. Was something the matter with Miz Hyacinth? That's the only cause Celia could imagine for such earnest sobriety . . . unless there was something scandalous, something tragic or unimaginable, something compelling for her to investigate.

She crept closer. Dusk gathered among the hills and spilled through the valley. It wouldn't hurt to get a little nearer . . . near enough to hear Reverend Willard.

"Perhaps you know who she meant. I don't know who this relative is — no one from

112

around here, surely. How she came and went without Ida Mae reporting it is anybody's guess. I don't think anyone even knew Miz Hyacinth had living relatives until you came. The thing that concerns me is Miz Hyacinth's heart. I'm worried she might work herself up into another stroke. Dr. Vishnevsky said that after one stroke it's not unlikely to have another."

Miss Grace stopped in the middle of the road. "I should never have come."

"Please, you misunderstand me! Miz Hyacinth has not been this engaged or looked so well in these two years since her stroke. Except for today, she's happier since you've come than I've seen her since I was a boy. You're a spring tonic for her, Grace . . . for all of us. A breath of fresh air." He shifted the parcels and Celia saw he was searching for words — an uncommon challenge for the reverend.

"You'd think with all this good air flowing off the mountain we'd be a spritely bunch, but the truth is, we're not. We need new blood and the culture and refinement you and your cousin bring. Please don't regret coming. I'm glad you're here and hope you'll stay." Even in the gloaming Celia could see that speech had cost the reverend and caused him to blush.

Miss Grace didn't seem to notice but, agitated, walked on. Celia knew she should break off and head for home, but a lightning bolt flashed across her mind that stopped her in her tracks. *Reverend Willard's sweet on Miss Grace. He's never looked at any of the local women like he looks at her.*

Celia gave a low whistle to think of all she'd uncovered in one night: Somebody'd grieved Miz Hyacinth. Miss Grace was a spring tonic not only for Miz Hyacinth, but for the reverend. Why didn't Miss Grace seem glad about that? Any woman in No Creek would give her eyeteeth for the preacher's attention. He was a looker, as Ida Mae always said, and Miss Grace was a stunner. They didn't look far apart in age. Why wasn't this attraction producing sparks? And who in their right mind would worry Miz Hyacinth into a stroke?

Celia breathed deeply and headed home at a clip. She had some serious sleuthing to do.

CHAPTER FOURTEEN

By the time I reached Garden's Gate and relieved the reverend of my parcels, I was spent. Though he stood a long moment on the front porch, I would not invite him in. Evening had settled and it would not do for neighbors to talk. Why he didn't seem to think on that was a puzzle to me. Besides, no light shone in the windows, and though that might mean Aunt Hyacinth was sitting in the dark, still dressed and imagining it was day, it might also mean she'd gone to bed early, especially after such an upset as Reverend Willard had revealed.

Gerald was surely her upset. From what the reverend had overheard, it had been my husband on the telephone, rather than my father. Yet the only way Gerald would know Aunt Hyacinth's full name or address was from Father. Further evidence of how the two worked in league. The thought sickened and frightened me.

The evening was warm, but I shuddered to

imagine his call. In Gerald's search for evidence that I wasn't stable, he'd gladly construe my running away as, in legal jargon, "desertion." Either way, it did not portend well for me, or for Aunt Hyacinth, if he pursued his search.

By the time I'd entered the foyer, found the light, and deposited my packages on the table beside the stairs, I knew I needed to move on before Gerald or Father came looking for me. I couldn't put Aunt Hyacinth in danger or through humiliation in No Creek, and I certainly did not want to be caught and dragged back to Philadelphia for public disgrace or to be "put away." The very thought sent shock waves through my system.

"Who's there?" Aunt Hyacinth's voice came from the dark parlor, causing me to jump.

"It's me, Aunt Hyacinth. I'm alone."

"Thank heaven. We need to talk."

I turned on the Tiffany lamp by her chair. It wouldn't matter to Aunt Hyacinth, but I needed light to chase away the demons. I sank into the chair opposite her. "Reverend Willard met my train. He told me what happened."

"I don't know how much he overheard."

"Enough to know that you have some crazy relative who ran away from her dangerous husband."

"He doesn't suspect you." It was both statement and question.

"No, I don't think he does. But he surely will, once he thinks things through."

"I don't believe he will, and I don't believe he'll share what he heard with anyone else. He's smitten, you know."

"What?" But I did know, or at least I'd begun to suspect. I didn't know the reverend well enough to know if his attentions to me were singular or if such solicitude was habitual for him, but I'd been on my guard since our first meeting.

Aunt Hyacinth sighed. "He's never fallen for anyone — at least no one here in No Creek. I think there might have been someone when he was away at seminary, but for whatever reason it didn't work out, and he came back to us. He doesn't know you're married, and because he doesn't know, I think he feels rebuffed."

I closed my eyes, weary to the bone. "I can't help that. You know I can't encourage him and I can't tell him why not. That's one more reason."

"For what?"

"Reason that I must go. Believe me when I say that Gerald is dangerous. He won't give up because you told him to. And threats won't keep him away. He's fearless. His typical response to a challenge is to rise to the occasion and thwart any and all in his way, and I'm afraid, from what Reverend Willard said, he might see you as that challenge. He won't trust that I've left. He may very well show up here, and soon."

"But he may not."

"We can't take that risk. I can't put you in danger, and I won't, I absolutely won't, go back to him." The trembling came through my bones.

"I'd never expect you to or want you to. But I do want you to stay."

"Aunt Hyacinth, you don't know him. He can be oh so charming but turn on a dime. And when he comes here, everything will come out. Everyone in No Creek — Reverend Willard, Gladys Percy, Olney Tate — Ida Mae, for pity's sake — will know that we've both lied to them. It will be awful, a scandal for you. You've lived here your whole life. You're the most dearly loved and highly respected member of this community as near as I can tell. I won't take that from you."

"You wouldn't be. Gerald's the one —"

"Yes, Gerald, my husband, my infernal mess." I shook my head. "No, I love you, Aunt Hyacinth. These few weeks have been the best of my life and I'll never forget them. I'll never forget you or your love and kindness. But I must go, for your and my protection, before he gets here."

Aunt Hyacinth's shoulders slumped. She looked as if she'd shrunk two sizes during my tirade. "Please," she said. "Please, Lilliana, my darling Lilly, don't go."

118

My heart nearly burst and I knelt before her, taking her weathered hands in my own. "It's for the best. Don't you see?"

"No, I don't see. I only know that I'm not long for this world and —"

"Please don't say that."

"I'm not the one saying it. Dr. Vishnevsky told me — two or three months at most, and Granny Chree, my dear old friend, my nanny from childhood and the mountain's best midwife and herb doctor, has confirmed it."

"What? Because of today — because of Gerald's call?"

"No. That shock didn't help, but it's my heart. It's giving out. I won't be here long, and I don't care two cents what people think or say. I love you and I want you here with me, if you're willing to stay. I know it's a risk to you if you're afraid he'll come. I can't even give a name to a man who hits his wife. But if you could stay, if you would share these days with me in my time that is left, and if we could restore Garden's Gate together — make it what we'd both like it to be again — it would be a gift beyond measure.

"After I'm gone, as long as you're free of that man, you'll be able to do what you want with the house, the land — to stay or sell, whatever you wish. I've already talked with Rudolph Bellmont, my lawyer, and explained everything. His office is in North Wilkesboro. He'll administer the trust in your interests alone. Any questions you have, and anything you need, just go to him. We're making certain through a discretionary trust with a spendthrift clause that Gerald doesn't inherit or benefit from a penny, and he can't force you to sell. While you're married to him, you'll receive enough to pay for repairs and taxes on the house, pay Gladys and Olney for their help, and collect a stipend for your living expenses — nothing more. If that man should outlive you, everything I own goes to someone else I've designated. I won't say who, for I expect you to live a long, full life."

I didn't know what to say — not about staying or inheriting Garden's Gate or all that Aunt Hyacinth had set in place for my welfare. It was too much to think on. What I cared about more, what tore at my heart, was all she'd said about her dying — expecting to die so soon. I couldn't take that in, couldn't cope with the horror. Not after Mama's going. Losing Aunt Hyacinth would be like losing Mama all over again. She was the last of Mama — of my mother's family.

More than that, Aunt Hyacinth had grown precious to me in her own right. I closed my eyes. Leaving now might be as dangerous for Aunt Hyacinth as staying. Either way, Gerald or Father might come, bully her, hoping to get information of my whereabouts. That idea was untenable. I must protect her, though I couldn't fathom how. I pulled myself together as best I could and whispered, "Of course I'll stay. I'll stay as long as you want me. We'll pray he doesn't come."

Aunt Hyacinth squeezed my hands. "Thank you, my darling girl. Thank you. We'll do all we can in the time we have, and we'll trust, and we'll pray, God's will be done."

I didn't answer that. I feared God's will if it was anything like Gerald's or my father's or Pastor Harding's. They'd proclaimed it so. Their will had ruled Mama's life until her dying day, and mine until the day of her funeral.

I helped Aunt Hyacinth up the stairs to her room, then helped her prepare for bed, tucked her in her grand four-poster bed, and kissed her good night. My heart rose in my throat. Her smile was so like Mama's. *Dear God, I don't want to lose this dear woman. Not now. Not so soon. Please, please give us time.*

Bone tired, I headed toward my room, leaving wallpaper books and parcels unopened. Passing the gilded hallway mirror, I stopped and stared. The woman looking back at me, weary and surely older than her appointed years, resembled in bone structure my mother and my grandaunt. I was glad and sad of that, realizing I'd all too soon be the last of the Belvidere women.

CHAPTER FIFTEEN

Celia had never seen her mother or Olney Tate work at the pace they did. Olney and his nephew, Marshall, had stripped peeling paint from the clapboards of Garden's Gate and sanded the whole thing, roof to ground, inside two weeks. Her mother and Miss Grace had scrubbed every inside wall and inch of woodwork on three floors by the day the paint was delivered. It reminded Celia of news she'd heard on Miz Hyacinth's radio about the German army's march into Russia — *whoosh, and in one fell swoop*!

Miss Grace, Olney Tate, Marshall, and Celia's mother formed an army of painters and wallpaper hangers inside. Miz Hyacinth sat in her chair by the parlor window, smiling from ear to ear, every once in a while encouraging her workers along with a hum or a song or a "Don't forget the corners. You'll need to move that heavy china cabinet. Celia, you and Chester empty it. That will help. Just be mindful of the crystal. It's older than you can count."

Celia wasn't partial to handling crystal and delicate things. She was more comfortable juggling abandoned birds' nests and rocks dotted in flecks of shining mica and pine cones dried and split wide-open — real treasures, like those she'd lined across the ledge above her sleeping spot at home. But she and Chester did their best with Miz Hyacinth's whatnots and only broke one crystal vase and a china teapot. Considering all there was, that didn't seem too bad.

Celia noticed that Miss Grace worked as if burning was shut up in her bones, as if every inch of that old house must be scraped and painted and polished and scrubbed yesterday, all the while keeping a worried eye on Miz Hyacinth.

Celia's mama said Miss Grace would work herself into an early grave at that rate and then where would Miz Hyacinth be.

But at long last, when the purple and white rhododendron and the oxeye daisies bloomed full in the garden and butter-yellow roses spilled over the picket fence, when turkey beard covered the surrounding meadows and fire pinks carpeted the woodland floor, it was finished.

"Thank You, Lord," pronounced Miz Hyacinth, satisfaction in every syllable. "The bones are in place. Now the real work begins."

Chester's eyebrows waggled at Celia. Celia had no idea they hadn't been doing real work, but the potential of what that might mean came intriguing.

Tired and dirty as the work crew was, Miz Hyacinth called on Celia's mama to make a full pitcher of sweet lemonade poured over ice shavings for an immediate meeting with her, Miss Grace, and Olney Tate. Marshall, Chester, and Celia sat on the sidelines, watching. Miz Hyacinth ordered Miss Grace to sketch the house and grounds as she described them and encouraged Celia's mama and Olney Tate to fill in all the plants and flowers and shrubberies and "appointments" they could remember of Garden's Gate's glory days when they were children. She even had Miss Grace write up an order for a fancy wooden swing like the one she remembered. Olney offered to build it for her, but she said she had other things for him to do. She remembered just where the wooden swing had hung when she was a girl — "The one Camellia and I shared — so many happy hours. Blindness only means my eyes can't see now," she said. "The sight of my memory is vivid."

Celia closed her own eyes, remembering run-down Garden's Gate as it had been a few weeks ago. Already on its way to glory, it was easy to envision the swing Miz Hyacinth talked of. *I reckon she's right about sight and memory.*

Olney and Marshall pretty nearly tore up the yard and gardens weeding and replanting, trimming every tree and shrub, even though it meant many wouldn't bloom till next year. They dug and burned with the intention of starting new beds from scratch.

It was an amazing thing for Celia to pass Garden's Gate in the morning, on her way to the widow Cramer's, and see it one way, then come home in the later afternoon and witness a new landscape. "Spring," declared Olney, "would have been the proper time to plant and do all Miz Hyacinth's outdoor bidding, but summer means longer workdays. We just keep on doing all we can. Next year will bring the harvest." He seemed worn but mighty proud to do it.

Miz Hyacinth didn't stop with the outside or the painting and papering of the inside. Once she had Olney and Marshall working like a house afire outdoors, she ordered Celia's mama and Miss Grace to her library. Celia and Chester sat again on the sidelines.

"We must decide about my books. I so loved sharing them with the children when I taught school. Sometimes I even loaned a few to parents. But since my stroke, since the school here closed, there's been no opportunity to reach the children, to see them

125

day by day — at least I've made no effort." Miz Hyacinth seemed to shrivel down a little at that confession.

"This is no ordinary library, you know. I've told you that I've acquired in my lifetime . . . oh, I suppose hundreds of books, and have done my best to keep up with both classics and the current writers of the day for children and adults. But there is so much more — there are books on these shelves from every generation of Belvideres reaching back to England and Scotland with our first ancestors to set foot on the soil of the New World. First editions, books autographed by authors — a veritable treasure trove of poetry and literature and plays, theological tomes and histories. I could go on, but you must understand what is here, and what it is potentially worth, especially once this horrid Depression is over. They are valuable as books, but books are only truly valuable as friends when they're read and their contents devoured and treasured. What will you do with all these books, Li— Grace?"

Miss Grace's eyes went wide. When she spoke, it came out more as a sputter. "Wh-what would you like me to do with them? They're yours, so I have no idea."

Celia had *lots* of ideas and it had been all she could do to keep her mouth shut and sit on her hands while Miz Hyacinth spoke. "I know!"

126

"Celia!" her mother hissed. "Hush, now! Miz Hyacinth knows what she wants done. She'll tell us in her time."

"But I have the answer — the perfect, most brilliant solution!" Celia loved the word *brilliant* and she loved the word *solution.*

Celia's mother turned her back on her, but Celia, undeterred, pushed between her mother and Miss Grace to lay her hand on Miz Hyacinth's arm and speak with her face-to-face.

"What is it, Celia?" Miz Hyacinth smiled as if she had all the time in the world. "What is your brilliant idea this time?"

"A library."

"Yes, that's just what it is, a library."

"No, now it's your library — yours and Miss Grace's. I mean make it a library for everybody."

"For everyone? Everyone in No Creek?" Miz Hyacinth's smile faded, but her sightless eyes paused and her head tilted to one side. "A lending library. What an interesting, big idea."

Celia's mother shook her head. "Now hold on. Think about that, Miz Hyacinth. You'd have everybody and their brother traipsing through your gardens and knocking on your door all times of the day and night. They'd never care for these treasures as you do. Why, I've seen the books Celia brings home from the school library — covers torn off, pages dog-eared and thumbmarked and soiled. No. That won't do."

"Hmmm," Miz Hyacinth considered. "Well, that won't be my problem. Grace, what do you think? Would you want folks traipsing in and out? Would you trust them with our books? Would you even want to own or run a library for the community?"

Celia, holding her breath, turned to Miss Grace. It was all she could do not to press her hands together in a pleading prayer.

Miss Grace blinked, her eyes open wider yet. "Why — I never — that is a big idea. A very big idea, and I'm not sure I'll be —" She stopped short. "I need to think on it." She sat down as if the weight of such a thought liked to do her in.

Celia didn't waste the advantage of now standing just above Miss Grace's eyeline. "Miss Grace, when Miz Hyacinth taught school here, she read to us every day — books from her library, books we had no chance of owning or ever borrowing from anyplace else. She read us *The Secret Garden*! And *Treasure Island*! Sometimes she'd let us hold them in our hands. On her really old books we'd rub the engraving on the outside of leather covers, trace our fingers in the gold-leaf words on the bindings. Her new books smelled of ink. And we never hurt one, did we, Miz Hyacinth?"

"Not one." Miz Hyacinth smiled in

memory, clearly delighted that it had meant so much to Celia.

"We'd be real careful, and you wouldn't have to let folks come day and night — just whenever you want. There's books here I'd give my right arm to read, and I swear I'll be careful."

"That's not a good idea," said Chester. "You'll need that right arm for stickball, and you're not supposed to swear."

"It's an expression, stupid."

"Mama, she called me stupid!"

"Children, hush now!" Celia's mama looked beside herself. "You're wearing Miz Hyacinth to a frazzle."

"It's all right, Gladys. Let them be. I enjoy them more each day." Miz Hyacinth beamed in the direction of Celia's voice. "It's a good idea."

"Well, they wear me to a frazzle," Gladys mumbled.

"Then I guess they need a job." Miss Grace sighed the kind of sigh grown-ups heave when they're about to give in and leveled a scrutinizing eye at Celia and Chester. "A job that may take quite a long time, if you'll agree, Gladys."

"If it will keep these two busy and out of mischief, they're all yours," Celia's mama declared, fists dug into her hips.

"I think a library — with limited hours — might be doable. Might be just the thing for everyone." A slow smile started at the corners of Miss Grace's mouth. "If it doesn't work out, we can always close. But we'll need to organize the shelves first and find a way to keep track of who borrows each book."

"Categorize — the Dewey decimal system," Miz Hyacinth proclaimed. "Order the books that way and you'll be able to keep track."

"The Dewey decimal system? All these books?" Miss Grace paled and looked like she might croak.

"I just mean organize the nonfiction into those general categories, then alphabetize the fiction by author."

"Yes, I can see that," Miss Grace mused, turning slowly, taking in each and every shelf. "You've already done that for the most part."

"What about kids' books?" Chester caught the fever.

"Yes," Miz Hyacinth enthused, "there must be a separate room for children. Perhaps the dining room — or the front parlor."

Miss Grace smiled. "A children's library. I think the front parlor, if that's all right with you. We'll keep your chair there by the window, of course, but the light is wonderful and the room's so cheery, and there's the piano. I can imagine we might want to play some songs and create some children's programs at times; what do you think?"

Celia couldn't keep the springs out of her shoes. She jumped up and down, threw her arms in the air, and shouted, "That's a stupendous idea! This is the best day ever!"

Her mother caught the vase Celia knocked over just before it crashed to the floor. "Mercy sakes! Can we put these children to work right now?"

Miz Hyacinth clapped her hands and laughed her full repertoire of bells, the high ones and low ones, the deep warm ones and the silvery tinkle of fairy bells. "What joy! I knew there was a reason I heard the whip-poor-will sing last night!"

Celia grinned so she thought her face might split. Never had a prospect sounded so wonderful; never had a grown-up listened to her big ideas and acted on them straightaway. Miss Grace rose ten feet in her estimation, nearly as high as Miz Hyacinth.

CHAPTER SIXTEEN

I saw in Aunt Hyacinth a moment-by-moment transformation as we worked in her library each day. It was a mammoth project, one I knew might last the length of her life, but it kept us all together, bustling around her, busy and happy. That was worth every minute, every strained muscle from moving bookshelves and nose full of dust from the upper reaches — shelves that probably hadn't received attention in ten years.

Celia's excitement and growing sense of purpose made my heart sing. What it would be to live with such joy and purpose each day — to rise every morning looking forward to work that would benefit an entire community, bring us into relationship with one another and use the natural gifts and inclinations we'd all been blessed with. It seemed like heaven opening to me, and that was confusing.

How could something so lovely, so inviting and welcome come to me? How could it seem that God was blessing everyone around me, allowing me to be part of this amazing gift, when He couldn't possibly look on me with favor? I didn't know, and I dared not look too closely for fear the gift might be taken away. Any day, Gerald could waltz through the front door, or there would be a knock, and when I opened it, his smug power would bear down on me.

In the meantime I determined to do my best for Aunt Hyacinth and the people of No Creek who might benefit from the library, and to take advice from an expression of Olney Tate's: "Don't look a gift horse in the mouth. You might find the teeth are rotten or you might find them fine; it's a gift horse just the same."

I could tell by Reverend Willard's longing gazes at the books and his concern for Miz Hyacinth that he wished he could be part of tearing down the old and setting up the new, but he hadn't time. He tended the congregational needs of a full church in No Creek on Sundays and Wednesday evenings as well as a church in Ridgemont on Saturdays and Tuesday evenings — besides visiting the sick and homebound and settling local disputes. All that plus another job writing a column of sermons printed in a Charlotte newspaper kept him busy and solvent.

Aunt Hyacinth and I could lift the window most late afternoons and hear him practicing his sermons to the tombstones in the churchyard. We couldn't hear enough to know all he said but caught the inflection in his voice, the passion of his heart. It seemed to do Aunt Hyacinth good, so daily I raised the window by her chair. Sometimes we'd share a giggle over our eavesdropping or at amusing things he said.

It was fun at the time, but later I felt guilty — as if we were being sacrilegious. And yet, when Aunt Hyacinth surprised me by telling Reverend Willard we did that, he laughed as if it was the best joke in the world and said he figured it a great compliment that we'd listened so attentively since, after all, he'd not been able to raise the dead with his preaching.

It was on a Tuesday that we finally finished organizing the adult nonfiction. Alphabetizing the fiction and setting up the children's room would be pure pleasure after that.

"How will we let people know when to come?" Celia asked the question that had troubled me. As a newcomer I didn't think I was the one to spread the word. And I feared, as the time drew closer, opening up Garden's Gate to the scrutiny of strangers and the litany of questions regarding my relationship to Aunt Hyacinth and the Belvidere family that would surely come with daily visitors. How could I answer them truthfully without revealing too much, without running the risk that word of my whereabouts would somehow get back to my husband or father?

"Reverend Willard can announce it on Sunday," Chester volunteered, which sounded like a very good idea.

"But then it just sounds like something the preacher wants us to do that's good for us." Celia stuck out her lower lip and pinched it. "Nobody's likely to take to that."

"We could post a notice at the general store. Ida Mae's good for spreading any word we want." Gladys flicked her dustrag across the bottom row of novels authored by writers whose names began with the letter *A*.

But it was Chester who came up with the idea Celia seconded and championed. "A party, like they throw after a working — that always gets people to come."

"Clogging and Joe Earl's fiddle — here?" Their mother frowned.

"Perhaps not, but a party," Aunt Hyacinth mused. "A summer tea party to show off Garden's Gate and welcome our friends to the library. That's not a bad idea. What do you think, Grace?"

"Well, I —"

"We could show them all the books and how they're arranged and teach them how to check them out!" Celia looked near to bursting. "I can be the librarian and sign everybody up! And lend all the books out!"

Her mother fussed, "Settle down, Celia. You're hopping like a pogo stick. I don't know that an invitation to view books will bring people out, Miz Hyacinth."

"They'll come if there's cake!" Chester asserted. "I'll come, if there's cake."

Aunt Hyacinth's bells went off again. "Then cake there will be!"

"And lemonade for the kids and sweet tea for the grown-ups!" Celia was already making a list. "And everybody can come, right? Right, Miz Hyacinth? We can help spread the word."

"Grace?" Aunt Hyacinth deferred.

"It sounds like a good idea — more work, but a good idea."

"Excellent! I do think posting a notice in the general store and post office is the thing, and if Reverend Willard would make some sort of announcement and mention on Sunday that he'll come, that would certainly bring folks out."

"At least women with unmarried daughters," Gladys said under her breath.

So our plans were underway, and Celia, true to her word, set about inviting everybody she knew.

136

CHAPTER SEVENTEEN

Jesse was delighted with the library idea and more than glad to make the announcement in church, extending the invitation to Miz Hyacinth's house on Sunday. The tea party and library reception would take place that very July afternoon, and all of No Creek was invited.

Ida Mae and those attending church who'd seen the notice all week tacked up in the post office took it for granted that only the white people of No Creek would come. Jesse knew and accepted that. It hadn't occurred to him that it would be otherwise.

Notwithstanding a shred of misgiving when he saw Ida Mae's face, Jesse wholeheartedly expressed joy and offered a firm handclasp when he met Reverend George Pierce of No Creek's colored church, Saints Delight, leading his flock to Miz Hyacinth's door.

Reverend Pierce was one of the finest men and most gifted pastors Jesse knew. Miz Hyacinth and Miss Grace already ranked high in Jesse's estimation. Their invitation to the members of Saints Delight Church despite No Creek's known prejudice shot that standing over the moon.

Olney Tate was not among those attending, but Jesse saw his wife and children right behind Reverend Pierce. Olney and Marshall, Jesse knew, were working that afternoon for the widow Cramer, who desperately needed a new well dug.

Jesse and Ida Mae were latecomers, as were the folks from Saints Delight. They entered through the front door together, Jesse pulling Ida Mae, who'd become a mite standoffish, right along with him. Celia welcomed them all into the parlor — now the children's reading room — like they were long-lost cousins and she, lady of the manor.

Jesse went through to the kitchen and saw out the window that everybody else who'd come was milling about in the back garden, where the eats were spread on sawhorse tables covered with Miz Hyacinth's best damask tablecloths. Miz Hyacinth, leaning on Grace's arm, was just finishing up a speech about the new lending library and introducing her "dear relation" as the woman in charge.

It was a beautiful summer's day, just right for admiring the roses in full bloom and all the new plantings and old trimmed shrubs that Olney and Marshall had brought back to shape and life. Even the new swing, big enough for two sets of two at a time, had been painted white and stood ready for guests.

It was a veritable Garden of Eden, a grand day outside and a grand and astonishing day inside as Celia opened to the congregation of Saints Delight Church the wonders, the breadth and generosity of Miz Hyacinth's library. Jesse could hardly decide where to perch it was all so fine.

"Yes," he heard Celia expound to Reverend Pierce after he'd lamented that many of the books were beyond their children's reading level, "maybe they are now, but I'm certain that Miss Grace will be right glad to help any of your church's children with their learning. She wants everybody to enjoy the pleasures of reading!"

"That's mighty generous!" Reverend Pierce looked at her, surprised. "Some of our young ones have fallen behind since our schoolhouse teacher moved on. The children need more books, but more than that, help with their reading. Some of the parents of our young-sters — those who've had some schooling — have been taking turns, but most of our ladies are busy with their housework and take on extra work besides. If Miss Grace could see her way to help, that would be magnificent."

Celia declared that she loved that word, *magnificent,* and promised more than Jesse knew was possible to deliver, more than she could possibly have been authorized to offer by either Grace or Miz Hyacinth.

Ida Mae tried to intervene numerous times, but Celia was on a roll and not to be deterred. By the time Miss Grace led the group from the backyard in through the front door to introduce them to the "inner workings of the library," the Saints Delight congregation had moved on into the grown-up section of books and was just about to work up enough nerve to take a book or two off the shelf to view. The excited conversationalists of each congregation became slowly aware of the other until all came to an abrupt halt and a dead silence.

Janice Richards, Celia's archrival in school and life, gasped. Mrs. Richards turned to see the reason, gasped herself, and pulled her children behind her, whispering just loud enough to raise the hairs on Jesse's neck, "What in the world are *they* doing here?"

It was the first Miss Grace seemed to notice anyone else in the house. She started, as if she had trouble taking everything in, as if she didn't want to be drawn into whatever tension was clearly growing in the room, as if she didn't want to claim the center of that attention. To her credit, Jesse thought, she visibly swallowed, smiled tentatively, and stepped forward, extending her hand to welcome Reverend Pierce, who stepped up to shield his flock. "I'm so glad to meet you. I'm Grace."

Jesse's heart raced as Reverend Pierce held back only a moment before clasping Grace's hand in an uncertain handshake. "Reverend Pierce, ma'am. I'm mighty pleased to meet you, Miss Grace, and I thank you for this kind invitation."

"Just Grace, please." She smiled warmly.

It was his moment, Jesse's opportunity to bridge the gap. "Reverend George Pierce is pastor of Saints Delight Church, and he's brought his congregation here today to welcome you to No Creek and to see this wondrous library." He ran out of words then.

"Did I misunderstand?" Reverend Pierce kept his smile, but the nervous tick in his eye reacted to the shudder of Mrs. Richards and the lift of Ida Mae's chin.

Before Grace could respond, Celia pushed forward. "You didn't misunderstand nothin', Reverend Pierce." She turned to Grace. "I invited him, Miss Grace. I invited everybody, just like you said!" She spread her arms wide, but Jesse saw the momentary uncertainty in the girl's eyes.

"And quite right you were to do so, Celia!" Miz Hyacinth and her white-tipped cane pushed through the crowd. "Reverend Pierce, I can't see you but I hear your welcome voice. Come and shake my hand, sir."

The crowd in the parlor parted like the Red

Sea, and the matriarch of No Creek stood, waiting for her Moses to cross the divide. When he'd reached her and taken her hand in both of his own, Miz Hyacinth called out, "Is Joe Earl here?"

"I am indeed, Miz Hyacinth!" Joe sounded sober, much to Jesse's relief.

"Did you bring your fiddle?"

"Don't go nowhere without it."

"Then play us some hymns. It's Sunday, after all. And, Reverend Pierce, is enough of your choir here to do those hymns justice?"

"Yes, ma'am." Reverend Pierce beamed from ear to ear. "We'd be mighty proud to bless this endeavor."

"Then I wish you would. Joe, start us off with 'I Love to Tell the Story.' That's a fitting one for a room full of books, don't you think?"

Jesse stood back then and watched the choir come to life. Miz Hyacinth, smiling broadly but pale with the exertion of it all, took her chair by the parlor window.

Jesse glanced at Grace, who stood with eyes lit in awe and appreciation of Miz Hyacinth's natural ability to deflect tension, her generosity of spirit. Still, Grace appeared a little breathless with the tension in the house. But her face froze when Mrs. Richards grabbed her elbow and pulled her to one side, whispering intently in her ear before standing back to glare at her full on.

He couldn't hear, but Jesse saw Grace flush and her hackles rise, saw her shoulders pull back and her spine stiffen. Still, she grit-smiled, tilted her head, and whispered something in Mrs. Richards's ear that made that woman stand back pinch-mouthed, shove the empty crystal punch cup into Miss Grace's hand, grab the hands of her son and daughter, and nearly yank them out the front door. They pushed directly through the choir that had already finished "I Love to Tell the Story" and was on the second verse of "Bringing in the Sheaves."

"Sowing in the sunshine, sowing in the
shadows,
Fearing neither clouds nor winter's chilling
breeze . . ."

Jesse figured "winter's chilling breeze" an appropriate line for the woman's exit but was sad that more of the Shady Grove congregation followed her — more folks than Jesse cared to count. He could tell by the tilt of Miz Hyacinth's head that she knew some had left and he was certain she knew why, but she just kept smiling in the direction of the singing and tapping her fingers to the music on the arm of her chair.

The party went on for another half hour and the singing, warmed up and rattling the windowpanes, might have gone long into the night, but Gladys Percy invited all the Saints Delight folks into the back garden for a freshly spread table of eats. Jesse marveled at Gladys, never understanding how she could create a banquet from a sow's ear, but she was famous for it and had done it again. Joe Earl seemed like he'd play from then to eternity, but Grace kindly hinted that Miz Hyacinth was looking a mite weary and had best call it a day. Perhaps he could play in the garden for the guests there.

There was no hesitation. The parlor and library emptied in a moment; every person said their goodbyes and thanks to Miz Hyacinth and Grace, then left by the front door or stepped into the backyard to continue the party.

In another half hour Grace had guided Miz Hyacinth up the stairs to bed. The last few guests helped tote empty platters into the kitchen, fold the spotted damask tablecloths, and break down the boards and horses that formed the long line of outdoor tables.

Then it was Celia, Chester, Gladys, and Jesse in the kitchen, washing up the dishes. They didn't expect him to stay and do that, he knew. But it felt homey to be among them in the heart of Miz Hyacinth's dwelling place and he was glad to be a part of it. He didn't mind wearing the old dish towel around his waist or bending over the dry sink that sat too low for the ache in his back.

Grace came in then, her face set in a peace that Jesse had not seen before, and she smiled. His heart quickened. He thought in that moment that he wouldn't mind waking up every morning of the world to that smile. He turned quickly away, grabbing a dish to wash that he'd already washed, anxious and chagrined and delighted that he'd conjured such a thought.

The women were just setting up the last of the platters and plates when a scrape came at the back door. No one bothered with it at first, not even sure it wasn't the wind or a field mouse come calling. But it came again, a timid knock.

Gladys opened the door. "Why, Ruby Lynne Wishon! It's near dark. What are you doing here, child?"

Ruby Lynne glanced at Jesse and her color rose, but her eyes swept the room, coming to rest on Grace. "I've come to see Miss Grace."

"Well, it's getting late. Don't you think — ?"

But Grace stepped forward. "We met today. Ruby Lynne, I'm so glad to see you again. How can I help you? Did you want a book tonight?"

"No, ma'am. I mean, yes, I'd like a book, but I don't need help." She twisted her hands.

"Please come in. You may browse all you want."

Gladys huffed. "There's library hours for such business. Miss Grace isn't open all hours of the day and night, you know."

"Gladys," Grace admonished gently, "Ruby Lynne is my guest and I'm so very glad she's come."

Gladys shook her head and stood back, letting Ruby Lynne enter.

"It isn't really that I want to borrow a book. I mean I do, but not tonight. I want to help in your library."

"I'm the library helper." Celia spoke up right away and Jesse knew she was fearful of losing her special place.

Ruby Lynne ignored her. "I heard Reverend Pierce say some of the children in his congregation need help with reading. Celia said you'll help them — tutor them, I guess."

Grace's eyebrows rose. It was the first she'd heard about it, Jesse realized, and he almost grinned.

Celia stepped forward, looking up with big brown eyes. "I was gonna tell you about that."

"I see. And what else did you say?" Grace waited patiently, so like Miz Hyacinth, Jesse thought.

He saw the lump in Celia's throat go up and down. "I'm not exactly sure. It was all so exciting and everybody was happy and everything seemed like a good idea . . . at the time."

"The thing is," Ruby Lynne broke in, "I want to help. I have it in mind to one day be a teacher, like Miz Hyacinth. I was in her last class, you know, and I never had a better teacher. I never had another teacher. My daddy said there's no reason to bother with me going to the high school. But I loved school and I loved everything she taught me. I want to teach school someday."

"That's a laudable ambition." So few of his congregation nurtured ambitions beyond their next meal, which was challenge enough. Few, outside of the Maes and Miz Hyacinth, had completed school or set foot outside of No Creek unless they'd left for work in the tobacco factory in the city of Winston-Salem or for one of the mill towns across the state, or ran 'shine into another county. Factories and mills meant long hours of backbreaking labor amid heat and dust with no union to advocate for safety or protest the pitiful pay or deplorable working conditions — or to keep them from near indenture to the company store. None of those "opportunities" provided a path beyond poverty.

Ruby Lynne's color rose even brighter at the preacher's praise. "I can help some of those children learn to read better. I'm a fair reader myself."

"That's a brilliant idea, Ruby Lynne." Jesse couldn't contain himself. But he was taken aback by Grace's set mouth. He felt his eyes go wide. Had he spoken out of turn? Did she not want to encourage the tutoring of Saints Delight children?

But Gladys spoke out loud, looking first at

Ruby Lynne and then at Jesse. "Will your daddy see it that way, Ruby Lynne? He might not like you teaching colored children. And where would you do it? You can't be going down to their schoolhouse or into their homes. Your daddy'd never stand for you going down to Saints Delight, even if Reverend Pierce opened up the church for just that purpose. Have you asked him about this?"

"You may teach them here, Ruby Lynne." Grace said it kindly but firmly, just as if she hadn't heard a word Gladys said. "We'll work out the days and times with your schedule and mine, and we'll need to talk with Reverend Pierce, find out who needs help and what kind and when they can come. It may be that some need more than reading help — arithmetic and such."

"Reverend Pierce said that the children have fallen behind since their teacher left." Celia spoke humbly, but Jesse knew that was a conniving measure on her part. Still, Grace ignored all but Ruby Lynne.

"Would you be willing to help with arithmetic?"

The smile that broke across Ruby Lynne's face would shame the sun. "I would, Miss Grace. I will! I'll help with anything."

"Good. That's settled. Now you'd best get home before real dark comes on. You don't want to be out alone so late."

"No, ma'am. I mean, yes, ma'am! I'll come

148

by Wednesday and we can talk more, all right?"

"Yes, all right. That's a fine idea."

Ruby Lynne all but twirled out the door, dancing light on cat's feet. Just before she tripped through, she stopped in her tracks. "Oh, I almost forgot. Ida Mae was on her way here and saw me on the road. When I told her I was coming, she asked me to give this to Miz Hyacinth — said it came in yesterday's mail and she had to sign for it. She said she doesn't know who this is for, but since it was sent in care of Miz Hyacinth, she figured it was all right to sign and send it on. She meant to give it to her this afternoon — it looking official and all. Said she's sorry she clean forgot once she got here." Ruby Lynne handed Grace an envelope — a long, business type of envelope. Even from across the table Jesse could see the formal black script.

Grace read the address. Her face washed white. He was certain her breath caught and that the hand that reached for a chair back was meant to steady herself.

Ruby Lynne left, her every step still lighter than air.

Gladys locked the door the moment the girl was gone, as if that would change anything. She turned to Grace, ignoring the fact that Jesse was still there, ignoring the sudden weariness that had dropped over Grace like a

149

veil. "Do you know what you're doing? Rhoan Wishon won't stand for it. This isn't Philadelphia or New York or even Washington, DC. Whites and coloreds don't mix here — not in one another's homes — and live to tell it."

Grace looked at Gladys as if she'd just realized she was not alone in the room, then glanced at Jesse, who couldn't take his eyes off her. "I'll help," he said, "in any way you want."

Grace stood silent — frozen — for a moment, then took off her apron and hung it on the hook by the door. Jesse could no longer see her face but saw the shudder of her sigh. Even so, it seemed to him that a ramrod inched up her back. She didn't turn but said quietly, "This is my fight."

Chapter Eighteen

The letter sat on the small secretary in my room for an hour. It took me that long to gain the courage to slit the seal. I'd rather face a hundred Velma Richardses and Ida Maes and even Ruby Lynne's father than its contents.

My dear Lilliana,

This is to inform you that I will arrive in No Creek on Tuesday to bring you home.

Your father and I understand you were distraught over your mother's death, but deserting me at such a time was not the best means for you to cope; you must see that. Rest assured we will find you the help you need. We realize that we can no longer hope you will recover on your own.

Convey to your aunt my sincere apologies for the imposition she has experienced and assure her that I will reimburse her for

expenses incurred during your protracted
stay.

Your concerned and loving husband,
Gerald

Every word calculated. Every word bent
toward his intended end. Even the delivery of
the letter, requiring a signature, could be
used in court against me.

Home. As if *home* was where he truly
wanted me. As if *home* was with Gerald.
Memories of Father physically dragging
Mama from Aunt Hyacinth's arms all those
years ago flashed through my mind.

It was already the early hours of Monday.
He'd be here tomorrow. I could run, but
where? And if I did, it meant Aunt Hyacinth
would be left to face him alone. Chills raced
through me at that imagination.

For weeks I'd dreaded the moment I might
open the front door to find him standing
there — so much so that I'd hated to fall
asleep for the nightmares that came. Now,
unexpectedly, he'd given me warning. Why?
Was it to establish a paper trail for legal
purposes? Did he intend to give me time to
run? Would my running add weight to his
case?

I had no idea what had transpired within
the church or what had come of Gerald's
privileged workings within the legal system in
the months I'd been gone. Retrieving me was

evidently his next step. What else had he set in motion to have me committed or accused of adultery or both?

Yesterday's tea and opening of the library had unfolded a future — glorious, hopeful. Even Velma Richards's snubs had served to foster streaks of determination in my spine — something new and wondrous or, dared I hope, long dormant and now roused. I'd been incensed by her unkindness and injustice and annoyed at Gladys's fear in the face of something so important as teaching children to read, as helping Ruby on the road to achieving her dream.

It reminded me of my regret over Sarah — how little Mama and I had done for her. I didn't know if Sarah knew how to read. I didn't even know her son's address in Chicago. *How could I not know those things after all she was to me? How could I not have thought to ask after her family, to offer to teach her to read if she didn't?*

By committing to help the children of Saints Delight and to mentor Ruby, I'd felt a kindling of fire inside my heart — a good fire. Then, in hardly the space of a breath, everything of that all-important day had vanished, slamming the door in one terrifying note.

I didn't undress but lay staring out my window at the dark. A whip-poor-will called from the edge of the woods. It sang off and on for hours, keeping me company as the moon made its way across the sky, reminding me of the night I first came to Aunt Hyacinth's. That night bird's call had drawn memories of the year Mama and I had come to Garden's Gate. She'd said as we'd stood on Aunt Hyacinth's front porch that a whippoor-will's call signals comfort in the night. Even as a child I'd hoped it meant new beginnings. But what did those new beginnings mean now?

By the time gray light crept through the trees, I'd determined my course.

There was no question Gerald could force me to return to Pennsylvania with him. Aunt Hyacinth might offer me sanctuary, but Gerald was even more to be feared than my father. My father had bullied and terrified my mother; Gerald bullied and terrified me, but he was also physically stronger and more persuasive to those around him. He could convince others of whatever he wished, through gentlemanly charm or tears or vows to change — if any doubted his sincerity. If that didn't work, he could, and had, physically carried me off.

I could run away again, but where would I go? Eventually he would find me — as he'd found me now.

There was nothing for it but to return with him and endure whatever public humiliation he'd planned to permanently rid himself of me. Only when I no longer hindered his plans or reputation could I hope to escape for good. Whether I'd be able to return to Garden's Gate before Aunt Hyacinth's passing, I didn't know — could hardly expect — but I needed to do all I could for her before I went. She would be heartbroken with this loss on top of all else.

I packed my few belongings. I'd arrived with nothing. Aunt Hyacinth would have no use for the clothes I'd purchased here, but Gladys might. We were close to the same size. Gerald would never permit me to keep them anyway. It would look too much as if I'd found a way to manage on my own.

Though I'd been terrified Gerald would find me, now that the letter had come, now that I'd read it and laid it aside, I was not so frightened as I was numb. Numbness was my defense against Gerald's fists and shouting tirades, against his throwing things and biting and kicking my legs and stomach. Shutting down and folding inside myself was the only way I'd survived seven years of his outbursts. Numbness was the only means of surviving to move forward another day.

There was no way I could spare my precious aunt sorrow. And she deserved to hear everything from me first.

Midmorning I took tea into the parlor, now also the children's library room, for Aunt

Hyacinth and me. I'd baked biscuits early and, after pouring her tea, spread the warmed-over biscuits thick with butter and Aunt Hyacinth's raspberry jam. I set the plate beside her tea and guided her hand to it. Oh, how I would miss these precious moments with her!

"What a treat! I smelled those biscuits baking, you know, and wondered when you'd bring them out." Bells came through the smile in her voice.

"There's something I must tell you, Aunt Hyacinth."

"Yes, my dear? About the library? I think yesterday's opening was splendid! All things, and all people, considered, I don't think it could have gone better."

"No," I conceded, "you're right. It was wonderful. But that's not it —"

A knock came at the door. It occurred to me in that moment that perhaps Gerald had deliberately misled me, that he'd given me a date but all along meant to show up early, to throw me off my guard.

The knock came again, this time louder.

"Who could that be?" Aunt Hyacinth asked. "An eager library patron already?" She smiled, but I didn't move. "Is everything all right, Lilliana?"

I stood, swallowing. "I hope so." I smoothed my skirt, drew a deep breath, and walked to the door. Another pounding was in progress when I pulled it open. "Coltrane? It's Coltrane Richards, isn't it?"

"Mama said to give you this, Miss Belvidere." Coltrane shoved a pink envelope into my hand and all but dove off the porch as if his feet might burn if he stayed a moment longer.

Relief washed over me so that I almost laughed into the morning sun.

"Did you say Coltrane is here?" Aunt Hyacinth called.

I closed the door and slit the seal on the envelope. "He's gone now. He brought a note from his mother."

"Oh, dear." Aunt Hyacinth clucked her tongue. "What does she have to say now? Nothing helpful, I'll wager."

As I pulled out the note, a waft of perfume — something strong and pungent — filled the air. I read aloud to Aunt Hyacinth.

"Dear Miss Belvidere,
Thank you for yesterday's tea and the opening of Miz Hyacinth's home to form a lending library for our community.
I trust that yesterday's mistake, which I attribute to Celia Percy's rashness and apparent misunderstanding, won't happen again. You must realize that inviting coloreds into Miz Hyacinth's home will inevitably stain your reputation and hers. As you surely know and as Miz Hyacinth can tell you, such

157

stains carry lasting consequences.

To make myself perfectly clear, I must repeat that neither my daughter, Janice, nor my son, Coltrane, will be allowed to attend your lending library or to play with the Percy children if you and they do not properly separate yourselves. I am also writing to Mrs. Percy in the same vein. You will agree that we must protect the reputations of our children, especially our daughters. It is my Christian duty to make certain the other mothers understand the severity of the situation and do the same. Trust that I will.

Sincerely,
Velma Richards"

"Of all the nerve!" Aunt Hyacinth sputtered. "It's just like her, I'm sorry to say. Well, you can't kowtow to her or anyone else."

I almost gasped. *Kowtow?* I'd become very good at kowtowing. But Aunt Hyacinth knew nothing of Gerald's letter. I had to focus on the matter at hand — and yet, what would Velma Richards matter to me if I wasn't even here?

I knew the answer. If it weren't consequential for Celia and Chester and for the other youngsters, colored and white, who so wanted to come to the library, I could have ignored the woman. For their sakes I needed to stand up to Velma Richards without alienating half of No Creek. Aunt Hyacinth and I needed to stand up to her. But how? How could Aunt Hyacinth manage the library with me gone? Ruby Lynne had offered to help, but she was too young to take over and certainly couldn't be here all the time. It was too much to expect of Gladys.

"Never mind her. I surely enjoyed Reverend Pierce and his choir yesterday. Such splendid voices. Such heart! It thrills me to know they'll be using this library. It wouldn't have happened without you, Lilliana."

"Yes." I wasn't sure I should inject too much enthusiasm. "Yes, they have splendid voices."

"You seem less than excited about our day."

I sighed. "I don't know what to do. Velma Richards seems like a woman who will carry out her threat."

"No doubt. It's a crusade for her." Moments passed. "Not much Christian about it, is there?"

I felt like snorting. "I don't know. It pretty well fits with what I've come to expect of Christians."

"Then you've only known people who take the name of the Lord in vain."

That caught me short.

"Jesus called Jews of every social rank. He called women and children and people from Samaria and tax collectors and prostitutes and the down-and-out to Himself. He called unlearned fishermen for the greatest work in the history of the world. He called the humble and the penitent and those who were smart enough to recognize their need of a Savior and to see that need fulfilled in Him. Those people followed Him, surrendered their all to Him, and obeyed His commands. They are the ones who deserve the name 'Christian' — Christ followers. Anything less, anything Pharisaic and legalistic and arrogant, takes His name in vain. Velma reminds me of the elder brother in the parable of the Prodigal Son — totally unaware that her position in the community was given her."

"Are you saying Velma Richards is not a Christian?" I was astonished by Aunt Hyacinth's lengthy tirade and perversely thrilled with her defiance.

Aunt Hyacinth chuckled. "Well, not to her face." She grew serious just as quickly. "But I'm saying that you need to recognize the difference between what people claim to be and what they are, and take that into account when you make your decision."

"My decision?"

"Yes. Whether or not you'll allow everyone to come to the library, whether or not you'll tutor children at all, and if so, will it be all children who want to read better or only the children who are acceptable to the Pharisees? Gladys told me about Ruby Lynne when she came to say good night — and Celia's offer to Reverend Pierce. It's up to you, Lilliana."

"It's not up to me, Aunt Hyacinth. This is your house. No Creek is your home. These are your people." Knowing I would be leaving, it was more important than ever that Aunt Hyacinth decide for herself. "Mrs. Richards said that if we continue to allow colored people into the house, it will stain — will ruin your reputation and mine. I think she means to shun us. That could be so uncomfortable for you at church, and maybe no one would come to use your library."

"Shun me at church? It won't matter much longer for me. And Reverend Willard would never stand for that."

"He may not be able to stop her."

"No, he may not. People here are well-set in their ways. Answer me this: are you afraid of Velma Richards?"

"Afraid?" That raised the ire in me. "No, I'm not afraid of her. I'm angry — infuriated. But I am afraid she'll do what she says. And there are so many things to consider." Was now the time to tell her? *I'm running out of time.*

Aunt Hyacinth shrugged. "Let her try. Let her, and see how things unfold." She leaned back in her chair and closed her eyes. "Aren't you tired of being afraid, Lilliana? Aren't you bone tired?"

Chapter Nineteen

Jesse had just laid his Sunday pants between the bedsprings and mattress, hoping to hone a crease down the center by the Tuesday evening service in Ridgemont, when a knock came at the parsonage door. He checked his watch. Eight o'clock on a Monday night was late for callers. Most folks in No Creek rose and went to bed with the sun and, except to frequent the Whistle Stop or a hidden still in the woods, rarely set foot off their front porch after a weeknight supper.

He flipped on the porch light and opened the door. "Grace! What a welcome surprise." He was surprised, even confused to see her standing there. She'd never come to the parsonage, not once. "Is Miz Hyacinth all right? She's not taken a turn, has she?"

"No, no. Hyacinth is fine. It's me I've come to talk with you about, Reverend Willard. Me, and it bears on Hyacinth — Aunt Hyacinth."

He had no idea what she meant, but he was gladder than peach pie on Sunday to have her. He noticed her use of *Aunt.* "Forgive my manners. Won't you come in?"

"Is it . . . is it all right to see you here, now? I know it's late."

"It's fine — fine." But then he realized he must consider her reputation. "Unless you'd rather we talk in the church."

"No. It's a matter of some delicacy. I don't want anyone to walk in on our conversation or to overhear just yet."

He'd not seen Grace Belvidere so divided from her confidence, so strained in her speech yet so determined to talk. "Please, come in. Can I offer you a cup of tea? Coffee?"

"No thank you. Please. I need to get this out, and it's hard for me but important, and there's not much time."

"Have a seat."

She sighed as she sank onto his settee. He took the rocking chair adjacent.

"I've thought about this all afternoon and still, I hardly know where to begin."

"The beginning's always been a favorite of mine." He smiled.

She smiled, a bit sadly, in return. "I'll start with my name. It's not Grace Belvidere."

If he'd expected anything, it wasn't this.

"My name is Lilliana Grace Swope. My grandmother was a Belvidere — Aunt Hyacinth's sister, Camellia Belvidere, before she married. Grandmother's daughter — my mother — was Rosemary."

"Miz Hyacinth's niece, the one she raised — the one who —" He stopped short.

"Yes. The one who ran off to get married and broke her heart. And now I'm about to break my grandaunt's heart again."

"You're running off to get married?" Jesse's heart plummeted to his feet.

"No . . . no."

"I'm sorry. Please go on."

"Mama died earlier this year."

"I'm sorry, Grace — Lilliana. I didn't know."

She smiled, now a worried smile. "Thank you."

"Lilliana is such a beautiful name. Lily — a flower name — like all the Belvidere women. Was Swope your mother's married name?"

"No. It's my name — my married name."

Jesse felt as if someone had punched him in the gut. His head reeled and his body stiffened. *Married? She's married?* He willed his face not to react. *She came because she's in need. I'm her pastor, as much of a pastor as she has. It's my job — my duty — my privilege to listen to what she has to say.*

"I ran away after my mother's funeral." She pressed fingers to her temples, pushing her hair and the combs that held it back, leaving it standing up on one side. "It's a long story, and I'm not making excuses, but I didn't

164

know where else to go. Aunt Hyacinth had been so good to my mother and to me when I was a little girl — the summer we came here."

"Does Miz Hyacinth know — ?"

"Yes, she knows everything . . . Well, as much as . . . The thing is, I received a letter — the letter you saw Ruby Lynne de —"

She was interrupted by a second pounding on the door that made them both jump.

Jesse couldn't imagine who else could be on his doorstep at such an hour. Nobody was near dying, as far as he knew. No imminent births. An accident? "I'm sorry, Grace — Lilliana." Her new name would take some getting used to. "I'll see who it is and be right back."

She nodded, turning her head, swiping at tears that threatened.

His head still spinning, Jesse opened the door to a man he'd never seen — and Ida Mae standing off to his side. "Ida Mae? Is everything all right?"

"Not by half, Reverend." Ida Mae looked like the cat who'd swallowed the canary and pretended to be sorry about it.

The man pulled open the screen door before Jesse could offer. "Gerald Swope." Jesse heard Lilliana gasp from the sitting room. "I see that my wife is here."

Jesse could not have been more surprised if the man had claimed to come from the moon or if he'd delivered a right hook to his jaw.

Ida Mae's eyes widened. It was the light of the gossip in them that irked Jesse most. "Mr. Swope came looking for Miz Hyacinth's house, and it being near dark and him a stranger to No Creek, I offered to show him. When we passed your house, we couldn't help but see through the window — he's come looking for his wife, to take her home — Lilliana Swope." Ida Mae poured it out all in a rush and enunciated the name loudly, looking significantly past Jesse toward the sitting area. "I told him that as far as I knew only a relative named *Grace Belvidere* was living with Miz Hyacinth, but of course, he explained the truth of that."

Jesse realized their interpretation of what they'd seen through the front room window. Nothing could have been more innocent or possibly looked less so if a person was so inclined.

Lilliana waited on the settee, her hair still standing up on one side. He glimpsed her attempt to stop the trembling in her hands. Instantly, he disliked the man and his assumptions. Not an appropriate initial response for a man of God, he knew.

"Thank you, Ida Mae. We won't keep you. I'm sure you'll want to close up the store and get home to your family. Would you like to come in, Mr. Swope?" As Gerald Swope shouldered past, Jesse pulled the screen door closed, cutting off Ida Mae's intended entrance. "I'll see you at the Wednesday evening prayer meeting, Ida Mae." Before she could close the wide O of her mouth, he closed the inside door, all the while praying for discernment, understanding, wisdom, strength, patience.

But Ida Mae pushed it open again and walked right in as if she lived there. "Mr. Swope gave me a ride up the hill in his car as I offered to show him the way. He assured me he'd see me safely returned to the store. Any gentleman would."

Jesse couldn't argue with that, even though he knew Ida Mae and every citizen of No Creek walked every inch of the surrounding hills by the light of the moon without so much as a stumble.

"Lilliana, it's good to see you." Gerald stepped forward to embrace his wife, but she stepped back.

"Your letter said tomorrow — that you were coming tomorrow." Lilliana's words sounded hollow, betrayed.

Gerald removed his hat. "I couldn't wait another night. I drove all day to get here. We can spend the night with your aunt and be off in the morning. It will give me a chance to meet Aunt Hyacinth." His manner turned solicitous, even charming.

"Aunt? Miz Hyacinth's your aunt?" Ida Mae raised her eyebrows. "Rosemary's daughter."

"Ida Mae," Jesse interrupted, "I think Mr. and Mrs. Swope may need some privacy. Perhaps I can walk you home."

"No! Please don't go — not yet," Lilliana all but begged.

"Lilliana, we need to speak alone. Let's go to my car. The reverend has offered to see Mrs. Mae home." Gerald reached for her.

"I won't go with you."

"Please, Lilliana, don't make a scene. No more scenes. We'll go for a drive. We can talk things out in private." The charm thinned.

"I don't want to talk. I won't be alone with you. I heard what you and my father were planning. I heard you that night in the church — after Mama's funeral."

Gerald's jaw tightened, but he pressed on. "I don't know what you heard or think you heard. You disappeared after your mother's funeral. What was I to think? I understand you were upset, distraught, that you might have imagined things that simply weren't so. Your father and I've been looking for you day and night ever since."

"And you've only just found me. After all these weeks." She clearly didn't believe him.

"Come home. We can work out whatever it is that has you worried. We'll get you whatever help you need. I promise."

But Lilliana stepped back, shaking her head. "I'm not the one who needs help."

Jesse thought that if she could disappear into the woodwork, she would. He didn't understand. She looked at her husband with eyes of terror, as if he was a monster, but he didn't seem like a monster — just a very concerned, possibly controlling man looking for his wife. Although something about his story, about the elapsed time frame, didn't add up, and Jesse had never thought of Grace — or Lilliana — as troubled, at least not in an unstable way. If this was indeed the man who'd so upset Miz Hyacinth on the telephone, there must be more to the story than he portrayed.

"Why are you here now — in this man's house?" Gerald changed from the concerned spouse to the injured party. He glanced from Lilliana to Jesse and back. "Have the two of you been living here — together — all this time?"

Ida Mae went bug-eyed. She looked as if she might speak but forcibly closed her mouth.

"Grace — Lilliana lives with her aunt. I believe you know that, Mr. Swope," Jesse said firmly. "You said you were on your way there to see her."

"Then why is she here with you now, after dark?" He turned to Lilliana. "Why did Hyacinth Belvidere tell me that you were not living with her?"

"I came to say goodbye and to ask Reverend

169

Willard to look in on Aunt Hyacinth after I'd gone." Lilliana drew a deep breath as if relieved she'd finally gotten out her real purpose for coming. "But now I know. I'm not going back with you, Gerald. I won't leave Aunt Hyacinth. She's not well — and I'm not going with you."

Jesse saw that it took every ounce of courage Lilliana could muster to deliver that speech, but her husband dismissed it.

"I'm sure your aunt doesn't expect you to stay with her rather than return to your own home, to your own husband."

"Aunt Hyacinth's not the reason I won't go with you —"

"Unless there's more going on here than you're telling me. Unless this has little to do with your aunt." He looked pointedly at Jesse.

"Don't misrepresent what you see here, Mr. Swope. That's an insult to your wife and to me." Jesse's inner conflict was his own. He didn't want it to cloud the situation.

"If that's true, then there's no reason we should delay. Come with me now, Lilliana. We may just as well head home tonight." Gerald grasped her by the arm, directing her toward the door.

"Let go!" But he didn't seem inclined. She jerked away, digging her fingernails into the hand that had gripped her arm so tightly.

The flare in Gerald's eyes showed a different man — a flare he quickly got under

170

control. "What's got into you?" He made a production of pulling a handkerchief from his pocket to wrap his hand — a hand that Jesse noticed wasn't bleeding, but that Ida Mae was all too willing to help him tie the makeshift bandage around.

"Really, Lilliana — or Grace — or whatever name you go by. Resorting to violence!" Ida Mae shook her head. "He's your husband, after all."

"That's enough!" Jesse saw it all falling to pieces.

"You're trying to turn the tables — like always. I won't give in to you anymore. I'm done, Gerald. I've done nothing wrong and you can't pretend I have." Lilliana stood back, further yet, though unsteadily, Jesse saw.

"Nothing wrong!" Gerald half laughed, looking around the room as if seeing in its meager and threadbare offerings things that no one else saw.

Something in his laugh reminded Jesse of one of Dickens's villains. *Fagin, is it? Or worse, Bill Sikes?*

"Besides falsifying your name, did you forget to mention here that you're already married — seven years, to an elder in your own church?" Gerald watched her until the silence in the room became more uncomfortable than the voices. "I imagine, Reverend Willard, you believe yourself her needed protector. Is that what she's told you? Lilli-

171

ana doesn't need you. She has a husband, a husband whose patience has been sorely tested." He shook his head, now nearly pleading. "Lilliana, I can see you believe yourself injured. Whatever it is, can't you find it in your heart to forgive me and come home, give us another chance?"

"I told you I won't go with you. I will not go with you — ever again." Lilliana repeated her words as if the repeating gave her needed courage to stand by them.

"Hard-hearted, willful," Ida Mae mumbled, shaking her head with her hand against her cheek. She took a seat in a straight-backed chair near the door.

Gerald sat down heavily on the settee Lilliana had abandoned, a look of abject sorrow on his face. "You can't be serious . . . after all these years. We're married. You know I love you."

Lilliana didn't speak but edged toward the window, her back to the wall.

"Perhaps we should end this for tonight. Let's everyone go home and get some sleep and see how things look in the morning." Jesse didn't know what else to suggest. It looked as if the stalemate could go on a long time.

"Maybe so," Gerald sighed. "At least that will give me a chance to meet Hyacinth, talk things over as a family."

"Leave Aunt Hyacinth out of this. Her

heart can't take —"

"Your aunt surely won't turn me out of my wife's bed — our family's home!" Gerald stood up. "There's a limit, Lilliana."

"You said you wanted a divorce. You told my father. You can have it — or a permanent separation — anything. Just stay away. Leave me alone." The hurt and fear and resolve in Lilliana's eyes nearly undid Jesse.

"Divorce?" Ida Mae gasped.

Lilliana's cheeks burned bright.

"Lilliana." Gerald spoke softly, walking close to her. "You're overwrought. You don't know what you're saying. This is our marriage we're talking about. Tomorrow we'll go home. If you believe you have a grievance, we can take it before our church if that's what you want. Let them judge."

"*Our* church!" Lilliana laughed in disbelief.

"That's the biblical procedure for grievances that can't be resolved. Your own father is one of the elders. You know there will be a fair hearing. He's going to marry again, by the way. You'll want to be there for his wedding, surely."

Lilliana gasped. Jesse figured that last part was unwelcome news.

"You can't get a divorce for no good reason," Ida Mae insisted.

"Ida Mae, this is not our affair," Jesse cautioned.

"No, Reverend, it's certainly not." Gerald's

eyes flashed.

"You're welcome to stay here for the night, Mr. Swope. I'll give you my room. The settee is fine for me. Miz Hyacinth, you must remember, is an elderly maiden lady and not used to having men under her roof." Jesse wouldn't use the word *gentlemen.* He was becoming more and more certain it was an appellation Gerald Swope did not warrant, no matter that Ida Mae seemed convinced otherwise.

"Please take me home now, Mr. Swope. I've heard quite enough, and I've certainly earned the ride." Ida Mae lifted her chin, looping her purse over her arm.

Gerald looked as if he would say more, as if he meant to stay, but finally stood. "Of course, Mrs. Mae." He picked up his fedora. "I came here in good faith, intending to take my wife home and get her the help she needs, but I see I'm too late. Even you've come under her spell, *Reverend.*" He placed his hat on his head.

Lilliana stood straighter but didn't say a word.

Gerald stepped closer to her, but Jesse could still hear his words. "Remember what I've always told you. My promise stands — every word." He stroked her cheek. She turned her face away, refusing to look at him. He turned to Jesse. "More than desertion is evidently going on here. Expect to hear from

174

my lawyer, Reverend. Mrs. Mae?" He offered Ida Mae his arm and the door closed behind them as he ushered her through.

Jesse drew a ragged breath. It was as if a tornado had torn through his house, blowing out all the windows and doors, and now a terrible silence reigned in the destruction. "Well." He couldn't think what else to say.

"I'm sorry. I'm so sorry," Lilliana whispered. "He'll do what he says. I know he will."

"There's nothing he can do. He doesn't live here, and nothing untoward happened between us. I'm your pastor. You came to talk!" Jesse felt his voice rise against his will.

Lilliana shook her head. "The truth has never mattered. He's always the injured party, the one in an outrage. Whatever it is, it's always my fault. He knows men in high places. He'll ruin you. He'll —"

"I'm not afraid of him, Gra— Lilliana."

"You don't understand. He's so convincing. You don't know how convincing — how charming he can be when he wants. You saw Ida Mae. She believed everything he said."

"Ida Mae believes what she wants to believe."

"Yes, and she talks — all the time — and convinces people."

"She feeds their desire for gossip." Jesse felt his head throb.

"In the end, when people hear something ugly long enough, they believe it's true. They want to believe it — to set it in a box they can understand and label. That's how it was in Philadelphia. I'd hoped it would be different here."

Jesse pushed his fingers through his hair. She was right, of course. He'd spent a lifetime building a strong reputation among the people of No Creek. But they'd be all too willing to believe the eligible Reverend Willard — who was not courting or marrying one of their daughters — had had his head turned by a Northern vixen, a married woman to boot. She was an outsider and a cultured one, which was another reason to take her down a peg or two. He could see his fall from grace and their condemnation of her like the handwriting on the wall, no matter that nothing had happened.

The truth was that he'd wanted to court Grace — or Lilliana. But that was before he knew she was married. Now it was out of the question. If that was so, why did he feel so protective, so desirous of rescuing her?

Lilliana rubbed her arms, up and down, as if cold. "He — he was going to have me committed as insane and pretend I'd been unfaithful so he could divorce me. I couldn't stand up to him as broken as I was over Mama's death." Now that the confrontation was past, she couldn't hold back the tears.

Confused and conflicted, Jesse handed her his handkerchief.

She drew a shuddering breath. "Being here — it's the first time I've been able to wake each morning without being afraid. But when he sent the letter, saying he was coming tomorrow, I thought I had to go back with him to save him confronting Aunt Hyacinth. I couldn't bear what his coming might do to her — to her heart and to her spirit — or the humiliation he might bring her in No Creek. But now that I've seen him again, I can't. I know I can't go back. And now look. I've ruined life here for you and for Aunt Hyacinth."

"You've not ruined anything. This is not your doing."

Lilliana shook her head, her eyes round in a sad knowing. "You don't know him. He won't simply walk away. He'll wheedle and whine and win people over."

Jesse couldn't imagine what Gerald Swope had done to make his wife so afraid, but it was clear that she was. He wanted nothing more than to take her in his arms, to hold and comfort her, to reassure her that everything would be all right. But under the circumstances that would be the worst thing he could do, and assuring her of a good outcome was quite possibly not true. So he did nothing as she cried, and hated himself for it.

CHAPTER TWENTY

I spent the night pacing the floor of my room — thankful beyond words that I still had a haven to think, a place safe from Gerald. Where he was at that moment, I had no idea.

I couldn't imagine he would go back to Reverend Willard's to spend the night, not after the threat he'd left dangling in the air. But No Creek boasted no hotels or boarding-houses. Would Ida Mae take him in?

That would be like Gerald — to create an impossible situation, then make himself piti-ful so someone would insist he stay with them. Gerald could effectively play the martyr, insisting that he sleep in his car to avoid putting anyone out. He'd done that on trips to church conferences before, demand-ing I sleep in the car with him — even on freezing nights. It built his reputation as a suffering servant.

Staying the night in No Creek would most certainly give him the opportunity to build his case as wronged husband with a heartless, disturbed wife who refused him. He could pour out his woes over the generous breakfast his host pressed upon him. Ida Mae would be only too eager to listen, to sympathize and broadcast.

I gave up pacing in the dark and turned on my bedside lamp.

Reverend Willard was naive to think that Gerald couldn't make anything of our conversation. Gerald was a master at garnering pity and creating innuendo. Before long Ida Mae would see the picture as he painted it, regardless of what she'd seen with her own eyes.

I jerked my hair by its roots, wishing I could truly pull it out and suffer that pain instead of the mental anguish that wouldn't go away. What had I brought on Aunt Hyacinth in her last days? What had I done to Reverend Willard and the entire congregation that would suffer from the loss of him? He was the guardian voice of No Creek. He was Shady Grove church at its best. He'd grown up among the people here and knew them. No outside minister would understand them or help them or champion them as he did.

Dear God, please. I'm afraid and ashamed and desperate. Do You want me to go back to Gerald? The very thought, let alone the prayer, made me shudder. *If You do, please make that clear to me and give me the strength to do it. I love You and want to do what You want me to, but I would rather die than go back to him. Please, God, please help Aunt Hyacinth and Reverend Willard. Protect them from Gerald. They're good people and they love You with all their hearts. They're worthy of Your love and protection. In Jesus' name, amen.*

Gray dawn broke as I dressed and pinned up my hair. I waited until almost seven. If Gerald was at Reverend Willard's or the general store, I'd see his car.

If he'd slept in his car, I'd rather confront him outside than inside. There would be safety inside, in the presence of other people, but also listening ears. I didn't think he'd hit me where neighbors might see out their windows, and his hitting me wasn't the worst that might happen.

I slipped out the back door. Just as quickly as my foot found the step, I felt another presence. There, across the garden, was a dark form, a dark-blue billow of fabric, teetering on the edge of the woods. *Gerald? No, it can't be.* The form rose up, and though I couldn't see the person's eyes clearly, I felt them bore into mine. My breath caught in my throat, but just as quickly as I blinked, the form was gone. Unsettled, I grasped my arms around me and hurried down the hill.

Gerald's long automobile was nowhere near the church or parsonage. I found it parked outside the general store.

He was not in his car. There was no sign that he'd slept there. The door to the store and post office was not yet open, but people would be coming by soon.

I didn't have long to wonder or wait. Gerald waltzed around the corner of the building with Ida Mae on his arm. She looked five years younger, smiling and chatting with the handsome man who'd captured her every attention.

"Lilliana!" Gerald spoke my name as if surprised to see me. "You've come."

"We need to talk, Gerald." I looked at Ida Mae with her arm still wrapped around Gerald's.

Ida Mae's face turned from smiling to smug to grim, then slightly pink in the space of a moment. "I'm sure there's a great deal you need to explain to your husband. I must say that I don't know whatever possessed you to leave such a man."

Heat rose from my toes through my torso and up to the roots of my hair. "You're right, Ida Mae; you don't know."

"Ladies, please." Gerald spoke masterfully as if stepping between a catfight. "Ida Mae, I cannot thank you enough for your hospitality or for your understanding. I won't forget it." The charming but sad near smile he gave Ida Mae would melt any woman's heart.

"You come back anytime you want, Mr. Swope. Our door is always open to you." She patted his arm, gave me a scathing look, and mounted the steps to the store and post office.

I waited, uncertain how to begin. "You stayed in Ida Mae's house?"

"The hospitality of a fine woman and her husband eager to help after my wife turned me out."

"Why have you really come?"

"I came to get you, of course, and take you home. You're disturbed, Lilliana, and I intend to find you a place where you can get the help you need."

"I won't go back with you."

"I saw that last night when you were sitting in the good reverend's house, your hair mussed up as if the two of you had been doing more than talking. Something Ida Mae noticed as well."

"Nothing happened."

"I doubt the court will see it that way." He looked over his shoulder. The door to the store stood slightly ajar, though the window shade was still partially drawn. Ida Mae surely stood on the other side, listening. Gerald took my hand and pulled me toward the street. "Let's walk."

I tried to pull away, but he gripped my fingers so tightly I feared he'd break them. Once he'd nearly crushed my fingers until forcing me to return his hand squeeze three times, meaning *I love you*. I knew his strength.

"Pennsylvania courts are particular. I don't suppose you know that. But the law allows divorce for only a few reasons. One, of course, is insanity . . . something that can be rather cumbersome to prove, but not impossible, given credible witnesses. A decree of insanity does have the advantage of putting the culprit away where they no longer create a nuisance, and it does garner sympathy — or at least pity — for both parties."

I stiffened, remembering his words to my father.

"That would require me to take you back to Philadelphia and go through some psychiatric tests, perhaps a few shock treatments — whatever the good doctors might need to determine their diagnosis. I believe it can be arranged for the state to care for you in one of their institutions for the rest of your natural life."

My heart pounding, I jerked away again, but his fingers dug through my flesh.

"I'd wanted to do this quickly, but I understand your dear aunt is nearing her end. I realize you won't want to leave her, and I don't mind being tethered to you long enough to share in our inheritance."

"Our inheritance? You'll never get a penny. Aunt Hyacinth has already seen to that."

"If I'm the survivor of this marriage or your legal guardian, there's nothing she can do —"

"Not even then! If anything happens to me, every penny goes to someone else."

Gerald's eyes burned. His jaw set. "Then we need to change her mind. There are other just causes for divorce that may not require the messiness of returning you to Philadelphia. Adultery, for one. I don't think that would be too difficult a case to make, now that I've seen you with the good reverend."

"You're the one who —"

Gerald chuckled. "Ida Mae thinks it's quite possible you seduced him. You evidently have cast quite a spell over the man — much as you did me. Pity, that fall from grace. Scandal will be his ruin in this backwater town — and your fault, like everything else."

"Don't do this, Gerald. He's a good man and he's not done anything to —"

Gerald stopped in the middle of the street and turned me toward him. To anyone passing, or to Ida Mae peeking beneath the window shade, it would look like a lover's plea. "Truth is relative in this case, don't you think? Allegations of promiscuity, adultery, with the affidavit of credible witnesses like your father — and Ida Mae — will probably be much easier and less time-consuming to accomplish."

I pushed aside the painful certainty that my own father would testify against me. "You're the one with the uncontrollable temper. If there is insanity or adultery, it's —" But he cut me off.

"Have you forgotten my promise? If you ever tell anyone about my upsets — outbursts brought on by you — I will kill you. I swear I will kill you, Lilliana, and then I will kill myself. What would I have to lose at that point? If you speak out, it won't matter that you're hiding away here. I will come. I will find you wherever you go. Do not doubt that I will go through your aunt to find you — whatever it takes. Do you understand?"

I tried all the harder to pull away, unable to stop the tears streaming down my face.

"Crying is a sign of weakness. You always were a weak woman. I said —" his grip nearly brought me to my knees — "do you understand?"

I wished I could spit in his face, but I was too afraid.

"Miss Grace?" Reverend Pierce, with Celia and Chester at his side, appeared on the road behind us. "You all right, Miss Grace? Is there anything we can do for you?"

Gerald released me in a moment. The concern on Reverend Pierce's face and the worry in Celia's and Chester's eyes caught my breath.

"My wife and I are having a private discussion."

I took the opportunity to step back, nearer Reverend Pierce and the children. "This is Reverend Pierce of Saints Delight Church." I didn't introduce Celia or Chester, didn't want to bring them to Gerald's attention in any way.

"My name's Celia, and this here is my brother, Chester." Celia hung back by Reverend Pierce but wasn't about to be excluded. I should have known. "You're crying, Miss Grace."

"And I'm Gerald Swope, Lilliana Grace's husband." Gerald said it with the force of a decree, ignoring Celia's observation.

Confusion swept Reverend Pierce's face, but he extended his hand. "Welcome to No Creek, Mr. Swope."

Gerald hesitated a moment too long but loosely took the reverend's hand.

In that moment Celia slipped her fingers into mine. "Chester and me — Chester and I — are on our way to weed garden for the widow Cramer. Want to come with us, Miss Grace? Is that your whole name, front and back, Lilliana Grace?" She didn't wait for an answer. "That's the prettiest name I ever heard. I shoulda known you'd have a name that sounds like flowers."

Gerald looked like he might blow a gasket.

Reverend Pierce's hand passed across his brow. The man looked bone weary and swayed slightly.

"Reverend Pierce, are you all right? Do you need to sit down?"

"I need to get on up to see Reverend Willard. My people have had a bad night — a real bad night."

"What is it? Can I help?"

"Maybe so, Miss Grace — Miss Lilliana Grace — but we need Reverend Willard in on this." He looked at Celia and Chester. "It's not for young ears."

Thankfully, a local wagon crested the hill at that moment and rolled to a stop by the store. *Safety in numbers.*

"I want to stay, but we got to go or the widow will come lookin' for us and Mama'll skin us! See you this afternoon, Miss Lilliana!" Celia and Chester took off at a run, my name ringing behind them. I was never so thankful to see them come or see them go.

"Come by the house for cookies and milk when you've done your weeding!" I called, making certain everyone within earshot understood I was not going anywhere and that Aunt Hyacinth and I would not be alone.

"Lilliana, we're not finished." Gerald stepped closer, but I took my stance near Reverend Pierce.

"Yes, we are. That's what I came to tell you. Goodbye, Gerald." I turned then and would have taken Reverend Pierce's arm to steady him and myself if Gerald had not been there and if Ida Mae hadn't been peeking through the store window. I didn't want to make matters worse for either of us. "The parsonage is on my way home. I'll walk with you, Reverend Pierce."

I'd never turned my back on or walked away from Gerald. I knew he was angry, but he didn't come after me, not in front of Reverend Pierce.

Reverend Pierce didn't say a word, but after we heard Gerald's footsteps recede and his car door open and slam closed, he passed me his handkerchief.

"Thank you." The sigh came from my toes, sending a shudder through my voice.

" 'I will praise thee, O Lord, with my whole heart; I will shew forth all thy marvellous works. I will be glad and rejoice in thee: I will sing praise to thy name, O thou most High. When mine enemies are turned back, they shall fall and perish at thy presence. For thou hast maintained my right and my cause; thou satest in the throne judging right.' " Reverend Pierce's voice, weary at first, strengthened with conviction as he spoke.

His words, I knew, were for me, but there was something more. "What's happened?"

He stopped in the road, catching his breath. I returned his handkerchief. He needed it more than I. "Miss Lilliana Grace, I don't know a thing about your husband, but I say this: Remember, no matter what the evil of man, 'The Lord also will be a refuge for the oppressed, a refuge in times of trouble. And they that know thy name will put their trust in thee: for thou, Lord, hast not forsaken them that seek thee.' "

" 'A refuge for the oppressed.' "

" 'For the needy shall not always be forgotten: the expectation of the poor shall not perish forever.' "

Not forgotten. All the times I'd hidden from Gerald in our basement in Philadelphia or hidden in the ladies' room of the church or fled to my parents' house and hidden in my mother's closet to escape his tirades, I'd been alone, certain I was forgotten by the Lord.

But now, despite Ida Mae's suspicions and Gerald's threats, Reverend Pierce and Celia and Chester had appeared in my need. Reverend Willard was just up the road, and Aunt Hyacinth waited at Garden's Gate, where I knew she'd be worrying and wondering where I was. *Can that be God's doing? Can it mean that He reached down and stirred them to befriend me, to help me now?* It was a new thought, a flicker of light. Shaking, I breathed, relieved beyond words by the plume of red dust Gerald's passing car left on my shoes.

CHAPTER TWENTY-ONE

The next afternoon Celia swept the porch and stone walk at Garden's Gate. She wanted everything to look pristine and orderly for the library's first afternoon of business. She'd hated being sent to weed the widow's garden, knowing she'd miss the first library customers — or patrons, as Miss Grace, or Miss Lilliana Grace or whoever she was, had called them. But her mama had insisted and then insisted she and Chester each spend an hour at home reading before going to Garden's Gate. As if she couldn't learn more spending the day among the stacks of Miz Hyacinth's books and soaking up all the learning in the world. Still, summer was long and she could be at the library part of every day now.

And another thing. Her mama had explained, after talking things over with Miss Grace and Miz Hyacinth, that Grace was Miss Grace's middle name and that from now on they should all call her Miss Lilliana, although she was really Mrs. Swope. The married part ranked a scandal in the general store and post office; Ida Mae whispered that Lilliana Swope had run clean away from a perfectly good husband and come here pretending to be somebody she wasn't, and shook her head that poor Reverend Willard was an innocent around conniving women.

After seeing the way Miss Lilliana had cried and the way the man had near crushed her arms the morning before, not to mention the bruises that sprang up afterward, Celia wasn't sure Gerald Swope was a "perfectly good husband," but the Lilliana part pleased her. Lilliana was closer to a flower name, more befitting the Belvidere ladies. What did Celia care about Ida Mae and her rattling of "skeleton husbands in the closet"? Why should anybody care? But Celia knew they did, especially about Reverend Willard, just as they whispered about her daddy in jail and her mama being the wife of a jailbird and what did she do all those long and lonesome nights without a man? It didn't seem to matter that half the county men ran moonshine — married or not — leaving their wives alone for nights on end; her daddy'd been caught. Being caught was the sin.

Celia's mama made it clear that Celia and Chester weren't to ask Miss Lilliana a single question about her husband or the name change or any of it, nor were they to mention it to another living soul. But Celia figured a person could still think on it.

Celia tucked the broom away and sat on the front step with her chin in her hand. An hour passed and no one came. Finally Ruby Lynne Wishon stopped by.

Celia was glad for company. "Care to pass the time of day? Want a book? I can check you out a book. That's my regular job here."

Ruby Lynne shook her head. "No thanks, not today. I'm here to see Miss Grace."

She was dressed fit to impress and looked happier than Celia had seen her in a month of Sundays.

"Miss Lilliana — that's what she goes by now, though sometimes I call her Miss Lill — is pretty busy, what with the library and all. Maybe I can help you," Celia offered, eager to stay in the middle of things, even though the part about calling her Miss Lill was a lie. Still, it seemed like a good name.

"She's expecting me. Could you tell her I'm here, or should I just go on in?"

"Oh, all right. Follow me. I'll find her." It was the perfect excuse to learn what Miss Lill would give Ruby Lynne to do. Celia'd been looking forward to checking out books to folks ever since they'd dusted and rearranged the first bookcase. She hoped Miss Lill wouldn't give Ruby Lynne that job.

What Celia never expected was to find Miss Lilliana and Marshall Raymond sitting in the kitchen, their heads hunched together over a

192

newspaper. The moment Celia and Ruby Lynne walked in, Marshall jerked his head up and jumped to his feet as if he'd been snakebit.

"Ruby Lynne!" Miss Lilliana looked surprised and undone at once. "I didn't expect you so soon."

"I know I'm a mite early, Miss Grace — I mean, Miss Lilliana, but I was able to come and I'm so eager to get started. Do you have any students for me?"

Now Miss Lilliana stood. "Well, as a matter of fact, I do. It's why Marshall is here. He'd like to learn to read . . . better."

Marshall kept his eyes on his feet. Ruby Lynne's eyes went as wide as Celia's. You could have heard ants crawl. Celia swallowed, knowing this was trouble. *Talking about teaching colored little bitties is one thing, but doing it in living daylight with a boy taller than her — near a man growed — is another.*

"I'm working with Marshall now to see where he is in his reading and writing. Perhaps you'd like to take a seat and join us."

Ruby Lynne stood stock-still as if her feet were tarred to the floor. The silence went on so long that Marshall raised his eyes and looked at Ruby Lynne, then at Celia. Celia slipped her hand in Ruby Lynne's and guided her to the table. "Can I help, too, Miss Lill? It'd be fun to do it all together. I could learn how to teach, too — by watchin'."

Miss Lilliana smiled, a mite nervous, but Celia knew she'd done right to offer.

"Yes." Ruby Lynne pulled out a chair and sat down, decided. But Celia knew that she was playing with fire — not fire from Marshall, but from her daddy if he ever found out she was helping a teenage colored boy, that she was even spending time in the same room.

Why Miss Lilliana didn't seem to catch on or care about that was a further mystery to Celia. Or maybe she did, and maybe she was just determined to help Marshall, or maybe she meant to stir things up in No Creek so they'd never be the same, now that she'd gone and made news by leaving her husband. Change could be good; that's what her mama said President Roosevelt intended for the good of all, what Mrs. Roosevelt advocated. Celia liked that word, *advocate.* She only hoped Miss Lill's advocated changes would make things better, not turn deadly.

Celia wasn't afraid of much, but she knew the noises outside their three-room cabin that night didn't come from coons or possums. They were human feet, unsteady and jerking through the underbrush. Drunk. She'd heard her daddy's footsteps sound just like that on a Saturday night before Mama'd open the door and drag him in to bed. But Daddy was in jail, and there ought be nobody else roaming outside their door that time of night.

"Gladys! Gladys Percy!" the drunken voice called. "You come on out here and talk to me, little darlin'!"

Celia peered over the side of her bunk and could see the pale cast to Chester's face in the moonlight that streamed through the window. He pulled the feed-sack sheet up to his eyes and peeked out as if that might protect him. She didn't want to see Chester scared. She was scared enough for both of them. "It's just old Troy Wishon, drunk as a skunk. Don't you mind him, Chester."

"I wanna talk to you, Gladys!" The call came again, this time closer to the house.

Celia's heart beat faster when she heard his boot thump on the front porch. "Mama, don't open the door!" she whimpered.

"You children stay there and go back to sleep. There's safety in numbers." Mama kept her voice steady but firm and shut the bedroom door.

Celia slipped from her bunk and climbed in beside Chester, wrapping his fingers tight in her own. "There's safety in numbers," she whispered.

A pounding came on the front door.

"Troy Wishon, you go on home. You're drunk and I won't have you scaring my children. You should be ashamed of yourself." Celia loved the authority in her mama's voice, but she also caught the quaver.

"Your girl ought to be scared, Gladys. I heard what she did over to Miz Hyacinth's new lendin' library. What I want to know is just what you ladies are lendin' out!" He laughed till he near choked over his own foul joke. "You teachin' your girl to let anybody and everybody in? I just come by to see." Celia heard the solid door rattle, but Mama had pulled the latch in and set the bar.

"I'll tell you once more, Troy, go home!"

"Or what? You got no man in there to show me different. Fillmore's been gone a long while, little darlin'. You gettin' lonesome? I could help you out there."

"You're a boy, Troy, and a drunk one. Go home!"

The door thundered with the pound of Troy's fist and his boot. Chester cried out and Celia screamed.

"I'll show you what kind of man I am! If you think I'm a wet-nose boy, maybe I should show that sassy-mouthed girl of yours. She's not much, but she's growin'."

Mama didn't say another word to Troy, but she opened the bedroom door and slipped inside. She pushed a cane-back chair against the door and up into the knob, pulled down the window, and closed the curtains. Then she took up vigil by the side of the window, a cast-iron skillet in one hand and a hammer in the other.

■ ■ ■ ■

Celia and Chester walked to the widow Cramer's for chores the next day. Their mama walked with them as far as Garden's Gate. None of them had gotten much sleep.

"You and Chester keep close coming and going. You know what I told you."

"There's safety in numbers, Mama," Chester piped up. "Do you think he'll come back?" It broke Celia's heart to see the worry in Chester's eyes.

"No, I don't." Their mama was emphatic and that bolstered Celia's courage. "Troy was drunk and on a rampage last night. We just happened to be in his path. He'll sober up and likely not even remember he was there. Don't give it another thought."

But it was all Celia could think about until the widow gave them each a nickel to spend at the general store, and then there wasn't room for the two thoughts.

Later, pockets filled with candy, they began their walk home. *If only we didn't live down such a lonesome stretch.* Celia kept watch along the sides of the road for Troy. Chester kept his slingshot at the ready.

By the time Celia and Chester reached home, it was nearly four o'clock. Their mama was not there, and that raised Celia's worrywart, bringing all her thoughts back to home.

"She's probably up to Garden's Gate," Chester moaned, hungry for more than candy. "Mama's always up there anymore. We might as well go live there."

"That's the best idea you've had in a while. Let's go tell her."

"Wait, Celia — I just want Mama home, that's all."

But Celia was already out the door and on her way. She knew Chester would follow and that seemed a far sight better than sitting in the empty cabin all alone, wondering if Mama was all right, skittish that Troy might return.

Besides, Chester's idea was a grand one — a solver of all their immediate problems. The joyful notion of living at Garden's Gate with Miz Hyacinth and Miss Lill and their library full of wonderful books grew as Celia pounded the red dirt road.

Mama will appreciate saving the rent and all those steps between houses. She can cook one dinner every day instead of two. When she makes cookies for Miz Hyacinth and Miss Lill's afternoon tea, she can tuck one or two away for me and Chester — like Janice Richards's mother bakes for her kids. We'd be a bigger family — and we'd be safe from the likes of Troy Wishon till Daddy gets home, if he ever comes home.

Celia had it all worked out, so she wasn't prepared for her mother's reaction when she explained her bright idea.

"Have you lost your mind, Celia Percy? You've certainly lost your manners. We have our own home. This is Miz Hyacinth's home and Miss Lilliana's."

"But they're all alone. Don't you think they're wanting for company?"

"They're company for one another — and family."

"But you're always here anymore, Mama. We have to come find you. If we lived here, that Troy Wishon wouldn't be comin' around, botherin' you. He wouldn't dare come to Miz Hyacinth's house. There's safety in numbers — that's what you tell us. And besides, Miss Lill's always inviting Chester and me for cookies and milk. I help out in the library and I could help —"

"Hush, Celia. They'll hear you. You're shaming me."

A bell tinkled from the parlor.

"Can I go?" Celia begged.

"Reverend Willard is in talking with Miz Hyacinth. Run see what Miz Hyacinth wants — ask if they want tea, but don't you dare say —"

"I won't, Mama; I promise!" Celia tore from the room as much to avoid her mother's chastising as to answer the bell.

She stopped just before entering the parlor. Reverend Willard's back was to the door, but Miz Hyacinth sat in her chair by the window, as usual. Miz Hyacinth's silver-white hair was brushed and curled, her dress neat and clean and pressed, her shoes polished to a spit shine. All that Celia noted in a moment and appreciated the change Miss Lill had brought to Miz Hyacinth. But the ashen cast to the older lady's face wasn't at all usual. Celia'd never seen anyone look that way, only ever read the phrase "bore the pallor of death," but she was certain Miz Hyacinth did. And it caught her short.

"Celia? I can tell it's you by your footsteps, dear. I'm glad you're here. Come in. Reverend Willard and I were just talking about you. Come here, child." Miz Hyacinth's voice was weaker but still authoritative.

"Yes, ma'am." Celia walked up to her chair and placed a hand on Miz Hyacinth's arm. Miz Hyacinth covered Celia's hand with her own. She nodded to Reverend Willard. He smiled, but the worry lines on his face were evident to Celia. She figured that worry was for Miz Hyacinth.

"I want you to tell me something, and I want you to tell me truly. Will you do that?"

"Yes, ma'am."

"Good. I'm asking you because I believe you will tell me the truth and not try to hide anything because you think you need to protect me. And I am going to tell you the truth because I believe you can accept it and act wisely upon it. Do we understand one another?"

"Yes, ma'am." Celia glanced nervously at Reverend Willard, certain now she was wading into dangerous waters.

"Reverend Pierce told Reverend Willard that he and several members of his congregation found crosses burning in their yards Monday night. I want to know, was there a cross set on fire in your yard?"

Celia felt her eyes go wide. She'd never seen a cross burning, but she'd heard plenty — when grown-ups thought she wasn't listening — about the Klan setting crosses alight. She'd even seen Klansmen holding torches and marching down by the railroad platform once. "No, ma'am," she answered truthfully. "Why would anybody do that?" But Celia knew why, even as she asked the question, and she knew, deep in her soul, that she might have been the cause.

"To scare some people away from using the library, I presume. To keep the library for themselves, perhaps, or more likely just to frighten folks because they believe they can."

Celia thought that through. "You think they'll set a cross burning in our yard because I invited Reverend Pierce and his church here?" She swallowed what felt like hot coals. Could the Klan have found out about Miss

201

Lill and Ruby Lynne helping Marshall read? "Did they hurt anybody?"

"Only their spirits for now, but Reverend Willard and Reverend Pierce and I are concerned they might not stop there."

"Reverend Pierce is very concerned for his people," Reverend Willard spoke up. "You're sure nothing bad happened at your house? No one has threatened you in any way?"

Celia swallowed. She'd thought of little else since Troy Wishon's midnight visit. But her mother had made her promise not to say anything — about anything — to Miz Hyacinth. She knew who could, though. "Maybe you'd best talk to Chester."

"Chester? Reverend Willard and I are talking to you, Celia."

"I'm not supposed to talk about who came or what happened or anything at all."

Miz Hyacinth breathed deeply. "I see. Mama's orders?"

"Yes, ma'am."

"And what else did Mama order?"

"I'm to ask if you and Reverend Willard want tea."

Miz Hyacinth smiled. "We do, and some of that delicious shortbread your mama baked this morning, thank you. And please say that I want Chester to bring us the shortbread. Tell him we'll share."

"Yes, ma'am." Celia scooted through the door, sure she'd dodged bullets but not sure she wouldn't get in trouble anyway.

Chester delivered the shortbread, Mama brought the teapot, and Celia carried the tray with sugar and cream.

"I need to get back to the kitchen and finish up, Miz Hyacinth. Are you and Reverend Willard certain these children aren't bothering you?"

Celia looked down innocently and humbly, certain if she raised brown orbs to her mother, they'd give her away.

"We'll enjoy them, Gladys, and we have shortbread to share."

Celia's mother didn't look convinced, but she dried her already-dry hands on her apron, gave Celia and Chester a warning glance Celia caught from the corner of her eye, and turned to the kitchen.

Miz Hyacinth plied Chester with thistle-imprinted shortbread — Celia's favorite because of the pretty design — before Reverend Willard asked his questions, smiling all the while.

"Chester, I understand you had visitors to your house last night."

Chester looked like he'd swallowed cardboard. He looked desperately to Celia for direction, but she looked away.

"Is that right, Chester?" Miz Hyacinth asked. "Did you have visitors?"

He nodded, but Celia knew Miz Hyacinth

couldn't see that. "He nodded yes, Miz Hyacinth."

"Is that so? How many?"

Chester frowned and held up one finger.

"Can you speak up, Chester? I couldn't hear you."

"Just one."

"One?" Reverend Willard set his teacup down. "And who was that?"

Chester looked so miserable Celia felt sorry for him. "Mama didn't say you couldn't say. She just said I couldn't say."

That seemed to relieve Chester a little. "Troy Wishon." He leaned forward and whispered, "He was dead drunk and scary."

"Troy Wishon," Miz Hyacinth mused. "He and that brother of his are both — both drinkers."

But *drinkers* was not what she'd been about to say, Celia was certain.

"Did Troy Wishon say anything, Chester?" Reverend Willard laid his hand on Chester's shoulder.

Chester set his shortbread down and for the first time Celia saw his crumb-sprinkled chin quiver in rage. "He scared Mama and Celia and said he'd come back if . . ."

"If what?"

"I'm not sure. He kept saying things to Mama about Daddy bein' gone and about Celia bein' a nearly growed girl and how they

204

must be lonesome with Daddy gone. I didn't like it."

"No, I'm sure you didn't. That should never have happened, Chester. You were right to tell us." Reverend Willard looked more worried than ever.

"Mama doesn't want us talkin' about it."

"Your mama's very brave."

"She don't have a gun, but she has a frying pan and a hammer. She sat up by us all night, one in each hand."

"You've a good, good mama." Miz Hyacinth looked paler yet.

"I do. Mama says there's safety in numbers."

"Your mama's right. You and Celia and your mama stick together, and if ever any of you need help, come and get me." Reverend Willard leaned down to look in Chester's eyes. "I'll come right away, day or night — anytime."

Chester nodded. Celia knew he believed Reverend Willard, and she knew Reverend Willard meant what he'd said. But some things, she knew, even Reverend Willard couldn't stop.

Chapter Twenty-Two

Reverend Pierce had not confided in me Tuesday morning when we'd walked from the general store. I was so preoccupied with Gerald's threats and the great relief that he'd left No Creek and then the significance of the Scriptures Reverend Pierce quoted that I hadn't pressed. After tutoring Marshall on Wednesday, I'd spent most of Thursday in Winston-Salem, following Aunt Hyacinth's suggestion that I pick up some early readers for the library and the children of Saints Delight. I was without local news until I returned on the train that afternoon and ran into Reverend Willard, just leaving Garden's Gate.

He shared his worries for Reverend Pierce's flock, for the church, for Gladys and her children.

"It's like something out of a novel," I fumed. "I can't imagine how terrifying those cross burnings must be or how frightening that was for Gladys and the children."

"Cross burnings are only the beginning. I don't know where this might lead. Maybe it's just to terrorize — horror enough . . ." Reverend Willard kneaded the back of his neck. "Right now I'm more worried about Gladys and the children — out there alone in that cabin. The Wishons are mostly talk and bluster until they're drunk, but they can be mean then and carry on without restraint. The problem is, they're drunk far too often."

I believed all that Reverend Willard said. Gladys and the children must be scared half to death to go home. As far as the KKK and their cross burnings meant to terrorize, I could barely imagine. I'd only seen a person in Klan regalia once, in a photograph in the Philadelphia newspaper. It had seemed outrageous and looked silly, if garish, at the time.

I ridiculed the notion of grown men parading around in white robes and pointy hats as Aunt Hyacinth and I talked it over in the late afternoon. She made certain I never ridiculed them again.

"You know nothing of the Klan, Lilliana. You don't know their self-righteousness or their hatred or the wicked things they've done. Right here in No Creek not twenty years ago they tarred and feathered a white man who dared to take the witness stand in defense of a colored man arrested for raping a white woman. His defender was with the accused at the time the woman claimed it happened. He testified that the woman lied in anger after the colored man had not removed his hat in her presence, not shown her the respect she demanded. He openly defended the accused man as to what happened that day, but everyone in No Creek knew there was more to the story.

"That colored man had worked the fields for the woman's family. She'd flirted shamelessly with him so even the neighbors saw, but he'd refused to go near her and she couldn't stand that. The Klan formed a mob and pulled that poor man out of jail, then hung him by the neck until he was dead — and they did it slowly. Then they tarred and feathered his white defender; the man died of his burns."

I could barely fathom such a thing, but Aunt Hyacinth wasn't finished.

"They beat and hanged Olney Tate's father to death not fifteen years ago for daring to bid against Rhoan and Troy Wishon's father for a prime piece of tobacco land gone to auction — land that I'm sure should have been his anyway, though I could never prove it. They invented some story about him having stolen the money — money he'd saved all his life, an inheritance from his daddy. It was Wishon jealousy and greed — that's what did it, and I'm ashamed to say . . . Never mind." Aunt Hyacinth's voice rose and trembled with the tellings. "He was fifty-six years old and should have died an old man in his bed."

"What did the police do?"

"The police? The sheriff, who turned a blind eye, is likely a Klansman himself."

"So that's why Olney's skittish about coming into the house, why he worries so about every little thing Ida Mae says . . . why Marshall is afraid for his uncle to learn he's come for reading help. And Ruby Lynne . . ." It all made sense now.

"I'm certain that's why Olney chose to dig the widow's well the day our library opened. He didn't want to be here or to allow Marshall here in the house with whites, even though I'd asked him myself to come and be our guest that day. I doubt he liked it that Mercy and the children came, but she so craves learning for her children. He'll help me with anything I need or ask, but he won't mix outside this house."

I shook my head. I'd never heard of such things in Philadelphia. I'd read about troubles in the South, but they hadn't affected me. I'd hardly known any colored people, other than Sarah. Why was that? Sarah was like family in my book. I'd realized too late that while she'd acted as family to me, my family — my father, who possessed the means — had done nothing for her outside of employment. "You say that happened fifteen years ago. Surely they don't do those things now. This is 1941."

"Cross burnings are warnings — intimidation to keep people 'in their place.' Right now they're stirring the pot. Once the Klan gets worked up and going, it's like a fire; it smolders and smokes, looking for a place to vent, until it explodes. It's that venting, that explosion that worries me."

"Then why didn't they burn a cross here? This is where we welcomed everyone, where everyone 'mixed.' If they considered it anyone's fault, it should be mine."

Aunt Hyacinth sighed. "I'm why. I've never explained that to you and I know I should. Still, it doesn't mean it won't happen. For the moment I'm more worried about Gladys and the children. I'm worried about you being alone here after I'm gone. It's not good for a woman to be alone, especially one the Klan has their eye on."

If community respect for Aunt Hyacinth kept us both safe, I didn't see what we had to fear. "They don't know anything about me. I'm a stranger to them."

"In their minds you're a dangerous stranger, Lilliana — someone trying to change the way they've always done things. Opening the library and welcoming coloreds and whites on the same day is inconceivable to them. Separating from your husband for any reason at all is scandalous in their eyes. They claim to be Christians and strong supporters of their families. They won't want their wives to think such a stand as yours is tolerated, no matter the cause. I hate to say it but they don't consider wife beating a reason to leave a marriage. They've forgotten or don't know what God says about oppressors. I shudder to think how many of them do it behind closed doors, drunk or sober."

I gritted my teeth. I wouldn't go back to a life of shouting and beatings and intimidation from Gerald because the Klan believed I should. "From what Reverend Willard told me about Troy Wishon, it's Gladys who needs protection right now. How long until her husband is released from prison?"

"Six months, give or take. I'm not sure what will happen between them once he's released. She doesn't speak of it."

"What would you think of inviting Gladys and the children to live here until then?"

Aunt Hyacinth's cheeks wreathed in smiles. "I hoped you'd say that. Wouldn't it be grand to have children in the house? They'd be such helpers, too. We could have our own chickens again — not just the leftover strays that roost in the trees. Maybe even a milk cow. Celia's just the one to take them on."

I didn't know why we hadn't thought of it sooner. By making Garden's Gate their home, Gladys and the children would surely be safer, and with them here, Gerald would be less likely to push his way in. It would be good to have Gladys's company and steady hand, and Aunt Hyacinth was right: the cheerfulness of Celia and Chester was nothing short of contagious. "Do you want to invite her, or should I?"

"I think it's best that it come from you, and I second the invitation — as long as you're sure. It's an arrangement you may or may not wish to continue after I'm gone. I want to be certain that you're entirely comfortable with it. We mustn't go forward if you feel any hesitation. First and foremost, this is your home, my dear."

I closed my eyes, thankful Aunt Hyacinth couldn't see me in that moment. "Please stop talking about not being here —"

"It's a matter of time, Lilliana. I feel it in my bones — and my heart." She reached her hand into the air, searching for mine. "We must speak frankly."

I took her hand and held on tight. "It will be a relief to me to have Gladys here. She's so capable and knows everyone in the area. She knows just what to do in a crisis and even how to handle Ida Mae — which I certainly haven't mastered. She's become a good friend, and I love Celia and Chester. Unless . . ."

"Unless, what?"

"Unless you think she'd feel tainted by me or that the community might make things harder for her — because I lied about my name and because of my separation from Gerald and the library and . . . everything."

"We both lied and I put you up to it. I'll tell Gladys that. I believe she understands more than you can imagine. She's been through so much in her own life. But we won't know until we ask her."

"I suppose not."

"Then it's settled. You'll take care of it."

"Right away. If she's willing, they don't need another night in that cabin by themselves."

The name Wishon had sounded familiar when Reverend Willard met me on the road and told me about Gladys's troubles, asking that I keep an eye out for her and send for him if I thought he was needed. Now it dawned on me. "Is that man — Troy Wishon — related to Ruby Lynne?"

"He's her uncle — her father's younger brother. Younger by a good bit, born late as a surprise, and spoiled all his life. Their mother died in his childbirth and the father took to drinking hard. The boy was raised mostly by Rhoan, Ruby Lynne's father. Both of them drink and have tempers, especially Rhoan. You'll want to avoid the Wishons."

"Except Ruby Lynne."

"Except Ruby Lynne. That dear girl has a hard row to hoe. If her father allows her to step outside of No Creek, it will be a miracle."

"Her heart's set on going to college — to teach, like you."

Aunt Hyacinth shook her head. "That will

213

happen when pigs fly. She hasn't even been allowed to graduate high school. Rhoan thinks women are bred to breed and not worth education beyond simple reading and calculating a market bill. Being able to sign their names is enough in his mind."

"That's why Gladys cautioned me about having her help with reading lessons — and asked Ruby Lynne if her daddy knew what she was up to over here."

"Ruby Lynne's such a bright young thing. One of the best and brightest in my class. She cried when I retired. I'd so hoped that she would join the other children on the bus and continue her education. But her father treated her every academic achievement as if it wasn't worth the paper it was written on and forbade her going on. I'm afraid when he learns that Ruby Lynne's coming here — especially if she continues to tutor Marshall — he'll not only be angry but punish her."

"Punish her?" Knots formed in my stomach, worry knots of remembrance — my father's belt and my husband's fists. "Punish her how?"

"Years ago I saw bruises on that girl's arms and neck that couldn't be explained by bumping into things or being accident-prone, though that's what she claimed at the time."

I knew exactly what that meant, how hard it was to keep up the pretense — the daily, hourly waiting for the proverbial shoe to drop, wearing long sleeves and dark stockings or longer skirts in the heat of summer . . . and I was sick at heart for Ruby Lynne. I mentally counted the second-and third-floor bedrooms. We might need one more.

drop, wearing long sleeves and dark stockings or longer skirts in the heat of summer . . . and I was sick. I mean, Sue Ruby turned I mentally around the second and third floor bedroom. We ended up at my

Chapter Twenty-Three

Celia saw Miss Lilliana's invitation as a gift from heaven and a sure sign that the Lord loved them. Her mother's smile said much the same.

"You have no idea what this means to me, Miss Grace — Miss Lilliana."

"Please, Gladys, call me Lilliana. Aunt Hyacinth deserves the 'Miz,' but it makes me feel old. We're friends and equals. By moving in, you'd be doing me such a favor."

"I don't see how, what with all the noise and commotion my children make —"

"Don't you?" Miss Lilliana leaned close. "It's not been three months since my mother died in my arms. I can't bear to lose Aunt Hyacinth or to be alone when the time comes. I see the signs. I'm afraid it won't be long, and I'd love for you to stay on. Please say you'll stay — unless there's some reason you don't want to. I understand if you'd rather not. You don't have to explain anything. I know what the community thinks of me."

216

She twisted her fingers in a knot.

Celia saw that her mama could hardly hold her chin steady, she was so relieved and touched. She blinked to think how much her mama had been holding in since her daddy'd gone away, surely trying to spare her and Chester. Well, now they'd not be alone in that cabin, and Troy Wishon wouldn't dare come to Miz Hyacinth's house. She was greatly respected, and the preacher lived just down the lane. They'd be all together, like a real family, where there was electricity and books and conversation and safety in numbers and indoor plumbing and even a piano in the parlor — a grand piano. Maybe Miz Hyacinth would teach her to play, or maybe Miss Lill knew how.

Celia went to sleep in a real bed in a real room all her own that night, believing, at least hoping, that despite Europe's worries pouring through the evening news over Miz Hyacinth's radio, God and the world smiled.

Ruby Lynne came to Garden's Gate every Wednesday, Friday, and Saturday, when her daddy drove into the next county and she knew he'd be gone a couple hours or overnight and not need her for anything. That's what she told Miss Lill. He might be mean as a grizzly, Celia decided, but Rhoan Wishon was predictable, sort of like her own daddy. She understood about sneaking around drunk tirades and moonshine runs.

As Celia watched Ruby Lynne teach Marshall at the kitchen table, she saw something more than a girl running away from her daddy. Ruby Lynne had a real gift for seeing what Marshall didn't understand and then explaining it. And Marshall was driven to read and to write.

Celia wondered — even feared — he might get to be sweet on Ruby Lynne, but she saw no sign of that. Only a big boy embarrassed that he was nearly grown and unable to read worth spit, at least when the lessons first began. He worked hard. Every time Ruby Lynne assigned him some homework, he came back with it done and done right. He was polite to everyone in the house and always thanked Ruby Lynne and Miss Lill for helping him on.

But Celia knew the lessons were best kept secret. She knew it without being told. She just wasn't expecting Janice Richards the day she came calling.

The bell Miss Lill had hooked over the front door to let the household know someone had entered the library jingled. Celia rushed from the kitchen to see who it was, forgetting to close the door behind her.

"Janice!" Celia was astonished to see her archnemesis. *Archnemesis* was the new word she'd just read and she figured it meant *enemy.* "What are you doin' here?"

Janice flipped her perfectly curled hair over her shoulder. "Anybody can come to the library. My mother said so."

Celia's heart beat a little faster. " 'Course they can."

Janice's chin lifted.

"I thought your mama didn't want you to come." Celia shifted her feet. "You want to check out a book?"

"Maybe. Mostly I'm here to see Miss Grace — I mean, Miss Lilliana Grace. Mama heard she plays Miz Hyacinth's piano from time to time and figured she might give me piano lessons."

Now Celia raised her chin. Who was Janice Richards to ask Miss Lill for piano lessons? Miss Lill hadn't said anything to her about teaching piano, and Janice's mama had not made Miss Lill or the library welcome in the least. "Miss Lill's not here just now, and she doesn't have time to teach piano lessons."

"Mother said that if *Miss Lilliana* has time to teach coloreds to read, she certainly has time to teach me piano."

Celia clamped her lips.

"Where is she? She can't have left you alone in the house with Miz Hyacinth. Where's your mother? Isn't she supposed to be working here — scrubbing or something?" Janice wrinkled her nose, and Celia knew it was because Janice's mother had never had to work outside the home a day in her life. Prob-

219

ably didn't work inside the home, come to think of it.

Celia felt her dander rise. The desire to protect her mother flared within. "Mama's down to the store and Miss Lill is out back in the garden, busy with Miz Hyacinth, helping her get some air. Now, what book do you want? I'm the person to check one out to you." She couldn't stop herself from adding, "As long as you bring it back on time. If you think you can remember."

Janice swept past her then, as if she were queen and Celia just some little peon in the way of her grand entrance. She ran her fingers over the books lining the shelf. Celia cringed at the way Janice acted like she owned everything, more like a dog leaving its mark than curiosity about the treasures within the covers of books.

Celia felt the hairs on her head tingle as Janice strolled from shelf to shelf, through the children's room parlor and into the grown-up portion of the library. She didn't even bend down or look up to read titles and barely bothered with what was at eye level. When Janice finally chose a book, Celia knew it was one beyond her reading level — a book of essays by Ralph Waldo Emerson with no pictures except the one of Mr. Emerson in the front. Celia had tried reading it herself, and though the essays sounded poetic, they were mostly beyond her.

"You sure you want this book? It's a mite hard for . . . for reading."

Janice smirked. "Maybe for you. Not for me. Check it out."

So Celia did. She took the book to the desk and took her time pulling a card from the file box, writing down the name of the book and author and the date. She pulled a pen from the penholder with a flourish and held it up for Janice to sign.

But Janice was no longer there. She'd left the desk and was standing in the hallway, staring through the open kitchen door. Celia saw Janice's shoulders square. A chill ran up Celia's spine. When Janice turned, her face was flushed red and her green eyes stood wide as the tires on Troy Wishon's fast car.

Celia blinked, understanding. She stood, heart racing, and handed Janice the book and card and pen. "You want your book?"

Janice's lips formed a thin line, but her eyes gleamed as if she'd struck gold. She scratched an illegible signature across the note card, took the book, and fled, leaving the front door open and the bell jingling.

Ruby stood in the doorway of the kitchen, her face pale.

"She's gone," Celia whispered.

"She saw us," Ruby Lynne returned.

Celia swallowed. "Just the two of you reading."

"That's not what she'll say."

Celia nodded. It was the truth. And if she knew Janice Richards, she'd make much more of it than could possibly be.

222

It was ten thirty at night when the pounding came at our door and woke me from a sound sleep. Before I was out of bed, Gladys stood barefoot in the hallway, bathed in the light of the overhead lamp. By the time I'd tied my robe around me and groped my way down the steps, Celia tucked into my elbow, whispering, "Don't let him in, Miss Lill! Don't let him in!"

"Celia Percy, get back here!" Gladys hissed, pulling her daughter up the stairs. "You and Chester go to my room and stay there till we get back."

"But, Mama —"

"Don't 'But, Mama,' me! Do as you're told — and lock the door!"

I heard Gladys's bedroom door slam closed and Aunt Hyacinth call weakly from her room.

"Gladys, I'll take care of this. Watch over Aunt Hyacinth. She needs you."

"Don't open that door, Lilliana. Whoever it

223

is, he's likely skunk drunk this time of night and nothing but trouble."

I knew about trouble. I was scared, terrified nearly out of my mind. But I also needed to protect Aunt Hyacinth and Gladys and Celia and Chester. They were my family now.

The banging came again. I was almost to the door when I realized I didn't want to open it or challenge whoever it was empty-handed.

"Open this door, you city slut, or I'll break it down!" The slur came, enraged.

I grabbed the fireplace poker. A moment later I realized that Gladys stood beside me, a cast-iron skillet in one hand and a hammer in the other.

"Weapons of choice." I heard her half smile.

I squeezed her wrist in gratitude and just to make certain she stood flesh and blood beside me.

"Don't open it. Just talk. Talk him down."

I nodded and called, "Who's there?"

"You know who it is! Open this door!"

"No, I do not know. Tell me who you are and state your business."

"Rhoan Wishon! And I'm here to deal with you about my Ruby Lynne." His banging rattled the front parlor windowpanes.

I swallowed. Celia and Gladys had warned me this might happen. "Mr. Wishon, no gentleman comes calling this time of night. If you'd like to speak with me, you must come back sober and in the daylight. You're welcome to bring Ruby Lynne with you."

"Ruby Lynne will never set foot in your whorehouse again!"

I felt Gladys tense beside me. "This is Miz Hyacinth's home, Rhoan Wishon, and you've no call to speak to her niece that way. You are drunk and should be ashamed! Go home before you say things you'll regret."

"It's my Ruby Lynne that's regrettin'. It's all over No Creek how you're running a courtin' house between our white gals and colored bucks — how you used my Ruby Lynne as bait. I ought to burn you out! We ought to string that boy up!"

"This is no 'courting house,' Mr. Wishon, and nothing but reading goes on here. This is a lending library where we help anyone who wants to learn to read and write. Your daughter was helping a young man learn to read better — that's all. She's a truly gifted teacher. You should let her go back to school."

"My girl's dumb as a milk can and already wasted years on the schooling she's got. She ought to be married. She'll be lucky to get a good, clean man to look at her now, thanks to you and your —"

That did it. I flicked on the outside porch light and unbolted the door, all the while with Gladys tugging at my waist, trying to pull me away. But my dander was up and I flung open the door, stepping forward and brandishing my poker in the man's face, half a foot above me, so he stumbled backward and down a step, near blinded by the sudden light. "Your daughter is still a child. She's too young to marry. She's fifteen! And she's brilliant. She's capable and has a caring heart. She just wanted to see what it would be like to teach. She's a wonderful teacher — would be a wonderful teacher given a chance. You should send her back to school, Mr. Wishon, and then to college for a teaching degree. She can make something of herself if you don't hold her back."

My long-winded speech momentarily rendered Rhoan Wishon speechless, but he summoned his wits and stepped up again, reeking of whiskey. "It's you putting fool ideas in her head. College — a waste of hard-earned money."

"I hear you have money. Don't you want to use it for your family? Ruby Lynne's your own daughter."

"Use it? Waste it! Spend all that money on education and then she marries and stays home poppin' babies? That's what women are made for, Miss High-and-Mighty, or didn't nobody ever tell you that? No, I don't s'pose they did."

"Mr. Wishon —"

"My girl's not to set foot here again. She's old enough to court and here you've ruined her reputation havin' her spend time with a colored boy — whatever they're doing. Well, never you mind. I'll take care of him myself. Is that clear, *Miss* Belvidere? Oh yeah — it's not even *Miss,* is it?" He snorted.

I gritted my teeth and gripped the poker all the harder — now in fear. He stepped onto the porch again, too close, staring down into my face. I trembled from the inside out, just as I'd done whenever Gerald stood over me, brawn and strength intimidating my every breath.

He slammed his fist against the doorpost. "I said, do I make myself clear?" I couldn't have told if he shouted or whispered, his words and fist and presence reverberated through my soul with such intensity.

"Clear." It was all I could squeak out. He loomed over me so that I might have swooned from fright if I didn't feel Gladys beside me, her arm snaked around my back for support.

Rhoan Wishon glared at both of us — two thin women in nightclothes armed in domestic weaponry. He looked us up and down, assessing every inch, smirked as if we were no longer worth bothering about, and stepped off the porch into the dark.

Nobody slept that night. Gladys drew her children into bed with her and locked the door. I kept to the chair by Aunt Hyacinth's bed, our hands clasped. The whip-poor-will sang all night. By dawn, when Gladys came with a breakfast tray, Aunt Hyacinth had failed dramatically.

"She's so much weaker," Gladys whispered. "We can't sit her up to dress. She doesn't even want to sip tea. I think we should send for Dr. Vishnevsky . . . and somebody ought to warn Marshall about Rhoan. I'll send Celia down to Olney's."

I agreed on both counts, but all I could think of at the moment was Aunt Hyacinth. With trembling fingers I dialed the operator for the doctor's number. I felt like a child, playing telephone, so inept and unprepared was I for Aunt Hyacinth's sharp decline.

Dr. Vishnevsky came within the half hour. Aunt Hyacinth asked to be left alone with the doctor. I respected her privacy but anxiously paced the hallway outside her door.

Their voices, muffled, went on a long while. When at last the doctor came from the room, he removed his glasses, wiping his eyes with his handkerchief.

"Her heart?" I whispered, wringing my hands.

He nodded. "It won't be long now. Last night's shock did not help, but she has been nearing her time. Do all you can to make her comfortable. Offer liquids if she wants, but don't force food. Her earthly shell is shutting down, getting ready."

I couldn't swallow the painful lump in my

throat. "I'm not ready. I'm not ready for her to go."

Dr. Vishnevsky replaced his glasses, looked sadly, compassionately in my eyes, and half smiled. He took my chilled but sweaty hand and pressed it in his own. "We never are." He hefted his bag. "Lilliana Grace. A beautiful name. Call me if you need me, when there is change." He scrutinized my face. "She loves you. Do not underestimate the good of your coming here. You've given her all her heart desired in her last days."

His words were balm and knife.

"Go in now. She wants to see you. But then you must sleep, Lilliana Grace. You will need it in the days ahead."

Sleep. I couldn't imagine losing a moment of Aunt Hyacinth's precious life to sleep.

"Thank you, Doctor." I prepared to show him out, but he held up his hand.

"I know the way." He hesitated, his hand on the newel knob of the staircase, his back to me.

I waited.

He spoke quietly. "Do you know what *shanda* means?

I shook my head.

"It is the Yiddish word for 'shame.' Your aunt feels it keenly."

My breath caught. *What shame could Aunt Hyacinth feel? Is it shame of me?*

"It is shame to live life and to have no one

remember it. In the Jewish culture we have an expression, *dor l'dor* — from generation to generation. We want to tell our stories, to be remembered by our children's children, to be known and to tell how Adonai has led us and leads us still. Your aunt bore no children. The child she raised is gone. She needs to give you her stories, your family's stories. While there is time, if there is still time, listen. It is the gift that matters most to her." He didn't wait for me to answer but made his way down the stairs and out the front door. The bell jingled, then fell silent.

I stood in the upstairs hallway, dust mites dancing before the far window. Something passed through the garden below and into the woods — a shape similar to the form I'd seen — and sensed — on the way to find Gerald that morning not so long ago. I shivered. *A premonition? An omen?* If only I could stop time — freeze time in this place. But the sands of time did not slow. I turned the knob and went in to my aunt.

Aunt Hyacinth lay on the center of her bed beneath an ivory coverlet. Embroidered pink roses connected by loden-green ribbon vines bordered the edges. Bouquets of roses and violets, lilacs and daisies filled each square, each one tied with garlands of pink ribbon. I'd never seen the coverlet before — nothing like it.

Aunt Hyacinth's eyes opened as I pulled a chair to her bed and sat down, running my fingers over the raised threads. Her frail hands smoothed the coverlet, fingering the stitching.

"This is beautiful, Aunt Hyacinth. Where did it come from?"

"I made it for my wedding day. Every stitch, filled with love."

"Your wedding day?"

A cloud, a sadness passed through her eyes, and she took a breath that barely lifted the coverlet from the bed. She opened her hand. I placed mine in it. "There are so many things I should have told you. And now . . ."

"What is it you want to tell me?"

She nodded, then closed her eyes. I waited, glad Dr. Vishnevsky had spoken to me. If he hadn't, I might have tried to quiet her, urged her to save her strength.

"First, about my Henry."

"The ring I brought back to you. You said it was Henry's ring."

Aunt Hyacinth smiled. Her thumb twisted the ring on her finger, setting it so she could feel the ruby. "You'll see to it that I wear it — always?"

"Yes." I tried hard to keep my voice steady. "Of course. I promise."

"Papa took us to the seaside each summer, Camellia and me, even after we were old enough to begin the tours . . . New York,

Canada, Europe. New York is where I met Biddy. You'll write her for me?"

I squeezed her hand, not trusting my voice.

"Good. Mama died when Camellia was born. That took half of Papa's life. When Camellia married, he no longer had the heart to 'traipse the world,' as he said." Aunt Hyacinth paused, her breathing seeming too much a chore to continue.

"Maybe you should tell me later, Aunt Hy—"

Her hand squeezed mine. Obediently, worriedly, I waited. She spoke between labored breaths.

"It was the first summer after Camellia married. Papa was so distracted — with his regrets and worries, I suppose. He said he had family business to see to and that he was no longer up to keeping track of me, no longer insisted on a chaperone to accompany me. I was allowed to roam on my own, and roam I did. I met a young man, a handsome young waterman who worked for the Chicamacomico Life-Saving Station in Rodanthe — along the Outer Banks." She smiled in memory. "His chest was broad and his arms like steel from the rowing he did each day. His eyes were the color of the sea, just before a storm."

Aunt Hyacinth didn't speak for several minutes, and I thought she'd fallen asleep from the exertion. I hoped it was in the peace of happy memory. But then she opened her eyes, still looking toward some far-off place — perhaps Rodanthe, long ago.

"We fell in love, deeply in love. He gave me this ring and asked Papa for my hand — all very proper."

"What happened?"

"Papa refused — furious. He was still grieving Mama all those years later and then that Camellia had recently married and left us. I was all that he had left . . . and he thought Henry — a waterman from Dare County — beneath the Belvidere family name." Aunt Hyacinth sighed wearily. "I could hardly wait to marry Henry or to get away from Papa. We were going to run away — elope."

"Like Mama."

Aunt Hyacinth smiled. "Yes, in a way it would have been like your precious mama. But there was more to her running away than marriage. I suppose she never told you our family secret, our shame. I should have told you, but I've put it off, still so ashamed — and yet it didn't start out that way. Not all the Belvideres were like Papa. I'll tell you now, my darling girl, and pray you'll forgive our family. I understood Rosemary's going better than she knew, though I grieved every day for her — the daughter I never bore."

I couldn't tell if Aunt Hyacinth was imagining or remembering in her rambling. I couldn't imagine what "family secret" she might have held or how that could have influenced Mama. Mama never said. But it was Aunt Hyacinth's love story that seemed to matter most. "You didn't go with Henry?"

"Papa had gone to his business meeting — whatever that was, he never said, then suffered a stroke that night — right there at the seashore hotel. It wasn't severe, but I couldn't leave him. I came back to No Creek to care for him that autumn, promising Henry we'd marry at Christmas. Despite Papa's protestations, I had my wedding dress made. You'll find it in the trunk at the foot of my bed, wrapped in tissue paper. This —" she caressed the coverlet — "was the wedding quilt I made for us. I worked on it every day I nursed Papa. I asked Gladys to lay it over me now. Henry and I were going to be married right here in Shady Grove Baptist. Papa was well enough to manage on his own by then, along with our hired help that came in, and nothing he could say would have stopped me."

"Then what — ?"

"There was a storm at sea — a terrible storm and a shipwreck. Henry was on duty that night. The rescue boat pushed out to sea and the men saved eight of the twenty passengers. Three of the rescuers were never found. My Henry . . ."

"Aunt Hyacinth, I'm so terribly sorry."

"I'll see him again. It won't be long now." Aunt Hyacinth breathed, a long but ragged breath, still holding my hand.

I stroked the tears from her weathered cheeks, so wishing I could wipe away her sadness and loss, wishing I could have given her a different life, a different ending.

"Eventually, one night, Papa suffered another stroke — a bad one. I stayed and cared for him till he died . . . nearly ten years. I don't know what I would have done if I hadn't had your mother to raise during his last years. She gave me such joy — made my life whole again."

"There was no one else — after Henry?"

"No one else for me." She turned her head. "There were other suitors, of course. Papa had seen to that. His money and his . . . his unique position in the community . . . drew suitors like flies to honey, especially when it was apparent that he was going to die and leave a fortune. But none of them were the sort of men I wanted to marry. I refused, which angered Papa no end, though he couldn't speak by that time. I preferred loneliness to — to what they were." She turned toward me as though she could look me in the eye. "You understand wolves in sheep's clothing, don't you, Lilliana?"

"Yes, I do."

"I wish you didn't — that you hadn't any need. Be careful, my darling girl. Be very careful. You were a child when you married that man. You're a woman now. Be careful, but don't be afraid to live your life. Take Paul's words to heart: forget those things which are behind, those things you cannot change, and press on. Don't let that man or any other beat your spirit down. God doesn't expect that of you. He doesn't want it. Your spirit belongs to Him, not Gerald, and Jesus loves you. He loves you so. He has plans for you, Lilliana, a future."

Tears streamed down my cheeks. I fought not to sob aloud. I knew Aunt Hyacinth believed what she said. But how could Jesus love me when my own father didn't? When my own husband wanted to be rid of me? I'd walked all the years of my childhood and marriage in fear. Hadn't my father told me over and over — *"Perfect love casts out fear. You're not walking as God's child if you don't love your husband, if you exasperate him to the point of losing his temper. How can any man tolerate a woman who quits performing her wifely duties, afraid or not?"*

I drew a shaking breath and summoned my voice to answer before I realized that Aunt Hyacinth was gone. Gone suddenly, her eyes still wide-open, her smile relaxed and peaceful, as if she saw something I could not.

CHAPTER TWENTY-FIVE

Miz Hyacinth's funeral made the most forlorn procession Celia could remember. Not that she'd lived long enough to see many funerals, but she counted no dry eyes, including Reverend Willard's — especially Reverend Willard's. Even Ida Mae's handkerchief hung limp and damp and rouge-stained.

Miss Lill walked from the church to the cemetery yard pale as a ghost. Celia had begged her to take just a little of the tea and toast her mama had sent upstairs that morning, but nothing she said moved Miss Lill. She just seemed numb in her grief.

Olney Tate, hat in hand and head respectfully bowed, stood a few rows of tombstones back, alongside his family. Granny Chree's dark-blue dress billowed in the breeze, just behind Mercy Tate, Olney's wife. Celia couldn't see their faces but knew their hearts were as bowed down in grief as her own.

It made her sick, and it wasn't fair, them not being welcome in the church for Miz

Hyacinth's funeral. Celia knew Reverend Willard would have opened his arms to each and every one, but she could name to a man — and a woman — those who would not, those who'd make their displeasure known in ways too dangerous to mention.

Janice Richards and her mother were at the cemetery, and Coltrane, pulling on his too-tight collar. For once, Janice didn't taunt Celia or Chester, and Celia didn't pay the girl any more mind than to wish the earth would open up and swallow her whole. Surely it was Janice who'd spread the gossip that had gotten Rhoan Wishon worked up about Ruby Lynne and Marshall reading in the kitchen. Only nobody cared that they were only reading, even if they believed it true.

It was Rhoan's banging on the door and his ugly threats that had sent Miz Hyacinth over the brink; of that Celia was certain. And yet there he stood — Rhoan and Troy and Ruby Lynne Wishon. Rhoan had the decency to look distressed, but Celia hated him for what he'd done and wanted to kick him in the shins and make him leave. "It's disgraceful and disrespectful, him bein' here after all he said and did," Celia hissed.

But her mother shook her head and whispered, "Those Wishon boys are grievin' like the rest of us, Celia. Miz Hyacinth taught everybody in No Creek for two generations, some families for three. They loved her, too."

"He sure had a funny way of showin' it!" Celia fumed.

"Miz Hyacinth's long been in the process of dying. Rhoan might have pushed her to the edge a little sooner, but he wasn't the cause and you mustn't blame him for it, or Janice. The good Lord knows what He's doing. It was just Miz Hyacinth's time." Her mother squeezed her hand.

That might be true, but Celia preferred to hold a grudge.

"If anything, maybe this will sober him up and he'll forget about Marshall."

Celia didn't believe it. He sure hadn't forgotten about Ruby Lynne. Maybe nobody else noticed, but Ruby Lynne was wearing long sleeves in the summer heat. Celia could bet dollars to doughnuts there was a reason for that — and for her split lower lip.

She turned away, unable to watch the graveside service. She heard Reverend Willard's prayers and the rope pulleys of the coffin being lowered. She sensed the gentle thumping of flowers, then louder dirt clods as they hit the coffin. People began to walk away. Chester tucked close beneath their mama's arm. Celia tucked close beneath the other, glad for the sun's warmth on her side.

When Celia looked up, she saw Miss Lill stood alone. Celia's heart gripped for her. *How sad to stand all alone, especially now.*

Now that Miz Hyacinth's gone, will Miss Lill

239

go, too? Will she go back to Philadelphia and that sorry excuse for a man she married? If she does, will we have to move back to the cabin? How long till Troy Wishon comes round botherin' Mama again? Who'll stand for us now?

CHAPTER TWENTY-SIX

What does a person do at a graveside? Or after a funeral? At home, back in Philadelphia, I'd cooked and baked for Mama's funeral luncheon. I'd served and welcomed and thanked people for coming — church members and strangers, businesspeople connected to my father. I'd washed every pot and pan until the church had emptied, putting off tears as long as I could. Then I'd fallen asleep in the pew. And then I'd heard my husband's plans, my father's disowning, and had run away.

I wanted to run away again when they began tossing handfuls of dirt on Aunt Hyacinth's coffin. I hated the *thud, thud, thud.* I wanted to scream, *"Open it up! She can't be gone!"* But I didn't, and of course she was. So I waited until they'd all said what they thought they should, what they needed to, what gave them peace, and left. I stood by the graveside for a time, remembering, trying to summon her presence, but it was no longer there. Finally I turned and, like everybody else, left Aunt Hyacinth's shell alone in the ground.

Reverend Willard waited for me a few steps away.

"I'm so sorry for this loss, Lilliana. Miz Hyacinth was —" He couldn't seem to go on.

"She was your friend, Reverend Willard. And you were hers. Thank you for that."

"I'll miss her," he said, sounding small, like a lost child. He coughed to regain his voice and tried to straighten.

I shook my head. It was no use pretending to be strong when you didn't feel it. I, of all people, knew that. I pressed his hand and walked away, just wanting to be alone.

Gladys and the children had waited by the church. We walked together back to Garden's Gate in silence. I was thankful that they didn't speak, thankful that I did not feel the need.

Opening the front door was like opening a vault. The house that had been so sunny with its front parlor, now a children's reading room, did not seem cheerful — only hollow. I tightened my lips, unable to think on any of that now, and headed up the stairs to my room.

"I'll fix some lunch, Lilliana, and have Celia bring it up . . . unless you want to join us down here."

I knew Gladys meant well, but the thought of food turned my stomach. "Please don't bother with me, Gladys. You go ahead."

"You need to eat something. You know —"

But I continued upstairs and closed my bedroom door. I didn't want anything, didn't know anything, didn't need anything, couldn't talk. Aunt Hyacinth was gone. Who was I in No Creek without her? Without Aunt Hyacinth to help me shape my new world, I couldn't imagine.

All I knew was that there was a ragged hole in my heart. A hole that could not be filled with Gladys's food or Celia's questions or Chester's smiles. It couldn't even be filled with teaching Marshall to read — as if that were still possible — or with fighting the likes of Rhoan Wishon on Ruby Lynne's behalf.

Empty. I felt empty, depleted of all that I was or had tried to become while remaining busy and purposeful in the restoration of Garden's Gate and the building of the library. It had all been to please Aunt Hyacinth and help those she loved — and perhaps as a memorial for my mother, who'd left here so young, and a project for people in need whom I was coming to care for. Now Mama and Aunt Hyacinth were both gone and the community was at odds with me. It all seemed futile.

The noon light came and went. Downstairs I heard a continual jingle of the front door library bell. The fragrance of a feast of casseroles and cakes wafted up the stairs and beneath my door. I figured custom had trumped anger. Still, I wanted to stuff something below the crack to keep the nauseating smells out.

The afternoon light faded. Dusk came on and the tree outside my window changed to silhouette. A knock came at my door.

"Miss Lill? Mama sent me up with a tray of food. Open the door, please?"

I didn't rise from my bed, kept my face buried in my pillow and turned toward the window. "I'm not hungry, Celia. Please tell your mama not to bother with me. You all go on and eat."

"I'm sorry, Miss Lill, but my mama won't stand for that. She says not to bring this tray downstairs till it's empty. Please, let me in."

The sigh within felt like it might swallow me. But I knew Gladys, and she'd not let Celia off the hook until she'd done her bidding. So I got to my feet, switched on the bedside lamp, and opened the door. Before I could take the tray, Celia pushed in, chattering a mile a minute.

"Thank you, Miss Lill. You know Mama. She won't take no for an answer, never could as far as I know. Wants you to eat every bite. Says you've got to keep your strength up. You're the Belvidere woman now."

That felt like a punch to my stomach.

"You might not like hearing that —" Celia looked me straight in the eye — "but we need you. We need a Belvidere at Garden's Gate."

The cold truth of Celia's words poked my spine and straightened it just a little. To be needed . . . to be wanted . . . And I was a Belvidere — not the Belvidere my aunt had been, but a Belvidere just the same. *The last of the Belvidere women. What does that mean?*

"So you gonna eat now?" Celia set the tray on my dressing table.

"I can't, Celia. I'm not hungry."

"I can't go downstairs till —"

"Then you eat it."

Celia's eyes widened.

It was the perfect solution. I pulled the pot lid off the plate and felt my own eyes go wide. Smoked ham, pot roast beef, stewed carrots and onions and scalloped tomatoes in a dish, two kinds of pie, and a cup of steaming coffee beside. "I'll never eat all this! Where did it come from?" *Where did these poor people get all this food? Nearly every family in No Creek lives on small or no wages and hard times.*

"Folks thought a lot of Miz Hyacinth. She taught most everybody in No Creek over the years. And now — with you — she opened the library. They want to honor her . . . so they do for you. Folks here do that with food . . . and sometimes 'shine."

Food and moonshine. Their best gifts, their only gifts. Gravel rose in my throat and lodged there. I'd felt so invisible, so lost and lonely and alone.

But the truth was, I wasn't alone, not here. Here was community that included me — even now that they knew I was a runaway married woman. They weren't afraid to show their curiosity or their disapproval, but they didn't lie about it. Despite Rhoan Wishon's drunken feud and the hatefulness of Mrs. Richards, here were people to stand with and people to stand up to — in the open, not behind closed doors with secrets.

Celia, Chester, and Gladys were my family now, Garden's Gate my home . . . *my home.*

"Maybe we can eat it together," Celia ventured, her eyes a little hopeful.

How could I not smile at that face? "Maybe we can."

I picked up the silverware beside the plate, not sure what to do. There was one fork and a knife. But that didn't deter Celia. She grinned, pulling a spoon from her dungarees pocket.

CHAPTER TWENTY-SEVEN

It took me three days before I could walk into Aunt Hyacinth's room. By then, Gladys had washed the sheets and lovingly packed away the wedding quilt. The room looked made up as usual, ready for Aunt Hyacinth to walk in any moment.

I sat in the morning sun that she loved, in her rocker by the window. I tried to imagine Aunt Hyacinth before her stroke, teaching school, living in this big house all alone . . . and before that, nursing her sick father, and before that, learning that her beloved was lost at sea, her only hope of leaving No Creek and forging a life of her own gone in a moment. Living forever with broken dreams — empty, alone.

Was that any worse — or better — than living married, every day in fear? I'm going to find out. For what else can my life be? Even if Gerald leaves me alone — and that's not likely unless he gets what he wants — I'll still be tied, still married to him. I'll never be free. The sentencing of that weighed heavier than before, now that Aunt Hyacinth was gone.

My eyes took in every inch of the room, trying to see it as Aunt Hyacinth had seen it. *Sanctuary? Prison? Both?*

The trunk at the foot of her bed beckoned. Her hope chest. Her wedding dress — she'd said it was there, tucked away in tissue paper. The urge to understand more of Aunt Hyacinth's last words, to see her as a woman my age, give or take a few years, came strong, so I knelt before the trunk and turned the key set in its lock.

Lifting the lid was like pulling back a tapestry. Pasted inside the lid were carefully scissored flowers from greeting cards and a large envelope containing notices of births and deaths — my mother's birth announcement, a write-up of Grandmother Camellia and Grandfather's car crash and obituary, and the write-up of the Chicamacomico rescue gone tragic, including pictures of the rescuers who'd drowned. I traced the lines of Henry's handsome face, wishing again that Aunt Hyacinth could have known the love she'd so desperately wanted, the marriage she'd so nearly achieved. I was glad I'd left the ruby ring on her finger. Ida Mae had chided me for leaving it there — *such a waste,* she'd claimed. But I had promised Aunt Hyacinth, and it would never fit another soul. It was where it belonged.

I found a framed sepia-toned photograph in the trunk that must be Grandaunt Hyacinth and Grandmother Camellia when they were girls in pigtails, standing beside their father, Great-Grandfather Belvidere. He looked a bit worn but severe, while the children looked as if they held back impishness.

I'd never seen those pictures, but I recognized the girls' likeness in my mother, in me, and my breath caught to think I came from a family past, though I bore no family future. I closed my eyes a moment, remembering Dr. Vishnevsky's words. *"It is shame to live life and to have no one remember it . . .* dor l'dor *— from generation to generation. We want to tell our stories, to be remembered by our children's children, to be known and to tell how Adonai has led us and leads us still."*

I could be that memory for Aunt Hyacinth, who'd borne no children. I could carry her memories, her story within me — at least those she'd shared — but I could not pass on her story or mine in our family line. Both would die with me.

I'd birthed no live children . . . My heart cringed at that memory and I slammed closed the trunk. My only child had died inside my womb, flushing itself from my body in a nightmare of pain and blood following one of Gerald's tirades. He hadn't wanted children, certain they would interfere with his profession and his call to public ministry, his life. He'd pronounced my pregnancy God's punishment on him for fondling me before marriage. He'd pronounced the loss of our baby God's punishment on me for allowing him to fondle me — such looseness and shame in a woman!

That terrible loss, that condemnation that could never be undone was my personal hell from a just and holy God. I must live with it and with the knowledge that I would never be allowed to bear a child. I'd long feared Gerald's touch, no longer dared to bring a child into our tumultuous marriage.

But now those memories must be forced aside. I needed to better understand Aunt Hyacinth, to know her heart and the life she'd lived before I came to her.

So pushing back my past, again I lifted the lid and carefully unwrapped the tissue paper. Her wedding quilt, never used before the week of her death. Now there was an envelope pinned to it. Gladys must have done that. But pins rust, could stain the fabric, and I didn't like the idea that Gladys had taken such liberty. When I unpinned the envelope and turned it over, I saw it was addressed to me — in Grandaunt Hyacinth's shaking script. Inside was a note in Gladys's handwriting. I recognized it from the grocery lists she kept tacked to the kitchen wall.

My darling Lilliana,

This wedding quilt is for you, my beloved. I hope someday you will find a good man to share your love and my wedding quilt will become your wedding quilt.

But please do not save it until then — enjoy it now. Enjoy the beauty of each new day and the life God has given you.

All my love,
Aunt Hyacinth

I sat back on my heels as the tears ran freely. *Oh, Aunt Hyacinth, there is no way for me to have that future. Why couldn't you understand that? But thank you for loving me. I love that you loved me.*

Aunt Hyacinth must have dictated the note to Gladys on her last day. How much had she told Gladys of my story, of my mother's story? What did it matter? Squeezing my eyes shut against the ache, I opened them again to lift out her wedding dress. Ivory satin . . . seed pearls intricately sewn into an embroidered bodice . . . the train so lovely and long. Belgian lace hemmed the veil. Even the shoes, heels dyed to match, lay wrapped in tissue paper in the trunk. Beneath that, a bundle of letters tied in pink ribbon. The postmark from Rodanthe. *Aunt Hyacinth's and Henry's love letters.* My chest tightened. *A treasure!* I wanted so to know that I came from good people who'd loved each other, who were gentle with each other and kind. *Dear God, what would that be like?* I'd save the letters. Perhaps when time had passed, it wouldn't feel such an invasion of my aunt's privacy to read them.

Beneath the letters were childhood books, surely favorites saved to pass on to her own someday children — books I could imagine Celia and Chester loving now. I removed each one and sat there reading stories I'd never read until the morning light had passed. The trunk lay empty. I knew Aunt Hyacinth better than I had that morning. At last I was beginning to set the books back in when I realized there was a finger-size hole in the back corner of the bottom and a little white peeking from the hole. Puzzled, I stuck my finger in and lifted.

A flat panel, exactly the length and width of the trunk, came out in my hands. Beneath the false bottom lay white cloth. Lifting the two pieces of heavy fabric, I shook out their folds and gasped. I'd never seen this up close but did not doubt exactly what it was. Full regalia — robe and hood — of the Ku Klux Klan.

CHAPTER TWENTY-EIGHT

Jesse could not understand why Lilliana Swope avoided him, why she refused to come downstairs when he brought the mail on Wednesdays — the day he'd been given to visiting Miz Hyacinth. He didn't think he'd offended her and hoped she wasn't embarrassed over the situation with her husband. That had been weeks ago. It had been awkward and, above all, disappointing on a personal level to his hopes and expectations, but it would be worse to lose her friendship.

He missed his regular visits to Garden's Gate. He missed his dear friend, Miz Hyacinth, and the Oswald Chambers devotions they'd shared . . . the letters from Biddy and the letters she'd dictated to him in response to her friend. He missed their tea and rousing discussions and the late-afternoon shadows that fell across his path as he made his way home content and satisfied — replenished and filled with a love of life and beauty, an hour of culture and music he didn't find elsewhere.

When he visited now, Gladys invited him into the kitchen for a cup of tea or coffee and a square of gingerbread glazed in pears or freshly baked oatmeal raisin cookies or the best biscuits smothered in preserves the world ever birthed, but it wasn't the same. It wasn't the same at all.

"I saw the front gate's come loose off the hinge," he observed during one such visit. "Can I fix that for you?"

"We'd be much obliged, Reverend. That was Rhoan's doing, the night he came here." Gladys poured him a second cup of tea. "Olney'd normally take care of that, but as you can guess, he and Marshall are layin' low, keepin' off to themselves for a while."

"Because of Rhoan?"

"Rhoan and the rest. I think he'd come by and be glad for the work, but Lilliana's not sent for him. If I had to guess, Olney may wonder does she blame Marshall for the trouble Rhoan caused."

"She wouldn't do that."

"No, but Marshall doesn't know that and Olney's scared. You know Marshall's daddy came to a bad end from a white man's wrath — the reason his mama sent him to live with her brother and Mercy. I saw Mercy picking blackberries the other day. She said Olney wants to send Marshall west. Since President Roosevelt signed that Order 8802, there's jobs for coloreds in defense factories. Now they can't be turned away for color."

Jesse shook his head. It cut his heart that men like Olney or Marshall feared the only way to live was to leave. "Lilliana needs to reach out to them, let them know she doesn't blame them. You ladies need their help and they need the work. Miz Hyacinth said she provided for that."

"She did. But Lilliana just stays up in her room. She takes no joy in us or the library anymore or even in the garden, rich as it is this time of year. She always loved that."

"I haven't seen her in church since Miz Hyacinth passed," he lamented.

"She won't come. I ask her every Wednesday and every Saturday night as we polish the shoes together, but she says no, that she won't set foot in another church, not ever again. I don't know why. She came with Miz Hyacinth."

"Because she insisted, I suppose."

Gladys smiled sadly. "Miz Hyacinth loved to go, loved to sing the hymns and hear you preach. She loved it when Lilliana lifted the window of an afternoon and they'd hear you preachin' to the tombstones." She blushed. "How they laughed at that idea."

"And how I loved to hear them laugh when they told me," he said. "Remember the sound of bells?"

"I do. Nobody laughed like our Miz Hyacinth. But Lilliana doesn't laugh anymore, not since our dear lady passed. I miss her so. I miss them both."

"As do I."

Gladys stood to refill the teapot. "I know you do. I can only imagine how much." As she passed him, she squeezed his shoulder. "You know, Jesse, she thought of you as the son she never had. She dearly loved you."

Jesse nearly choked, holding back the pressure against his eyes. Confirmation of Miz Hyacinth's mothering love, her special favor, overwhelmed him. Even to hear his given name spoken aloud was a wonder. Of course he was "Jesse" to those he'd grown up with. Certainly he was to Miz Hyacinth, though she never referred to him as anything but Reverend Willard from the moment he returned from seminary, and she insisted others do the same. She'd accorded him all the respect she'd have given an older, more experienced pastor, and never failed to let him know how his sermons blessed her. If only she knew how she had blessed him! He hoped she knew.

He'd hoped he could forge a relationship with Lilliana — perhaps one that included the reading of *My Utmost for His Highest* and the deep discussions that devotional had wrought and even a continued correspondence with Biddy, along with the music of an afternoon, the abiding peace he'd come to love at Garden's Gate. He missed those things, but more, he wanted to know Lilliana for the woman she was. At one time he'd imagined their relationship growing into something more. She was married, so that was not to be. But a friendship? Perhaps it was wrong of him to have imagined such a thing — to have presumed the character or even the platonic affections of another. Perhaps it wasn't possible under the circumstances. Perhaps it wasn't wise. Still, he couldn't help but wish it could be so.

On his way toward the door, he stopped to peruse the mystery section of the library. A good mystery these late-summer evenings might stand him in good stead, take his mind from some of the troubles he sorted amid the community by day. He'd just pulled the card to sign out an Agatha Christie when Lilliana came down the stairs, her hair disheveled and her skirt askew, a basket over her arm.

"Lilliana! I'm glad to see you."

"Reverend Willard — I thought you'd gone." She flushed, nearly tripping on the last step.

"Apparently not soon enough." He hadn't meant to sound sarcastic, but her clear wish not to see him cut.

She straightened. "I didn't mean that unkindly."

"Then why have you avoided me?" He sounded like a petulant child but couldn't seem to stop himself.

"I — I've not . . . I mean I —" She paled. Her face crumpled as she reached for the banister behind her but missed.

He crossed the space in three long strides and caught her as she appeared to stumble, but she steadied herself against him and pulled back, pushing him away at the same time.

"Don't touch me!"

"I'm sorry. I didn't mean to — I thought you were going to fall."

Gladys came running from the kitchen. "Lilliana, are you all right?"

Lilliana nodded, her face now flaming, her hands pressed against her cheeks. "Yes, I'm fine. I just . . . need to be left alone. I'm sorry, Reverend Willard. I didn't mean to accuse you."

"Lilliana — Grace — may we talk?"

She raised her hand before her face, refusing to look at him, and walked quickly down the hallway, through the kitchen and out the back door, letting the screen door slam behind her.

He spread his hands, appealing to Gladys, but she shook her head. "That's just how she's been — more than three weeks now. I don't know what to do. I don't know how to reach her."

Jesse didn't know either, but he believed it his duty to help those in need, even if Lilliana Swope wasn't actually a member of Shady Grove. Was she a believer in Jesus Christ as her Savior? Did she know she could turn to Him in her need even if she couldn't turn to another human being? Jesse didn't know. He'd assumed she believed, being Miz Hyacinth's niece, having grown up in a church — and above all because of her kind and loving heart. It went without saying, didn't it?

He wrestled with that question all the way home and finally came to the conclusion that he should have, would have reached out to Lilliana right after Miz Hyacinth's funeral if he'd not been so foolish, so blind, so smitten and nursing his hurt that she was married.

Lilliana was certainly a woman of purpose and conviction — willing to help Marshall and the children of Saints Delight Church learn to better read, regardless of the cost to her safety or reputation. And yet, faith and lofty purpose were not interchangeable. One could exist without the other.

He'd seen her come to life with the opening of Garden's Gate's library. That purpose had been challenged by the visit from her controlling husband, by the late-night tirade of Rhoan Wishon and the cruel gossip of Velma Richards and Ida Mae, then apparently derailed by Miz Hyacinth's passing.

He couldn't bring Miz Hyacinth back, couldn't undo Gerald Swope's actions or the ugly words from Velma or Rhoan, but he could encourage Marshall and the children of Saints Delight to appeal to Lilliana. The needs of others had spoken to her tender heart before. Surely those needs could facilitate the opening of that heart again.

Perhaps he could help Ruby Lynne Wishon at the same time. The girl had been in church with her father and uncle since Rhoan's "visit" to Garden's Gate, but she'd sat wan and pale between them, a shell of the joyful teen who'd been learning to teach.

Maybe, just maybe, the answer for all of them lay in one ball of twine.

CHAPTER TWENTY-NINE

I ran out the back door as quickly as my legs could carry me. I hadn't meant to insult or offend Reverend Willard, but he'd taken me by surprise. And when he touched me — *doesn't he know he mustn't touch me?*

I'm terrified of my heart — the direction of my thoughts. I should not be alone with him. He looks at me as if he sees right through my skin to my soul — as if he sees me in a way Gerald never did, and he likes what he sees.

Dear God, if You have any pity for me, any love for Reverend Willard, help him to despise me, to leave me alone. Association with me will ruin Jesse's reputation, and that will ruin his life here.

I was so lost in thought I didn't see the form on the ground until I all but tripped over her. Bent and kneeling at the edge of the garden, covered in a long, threadbare dress the blue-black color of faded juniper berries and wearing an old-fashioned black poke bonnet, a little woman — no bigger than

Celia — stopped her digging and lifted her spade. One keen brown eye and one grayed and sightless in a weathered face just as dark, framed in white wool hair, peered up at me. "Poor chile," she lamented. "Poor, poor chile."

I looked behind me, glanced around the garden for the "poor child," but didn't find one. She meant me. That made me bristle. "Who are you?" It was a rude question rudely asked, and I realized just as quickly that she must be Granny Chree — the granny woman Celia had told me about when I first came, the one Gladys said had long ago been Aunt Hyacinth's nanny, and before Emancipation a slave at Belvidere Hall. She was overdue to come dig herbs from Aunt Hyacinth's garden. She was also the form I'd glimpsed in and out of the garden from time to time — those moments I hadn't trusted my eyes or senses but had known someone was there.

The woman lifted an elbow and I helped her struggle to her feet. She must be one hundred years old, or nearly, by my accounting, but looked eighty-five and weighed no more than a child of ten. "You're Hyacinth's girl, Rosemary's child. You got your mama's eyes, the eyes of the Belvidere women."

Nobody'd said that to me since Mama had passed. Aunt Hyacinth couldn't see, so couldn't say, and who else remembered my mother's face, her eyes? It was good to be known for who I was, to have Mama remembered.

"Spittin' image. I knew her as a little bitty and as a young woman, before she ran off with that city man."

"My father."

"Hmmph," she grunted. She straightened as best she could. "I was right sorry to hear about your mama's passing, and then Hyacinth's a stone's throw after — mighty sorry. Your aunt was a good woman, a good, good woman."

I believed that, but what was a good woman doing hiding a white robe and hood in her hope chest? It was the most startling, most frightening thing I could have found. How could Aunt Hyacinth preach to me about the cruelties of the Klan and champion the notion of helping colored children in No Creek, all the while safeguarding a Klan robe among her most treasured possessions?

"Say what?"

"I didn't say anything."

"But you not sure about that? You don't believe ole Granny? Don't believe what you lived?"

"I just don't understand —" I stopped. I couldn't do this. "Aunt Hyacinth was so very good to me. She was dearly loved in the community. I just wish I'd known her longer, known her better — when she was younger. She said you and she were friends?"

"Pert near sisters. I slaved and later earned wages right here when it was Belvidere Hall. Knew your aunt from the moment she was born, raised her like my own. That's how it was in them days." Granny Chree chuckled, picked up two burlap bags at her feet. "Though you ought not tell that in town." She grinned. "Hyacinth understood the seasons and the earth. Once I moved out to my cabin in the hills, we'd meet over watermelon in summer and coffee or hot chicory come winter — depending on what year we're talkin'. Let me come here and dig some of her horehound betimes, and feverfew. I was the one planted them, after all. I brung her thistle and ginseng from the mountain, black walnut leaves for tea — she was partial to black walnut. Cleans the blood." She handed up a bag. "You know what to do with these?"

"No." I took the offering. "I don't."

"Gladys tell you. She's a good girl. She'll help you get on your feet."

That was truth. *I don't know what I'd do without Gladys . . . or Celia or Chester. And yet I can't ask them about that regalia. To connect Aunt Hyacinth with the Klan is an impossible idea — insulting to Aunt Hyacinth's memory. There has to be an explanation. Who in No Creek is part and parcel with the Klan?* Rhoan Wishon, surely. I'd assumed he might be numbered among the cross burners. Velma

Richards and Ida Mae had made their opinions on race clear, but somehow I'd never imagined women participating in the KKK. *Does that robe have something to do with our family secret — the shame Aunt Hyacinth spoke of? Is that what she meant about why Mama ran away?*

Granny Chree stood with her head tucked to one side. "You be a worryin' chile. Full of troubles and plumb wore out."

I am.

"You find it in your heart to let Granny Chree come dig herbs, like before?"

"Yes. Whatever arrangement you had with Aunt Hyacinth before, please continue. It will be fine. But . . ."

"What is it?"

Now I tucked my head to one side. "Did you always feel welcome here? Did you feel . . . safe?"

Granny Chree shifted her shovel. "With Hyacinth — and with her grandparents back in slavery days. Those Belvideres were cut from a different cloth than her daddy." She straightened, tilting her head to see me with her good eye. "I heard Rhoan Wishon come calling. He be by again. Wishons can't leave things alone."

It was an unwelcome prophecy, but a likely one.

"Don't you be bothered 'bout what come to pass. Can't do nothin' but meet trouble when it knocks on your door." She slung the other burlap sack over her shoulder. "You have trouble, you send for ole Granny."

Granny Chree stepped through rows of herbs and vegetables and around the corner of the barn, disappearing into the woods beyond before I could bring myself to press my question.

If I hadn't seen her with my own eyes and heard her speak, I might have thought her an apparition. I closed my eyes to chase away visions of robed and hooded Klansmen menacing Marshall and turned to the rosebush I'd come to find cuttings and solace in. *How could tiny, ancient Granny Chree help me in a world of cross burners and their secrets?*

CHAPTER THIRTY

Celia saw clear as day that Ruby Lynne was delighted to be teaching children again. How Reverend Willard had pulled that off, she couldn't imagine. Ruby Lynne no longer taught Marshall — nobody did — and everybody made sure that neither Olney nor Marshall was scheduled to work outside Garden's Gate when she came. Still, there were lots of younger children, colored and white, who needed "tutoring," as Miss Lill called it.

Ruby Lynne taught only the white children — her daddy's orders, though she left cookies for children of both colors and hair ribbons for the girls when they came in to use the library. Giving just seemed to brighten Ruby Lynne's soul and that raised her high in Celia's estimation.

Miss Lill had kept to herself for weeks through the summer and on into September, past the start of school. In the house she kept to her room. Outside, she took long walks up the mountain, never wanting company. Finally, one afternoon Miss Lill came downstairs and found Ruby Lynne at the kitchen table teaching the alphabet to seven-year-old Rebecca Mae, Ida Mae's grandniece by marriage. The child's laughter — like water bubbling over brook stones — seemed to wake Miss Lill, open her eyes and ears. Celia figured she still viewed the world a little cockeyed, maybe, but at least no longer looked like a woman in a trance.

Even so, Miss Lill wasn't the same as before Miz Hyacinth passed. None of them were. A light had gone from Garden's Gate, a light no one seemed able to find again.

Miss Lill took to sitting evenings at Miz Hyacinth's desk in the parlor to write letters of thanks to folks who'd tended her aunt in any way during her last days and to those who'd brought food or flowers to the house after the funeral. She intended to write to Biddy Chambers, Celia knew, because she'd heard Miss Lill ask her mama what she knew of the woman one afternoon in the kitchen.

"Only that Miz Hyacinth considered Biddy her dearest friend — 'friend of a lifetime,' she'd say. Reverend Willard knows more," her mama mentioned, peeling potatoes at the sink without turning round. "He's the one read all Biddy's letters out loud once she lost her sight, and he's the one wrote down everything Miz Hyacinth wanted said in return. I think he'd be proud if you asked him." Her mama turned to Miss Lill. "He misses Miz Hyacinth something fierce. It'd be a mercy to give him the opportunity to talk about her."

"I can't do that." Miss Lill shook her head. "I know you don't understand why. I'm sorry."

Celia kept quiet and stepped back into the hallway, just outside the kitchen door, knowing that the only way she'd hear more was to make herself invisible.

"Reverend Willard doesn't understand. Why do you shut him out so? He's a good man, Lilliana, a kind man, a man you can trust. And he's grieving, just like you. You'd be company for one another. That'd make Miz Hyacinth smile."

The sigh Miss Lill released as she pulled a chair from the table and plunked down sounded like the weight of the world rested on her shoulders. "Aunt Hyacinth might like it, but she wouldn't expect it."

Celia heard another chair slide over the floor and pictured her mama sitting across the table from Miss Lill. She peeked around the corner in time to see her mother clasp both Miss Lill's hands in her own. "Tell me what's burdened you so. You weren't this miserable the day we laid her to rest. What is it?"

Miss Lill choked back sobs. "You wouldn't

believe it . . . at least I don't think you'd believe it."

"Try me. Holding darkness inside never gave anybody peace."

"I'm so confused. My family is burdened in secrets. Aunt Hyacinth told me — oh, never mind. There's just so much I wish Aunt Hyacinth had explained to me, things I know she meant to — things I wish I could ask her. She was so in my corner, especially where Gerald was concerned, and now . . . Navigating this life without Mama or Aunt Hyacinth is so hard. It's . . ."

"Exhausting?"

"Yes!"

"I do understand that. Lilliana, I know you've endured terrible losses. I know Gerald is a horrible threat that you live under day by day — Miz Hyacinth told me and I see it in your face. But you're not alone in this.

"You have to know you're not the only one struggling with a man gone bad. My Fillmore ran moonshine for two years before he was caught and arrested. Every night he'd go out, I'd hold my breath, scared to death he'd be caught or shot. Every night he came home drunk from his victory over the run. He wasn't as mean a drunk as the Wishon boys, but nasty enough, and I was so ashamed. Ashamed to stay and afraid to go. Where would I go? I loved him and I hated him, wished him safe and wished him caught."

Celia swallowed. She'd never heard her mama talk like that, had never really known what she thought of her daddy's public shame.

"And every Sunday, I pinned my hat in place and marched into that church as if I were a God-fearing woman whose man worked a respectable job, selling honey from our bees and scratching a bare living from the garden dirt behind our cabin and selling pelts in Ridgemont." Now Celia heard her mother sigh. "That bit of work was all a sham, a cover-up for what he was really do-ing . . . running moonshine for somebody who paid him as much to keep his name secret as he did for running the risk of being arrested — or shot dead."

"You never learned who hired him?"

"He never told a soul — not even me, no matter that the revenuer said he'd let him go if he gave the man's name." Celia heard the weariness in her mother's voice. "I have my suspicions. I believe Fillmore was just too scared to say who — scared of what they might do to him or to the kids and me. I believe he bought some kind of protection for us by going to jail. How can I not love a man who does that?"

"There's so much I don't understand about this place."

"Well, now," Celia's mama said, "isn't it that way everywhere? The thing is, we can't

271

let our fears or things we don't understand weigh us so far down that they keep us from picking up and going forward. We're still on this earth for a reason. Your mama and Miz Hyacinth were called to their rest, but you weren't. Now, why is that? What are you here to do? I reckon that's the point to figure."

CHAPTER THIRTY-ONE

The morning after my heart-to-heart with Gladys, after rummaging through Aunt Hyacinth's closet, half-fearful of what else I might find, I came across her old school satchel tucked into the back of the top shelf. The leather was worn and even cracked, but the retired satchel still looked serviceable.

How many years, how many treks to the schoolhouse has this satchel seen? For all the confusion I carried since finding the robe and hood, I knew Aunt Hyacinth had been loved by the people of No Creek — people of all color — and that she loved them. *Whatever that Klan regalia means, or meant in the past, you and I were both willing — eager — to allow everyone to use the library and to help them read. That's still what I want. For as long as I'm here, as long as I'm able, that's what I choose.*

The idea that I was free to choose my course and not to have it dictated by Gerald or my father or Rhoan Wishon or Ida Mae and Velma Richards shot a thrill through my

273

bones. It was as if I were stepping into new shoes — my own new shoes chosen by my own self — and walking forward, not being led or directed where I didn't want to go.

I hadn't heard from Gerald since he'd left in July, though he surely knew of Aunt Hyacinth's death. Why he hadn't shown up again, I didn't know, unless it was because he believed there was no hope of his getting hold of Aunt Hyacinth's estate. He wouldn't have believed me but would surely have investigated that. Still, I knew better than to believe he'd just disappeared from my life. He wanted his freedom on his terms and would come again when he'd laid all his groundwork, when he had everything tied in a foolproof, legal bundle.

But it was September, coming on fall days with new beginnings. Children were off to school, at least those who could be spared from harvests. I couldn't sit around waiting, wondering when the shoe might drop. I had a life to live, for as long as I could live it.

Downstairs, in the library, I chose a primer and a simple reader from Aunt Hyacinth's many books, pulled a tablet and two pencils from the drawer of her desk, and tucked them in the satchel.

In the late afternoon, once I believed that labor for the Tate family might be finished, I set out for their home. I was half a mile down the road when Janice Richards called from her front porch swing. "Mrs. Swope!"

I drew a deep breath. I'd hoped to pass the Richards house without being seen. I didn't need questions and I knew Janice was trouble.

In a heartbeat she was walking beside me. "Where are you off to, Mrs. Swope? I'll carry your bag for you."

"No thank you, Janice. I appreciate it but it's very light, and I think your mother will want you home for dinner — supper — in a few minutes." I bristled at the use of my married name. No one in No Creek called me Mrs. Swope except Ida Mae on occasion and Velma Richards. Apparently Ida Mae and Janice's mother had compared notes.

"She won't care if I'm gone, long as I'm with you. You're almost like a teacher." Janice smiled a smile that told me she wanted to be included, but I dared not take her to the Tate cabin or into my confidence.

I stopped in the middle of the dirt road. "I'm sorry, Janice. I'd like your company another day, but I'm needing some time alone. I hope you understand." I gave my most convincing smile and patted her on the shoulder. "I'll see you at the library one day soon. You come by and pick out a good book. Bye now."

She frowned, but I turned and forged ahead, not waiting for her response, hoping she didn't follow. I'd walked another quarter of a mile before I looked back. She was nowhere in sight. Her feathers might be ruffled, but I couldn't help that. I'd pay her more attention another day. This mission couldn't be delayed or I might lose courage.

I'd never been to the Tate cabin, but based on a map of local homes and families that I'd found in Aunt Hyacinth's desk drawer, I had no trouble finding it. I imagined that Aunt Hyacinth's detailed map was something she'd created because of her teaching, wanting to know each of the families in and around No Creek, colored and white. At least, that's what I hoped it was for.

By the time I reached the rustic cabin tucked into the woods, my breath came out in vapored huffs. Whether that was from the trek uphill in the September cool or nerves watching for snakes in the underbrush, I wasn't certain, but I gathered my courage, climbed the porch step, and knocked on the door.

Mercy, Olney's wife, opened the door. "Miss Lilliana! What a surprise." She stepped onto the porch. "Everything all right over your way? You need Olney?"

"Hello, Mrs. Tate, everything's fine at Garden's Gate. That's not why I'm here. I wondered if I could talk with you a moment?"

Mercy kept her smile but cocked her head, taking in my satchel. "Of course. You want to come in? Or prefer to sit out here?"

"I'd love to come in." If I was going to make any inroads, I needed to show that I was as comfortable entering her home as I hoped she was entering mine.

Fatback sizzling, the strong smell of greens simmering, and the tantalizing aroma of corn bread baking met my nostrils the moment I stepped inside. The front room ran spare but was made cozy by a fireplace, a threadbare sofa, two wooden rockers, and a large oval floor rug — a colorful rag rug that must have taken Mercy weeks to braid and sew. A sampler embroidered with Scripture and flowers hung over the mantel, and a low fire burned in the grate to ward off the mid-September chill. Pressure pushed against the backs of my eyes. This was a real home, a cozy, welcoming home.

"You all right, Miss Lilliana?" Mercy laid her hand on my arm, concerned.

I shook my head to clear the pressure and smiled, taking her hand. "I'm fine. It's just . . . your home is so lovely and welcoming. A respite."

She smiled in return. "Well, it's not Garden's Gate, but it's ours."

"Yes, yes, it is. Thank you for allowing me to come in, Mrs. Tate."

She looked surprised at that, then tentatively offered, "You call me Mercy. Can I get you a cup of tea?"

"Thank you — Mercy. I would love that.

I'm chilled clear through from my walk."

"Fall's comin' on early this year, that's certain. I'll be just a minute. You sit and warm yourself."

By the time Mercy returned with a tray of tea and molasses cookies, I was sitting in one of her rockers, staring into the fire, more relaxed than I could remember.

Two sips of tea and two bites of her soft and scrumptious cookies put me in seventh heaven. "These are wonderful, Mercy. Thank you."

"I think you must be getting your appetite back at last, Miss Lilliana. I'm right glad." She smiled softly.

I felt myself blush and wondered if I was eating food they truly needed. "You are so very kind, Mercy. And please stop calling me 'Miss.' I'm just Lilliana."

Mercy shifted in her seat and I realized I'd made her uncomfortable. I was sorry, but such a title suited Aunt Hyacinth. It didn't suit me.

"I appreciate that, Miss Lilliana. You're very kind, but I don't believe that would be a good idea."

I swallowed, knowing she was right, hating that I even knew. "I should explain my visit."

Mercy nodded, waiting.

"I'm so sorry over what happened about Marshall with Rhoan Wishon."

"That's not your fault. Not your doing.

Rhoan Wishon's who he is, who he's always been."

"I understand that now, but it's not who I am, and I'm ashamed that I was intimidated by him. I know Ruby Lynne can't teach Marshall."

"It's too risky for either of them. Rhoan would beat his daughter to a pulp and do worse to Marshall. You can't ask them to continue, no ma'am." Mercy was firm, and I admired her — protecting her own as well as Ruby Lynne.

"No, of course not. But I can teach Marshall. I can work with him."

Mercy shook her head. "You'd never be able to convince the likes of Rhoan Wishon or Ida Mae that you weren't settin' up a courtin' school. I'm sorry, Miss Lilliana, but it won't do. It just won't do."

"I understand that, too, though I'm sorrier than I can say that it's so. But if you'd allow it, I could come here — tutor Marshall, and your children, if you want, in your home." It was a bold offer and the shock on Mercy's face told me so. "Nobody can fault us for that, can they?" I stopped talking, fearful I'd said too much, though my mouth wanted to run on.

Mercy knotted and unknotted her hands. "I don't know. I never know what those — those people will come up with, what they won't take to."

"Nobody besides us need know — ever. I could give Marshall a lesson, then leave the book with him so he could practice before our next one. I won't tell a soul."

Mercy compressed her lips, but her eyes spoke desire. I wondered if she knew how to read.

"Did Olney ever tell you why Marshall came to us?"

"No, he didn't, and I didn't ask. He's Olney's sister's son, isn't he?"

"Yes." Mercy nodded. "Marshall's father was beaten and hung by his thumbs in the woods for three days down Georgia way. On the third day they tied bags of stones around his arms and legs, rowed him out to the middle of a lake, and threw him in, still alive. They forced Marshall and his mother to watch him drown."

"What?" I heard her words, but my mind couldn't grasp the horror.

"Leticia, Olney's sister, sent her son here to save his life. She feared the same thing might happen to her boy."

"But why? Why . . . ?"

"Why does the sun shine? Why does the rain fall? Why does fall turn to deep winter? It's always been this way for our people. Every time one of our own steps out for betterment, that ax comes down. Some questions there's no use askin'." She shook her head, the weight of sorrow so heavy she looked away, into the fire. "Leticia said her husband wanted to pay off the man he worked for so they could move on, that he'd saved for two years to pay off what he owed in credit with the store for shoes and food. So many times they did without their meal in a day to save that bit of money.

"But the man didn't want Jody's money. He wanted his cheap labor — near slave labor. So he accused Jody of stealin' that money, and he worked up some of his friends with liquor . . . though I reckon it didn't take much." She looked at me now. "You come from a different world. What you want to step in our cow patch for?"

"Because I can read and I know what it means. I want that for Marshall. He's so bright, Mercy. Your children are bright. They deserve better and reading can help them. It's just a beginning, but still, it is a beginning. I don't want to risk you or Olney or cause you trouble. I'll only do it with your and Olney's blessing."

Mercy wet her lips, considering. "Olney won't take it for free. He'll want to pay."

"I don't want money."

"That's not what I said."

I stopped, understanding. "Could we trade? Marshall could cut me firewood for his lessons?"

The corners of Mercy's mouth turned up a little. "That might do. Yes, that might do. Let me talk with Olney."

I smiled in return. My facial muscles were beginning to ache and I realized I hadn't done much smiling of late. "In the meantime —" I pulled the primer and tablet and two pencils from my satchel — "I'll leave these. I know Marshall was working on them with Ruby Lynne. He can practice what he learned, reading and writing, and we'll go from wherever he is in the book. Perhaps he can teach your children what he knows, too. That will be good for them and it will reinforce everything Marshall learns."

Mercy looked as if I'd handed her a plate of Belgian chocolates. "What you're offerin' no firewood can repay. It's not just the book . . ."

"No, it's the beginning of a path out of here. A path out of No Creek to a better, fairer world . . . I hope."

"Is there such a thing?"

A way of escape? A new life, leaving behind fear and the abuse of the old one? Oh, I hope so. I clasped Mercy's hands and whispered, "God bless you, Mercy Tate," and meant it.

CHAPTER THIRTY-TWO

The calendar turned to October, and Celia's mama made plans without ever asking Celia's opinion.

Each night they listened to Miss Lill's radio — *Dick Tracy* and *The Lone Ranger* — before tuning in the news. Reports from the outside world sometimes confounded Celia, but Miss Lill explained all she could. The latest was that children in Moscow were working to enforce air raid precautions — *children*! In occupied areas children, even young ones, gathered intelligence and secretly carried messages. Older children fought Germans alongside their mothers and partisans.

In comparison, Celia knew that her life in No Creek was safe, tame, and boring. Still, she'd sooner deliver secret messages to cutthroat partisans in the woods than do what her mama had in mind.

To compensate for all that lay ahead, Celia packed the new Nancy Drew mystery Miss Lill had ordered for the library. Her mama insisted she pack clean socks and underwear for overnight.

Celia wasn't sure why she and Chester needed to scrub from head to toe and wear their Sunday best to visit their daddy in jail. After all, he'd be wearin' jailbird clothes, Celia was certain, and she doubted, after Miss Lill told her the plight of Jean Valjean in *Les Misérables,* that any warden insisted on baths more than once a week. She wasn't even sure she wanted to see her daddy, but her mama said he longed to see her and Chester, and that it was important so they wouldn't forget him.

Except for the photograph her mama kept on her nightstand, Celia would have forgotten what he looked like, what he smelled like, even the color of his eyes. It wasn't as though he'd been gone a short time for a family visit; it was as though he was long gone and Celia, for most intents and purposes, had written him out of her life.

Life as Fillmore Percy's daughter was humiliating at best. She was the girl mothers didn't want their daughters to sit with at lunch or bring home for overnights. Life at Garden's Gate with Miss Lill was not only a high step from where they'd lived before, but a genuine leap up the community ladder. Celia had no desire to return to the way things had been.

But on her last visit, her mama had applied

for and received special permission for the children to see their daddy. "It's a next step in his rehabilitation and an opportunity to begin to reestablish our family bonds. It's been over a year since either of you've seen him. It's time."

Celia wondered if her daddy had changed at all. *Reformed* was her new word. She wasn't counting on her daddy being reformed.

"Lilliana, there's cold chicken in the icebox and tomato aspic. There's a slice of apple pie and a little cheese in —"

"Gladys, I won't starve before you get back, and truth to tell, I do know how to cook. Not like you, granted, but I do, and I won't mind having a go in the kitchen. If I don't soon, I'm bound to forget how."

"I very much doubt that, but I know what you mean. It's good to keep your hand in. We'll be back tomorrow night. I believe we can just catch the last train."

"Just you take care of one another. Take my flashlight. I'll leave the porch light on tomorrow night, and I'll be glad to see you back, safe and sound." Miss Lill ruffled Chester's head of thick dark-brown hair and smiled at Celia. "Enjoy the train ride, Celia, and don't keep your nose in that book the whole time. The leaves are glorious now. You'll want to watch out the window."

"I will!" piped Chester, not to be outdone

by Celia. But Celia ignored him.

They were nearly out the front door when Celia heard her mama turn and whisper to Miss Lill, "Are you sure you feel safe here, all alone?"

"I'll be fine. Stop fussing. There's been no trouble since Ruby Lynne stopped teaching Marshall."

"But we've been a house full. I don't like you stayin' in this big ole house all alone."

"Aunt Hyacinth did it for years and years."

"She wasn't young and good-looking. She taught every hooligan in No Creek when they were boys, so they respected her, and she didn't go about stirring up trouble. You just have a knack for it."

Miss Lill smiled good-naturedly, if a little nervously. "I'll be fine. I always am."

Celia knew that was a lie.

CHAPTER THIRTY-THREE

Dusk settled over the mountain and seeped its way into Garden's Gate. It was my first night entirely alone in Aunt Hyacinth's house, and I wondered how she'd done it all those years. Every scrape of a tree limb against the house sent a shiver up my spine. Every creak in the floorboards unnerved me, and the ancient house just settling down for the night became something more. I pulled all the curtains and draperies tight, shutting out the world.

I wandered from room to room, turning up lamps and making noise. I wound Aunt Hyacinth's Victrola and played three of her Caruso records, once singing along at the top of my lungs. It only made me lonely for my aunt and Mama.

By eight thirty I decided I didn't want to sit up in an empty parlor — even if it was now rimmed in children's books and dotted with small chairs. I'd started reading Thomas Wolfe's *Look Homeward, Angel* the night before — a book Aunt Hyacinth had told me to order, but an author that Gerald and my father had forbidden. That made it all the more appealing and planted the hope of a good bedtime read tucked beneath the covers, though I'd found it hard to get into.

I'd just turned down the desk lamp when I heard voices — muffled but not distant. Suddenly all the electric lights went dark. My breath caught, and I peeked between the drapery panels across the picture window, just an inch or two, and saw a light — a dozen burning lights or more, dancing through the front gate. Something dark and tall rose in the middle of the front garden. There was shouting, hammering; then the thing burst into sudden flame — a blazing cross surrounded by a dozen or more burning torches, casting garish, writhing shadows over white hoods and robes.

Every hair on my neck, my arms and legs shot to attention, but before I could fully grasp all I was seeing, a pointed white hood bearing a torch jumped onto the front porch and pressed against the window, filling the space, inches from my face. Eyes glared at me from slits in the hood and a robed arm rose as if to fight. I screamed, heard the crash of the window's plate glass, smelled the stench of kerosene, and felt the strike of something hard and heavy against my head, then nothing.

■ ■ ■ ■

"She's comin' round. Quick, get a wet rag." Olney Tate's voice came from far away.

I heard footsteps pound, heard myself groan, felt a throbbing in my head, and lifted my hand to my forehead. I couldn't open my eyes but knew my hand came away sticky. The smell of burning wood and hair and paper reeked.

"Just lie still, Miss Lilliana. Just you lie still," Olney ordered. "I'm goin' for help and I won't be gone long."

Don't go. Don't leave me, I wanted to say, but no words came out my mouth.

"Hush, now. Lie still, now. Fire's out. Uncle Olney's gone for help. He'll be back directly. Just hang on. Please don't die on me, Miss Lilliana. Please — oh, dear God! Don't let her die!"

It was Marshall's voice — Marshall weeping and shaking and stroking my arm. I wanted to tell him I was all right, that I'd be all right, but I couldn't speak, couldn't open my eyes, couldn't move my arm. My leg felt pinned to the floor. I couldn't will it to move into a natural position. I ached. Oh, how I ached! I tried to open my eyes, but the light pierced. I moaned. Everything went black once more.

With no sense of time or space, I felt myself

floating, rising, falling on a sea of hands and arms. At last I lay still, quiet. My hands grasped the sheet of my bed. Cool hands bathed my face in cooler water. Still, my head pounded and my throat clawed, parched. "Water," I mumbled.

"That's it. That's right, chile," a voice crooned, lifting the back of my head, setting the rim of a cup against my lips. I drank, spluttered, and with help sank into the pillow again. I knew that voice from somewhere, sometime. Still, I could not open my eyes. Or perhaps I opened them but couldn't see. *Am I blind?*

"Settle down, now. There's nowhere you need to go, nowhere you need to be but here. You safe here. You safe and you gonna be safe."

"Granny . . . Chree." Had I said the words aloud?

"That's right. That's good, you know me. You know ole Granny. That's a good sign. You gonna be all right."

"Can't see." Panic tightened my chest. I was too young to go blind, too young to live out my days like Aunt Hyacinth had.

"That's right. Not now. You caught a nasty cut across your forehead, missed your eye by a horsehair. You all bandaged up now, but don't you worry. You'll see, by and by, baby, when those bandages come off. Just keep calm. Rest easy."

Smoke — from my clothes or hands or the air I breathed — permeated my nostrils. *The library! Aunt Hyacinth's books!*

I needed to know, but if Granny Chree said more, I didn't remember it. I faded in and out of nothingness. From time to time my head was lifted and something wet and cool pressed against my mouth. I tried to drink. The effort was supreme, and I lay back, exhausted.

At one point I woke and knew it was day, only because my arms were warmed by the sun as it poured through my window. "Granny Chree? Are you there?"

"It's me, Lilliana. Jesse."

The voice of Reverend Willard startled me. *What are you doing in my bedroom?* Every muscle tensed. Every nerve stretched taut.

"Take it easy. Take it easy. Don't move. Granny Chree just went to sleep a little and to get some more herbs for a fresh poultice from her cabin. She'll be back."

I tried to swallow, but my throat constricted. "Water."

Gently his hand slid beneath my back and neck, lifting me. The cup pressed to my lips felt cold, the water healing, refreshing. Pain still stabbed at my head, but I didn't hurt all over as I had earlier. Perhaps that was a good sign. "What . . . happened?"

"You don't remember?" He sounded worried. "We hoped you could tell us."

I lay still, forcing myself to concentrate on the in and out of my breath, conditioning my mind to accept his nearness and not cringe away, not fear. Gladys's words came to me: *"He's a good man, a kind man, a man you can trust."* And then my own doubt: *"Is there any such man?"*

"Lilliana?" he whispered, and I realized he might think me asleep. He couldn't see my eyes. I couldn't see him. That felt safer. I lay for a long while and might have fallen asleep again. There was a moment I felt him near, either dreamed or felt him lift my fingers and press his lips against them. I stirred, wanting to shake off the dream, and his nearness was gone.

He was reading aloud, and I recognized the words of Oswald Chambers in his voice:

"Jesus said, 'In the world ye shall have tribulation,' i.e., everything that is not spiritual makes for my undoing, but — 'be of good cheer, I have overcome the world.' I have to learn to score off the things that come against me, and in that way produce the balance of holiness; then it becomes a delight to meet opposition."

Could it be God's will for me to fight opposition — to score it off? Could meeting my challenges ever become a delight? The very thought hurt my head.

I reached for the bandages covering the top of my skull and eyes, down to my nostrils. My shoulders ached from the effort and I dropped my hands to my sides. *Helpless — I feel so helpless like this — the thing I've feared most. If Gerald came now, how could I — ?*

"Lilliana? Can I get you anything? Anything at all?"

The nearness of Reverend Willard, the sense of his hand on my arm undid me, but I couldn't respond. Speaking took too much effort. I lay still, pushing away thoughts of Gerald and trying to remember, trying to separate reality from the nightmare of fire and hoods. I remembered the lights, dancing through the garden. *A burning cross. Torches. A dozen or more — carried by white-robed and hooded men. Surely, men. A woman would never wear such a thing. Aunt Hyacinth, what was that robe and hood doing in your cedar chest?* A sob escaped.

"Lilliana." It was Reverend Willard's voice again. He sounded so grieved, so lost, so helplessly worried. But I couldn't help him. I couldn't help myself.

"Are you in pain?"

I couldn't answer.

"The library is saved. A few books were burned, but Olney and Marshall got here in time to put it out. We'll repaint the room, put everything to rights before you get downstairs. I promise."

If only everything was so easy to mend.

CHAPTER THIRTY-FOUR

Gladys hovered over me for days. Granny Chree came and went with her herbs and poultices. Dr. Vishnevsky visited, too, and finally removed the bandages from my head, checked Granny Chree's stitches — completed mercifully when I was out cold — consulted with Granny Chree and checked my eyes twice a week with his flashlight, then pronounced me "doing well . . . lucky . . . blessed . . . well cared for . . . a miracle of grace for Lilliana Grace" — his favorite pun.

It was almost three weeks before all my bandages were removed and I was allowed to walk down the stairs, then cautioned to rest frequently, stick close to home and others, and not worry. In all that time I couldn't read, but I listened to the radio. Gladys, Celia, and Chester toted it up the stairs together to my room so we could all listen of an evening as I rested.

Celia liked *Dick Tracy* best. I think that fussing over me and losing herself in stories and books and radio shows gave her an aura of busyness, an excuse not to think or talk about her father and their visit to the prison. Celia pretended otherwise, but I knew she was ashamed of her family's situation — and conflicted about her father. If only she could realize that I, too, was ashamed and conflicted about my father. But that wasn't something I could tell her. At least, I didn't know how.

War news dominated everything on the radio. The Atlantic had become a shooting gallery for the Germans intent on destroying Allied shipping lines. The USS *Reuben James* was torpedoed by a German U-boat on October 31 while escorting a British convoy across the Atlantic. My heart broke for the parents and wives and children and sweethearts of men who'd gone down on the *James.* I thought of Aunt Hyacinth and her beloved Henry, lost at sea.

Despite growing threats and accusations between Germany, Italy, Japan, and the United States — what Ida Mae called "a shouting match between that Hitler and Mr. Roosevelt" — we had not officially entered the war. As we listened to the radio during our evening hours, Gladys darned socks for the children and we knit scarves and socks for those bombed out in Britain. I didn't need to strain my eyes to do that, and it seemed the least we could do.

Fighting our own battles in No Creek, the

war seemed far away. Other times we felt it so near we found ourselves listening for bombers in the night. Celia and Chester learned to identify German planes from pictures posted in the general store. I longed for spring and summer and the whip-poor-will's call.

I lost count of time before my mind allowed me to recapture all the events from the night of the attack. My shared memories of that night reflected terror in Celia's and Chester's eyes. Ironically, I didn't feel that terror, at least not for myself. I remembered that Scripture, *"Fear them not therefore: for there is nothing covered, that shall not be revealed; and hid, that shall not be known. What I tell you in darkness, that speak ye in light: and what ye hear in the ear, that preach ye upon the house-tops. And fear not them which kill the body, but are not able to kill the soul: but rather fear him which is able to destroy both soul and body in hell. Are not two sparrows sold for a farthing? and one of them shall not fall on the ground without your Father. But the very hairs of your head are all numbered. Fear ye not therefore, ye are of more value than many sparrows."*

I'd been beaten, my home and life threatened, but for the first time I wasn't afraid. I was one of those, valued at least as much as a sparrow, that Jesus talked about. Those cloaked Klansmen and what they had done in the dark of night would one day be revealed for who and what they were. For all I'd been told throughout my life that I stood on the wrong side of God, I knew in this case I did not. They did.

This time I had been beaten not because I was willful or sinful or bad to the core or because I'd unwittingly prompted someone to lose his temper, but because I had reached out in love to others. This wasn't Gerald or my father, men whose authority I'd lived under. These were fiends in white sheets, breaking the laws of God and man, purporting to do it as Christians. Not all pain was the result of punishment from God. Men meted that out. It was a new thought worth pondering and it gave me a boldness, sending a kind of electric surge through every nerve. It was that boldness, a stranger inside my body, that thrilled and would not be shut down.

I dared not share those thoughts with Gladys. She was terrified for me and for her children, for the house itself. I couldn't blame her where Celia and Chester were concerned. People who would do this to a woman alone would not hesitate to hurt children, especially if that might help them frighten grown-ups into toeing the line they wanted. *Isn't life in Germany under Adolf Hitler a picture of that?*

But how did the Klan know I'd gone to the Tates? It seemed clear that my beating was in response to those visits, to my tutoring, unless they'd just been waiting all these months to find me alone.

I hadn't told Gladys that I'd been helping Marshall with his reading. I knew she'd think, after what had happened, that I should stop. I had no intention of stopping my reading lessons at the Tate house unless Olney or Mercy asked me to. And that's just where I was going the first time I felt well enough to walk out on my own.

Gladys guessed or perhaps Mercy had told her of my visits and begged me to stay at home. She even enlisted Reverend Willard's support when he came by to see how I was doing.

"Are you suggesting I do their bidding and hide? Or run away with my tail between my legs?"

He blushed. "Not at all. Leaving is the last thing I hope you'll do. But I do think you need to be careful. The fact that this was not one deranged person acting alone but an entire group of men means that they've egged one another on, and they'll be less afraid to repeat — or reinforce — their actions. When people cast aside restraint, they feel empowered. I believe you know that."

I turned away from his pointed stare. I did know. Once a person starts hitting or hurting another person, it becomes easier and easier to do. I had seen and lived it all my life, and

299

Aunt Hyacinth had warned me of the same.

Yet I still couldn't reconcile Aunt Hyacinth's apparent disgust and hatred of the Klan with what I'd found in her room. I needed to understand what that regalia was doing in my aunt's hope chest, if that had anything to do with the secret shame Aunt Hyacinth had talked about and Mama's running away. I needed to trust someone who'd long known my family.

Gladys had gone to make tea for the three of us when I asked, "Reverend Willard, have you always lived in No Creek?"

"Born and raised — until I went to seminary."

"And your parents?" It seemed an innocent question. I'd never heard him speak of them.

He looked away, then down at his hands, then back at me, searching my eyes. Finally he spoke. "I spent most of my life with a friend of Miz Hyacinth's — Lucy Newcomb. My parents were killed in a house fire. Burned alive."

Horror crept through my veins. I couldn't keep it from my face.

"I was eight, spending a week camping with a group of friends — out by Trout Lake near Boone. It was the first time I'd ever gone away from home. When I came back, our house was gone, my parents' bodies burned beyond recognition."

I couldn't get my words out. I swallowed

and tried again. "I'm sorry. So very sorry. I had no idea."

He stood and walked to the parlor window, newly replaced. "I don't speak of it."

"Was it . . . ?" But how could I ask him?

"An accident?" He snorted, a combination of disgust and sob. "The sheriff said so. Said lightning struck."

"Lightning?"

"No matter that there'd been no rain, not a cloud in the sky."

What does that mean?

"My parents came from rural New York, before I was born — a long line of abolitionists. Does that help?"

I tried to make connections. "Are you saying the Civil War was alive in No Creek?"

"The war'd been over for sixty years. Most of the folks hereabout sided with the Union, but they didn't object to slavery — at least not for the most part, not openly. Most supported it — a way of life that had always been, in their minds, and ought to continue. Some objected to forming a Confederacy for fear of losing their business dealings and profits in the North."

"I never understood that — that someone would have objected to forming the Confederacy, yet still supported slavery."

"There were only a couple of large plantations here — not like farther east. Most families who owned slaves held only a few.

301

But those who owned more ran the county. Slave trading, auctioning — before the war — was common. Even freed men and women weren't safe from slave dealers — or slave stealers. From what I've heard, pattyrollers ran a heyday here. They were ruthless if they caught a slave out after dark without written permission from his owner, and sometimes they didn't pay any mind to a man's plea that he was a freedman."

"What happened?"

"The war changed everything."

"No, I mean what happened to those caught out after dark by the — what did you call them?"

"Pattyrollers. Patrollers — always 'respected citizens' and property owners. They were known to hang the man or woman up by their thumbs and beat them till the blood ran. Then rub salt in the wounds. If they didn't know who they belonged to — or sometimes if they did — they might steal them and sell them downriver."

I thought I'd be sick. But it explained so much. This was where the people of No Creek had come from. This was the heritage that had birthed the Klan in their blood.

"There's even a story about a widow who owned slaves. She was good to them, but the local minister took her to court and had her declared 'a fit subject for the asylum' and incapable of caring for her property. He convinced the courts to declare him guardian of her estate, then sold her slaves. Neighbors said he wouldn't have cared a whit about her if she hadn't owned slaves."

My breath caught. Similarities in my story made me cringe. "A minister? And people tolerated that? The court tolerated it? The church?"

Reverend Willard sighed, weariness in the shaking of his head. "Of course they should have known better, done better. They made the law of the land their plumb line, instead of the Bible they espoused from their pulpit." And then he went quiet for a moment. "How different is it today? People want what they want and they find a way to make their sin palatable to society — or legal." He looked at me, and I knew he saw more than our words said. "We both know that."

I looked away. He went on.

"Most people, especially those farther up the mountain, were poor and too busy scrabbling out a living from the land to even think much about slavery. For them the war was about breaking up the Union, and the Union was sacred. Their ancestors, mostly Scots and Irish, had fought and died to help establish it. Few here cottoned to the idea of a Confederacy — until President Lincoln called for troops. They refused to fire on their own neighbors and kin, so they enlisted in the Confederacy in droves. Others were forced into it and resented it. Some even hid out in the mountains, refusing conscription, refusing to fight."

"But you said the war changed everything. Why, then, is it . . . how it is now?"

"Now they're the end products of forced Reconstruction and lauded Jim Crow laws. They deeply believe every created being has its distinct and God-given place, separated by color, class, clan, ethnic origin, religion — whatever they were born into was God's choosing, and those lines are not to be traversed. No middle ground. Just because the South lost the war and slavery, it didn't change people's thinking. Wars don't do that. Once the myth of the 'lost cause' became popular, folks even romanticized the war — if you can imagine."

"And your parents?"

"My parents' grandparents were active in the Underground Railroad into Canada and proud of it. Mama and Daddy taught me that color doesn't matter, that class is only a fallen man-made notion and that every man has the responsibility to better himself as he's able. I think they pretended not to see, not to hear what folks said behind their backs, as if that would make the snides go away. They never let it keep them from friendships they valued."

"And you think that's why — why they —"

"It took me a long time to understand what

might have happened. Even then, I couldn't comprehend it — who would do such a thing. My parents were good people, kind people. They didn't try to force their views down anyone's throat, but they did live their lives openly."

I heard the intensity in his voice.

"Trouble is, it was just their kind that the Klan was formed against — unwanted Yankee notions of progress and the fear of colored folks rising — becoming equals, owning land, being educated, voting, running for and holding political office."

He kneaded the back of his neck. "I've never told anyone this," he confided, still turned away. "But it was when I started asking questions about what had happened, how it could possibly have happened like the sheriff said, that a pastor who'd come to No Creek for revival befriended me, took me aside. He offered me the opportunity to go to school and seminary far from here. He changed my life. He was a good man, a great pastor. But I've often wondered if someone here sponsored my education. I don't see how he could have afforded all that on a pastor's salary."

"Aunt Hyacinth?"

Now he looked straight at me. "I've wondered. He was a good friend of hers. I even asked her once in a roundabout way, but she refused to talk about it." Minutes stretched between us. Finally Reverend Willard left the window and sat across from me. "She'd been my teacher. She knew everything that had happened to me and to my family — and to every other child in the community. She was the one who'd set things in motion for me to live with Miss Lucy, an older maiden lady, when my parents died. She's the one who deeded Olney Tate that portion of the prime tobacco land his father had hoped to buy before he was killed — the land he farms beyond his cabin. Wishons own most of the acreage out that way, the part that went to auction, but thanks to Miz Hyacinth, Olney owns his small plot, adjacent to the Wishons.

"By the time I started asking questions, Miss Lucy was too infirm to keep track of a growing adolescent boy. I believe Miz Hyacinth knew that. I think, if she was the one responsible, that she wanted to protect me from myself — from my questions and the repercussions they might bring. She knew a thing or two about the Klan."

What did she know? How did she know?

He sighed. "I believe I may owe her a greater debt than I know for certain. Greater than I was ever able to thank her for."

"I had no idea she'd deeded land to the Tates. Is that why Olney came whenever she called?"

"I'm sure he was grateful, but in my opinion, and I believe in your aunt's, he far more

306

than earned that land. Regardless, we both owe her a lot. A number of folks hereabouts do."

Aunt Hyacinth's hidden Klan regalia grew more mysterious in my mind than ever. "You were a wonderful friend to her, Reverend Wil — Jesse. That was the greatest possible gift. You were eyes and ears in her blindness and the community she craved."

"Until you came and enriched her life immeasurably. I hope you know how you gladdened her heart."

That made my own uncertain heart ache all the more.

CHAPTER THIRTY-FIVE

They were nearly to No Creek when Celia overheard Janice Richards, three school bus seats back, bragging to Norma Jackson and the cluster of girls beside her.

"So all I did was tell Ida Mae what I'd seen plain as day — Mrs. Swope goin' down to the Tates' one day with a satchel and another day with books — back and forth once, maybe two times in a week. Anybody'd know she was over there teachin' that colored boy to read. I never had to spell it out."

"But you heard what happened to her, didn't you? You reckon Ida Mae told? You reckon she knows who's who — in the Klan?" Peggy Sue Brown hoarse whispered.

"Doesn't everybody? Anyway, Ida Mae probably didn't tell a soul. There was a checker game goin' strong in the back of the store the day I was in. How could I help it if half the men in the county was there?"

"Ha! You mean the Wishons and their like!" Norma touted.

"Well," Janice giggled, "the good-looking one, anyway."

"You think he might have told — ?"

"How do I know who told what? She had no business goin' down there in the first place — especially not after Rhoan Wishon warned her. He showed Ruby Lynne the light of day all right. We keep to ourselves and they keep to theirselves. That's the way of things — my father said so — and Mrs. Swope best understand that."

Celia listened till she couldn't take any more. She pushed her way back to the seat in front of Janice, turned around so the bus driver couldn't see, and spit in her eye.

"Ack!" Janice squealed. "You pig!"

"Better a pig than a traitor! Miss Lill opened her home to all — even the likes of you — because she cares about sharin' Miz Hyacinth's books with everybody. And you trot your prissy britches around tellin' tales like a gossipy old lady, stirrin' folks up to no good. What does it hurt you if Marshall learns to read? You afraid he'll grow up and become mayor of No Creek? Afraid he'll steal your daddy's job and you'll lose your shiny patent leathers? You're slime, Janice Richards — slime lower than a slug, and anybody that has anything to do with you is slime, too. Doin' what you did and gettin' Miss Lill almost killed is near murder and like spittin' on Miz Hyacinth's grave at the same time.

You shame us all!"

It was the longest speech Celia had ever made and she meant every word. Jim Biggins, the tallest and handsomest boy in their class, who always sat in the back of the bus, began to clap his hands. "You tell her, Celia!"

Janice Richards's cheeks burned the color of ripe persimmons. She'd never care what Celia thought of her, but she cared plenty what Jim thought, and whatever Jim Biggins thought, the whole class followed. The gaggle of girls pulled away from Janice. Gratified, Celia marched off the bus and into the general store to pick up the mail.

When she returned to the store's front porch, Janice was waiting for her. The other kids, other than Chester, were gone. Janice stepped close as Celia hopped down the steps, doing her best to ignore her archnemesis.

"You think you're so smart, so clever, so much the favorite of everybody at Garden's Gate. But I tell you, Celia Percy, beware," Janice hissed. "You and your white trash family made an enemy today."

Chills ran up Celia's spine at the venom in Janice's threats, but she pretended not to hear and marched away, with Chester aghast at her heels. By the time she reached Garden's Gate, the hair on Celia's arms had settled down and the ire in her heart had risen. She flung open the back door and slammed her schoolbooks on the kitchen table. "Janice Richards is the meanest, nastiest girl in the school — in the whole history of No Creek going back five hundred years!"

Chester, out of breath, trailed behind and plopped his books on the chair. "No Creek didn't exist five hundred years ago. It was founded by the —"

"I don't care who found it! I only care who's gonna hog-tie and tar and feather that no-'count —"

"Celia Percy!" her mother exclaimed, running into the kitchen from the parlor. "Nobody talks like that in this house! I ought to Lifebuoy your mouth, young lady!"

"It's her fault, Mama! It was Janice Richards who told about Miss Lill helpin' over to the Tates'. She did it on the bus today, made it look like Miss Lill was doin' somethin' wicked —"

"It doesn't matter, Celia." Miss Lill walked in and Celia whirled to face her.

"It *does matter*! Don't you see? Those KKK would never have known if it hadn't been for her followin' you, tellin' on you. It was her got them riled."

"You can't blame Janice for riling them. Their own hate and hypocrisy and fear of what they don't understand got them riled."

"How can you say that?" Celia demanded, her anger forcing her eyes to well. "They like to killed you!"

"But they didn't. And if they'd meant to kill me, they would have. They just wanted to scare me."

"Well, they scared me!" Celia's jaw tightened. She felt like shaking Miss Lill. "*Don't you see?* If they scare you and you leave, there'll be nobody to stand up to them. We'll just go back to bein' who we were before you and Miz Hyacinth."

"Before Aunt Hyacinth? Before the Belvideres? Who are — who were the Belvideres? Because I'm confused. On the one hand everybody in No Creek treats the Tates like good folk as long as they 'stay in their place' and do their chores. But the moment they want to learn to read, to buy land, to work in the bigger world, they're pushed down, pushed back, and all the 'good folk' — maybe even the Belvideres, for all I know — turn away and pretend not to see." Miss Lill closed her eyes as if trying to get her bearings.

Celia circled the table and grabbed one of her hands. "How can you say that, Miss Lill? Miz Hyacinth was the only Belvidere outside you I ever knew, and she wasn't like that. And neither am I. Neither is Mama or Chester or Doc Vishy or Reverend Willard. We're on your side, Miss Lill. I'm your friend! Don't you see me standin' here?"

A shudder ran through Miss Lill that vibrated into Celia's fingers — a shudder she felt deep in her bones.

Miss Lill opened her eyes. "Yes," she sighed, her eyes filling. "I see you, Celia Percy."

CHAPTER THIRTY-SIX

Granny Chree didn't stop coming to see me when I recovered. I wouldn't have wanted it any other way. Her gentle but matter-of-fact doctoring had cemented our friendship. She showed up two or three times a week, just after the break of day. She never knocked but waited in a rocker on the back porch until I came out the door. Somehow, I always knew she was there. Her comforting presence drew me from a warm bed, like the tantalizing fragrance of biscuits baking.

There was something otherworldly but so down-to-earth about her — the timbre of her voice, her way with words and the gentle expression of her hands that pulled something from deep within me. Time spent with her made me want to cry and chuckle softly all at once.

She usually refused to step into the house, claiming she'd rather sit outdoors in God's great big world, but one October morning when the frost lay thick on the ground, I

314

pulled her into the kitchen and built up the woodstove before Gladys and the children rose. Together we sat at the table and sipped coffee strong enough to stand a spoon in. I told her again that I hadn't heard her come. I just knew she'd be there.

"You just respondin' to the Spirit, chile."

If anyone else had said that to me, I would've felt irritated. I wasn't convinced the Holy Spirit wanted anything to do with me.

"You kickin' against the goads, Lilliana. Won't do you no good. The Spirit's relentless. Won't be lettin' you go."

"The Spirit let me go a long time ago."

"You believe that? You suffered, chile, but you not the first."

"I don't mean this." I brought my fingers to my forehead, where I could feel the scar.

"I didn't meant that, neither." Granny looked as if she could read my mind. "That man beat you."

I swallowed, not sure I should open that door. "My father was a hard man, but it was my mother who suffered most by him."

"I don't mean your daddy. First time I met you, I seen that faint white ring on your finger. 'Pears to me you wore that tight like a shackle. Besides, a woman don't throw off her weddin' band for no cause. I see it in your eyes, in the way you stand and walk, the jittery way you look over your shoulder when you not engaged in somethin' goin' forward.

315

The way you sidestep every man in your path, including Reverend Jesse."

I wanted people to see in me strength and determination. I'd not imagined my defeated past written in my posture or on my face. "I ran away — maybe you've heard that. Even if I have to leave this place, I won't go back to him."

Granny nodded. "A man like that got no right to a wife."

"I wasn't much of a wife to him." It was the truth. After the first few months I could not stand to have him touch me, no matter how many times he said he was sorry he'd lost his temper, sorry he'd hit me or thrown something at me or bitten my leg, no matter how many times he'd begged for, then angrily demanded, my forgiveness.

Granny reached across the table and clasped my hand. "Be done with him, Lilliana. Did you not hear me? That man abandoned you in his beatings. He done broke his marriage vows. You free. Don't let him eat away at your life no more. He ain't even here. Let those ghosts rest and move on in the freedom God give you. Jesus didn't die so you can suffer. He died to free you from sufferin'."

Now I sobbed, shaking my head. "That's nearly word for word what Reverend Willard told me — what he read one day from Oswald Chambers. But, Granny, God didn't give me freedom. I took it. I made a vow to be married for life and I took it upon myself to run away. Isn't that the same as stealing? God doesn't condone separation but for a time before coming together again, and He doesn't condone divorce except for adultery. The Bible says so — at least that's what I think it means, what I was always told it means. I love God, Granny. I want to please Him. But I'd rather die than go back." And I meant it.

"The Good Word says for a man to love his wife as he loves his own body. You think God means for a man to berate and beat his own body? To crush his own spirit and try to kill himself over and over again? You don't think that man abandoned you? Abandoned you in all the ways God meant him to be there and protect you? Paul speaks to that, too, as a means to be done."

I shook my head. She just didn't understand. *I* didn't understand.

"Jesus say, if a man stumbles one of these little ones that come to Me, it's better if a millstone be slung around his neck and he be drowned in the depths of the sea. You want that man killed? You want a millstone slung over his neck and him go down forever?"

The whirring in my brain stopped. "What?"

"You wish him dead?"

I gasped.

"That make it clean and easy, Lilliana. You be free, then, in your mind and in the minds of those you worry over, wouldn't you?"

I squirmed in my seat. "I know it's wrong. It's wrong to wish him dead!"

"That what you doin' by goin' on, totin' that load of guilt like this. You stumblin', chile. That man is already dead to you. Leave him lie." She leaned closer. "You losin' sight of the love of Jesus and the freedom He died to bring you. You fallin' by the wayside because you believe Jesus is holdin' a sledge-hammer over your head, ready to let you have it if you don't toe that earth man's line."

The picture she painted was ugly. *Ugly and true.*

"As long as you lettin' that man stumble you into believin' Jesus can't love you, he's trippin' on down that road toward that millstone and that sea. It be bad enough for him what he's already done. The Lord don't look kindly on oppressors; you know that. But you fallin' away from the Lord under that man's shoe, livin' his victim all this life long, seals his fate. Don't you see Jesus don't want that for you — or him?"

I'd never considered that my pain, my stumbling, believing myself alienated and rejected by God because of all my father and husband had condemned in me could in any way harm them. Could that mean God wanted me free from Gerald for Gerald's sake — and for mine? *Is it even possible God could want what I want?*

Granny squeezed my hand. "You think on that. You think on that and you pray and ask God to show you your life now, from this minute." She pushed back her chair and rose slowly on stiff legs, hefting the bag of roots she'd dug earlier that morning, the last before the ground froze deep down. "Lilliana, you know anything about the love of God — how deep and wide and rich it is — or the freedom He bought you with the death of His own Son? Jesus showed us the kind of love a man is to give his wife when He died for us. That the vow your husband made and done broke. He broke that marriage vow in two and it's dead. You think on that."

CHAPTER THIRTY-SEVEN

It was the first of November when Celia found the locked box in the cellar, behind the budding Christmas cactus.

"It's a wonder that cactus is not dead and petrified. No telling how long it's been down there!" Celia's mama exclaimed. But Celia could see she was pleased. Her mama loved flowers, especially as the year and everything out of doors prepared to die. "It's God's reminder that miracles happen, that He can bring the dead to life." Celia knew her mama was talking about more than flowers. She was talking about her husband. Celia feared to think of him as "Daddy." Never would he or her mama understand the shame he'd caused Celia at school.

She wasn't the only girl whose father ran moonshine nor her father the only man in No Creek who'd been stopped by the law. But she only knew one other father who sat in jail. Leon Cutter was the only "convict child" besides her and Chester, and his mother was known to run around and even invite men to their home to keep Leon in shoes and their rent paid up.

"That's the way it is with jailbird families," Janice had declared during recess one day, loud enough for Leon and Celia both to hear. "Those women run loose when their men are away; that's what my mama said."

Celia had wanted to stuff dirt in Janice's nasty mouth, but at that moment Miss Ferrell, their teacher, had appeared at the school door and rung the bell for the end of recess. They'd all had to line up while Janice looked smug and Celia marched in and sat down for arithmetic, pretending she'd never heard. She wouldn't give Janice the satisfaction, but Celia hadn't forgotten. Her mother wasn't anything like Leon's mother, but it shamed her for people to talk like that, and it hurt her for Leon, who couldn't help being poor and couldn't help what his mama did.

Celia hoped her mama was so pleased by the find of the Christmas cactus that she wouldn't notice the locked box it sat on, but she did.

"Celia, what's that box?"

"I don't know, Mama. Just found it."

"Where'd you find it?"

"In the cellar . . . behind the flowerpots. Behind the Christmas cactus. That sure is a pretty flower. Bet it'll bloom like nobody's business come Christmas." Celia edged her way to the door, hoping to distract her mother.

"You come back here with that right now. It's not yours."

"Don't reckon it's anybody's, Mama. It's just an old, rusty thing."

"Which means it must have been down there a long time, which means it belonged to Miz Hyacinth."

"Yeah, and she's dead now. I can take care of it for her."

"Which means it belongs to Lilliana."

"Aw, Mama, Miss Lill won't care about some crusty old box."

"Don't you sass me —"

"What won't I care about?" Miss Lill appeared in the doorway and Celia's heart sank. *Outnumbered. Outgunned.*

"Celia just found this box — and this Christmas cactus — in the cellar. Looks like both have been hiding there a long time."

"Well, the flower can't have been there forever, but this box sure looks like it has."

Celia didn't hear disdain in Miss Lill's voice; she heard curiosity and knew that she'd never get to tackle the box alone. "Let's see what's inside it!"

"Now, Celia, Miss Lilliana might want to go through that in private."

"But I found it!" Celia wailed, exasperated and out of patience.

Miss Lill, thankfully, looked like she under-

322

stood. "Let's open it together — now, shall we?"

Celia sighed, grateful. "There's a lock, no key."

"Right. Hmmm. I guess we'll have to bust it open." Miss Lill frowned.

"No, now just a minute. Let me see." Celia's mama pulled the box toward her and pulled a hairpin from her bun. She stuck it in and fiddled the lock, folded her brow into a set of wrinkles Celia knew well, and cocked her ear toward the box. Celia didn't hear anything — no tumblers turning or anything clicking into place — but her mama drew a satisfied smile and lifted open the lid. Then her smile stopped, but her eyebrows rose, and Celia thought she might burst from wanting to know what her mother saw.

Miss Lill turned the box to face herself and Celia.

"A gun," Celia pronounced. "Who'd lock an old gun in a box like that?"

"Someone who wanted to hide it," Miss Lill said softly, as if to herself.

"Someone who wanted it gone — forever," Celia's mama said, snapping closed the lid of the metal box. "Which is just where it's going now."

CHAPTER THIRTY-EIGHT

The glorious colors of October's leaf showers had given way to November's stark and naked trees against a somber mountain sky. My aches and pains from the beating I took, especially the headaches, had eased, but not gone. My heart yearned for a good long ramble in the woods or up the mountain, but my head was still too light and my energy low. Each cold night after Celia and Chester finished their homework, we'd sit together in the parlor-library by the fire, reading stories aloud or playing Criss-Cross Words. Gladys was a formidable opponent, which delighted me no end. Celia wrote down every word over two syllables in her Eagle tablet of Amazing New Words while Chester pored over baseball cards he'd traded for at school and we all drank steaming cups of Ovaltine. It was my favorite time of day.

One night, just after supper, as lightning flashed and the wind and rain whipped the corners of the house, causing the fire to sputter, there came a pounding on the back door. I was setting up the board game and thought Gladys was still in the kitchen, so I didn't go at once, but the pounding came again. I heard Gladys's footsteps cross the room above and find the stairs. The pounding became a softer, more feeble knock. Panic stole into my heart, a premonition I couldn't explain. Celia and I glanced at one other and sprang to our feet. I threw the back door open to the rushing wind, the pelting rain, and a shivering Ruby Lynne Wishon. Her fair skin bloodless, her lips and cheeks bruised, she fell into my arms.

Our telephone line was out from the storm. It wasn't right to send Celia or Chester out into the rain for the doctor, and Gladys insisted I wasn't strong enough yet, but I couldn't let her go and leave her children.

"She'll be okay till morning," Gladys whispered. "Scared, more than anything."

But I wasn't sure. I recognized the brutality of a beating. It wasn't what you could see on the outside that worried me. There could be internal bleeding or broken ribs, not to mention the bleeding of Ruby Lynne's heart. But she was too frozen and too frightened to talk.

I had no doubt that Rhoan Wishon was at the bottom of this. My father had taken a belt to my back often enough, but the way Ruby Lynne clutched her stomach and sides, bent over, wincing without a sound, hinted at more.

Ruby Lynne's teeth chattered as we got her up the stairs, one painful foot in front of the other.

Gladys took charge. "Celia, heat some water and bring me a basin and a towel."

Flanking Ruby Lynne, Gladys and I guided her into Aunt Hyacinth's room and onto the poster bed. I pulled a fresh nightgown from the drawer, and together, Gladys and I helped her into it. The bruises extending down her back and torso were horrific. What terrified me even more were the blood and bruises between her legs.

When we'd finally gotten her settled under the covers, we called Chester to build up a fire in the room.

"I didn't know where else to go," Ruby Lynne whimpered, her teeth still chattering.

"You did just right, coming here. You're safe. No one can hurt you now."

Tears trickled from the corners of the girl's eyes and my heart broke for her. I knew if Rhoan Wishon stood before me now and I had that gun Celia'd found, I'd be tempted to pull the trigger.

Gladys placed a gentling hand on my arm. "Anger won't do her any good now," she whispered. "She needs to rest."

I nodded, barely able to contain myself. "I'll keep watch till morning. We can send for

Granny Chree then."

"Rhoan won't stand for Granny to —"

"Ruby Lynne needs a woman now. You saw those bruises."

"I did. But — I don't know. . . . I'll send Celia in with more blankets. You keep warm by that fire. You wearing yourself out won't do Ruby Lynne or anybody else good now. I'll make sure the doors and windows are locked."

"You don't think he'd come here, do you?"

Gladys shrugged. "He'll come looking for her once he sobers up. Only a drunken man would do this."

I knew better than that. Either way, I'd protect Ruby Lynne with my life.

CHAPTER THIRTY-NINE

It was a long night for Celia, who couldn't stop thinking about the bruises and cuts on Ruby Lynne or the horror etched on Miss Lill's face. Her mama took things more in stride, as if seeing a beat-up girl was nothing much out of the ordinary and they'd best just get on about the business of patching her up and going to bed. That bothered Celia, too.

Who'd do such a thing? Nobody in No Creek, sure and certain. Maybe one of those drifters who come by the store from time to time. But what good would beating up a girl do if you were looking for work or food?

The storm subsided. Celia was first to hear the knock at the back door, though it was still dark. "Mama, Mama! Wake up. Somebody's out back. Want me to see who?"

"No, I do not." Her mother was awake in an instant and pushed her away. "Leave that to me." But Celia felt her mother's cold hands and didn't like the idea of her opening the door and letting in the darkness. If that

328

darkness took human form — worse yet. Celia pulled her blanket round her shoulders and trailed her mama.

"Who's there?" Celia thought her mama's voice brave.

"Gladys Percy, it's a cold morning and I've walked three miles. You gonna let me in?"

"Granny Chree! Come in and warm yourself. I'll fill the coffeepot."

"Don't need no coffee. Make me some black walnut tea. I brought my poultices."

"How'd you know?"

"Just got the feeling I'm needed."

"You are!" Celia's eyes and mouth both went wide. "Upstairs in Miz Hyacinth's room. Ruby Lynne Wishon —"

"Ruby Lynne Wishon? I 'spected it might be Li—"

"No," Celia's mother cut Granny Chree off, pulling her inside and taking the damp blanket draped over her shoulders. "Ruby Lynne showed up at our door last night, bruised from head to toe."

"Beaten to a pulp!" *Pulp* was a new word for Celia and this was the moment to use it.

"Celia, hush that talk. The girl needs help, that's sure. I think she might have a broken rib or two and — I'm not sure what else. I'm mighty glad you've come."

"Rhoan won't stand for me tendin' his girl. Best send for the doctor."

"I told Lilliana. But I guess Rhoan's as like

to stand for a colored granny as he is for a Jew doctor. Besides, you're a woman — and here now." Celia's mama shifted. "Whatever that man says, we need you, Granny. Ruby Lynne needs you. I'm afraid the girl's been —" She stopped. "Celia, you get some fresh towels up to Lilliana."

"But, Mama —"

She swatted at Celia's behind. "Don't you 'Mama' me. You heard what I said."

Celia took to the stairs but leaned over the bannister, straining to hear what else her mother might say.

"Lilliana believes it's Rhoan what done it, but I have my doubts. I can't imagine a father doing such a thing to his daughter."

Celia couldn't hear more. She didn't know what they were talking about, but it must be bad. *Rhoan Wishon? Her daddy did this?* The idea sent shudders through Celia. *Better a drifter — somebody we don't know. What could make a man beat his own kin — his own daughter — like that?* Worse, Celia knew her mama and Miss Lill had hinted at something more. *But what? Beating her black-and-blue and bloody's bad enough. Can anything be worse?*

CHAPTER FORTY

Granny Chree soothed Ruby Lynne's spirit and body to peace and sleep, just as she had mine.

"You send for the doctor. Chile's been raped and it needs to be known. You keep this a secret from her daddy now, there'll be the devil to pay later."

"A secret from her daddy? Her daddy did this!" Wasn't it plain as day? I couldn't keep the fury from my voice.

"Rhoan Wishon? Did the chile say so?" Granny Chree pierced me with her one good eye.

"Who else could it have been?"

"She ought to say. And you send for Dr. Vishnevsky. I have a bad feelin' 'bout this."

"I'll not put her through more. That kind of examination by a man at her age? No, I won't do it."

Granny Chree grabbed my arm. "What if there be a baby? What then? Who her daddy gonna blame?" She shook her head. "It be better if it come out in the open now, what's done and who did it."

I didn't agree. What chance was there that a baby might result?

"If it come to that, I won't help her get rid of it." Granny Chree tucked the last of her herbs in the sack she slung over her shoulder. "So's you know. That not somethin' I do."

"I'd never ask you to."

Granny Chree raised her eyebrows. "This not about you — this about Ruby Lynne. Don't confuse that. You give this girl sanctuary, fair enough. But you not her keeper. You help her stand in the light of day, help her keep herself true — that the best thing you can do for Ruby Lynne."

I tensed and breathed deeply, both at once. She was right. This had been done to Ruby Lynne, not me. But it felt like a replay, as if I'd been there through the horror, lived it before, and I couldn't let this happen to Ruby Lynne again. She needed someone to protect her. How could Ruby Lynne — so young and vulnerable — keep herself in this horrific situation? How could she prevent her father from doing this again if she returned home? "Ruby Lynne needs a way out of No Creek."

"Did you have a way out?" Granny Chree asked quietly.

"Not till I came here. There was no one strong enough or able or willing to help me, but I can help her."

"You think on what you do here, Lilliana, and what you can keep on doing. You think on who you bring into this mess because the mess is here to stay. Are you?"

"You don't think I should help her?" That wasn't the Granny Chree I knew.

"I never say that. Don't be puttin' words in my mouth. Who you think they gonna blame for this? You think Rhoan Wishon take the blame — even if he did it — you got another think comin'."

And then I understood. "They'll blame Marshall."

"Sure as I'm standin' here."

"But that's not possible. He'd never —"

"Don't matter. He's colored. He's convenient and somebody easy to blame."

"A scapegoat."

Granny Chree nodded. "You get Dr. Vishnevsky over here and get him to write down everything she say before her daddy get ahold of her. It go better down the road if she been seen by a white doctor. They more likely to believe him."

"Yes, I understand." I hated what I understood, but I knew she was right. "Our phone is still out. I'll see if Celia can go for him."

CHAPTER FORTY-ONE

Celia raced like the wind for Dr. Vishnevsky, her feet pounding and slipping on the muddied lane up to his house. Her mother had said that Ruby Lynne was in a bad way and that Granny Chree needed the doctor to come quick. That didn't sound good. As far as Celia knew, Granny Chree could cure everything from croup to gunshot wounds. Whatever more had happened to Ruby Lynne Wishon, whatever it was that her mother and Miss Lill and Granny Chree frowned over so, must be worrisome in the extreme.

By the time she reached Dr. Vishnevsky's, the morning sun had stretched itself over the tips of the cedars flanking his cabin. Celia stumbled up the steps, her heart nearly bursting from her chest, and pounded on the door. It rarely took Dr. Vishnevsky long to open his door. This morning it seemed he'd been standing beside it.

"Celia Percy! What brings you here so early? Is your mother all right? Chester? Mrs.

Swope?"

Celia nodded, bending over, clutching her knees. She couldn't catch her breath but waved her hand from side to side to say that wasn't it. "Come. Please come now — to Garden's Gate. Ruby Lynne Wishon —" Celia couldn't finish but it didn't matter. Dr. Vishnevsky grabbed his coat and bag and was out the door and down the steps before Celia could turn around.

"My automobile's tire is flat! I'll see you there!"

Celia followed as best and quickly as she could, but the doctor's long strides left her far behind. That was fine with her. The sooner he reached Garden's Gate, the sooner the horrible could be fixed. He was, after all, the miracle doctor who'd saved Chester's life two years ago from that near-fatal attack of appendicitis. If it hadn't been for Dr. Vishnevsky's surgical skills, Chester would be dead. Hardly a week went by that Celia didn't think on that and thank God for Doc Vishy, even when Chester proved a pain in the neck.

By the time Celia reached Garden's Gate, the doctor was upstairs, conferring with Granny Chree and Miss Lill in the hallway outside Ruby Lynne's door. Celia wanted to join them, but her mother pulled her back.

"Oh no you don't, young lady. You've got chores and this is none of your never mind."

"But it's Saturday, Mama, and I found her

— almost — by the door. I want to know Ruby Lynne's gonna be okay."

"Dr. Vishnevsky's going in now. Ruby Lynne will be fine . . . in time. The best thing you can do for her is to go on about your business and not let on to anybody that she's here. You understand me? If word gets around, it could be terrible bad for her and for the rest of us."

Celia listened, trying to take it in. There was much she didn't understand and more she wanted to know.

"I said, do you understand me?"

"Yes, ma'am." Celia wouldn't do anything to hurt her mama or Miss Lill or Ruby Lynne for all the tea in China. *All the tea in China* was another expression she'd just read and she understood right well what it meant.

Jesse was no stranger to those unique tuggings on his heart and mind, the call of the Holy Spirit. He'd learned early not to ignore them. They'd never led him astray. That late morning, after a long night of walking the floor with an inebriated Joe Earl and consoling Joe's wife, those stirrings took him to Garden's Gate.

He knocked on the front door, intending to turn the knob and walk in, knowing the library bell over the door would ring, announcing a newcomer. But the door was locked — in the daytime — a thing he

336

couldn't remember happening since the library opened or even before Miz Hyacinth passed. He waited. When no one came, he knocked again, but still not a footstep within his hearing. He pulled back and noticed that curtains and drapes closed off each window — another peculiar thing for daytime.

Rather than knock a third time, he walked around back. Granny Chree was nearly through the wintered garden, into the barren fruit trees. "Granny Chree!"

She slowed but didn't stop.

He caught up with her as she neared the orchard's far edge. "Everything all right here?"

Granny hesitated, which was the third strange thing. At last she turned, settling her eye on him. "No, Reverend Willard. It's not."

"Is Lilliana all right?" He couldn't keep the dread from his voice.

"That chile on a long journey, but she be all right."

"Is she coming back?" He felt panic rising.

Granny let out something between a chuckle and a snort. "Not that kind of journey, Reverend." She shook her head. "You two ought to have your heads knocked together."

"There's not much I'd like better, but I'm afraid that's not possible."

"She got some travelin' in the mind to do and a heart that needs mendin'. Don't you give up on that girl now."

"I won't." He meant it. "But the curtains are closed. The front door's locked."

"Kitchen door's open. You go on in and see what they say. You might do some good."

Before Jesse could ask what she meant, Granny turned and stepped into the woods, disappearing amid the gray trunks of tall, naked trees and long needle pines.

That left him in an awkward position. He didn't want to just walk in on the ladies, but something was wrong. In a few long strides he was on the back porch and knocking softly on the door. It opened before his knuckles made their second rap and Celia Percy fell into his arms.

"Reverend Willard! You're here! I'm glad you're here!"

"What is it, Celia? What's the matter?"

Gladys pulled her away. "That's no way to carry on now, Celia. You go change your clothes. Widow Cramer's expecting you to help her clean house this morning; then get on to the store to sweep up. You don't want to lose that job with Ida Mae — but don't you say a thing about goings-on here."

"How can I go over there when — ?"

"You most certainly will go and you'll not say another word — here or there. Now go!"

The fear and uncertainty in Celia's eyes raked fingernails across Jesse's heart. He couldn't contradict Gladys, who turned away from him to the sink, but he couldn't imagine sending Celia off for the day distraught as she was. The moment he heard Celia's footsteps on the stairs, he whispered, "What is it? What's happened?" And then, as he realized he might be overstepping his bounds, "How can I help?"

Gladys braced herself against the kitchen sink. "I don't know what we've got here, Reverend Willard, but I'm afraid. I'm near scared to death for us all."

Before he could ask more, Lilliana walked in.

"Gladys, Celia needs you — upstairs."

"Lilliana," Jesse began.

"This isn't a good time for a visit, Reverend Willard. I'm sorry, but I must ask you to leave."

That felt like a punch to his gut. "I'd like to help — whatever is —"

"This is a family matter." Lilliana's eyes widened, as if that statement surprised even her.

"I hope I'm counted part of that family . . . if you'll allow me." Instinctively he reached toward her.

Lilliana hesitated, looking at him with what he could only interpret as longing, but pulled back, and a veil quickly dropped between them. "You should go now. Please." She turned away.

The lead in Jesse's heart sank to his feet,

but he lifted them and took himself out the door. *What could it be? Why won't she let me help? Why won't she let me in?*

But having no answers, he stepped off the porch.

Chapter Forty-Two

Two nights later, just before midnight, we were woken from a sound sleep by a pounding on the front door — a relentless beating that would not be stilled.

Gladys and I met in the hallway, she throwing a blanket over her shoulders and I cinching my robe's tie round my waist. Celia peeked out the bedroom door, but Gladys shushed her and sent her back in. Ruby Lynne stood in Aunt Hyacinth's bedroom doorway, her eyes wide and face pale and drawn. "It's my daddy. I know it's him. I don't want to go with him. Please, Miss Lilliana —"

"You're not going anywhere, Ruby Lynne. Get back to bed. You're in no condition to be up and around." I didn't know if that was true, but I had no intention of letting Rhoan Wishon anywhere near his terrified daughter.

"You don't know him, Miss Lilliana. He won't take no for an answer."

But she was wrong. I most certainly did

know his kind, and terrified though I was, trembling in my slippers the same way I'd trembled in my own home growing up, I was ready for a fight. Neither I nor my mother had been able to protect me from my father or Gerald, but I could help Ruby Lynne, a vulnerable young girl who deserved protection. At least my father hadn't done to me what Rhoan Wishon had done to his daughter. If I could help it, he'd never get another chance. "Get back to bed, Ruby Lynne. Don't come down. No matter what you hear, don't come down."

Celia poked her head out of her room again. "Chester's sleepin'. Please, don't make me stay alone."

"Go in with Ruby Lynne," Gladys directed her daughter. "You girls keep the light off and stay there."

"Gladys, stay with them. I'll handle this."

"Not alone you won't."

Never had I been so grateful. Together we tiptoed down the stairs, our footsteps tentative more from fear than concern for sound. The pounding on the door continued.

I switched on the porch light, thankful beyond words that Aunt Hyacinth had bought in once the electric lines had reached No Creek, even though she was already blind. Through the window I glimpsed the owner of the fist. Sure enough, Rhoan Wishon, all six feet and muscled arms, stood on the other side of our door. Without opening, I said, "What do you want, Mr. Wishon? Do you realize the hour?"

"I want my daughter! My Ruby girl! Is she in there?" His slight slur caught my ear.

"He's drunk," Gladys whispered. "Those Wishons hardly know what they're doing when they've been in the 'shine. Don't let him in."

I had no intention of letting him in. "Go away! If you want to talk to me, you'll return in daylight at a decent hour . . . sober."

"I say, is my Ruby Lynne in there? She's been gone two days, maybe three. You runnin' that courtin' school again, you white trash — you and Gladys Percy?" He beat on the door.

"Mr. Wishon, your daughter is here, safe and sleeping, which is more than can be accomplished in your house. If you want to see her or speak to her, if you want to speak to me, you must return in the morning — sober and without your cowardly white sheets to hide beneath. Is that clear?"

He stepped back, out of the pool of light. I saw that he ran a hand over his stubbled jaw as if mildly embarrassed. That surprised me. It also gave me a growing sense of power. He swayed a little, struggling to regain control of his senses.

"I'll be back, I swear it. You let that boy near my girl and —"

"Go home, you drunken fool!" I shouted,

nearly at my wit's end. The idea of him blaming Marshall for what he'd done was so repugnant I wanted to scream.

He stumbled off the porch. Then, from the darkened yard, he turned and called, "You talk so high-and-mighty, so hoity-toity. Let me tell you, you're cut from the same cloth as the rest of us. You understand me? You're no different and you best get that through your pretty head fore you get somebody killed!" He swore and swore again, then disappeared into the dark.

CHAPTER FORTY-THREE

Celia woke the next morning to find the bed she'd shared with Ruby Lynne empty. At first she thought Ruby Lynne'd gone to use the bathroom, but when she'd rubbed the sleep from her eyes and saw that Ruby Lynne's shoes were missing, that the nightgown Miss Lill had given her lay folded across the foot of the bed, Celia knew she'd run off.

"Mama." Celia shook her mother's shoulder gently. "Mama, wake up. Ruby Lynne's gone."

"What do you mean she's gone? Gone where?"

"Just gone."

Celia's mama pushed the covers aside. "That fool girl. Call Lilliana. We've got to find her. She's not well enough to be running home or anywhere else."

Celia woke Miss Lill and Chester and would have woken half the county if she could. "Mama, do you think we ought to get Reverend Willard? Ought we not go look for

345

her? Do you think she went home to her daddy? Maybe to the Tates?"

"Celia, hush now. We don't know and we won't know till we find her. Don't be after Reverend Willard with this . . . at least not yet. Get dressed. I want you to stay here with Chester. I'll go to the Wishons' come daylight. If she's not there, well, I'll try the general store, see if anybody's seen her."

Celia hated being left at home, left behind. And she didn't think Ruby Lynne would go home or to the general store. Ruby Lynne feared her daddy and she'd never run to Ida Mae for help or anywhere she'd be fodder for gossip. There weren't many Ruby Lynne trusted — not now. But she trusted the Tates, she'd told Celia, and she trusted Granny Chree.

By the time everyone was up and dressed, gray daylight crept through the sky. Celia's mama insisted on a hearty breakfast before beginning the search. "It won't do anybody any good if we go fainting by the wayside. I'll set a plate for Ruby Lynne in the warmer. She'll be chilled through."

"If we find her," Chester said, wide-eyed, gulping down the last bite of redeye gravy and biscuits.

"*When* we find her," his mother responded.

"I'll go to the Wishons'," Miss Lill said.

"Not alone you won't," Celia's mother countered.

"We'll cover more territory faster if we split up," Miss Lill insisted.

"That's true, but the Wishons' is a different place. A woman alone —"

"I'll go with her," Celia piped up. "That old Rhoan Wishon wouldn't do anything bad in front of a kid."

Miss Lill raised her eyebrows as if waiting for Gladys's response.

Celia's mama opened her mouth to speak, closed it, then opened it again. "I s'pose that's true. He's at least that concerned about his reputation when he's sober, though he sure didn't act it last night."

"He was drunk," Celia stated, matter-of-fact, though that didn't seem to make her mother feel any better. "He's not likely to be drinkin' this early."

"If Ruby Lynne did go home, you both showing up might put him on notice that he's got to behave."

Miss Lill gasped, "Ruby Lynne can't stay there! A man who'd do that to his daughter once will do it again. He needs to be brought to account — prosecuted!"

Celia's mama stood in the center of the kitchen, fists on her hips. "You think that's gonna happen? Here, in No Creek?" She shook her head and turned back to the stove. "Would that happen in Philadelphia?"

Miss Lill went white — whiter than she already was. It looked to Celia like her mama had hit the nail on the head, whatever it was they meant.

"Let's go, Celia." Miss Lill grabbed her coat on the way out the door. Celia gulped her last bite of biscuit and followed in her wake. It was a good two miles to Rhoan Wishon's. Celia knew that though Ruby Lynne was mending, she was in no condition to make that trek on foot.

They'd barely started before they met Marshall on the road, a rake slung over his shoulder. He tipped his cap. "Mornin', Miss Lilliana, Celia. You ladies out bright and early."

"We're off to the Wishons'," Celia piped up, "to see if Ruby Lynne went home."

Miss Lill gave her a look meant to shush. "You're out early, too, Marshall."

"On my way up to Shady Grove. Reverend Willard asked me to help him rake the leaves in the cemetery."

"Good. That's good." Miss Lill shifted her eyes but didn't look Marshall in the face. "Have you passed Ruby Lynne on the road this morning, Marshall?"

"Ruby Lynne? No, ma'am. You're the first soul I seen this mornin'. Everything all right over her way?"

"Till she got beat up," Celia offered. This time Miss Lill pinched her arm. "Ow! What'd ya do that for?"

Marshall set down his rake. "Beat up?

Somebody beat up Ruby Lynne? Who? She be all right, won't she? Please say she be all right!"

"She will. She'll be fine, but she needs to rest." Miss Lill wrung her hands. "And we need to find her. She was staying with us, but sometime in the night she left."

"I'll help you look — whatever you need. Reverend Willard would want me to."

"That'd be great!" Celia was relieved to think he might accompany them to the Wishons'. She'd talked big at breakfast, but after Rhoan's midnight visit, and after what had happened to Miss Lill with the Klan and the burning of Garden's Gate's books and now to Ruby Lynne, she wasn't anxious to go Wishon visiting with no more protection than pretty Miss Lill.

"I'm not sure that's a good idea, Marshall." Miss Lill looked worried. "I don't know what to expect from Mr. Wishon."

"Don't reckon he's there. He left out of here in his truck late last night."

"You saw him?"

"Heard him. He's got the fastest engine this end of the county. The road runs not far by Uncle's house. Not been by again."

"Celia, do you know what time Ruby Lynne left? Was it in the night — or early this morning?"

"Can't say. Went to sleep and she was there. Woke up and she's gone. You reckon she ran

349

off with her daddy?"

"I can't imagine — I hope not."

Marshall lifted the rake to his shoulder again and spread his feet. "Did Rhoan Wishon hurt her?"

"You should see the bruises!" Celia whistled.

"Celia, be quiet! Ruby Lynne hasn't said who it was, but . . . I'm worried for her. I'd like to go and be gone before Rhoan returns."

"Coulda been a drifter." Celia wanted it to be a drifter. She couldn't abide the notion of it being Ruby Lynne's own daddy who beat her that way. It was too much like saying any daddy could turn that mean from drink — so mean he'd do things unmentionable.

"I'm comin'. If that man lay a hand on Ruby Ly —"

"No, Marshall. Don't say another word. That's the last thing you or your family need. You showing up now could be the worst possible thing for Ruby Lynne."

"But —"

"No! I can handle this. He'll not dare hurt me or Celia."

"Miss Lilliana, Ruby Lynne's been good to me. She be the only person — black or white — ever take the time and patience to help me learn to read besides you. I won't let that man —"

"Then follow at a distance. Stay where you can't be seen from the house. If we need you,

I'll call, or I'll shout for you to go get help at the store. But for all that's holy, Marshall, don't let him see you, and stay back. You starting a war with the Wishons won't help Ruby Lynne."

"All right, then."

Just before reaching the house, Marshall hung back behind an old maple at the edge of the yard. Rhoan Wishon's truck was not in the drive. Miss Lill knocked on the front door. No one answered. She knocked again, louder this time.

From the corner of her eye, Celia saw the front room curtain move slightly to one side. "Somebody's in there," she whispered. "That curtain moved."

"Ruby Lynne?" Miss Lill called. "If you're in there, please come out. I need to know that you're safe." No answer. "You can come back with us to Garden's Gate if you want — stay as long as you want." Long moments passed. "Please, Ruby Lynne!"

The door never opened, but Ruby Lynne's voice came through, quiet and sounding scared. "I know you mean well, Miss Lilliana, and I thank you kindly for taking me in when I needed it. But I need to be home. Please, please go away before my daddy gets back. It won't do any good for him to find you here, and it'll be best for me that I came home on my own."

It was a long speech for Ruby Lynne. Celia

looked up at Miss Lill, uncertain.

Miss Lill leaned her forehead against the door and closed her eyes. "Ruby . . ." She spoke softly now, even though Ruby Lynne did not open the door. "Aren't you afraid to stay here?"

A minute must have passed. With such a question hanging in the air, a minute seemed forever.

"Every day." Ruby Lynne spoke through the door, so quietly Celia wondered if she'd heard right. Miss Lill half sobbed, and Celia, not knowing how to help, waited.

"Day or night — anytime you want — you come to Garden's Gate. Our door is always open for you, Ruby Lynne."

"I know, Miss Lilliana. I know."

And then the conversation was done. It took Miss Lill a bit to raise herself up, smooth her skirt down, and wipe her eyes. She didn't look at Celia but turned defeated shoulders and walked down the steps.

Celia followed at a respectful distance. Marshall had disappeared from behind the tree where they'd left him. Miss Lill kept her face resolutely turned toward Garden's Gate.

But when they were back on the road, Celia turned in time to see Marshall slip from the woods to the barn behind the Wishon house and to see Ruby Lynne round the corner, headed in the same direction.

Celia didn't say a word but caught up and slipped her hand between Miss Lill's fingers.

CHAPTER FORTY-FOUR

It was Monday, the week before Thanksgiving, when Ida Mae lowered her bombshell to Joe Earl at the general store and post office. Celia had just finished sweeping the floor and sat on the pickle barrel, chomping down on her dill pickle reward.

"I got a telephone call from my sister up in Olean, New York. She tripped over her little J. J.'s solar system project for school — something about Jupiter and the red eye of death — and broke her leg. Her oldest girl, LouAnn, is due any day now with her first and she's beggin' me to come and look after things for a month."

"A month! When?" Joe nearly swallowed his own pickle whole while plopping his seat on the flour barrel next to Celia.

"Now! This week!"

"This week! But Thursday a week is Thanksgiving. What about . . . what about Joleen and me?"

"I hate that I won't be here to cook for you

354

all and the reverend — not to mention my girls and Ray — but babies don't mind holidays and they don't come on schedule. She's not due till the end of December, but LouAnn's had trouble and they've put her to bed rest. Edna fears the baby might come early — or that they'll have to take it, and now she's laid up and can't do a thing.

"Celia, you reckon your mama might take a few more hungries Thanksgiving Day if we send some extra sweet potatoes and maybe a turkey or ham out your way?"

"I reckon. Sure! Mama always says, 'The more the merrier.' It's just poor what keeps her stingy from time to time." Neither thing was true, but Celia knew it wouldn't matter. Ida Mae'd do whatever she pleased.

"Well, I'd be much obliged. I was looking forward to having Reverend Willard over, but my daughters can't cook worth spit, and poisoning him might not help their prospects."

"Nor me, nor Joleen," Joe Earl piped up. "Can't you wait till after Thanksgiving, Ida Mae? It comes early this year, and I'd surely miss your sweet potato pie."

Ida Mae smiled at the compliment but shook her head. "Wants me to take the Carolina Special Wednesday morning from Asheville to Cincinnati. She said her neighbor can meet me at the station and take me on out to Clermont County in his market truck.

Her husband, Jim — Jim's got a job with the railroad — can get me a round-trip ticket and it'll be waiting for me at the Asheville station."

"You can't get over to Asheville that early!" Celia knew Joe Earl was throwing up roadblocks, hoping she'd wait till he'd had his Thanksgiving dinner.

Ida Mae sighed. "I hate to do it, I hate to ride with that man, but I'll ask Rhoan Wishon to take me tomorrow night. You know he drives over to Asheville late on a Tuesday night." She looked significantly at Joe. "Least, ever since someone we won't name was incarcerated."

Incarcerated was a word Celia knew applied to her family and she didn't appreciate it. Whatever her daddy had been, she'd seen on her recent visit to the jail that at least he was more than she'd remembered. It was one thing for her or Chester or their mama to bad-talk her daddy, but Ida Mae wasn't kin and had no call, and Celia was tired of it.

"Reckon I'll sleep on the bench at the station until time for the train to roll. Can't afford to miss it. I don't know why they up and moved north. I can hardly abide the shame of that. But family's family. You can't turn on them just because they've done foolish."

"When'll you come back?" Celia tried to keep her voice even and civil. If Ida Mae never came back, it would suit her just fine.

"Before Christmas, I hope."

"You hope?" Joe nearly fell off the flour barrel.

"More likely mid-January."

"Who'll run the store? Who'll get out the mail?" Joe Earl couldn't take hold.

"Who'll run the Christmas play?" That was much more Celia's concern than the business or the federal government.

Before Ida Mae could answer, the bell over the door jingled. All eyes turned to see a man — young, disheveled, and dirty — step inside, bringing the cold November wind and a swirl of brown leaves Celia had just swept from the porch.

"Close that door!" Ida Mae all but huffed at the stranger.

The man looked up, near sorry for existing, Celia thought, and closed the door. "My apologies, ma'am." He tipped his cap — a summer cap, Celia noted, and a lightweight coat not worth mending.

Celia's eyebrows rose and Ida Mae frowned, whispering, "Another dang drifter."

Celia flinched. She'd built a whole story in her head about how a drifter had found Ruby Lynne alone on the road at night and beaten her within an inch of her life. *Drifters are bad. Drifters are scary.* Celia told that to herself over and over, hoping it would drown out her fear of fathers able to turn mean on a dime.

But Celia knew in Ida Mae's eyes this

man's sin was more than drifting. He'd spoken as the words might be written — short on syllables for anybody born south of the Mason-Dixon.

Ida Mae cocked her head, then pretended to go back to her account books. Joe Earl rubbed his jaw, swinging his head around as if to stretch his neck but really to eyeball the stranger. Celia watched the man openly, wondering who he was and where he came from. *Must be on foot.* She'd not heard the gun of a motor or the brakes of an automobile.

For all that Ida Mae complained about drifters every week or so, few strangers passed through and nobody made No Creek a destination — at least, not since Miss Lill had shown up, and it turned out she had kin in town. But no matter. Every stranger was raw meat for the lions of Celia's imagination and Ida Mae's gossip.

"Can I help you find something?" Ida Mae asked pointedly, without looking up from her books.

The man all but dropped the sweet potatoes he'd been fingering into their barrel on the far side of the store — as if they were hot, as if he'd been caught stealing, which Celia wondered if he might be considering. "I'm just looking, ma'am." His shoulders rose and fell in what Celia took for a sigh. *He's hungry.* Celia knew the look and weight of hungry and this man didn't look like he could heft a sack of potatoes, let alone beat a girl to a pulp.

"Those sweet potatoes run forty-five cents for fifteen pounds. We carry only the best."

"Would you — would you sell me two?" he stammered.

"Two pecks?"

"No, ma'am." He blushed furiously. "Two sweet potatoes . . . maybe three."

Ida Mae's jaw dropped. She closed it. "Bring them over here and I'll find a paper sack."

"No need, ma'am. I can slip them in my pockets."

"I send my groceries out in paper sacks and boxes." Ida Mae snapped open the sack. "I suppose you're used to slipping things into pockets?"

Joe Earl nearly busted a gut. Celia thought that raw, but Ida Mae didn't shush him.

"I'm looking for work, ma'am. I work real hard — do anything. I'd be glad to sweep up in here for you, rake those leaves out near the road, give your store a new coat of paint — anything you want, anything at all. No need to pay me money. I'll work for food — whatever you give me."

"You're not from around here." Ida Mae ignored his plea.

"No, ma'am. My wife and I are passing through, on our way to Tennessee to work with family. We've just got to work our way there before the snow flies. We've come up a little short."

"You mean broke, don't you? Do you have money to pay for those potatoes or not?"

The man pulled a nickel from his pocket, a nickel Celia imagined had been worn thin with worry, and placed it on the counter.

"I know about hard times, young man. You don't have to tell me. No, I don't have work for you, and if I did, I'd give it to one of our own, not some Ya — some stranger." Ida Mae's eyes pummeled the man with a disgust Celia knew she reserved for strangers and Yankees and foreigners, the same she'd lavished on Dr. Vishnevsky when he first came to town. "You're wasting your breath asking anywhere in No Creek. Now, do you want to buy those potatoes or not?"

The man had kept his eyes on the three potatoes in his hand all along, but the color of his face had deepened from a cold rose to a deep-red flush, clear around the back of his neck. He pulled his nickel off the counter, the one he'd held his hand over throughout Ida Mae's long-winded speech. "No, ma'am. I don't believe I'll spend my money here." He looked up at her. "I believe I've earned them listening to your meanness."

Before Ida Mae could open her mouth to respond, the man had pocketed the potatoes and was out the door, leaving it standing wide with the November wind howling in her face.

Joe Earl whooped, "Whoeee!" glad for the climax of the show, and slapped his hand across his knee.

"Of all the nerve!" Ida Mae huffed, near speechless. She whooshed through the door, grabbed a porch broom, and brandished it round and round toward the man's head. "Thief! Thief! Get out of here, you confounded Yankee, and don't you come back!" She slammed the door, the bell jingling off its hook. "If there was any law within five miles, I'd call and set the dogs on him."

"Best let him go, Ida Mae." Joe still laughed and coughed, pretending he hadn't done the first. "That boy'll be three counties over fore you get the sheriff's feet off his desk."

Ida Mae huffed again.

Celia still sat on the pickle barrel, juice dripping down her hand from squeezing the pickle so hard while the conflicts swirled round her head. She licked her arm, scooted off the barrel, and peeked out the front window. No sign of the man. She'd like to have seen him again. She'd never known anybody to get the better of Ida Mae and live to tell it. Drifter though he might be, she hoped he'd get away, free and clear.

Still, she was a little surprised when, on her way home to Garden's Gate, she saw the very man and the back of a woman slip into the church. The man hadn't lied about having a wife. Maybe, she thought, they'd been to see

Reverend Willard. Maybe he let them stay in the church. Then she remembered that Joe Earl had said Reverend Willard had gone to Winston-Salem for two days. Joe Earl was doing his best to stay easy on the drink till the reverend got back to walk him sober if things got out of hand.

Celia hesitated near the cemetery. Should she tell somebody? The man was a thief, after all. There wasn't anything in the church worth stealing — nothing you could sell for food or drink. The church meant out of the cold, but there'd be no heat — not till Olney Tate brought a load of firewood for the stove early Sunday morning. Celia gritted her teeth and walked on. Maybe it was something she'd just forget. Only she couldn't.

CHAPTER FORTY-FIVE

"I don't know what's got into Celia. She's walking around in some other world, ever since she came home from her job helping out at the general store this afternoon." Gladys slapped a damp tea towel across the faucet to dry.

"Do you think she's heard something about Ruby Lynne? Something she's not telling us for fear of worrying us?" I couldn't stop thinking of Ruby Lynne.

"I don't know. She worries over everything these days — about the Klan coming back, about her father coming home, about the Germans invading by air and sea. The paper's full of talk about Mr. Roosevelt rattling his saber at the Japanese and telling them to leave those poor people in China alone, and about those blue and red war games in our own backyard, getting our boys ready to fight. They've gone and mined the Yadkin River bridge. Is that real? It worries me, but I know all that talk scares children half to death."

It sounded to me as if Gladys was the one scared half to death — which was unlike her.

"Chester asked me the other day if their school bus would explode if it drove over a minefield. Celia doesn't ask those things, but sometimes she wakes up screaming from nightmares. Next morning she doesn't remember or doesn't say. That girl carries way too much worry on eleven-year-old shoulders." Gladys rubbed her temples, then hung her apron on the hook behind the kitchen door and went upstairs to check on Celia.

I worried about the children some, too, but I worried constantly about Ruby Lynne. Celia had told me she'd heard nothing, seen nothing of her lately. She'd said that Troy, Rhoan's brother, stopped in at the store to pick up mail and groceries. That had always been Ruby Lynne's job. *Does that mean she's not well enough to go?*

Not even Olney or Marshall had seen Ruby Lynne about the Wishon place, and they passed it every day on their way into No Creek. I couldn't help but wonder if she'd gone somewhere. I would've loved it if Ruby Lynne really could get out of No Creek, if she could finish school and go to college, become the teacher she'd dreamed. But I feared that wasn't reality, and then I feared what was.

Over supper that night Celia poked peas around her plate.

"You eat those peas, Celia," her mother admonished. "Food doesn't grow on trees and you're lucky to have them. Remember those starving children in China."

Celia looked up, concerned. "I am lucky, and I don't even like peas. I don't need them."

Gladys set her fork down. "What a thing to say!"

"I mean, there are people in this world — really hungry people — who'd love to have peas, and they aren't all in China. I wish I could give them mine."

Gladys shook her head as if to dismiss Celia's new finagle to get out of eating peas. But I wondered. I'd come to realize that Celia usually worked a deeper thought behind the first one.

"Do you know somebody who's hungry, Celia?"

She looked up at me as if I'd caught her in a lie, then as if I'd struck gold. "Yes. I met him today."

"Who'd you meet today?" her mother demanded.

"A man at the store — a stranger from somewhere up north, Ida Mae said. Called him a confounded Yankee. Said it like she was sucking lemons. He stole some sweet potatoes."

"Stole! Ida Mae must have been mad as a wet hen!" Gladys huffed. "All that going on and you working down there. I don't like it. Maybe you shouldn't —"

"He wanted to work for those potatoes — for food, any food. Ida Mae said she'd never give him any work, even if she had it — that nobody in No Creek would." Celia frowned at her plate, then looked up, her brow creased. "Ida Mae was real mean to him, Mama. And Joe Earl just laughed."

Gladys smoothed her napkin across her lap. "Ida Mae's not known for kindness to strangers."

"She's got a mean streak," Chester agreed as if he were talking weather. "That's a fact."

"That's not polite, Chester," Gladys corrected him.

"Well, neither is she, Mama. She's mean and she was wrong!" Celia crumpled her napkin and threw it to the table. "I was ashamed of Ida Mae, and I was ashamed of all that I have. I can sweep up that store for a pickle or a candy, and I don't even need it. I'm not hungry and I'm not cold. I hurt for that man. You should have seen him. His coat wasn't near warm enough, and his shoes looked like they'd barely hold together . . . they won't hold together come snow."

"I'm glad you have a tender heart, Celia, but we don't know them, and we can't help everybody. Remember how Jesus said we have the poor always with us? Maybe that's what Ida Mae meant."

"I don't think that's what she meant, Mama. Besides, Ida Mae owns that store. She could help."

"She has to pay for the things she sells. She doesn't get them for free."

"She could still help a little. It wouldn't hurt her."

"Maybe we can help," I offered. "Do you know where he went?"

Celia hesitated, and I couldn't tell if she was conjuring a lie or simply not certain. "Not exactly, ma'am. He run off . . . but they might be nearby. He said his wife and him are workin' their way to Tennessee to be with family."

"Did you see his wife?"

"She wasn't with him at the store."

"Probably doesn't exist," Gladys sighed. "He might have made that up to get sympathy."

"No, Mama. He didn't. I'm sure he didn't."

"Let it be, Celia. I don't want you bringing home strangers or strays. Not one. You understand me?"

"You didn't see him, Mama. You didn't see him like I did."

I thought that a most profound statement. I doubted many people saw things as Celia did.

CHAPTER FORTY-SIX

The next afternoon Celia straightened her stack of books and pulled her skirt over her knees before she got off the school bus, hoping to look a little older, and marched into the general store and post office. The bell over the door jingled.

Ida Mae, near breathless, was running down a list with her second-oldest daughter, Pearl. "Now you've got to get the mail ready to go out in sacks — usually just one, but with Christmas coming, you never know. Have those bags over to the door by noon for Joe Earl to pick up. Even if he's late, don't you take the mail to the platform. There's no point with nobody to wait with it — train won't stop with nobody there — and you need to mind the store at all times. Joe Earl will tote it up to the depot in Roaring River — I already talked with him.

"If the snow flies fast and furious and Joe can't get here, give him grace. Don't go running him down. No point trying to call —

he's got no phone. He'll get here when he can. The train comes at 2:17 and he doesn't generally start drinking till four."

"Yes, Mama." Pearl pushed her glasses back up on her nose. "I'll try to remember all this, but it sure is a lot."

Ida Mae shook her head, exasperated, but her eyes lit when she saw Celia. "Celia can run errands for you if you need her to. You'll do that, won't you, Celia? While I'm away up north?"

The wheels turned in Celia's head. "I reckon I could."

"Wonderful!"

"How much?"

"Why, whenever Pearl needs you. I can't tell ahead how often that —"

"No, I mean how much you gonna pay me?"

"Pay you?"

"You're gonna pay Pearl, aren't you? You pay me peppermints and pickles to sweep up. Runnin' errands is more."

"Well . . ."

"How about groceries?"

"Groceries? Are you running short at Garden's Gate?" Ida Mae looked as if she didn't believe that, but what a juicy tidbit of gossip.

"Well, Reverend Willard and the Earls and who knows who all will be comin' for Thanksgiving dinner since you won't be here to cook for them. We could probably use a little extra."

"Does your mama know about this? Lilliana?"

"How could they? You just asked me. Fair is fair."

"All right, then. Keep a tally and we'll work it out."

"Yes, ma'am! And about the Christmas play at church . . ."

"I guess there won't be one this year."

"No Christmas play? That ain't right! It's the best part of Christmas Eve!"

"I know, darlin', and I'm sorry. But I can't be sure when I'll get back the way things are up there. And there's nobody else to —"

"I'll do it!" The words were out of Celia's mouth in a rush. Success with the groceries had gone to her head. Besides, there was nothing in this world she loved more than the Christmas play, unless it was reading and imagining, and she could imagine just how she'd run the Christmas play.

"You're eleven years old. You can't run the play. You have no idea the amount of planning and costuming and then coordination with Reverend Willard's sermon I have to do. And that's just the beginning. There's the roles to assign and the script to prepare — rehearsals and working out with parents what to bring. Directing is not the fait accompli you see on Christmas Eve. There's a ton of work goes into that."

"I don't know what *fait accompli* is, but I been an angel in it every year since I could walk. Mama even said that the year I was born, I was the baby Jesus. Let me try, Ida Mae. If worse comes to worse, I'll just have some kids read the Christmas story from the Bible. We got to have that. Even Reverend Willard would want that much." Though Celia had no intention of limiting her production to a stage reading.

"May as well let her, Mama," Pearl whispered. "There's nobody else and I can't take on more than the store and post office."

"Well, I don't know. I really should consult with Reverend Willard."

"He won't be back till tomorrow and you're goin' out to Asheville tonight."

"Oh, dear. No, I just don't think —"

"I'll get Miss Lill — Miss Lilliana — to help me. And Mama."

"Your mama's up to her eyeballs and Lilliana Swope doesn't even come to church," Ida Mae huffed. "I don't see that she — oh, land sakes! I nearly forgot. A letter came for her. I had to sign for it as I knew I couldn't wait till she came in with me leaving tonight. You give it to Mrs. Swope, Celia. Place it directly in her hand, you hear me? And don't get it all wrinkled."

Celia took the letter and carefully, under Ida Mae's watchful eye, laid it inside her schoolbook. "Yes, ma'am, soon as I get home." But one look at the return address and Celia knew she wouldn't. *Rupert Jennings, Attorney-at-Law, Philadelphia, Pennsylvania. This can't be good for Miss Lill. She's doing so much better, it would be a shame to darken her days just before Thanksgiving. It can wait that long, surely.* Celia straightened. "I meant I'd ask Miss Lill *if* I need help — you know, with costumes or something."

"Well . . ." Ida Mae stood, frowning, one hand on her hip. "Celia, you'll have to clear this with Reverend Willard. If he says no or seems hesitant at all, then you must nix this in the bud. You understand me? I think it's a terrible idea, but I can't think of anyone responsible who'd take it on such short notice. I know it won't be quality, but I guess we'll leave it to the reverend to decide if he wants to risk it.

"Pearl, you must make sure and certain you explain fully to Reverend Willard why I cannot be here. If I do return in time, I'll take it over, Celia, and undo whatever damage I possibly can."

"Yes, ma'am. Don't worry. You have enough concern over your sister and her daughter's baby. I hope your sister gets over her broken leg and that the baby comes easy." Those hopes were sincere, but no equal to Celia's desire to keep Ida Mae out of No Creek till the New Year.

Celia swept the store with extra vigor that afternoon and dusted every shelf under Ida Mae's watchful eye. Instead of peppermint or pickles as payment, she asked for a beet, which amused Ida Mae no end. But beets, Celia knew from Granny Chree, strengthened the blood.

On her way home from the store, Celia stopped by the church. Dusk and shadows gathered among the tombstones. No lights shone. The churchyard always seemed creepy that time of day. The cemetery sat between Garden's Gate and the church by the roadside, but the grounds in the back of the church sat largely empty except for a garden shed tucked way back against the woods. Celia reckoned that if enough locals died, even that part of the churchyard would fill up.

She stomped up the steps, pretty certain stomping shoes would scare off any ghosts that might be lurking and alert anybody who might be hiding in the church. Lifting the latch, Celia cast a glance over her shoulder, making sure no one passed by, and slipped through the door.

It took a minute or two for her eyes to adjust to the dimness. Everything looked the same as it had when folks had walked out after church on Sunday. Pews still sat there, and the reverend's pulpit. There wasn't much else, besides the little front table where Communion bread and juice were laid month by month and where the Bible lay open for anybody who wandered in to read.

Celia glanced around the church and felt the spookiness of empty. Yet a tiny rustle in the front corner told her she was not alone — a rustle too loud for field mice. Celia coughed and coughed again. She didn't walk up the aisle but spoke, loud enough to hear her own voice vibrate in her ears. "My name's Celia Percy. I was in the store yesterday when somebody came in and borrowed some sweet potatoes. I thought that somebody might like a beet I got here in my pocket. I'm gonna leave it on the pew back here, and I hope whoever needs it will come get it after I'm gone. I wish it was more. Tomorrow I'll bring more . . . if I can." Celia turned to go, then thought about Reverend Willard coming back to find visitors in the church. "Y'all will need a better place to stay. Reverend Willard'll be back tomorrow. I don't know what he'll say."

Hushed whispers came from the front corner of the church and a form rose from a darkened pew. Celia gulped. If she really believed in ghosts, she'd believe one stood before her.

"Thank you for the beet, miss. That's kind of you."

Celia breathed relief. It was the same man's voice she'd heard yesterday. "Y'all warm enough in here? Nights get mighty cold."

The man didn't answer at first, but his silhouette turned to the pew, and another form rose from the dark to join him. Together they walked to the center aisle. "Name's Clay — Clay McHone. This is my wife, Charlene."

"Pleased to meet you." Celia kept her manners, but the woman who walked into the last gleam of daylight through the church window and stood ten feet away looked ready to bust — seven or eight months in the family way if a day. Celia's mouth fell open.

"Thank you for the beet," the woman barely more than whispered, all the while holding her belly.

"Y'all can't be livin' in the church long."

"We'll be on our way soon as I can find some work and a place to stay. We mean no harm."

"I didn't mean you ain't welcome — if it was up to me." Celia mourned that it was not and she knew it. "I just mean you need somewhere to lay your head and be warm, a table to set your feet under."

"I've tried every farm we passed. No work. No room." Hopelessness subdued his voice. "We're trying to get to Tennessee."

"You got family there," Celia remembered.

"We hope," the woman said. "My mama's sister and her family moved out that way some years ago. We're not exactly sure where, but . . ." She shrugged. "We might not make it before the baby comes."

"I reckon not." Celia didn't know much about birthing babies, but this one didn't look far-off.

"You know of anybody who's got work? I'll do anything. I'm a hard worker."

"Wish I did — with all my heart." What else was there to say? "I might be able to bring some food now and again."

"We'd be much obliged, and I'll work it off, I promise."

"But we don't want trouble." The woman worried, though Celia knew she wasn't in a fit state to be worried about trouble. She'd have her own soon enough.

"When's your baby bound to come?" The question wasn't mannerly, but Celia figured the time for manners was past.

The couple looked at each other, and the man laid a protective hand on his wife's belly. "Within the month . . . we think. Is there a midwife here?" And then he pulled back, ashamed, Celia knew. "We have nothing to pay, but I could split wood or do some work to help."

"There's old Granny Chree. She'd do it, long as you don't mind colored. Then there's Dr. Vishnevsky, long as you don't mind Jew."

"We'd be grateful — much obliged, whoever can help," the woman said, her voice a little stronger with conviction now.

Celia licked her lips. It didn't seem right to go off and leave them in the cold church, but she didn't know what else to do. "You got blankets for the night?"

"One."

"I'll try to get another. Don't know if I'll get back tonight, but soon as I can."

"Thank you, Celia Percy. God bless you."

Celia winced. She hoped God would bless her, but she wasn't sure He'd look kindly on stealing, which was just what she was about to do.

Celia knew that keeping a secret in the church from Reverend Willard would be difficult, but keeping one from Olney Tate would be nigh impossible. She needed to get food to the McHones before Olney reached the church Saturday morning.

Olney kept the grounds outside Shady Grove Baptist Church and swept the sanctuary after Sunday service. In summer he trimmed the shrubbery around the church, trimmed grass in the cemetery, and washed the windows. In winter he split firewood and stacked it in the back of the church on Saturdays. Early Sunday mornings he started a fire in the woodstove. By ten o'clock, when services began, the chill was off and those who sat near the woodstove could doze, warm and sleepy, if Reverend Willard got wound up and went on too long.

Celia was careful as she could be and she already had a story invented in her head if she ran into Olney. It wasn't all that unusual for somebody to sleep through the night on a hard and cold church pew. That sometimes happened if a man drank too much hooch and his wife kicked him out for the night or if he just couldn't quite find his way home after a binge. The church was central for everybody. It had happened before with drifters — folks might spend a night or two, especially in rainy weather, then stop by a house asking for a plate of pinto beans or such.

Celia figured that a good story, and she was just beginning to embellish it in her imagination when she backed out the front door of the church and found Olney Tate inspecting three sets of footprints in the frosted grass.

"Morning, Celia."

Celia jumped and felt a flush race up her neck. "Mornin', Mr. Tate." She winced. Calling him "Mr. Tate" was a mistake.

Olney's eyebrows rose in curiosity. "You're out bright and early on a Saturday mornin'." He tilted his head as if he could just about see Celia's wheels turning.

"Did I tell you that Ida Mae's gone to see her sister? Her sister broke her leg and her daughter's about ready to bust a baby, and she's got to look after the whole passel, so

378

she asked me to direct the Christmas pageant. Did I tell you that?" Celia rattled off till she was out of breath and felt nervous as a cat walking a clothesline.

"No, I don't recall that you did."

"Well, it's so," she said, maybe a little too defiantly.

Olney scratched his head. "That's a mighty big job for a young'un."

"I'm not really a kid anymore. Soon I'll be twelve."

"True enough. Thought you just turned eleven."

Celia lifted her chin. "That was last December."

"I suppose you were just lookin' things over in there, planning out your Christmas program."

"What? Oh yes. Yes, I was. I meant to bring a paper and pencil to make notes but I forgot. Guess I'll have to come back another day."

Olney waited.

Celia knew he expected her to spill the beans sooner rather than later. She never seemed to help herself from doing that around Olney. Her stomach felt like she was full of beans.

"Well, I'll be seeing you." She hesitated, halfway down the stone walkway. "You know, things look just fine in there now. I don't think you need to bother inside before Sunday."

"Reverend Willard'll be wanting firewood come tomorrow morning."

"Can't that wait till Sunday to tote it in?"

"Best not. Give it a day to dry if I carry it in now."

"Now?" Celia felt her panic rise.

"Celia? You got somethin' to tell me?"

Celia licked her lips while Olney waited. The man had the patience of a hound tree-stalking a coon, Celia was certain. She couldn't think fast enough. "Olney, you know the Christmas story? The one in Luke?"

"By heart."

"You remember how it says there was no room in the inn for a poor man and his wife in the family way?"

"That's so, more or less."

"Well, do you think that was right? I mean, I know that was Mary and Joseph and the baby Jesus on His way to save us all, but it could just as like be some poor folks today."

"There's lots of poor folks today, that's certain."

"What if it was just some poor folks now — strangers that nobody wanted — about to pop a baby. Shouldn't there be room? I mean, Jesus said to take care of the poor and needy, didn't He?"

"Always. Said if we care for 'the least of these,' it's like we do it for Him."

"Then, shouldn't we?"

"Celia, who you hiding in that church?"

380

Celia sighed as though the weight of the world rested on her shoulders. "If I show you, will you run them off? They've got nowhere to go. Ida Mae called the man a confounded Yankee and run him off the store porch with a broom. He stole a couple of sweet potatoes, but they're starvin'. The woman's about to pop a baby."

"How soon?"

"Don't know, and neither do they. First one, I reckon." Celia's brow wrinkled further. "They're scared. On their way to family in Tennessee. They just need to hole up for a bit till the man can get some work and she can deliver her baby. Do you want to see them?"

Olney scratched the back of his neck.

Celia knew that as things stood now, he hadn't seen them, didn't have call to report them. But if he opened that church door, he'd be obliged to report to Reverend Willard all he'd seen. The reverend had a good heart, no doubt about it, but he didn't have the authority to take in vagrants, and if Ida Mae had already run the man off, the reverend would have her and her contingent to deal with. Celia knew she shouldn't have asked him, but she didn't know what else to do.

"Better if I don't. But they can't stay there. Folks'll be in early come mornin'."

"I told them so, but I don't know where they can go. Mama said I'm not allowed to bring home strangers or strays."

"Maybe Mercy knows a place," Olney mused.

"They're white. No offense intended." Celia didn't think that would matter to the McHones, desperate for help as they were, and she knew the Tates were generous to a fault, but she also knew they dared not bring notice from the Klan on the Tates or their neighbors. Celia saw the same realization in Olney's eyes. It went without saying.

Olney sighed. He leaned against the rake he'd toted around front, silent for a time, considering. "The shed behind the church. It's not much, but if a person was to move a few rakes and such to one side, then line it with newspapers and get a few blankets or quilts in there, it could keep the wind out for a night or two."

"I believe a person could do that." Celia's hopes rose.

"There might even be a stack of old newspapers in there that I meant to take down to the store. They're talking paper drives and such."

"This is a better cause."

"Where you gonna get food and blankets, Celia? What you gonna do if that woman's time comes?"

"Oh, I think they'll move on before then."

"Babies aren't real predictable. Best let Granny Chree or Doc Vishnevsky know."

382

"That's too many people. Maybe later. Anyway, I think they'll be movin' on before then."

Olney nodded. "Anybody see y'all slipping in and out of that shed or the outhouse, it's all over and I can't do a thing. You left footprints plain as day." He rubbed his unshaven chin as if that might help his thinking. "I'll speak to Mercy and send Marshall up with some victuals before dark. He can't be caught up in this, Celia; you know that. You say that man stole potatoes. No tellin' where that talk might lead."

"No, 'course not. Maybe Marshall could leave a sack behind a tombstone, and I'll come fetch it."

"The Belvidere family stone — sounds about right."

Celia grinned. "Sounds perfect."

CHAPTER FORTY-SEVEN

Why Celia volunteered to run the Christmas pageant was beyond me. Why she volunteered my services to help when she knew I didn't even attend church was beyond the pale and truly presumptuous. But the truth was that I'd always thought I'd like to be involved in a Christmas pageant — a thing not done at the church I was raised in and in fact frowned upon, as was anything theatrical.

I had no experience to offer and didn't want to take a moment of glory from Celia, who floated over the moon in her excitement. Still, I couldn't resist listening in on the auditions she ran in the children's library room the Saturday before Thanksgiving.

I stayed in the next room but heard the bell over the front door jingle time and again as several sets of boots stomped through. That went on to the tune of Celia's "Over there. Leave your boots by the door. You don't want to be stomping snow and dripping all over the library floor!" Next was "Come, sit down by the fire — in a line, that's right. We'll get to the auditions soon enough."

I heard some earnest grunts and then Celia say, "See there. Harvey knows to raise his hand to speak. What is it, Harvey?"

"My ma said I can use Grandpa's bathrobe if you want me to be a shepherd. She has an old broomstick would make a good staff."

"All right, Harvey. I'll write that down. We're gonna need lots of costumes. That sounds like a good one. Anybody else have bathrobes for shepherds or something fancier for kings — like maybe your mama has one of those kimonos or something? Any mopheads for beards? Not too dirty, but if they are, we can bleach."

It went on like this for some time and I marveled at Celia's creative efficiency and the enthusiastic offerings of the children. I guessed they'd done this every year, but the cooperation was wonderful. Until it came to the main roles.

"Now, of course, the main parts are Joseph and Mary and baby Jesus. The narrator does most of the reading from the Bible, and the angel of the Lord does the speaking. But for Mary we need someone gentle and mild, and we need a light-blue robe — all solid, no prints. I don't think they did flowers and checks in those days. And a white head covering. That's what Mary wears in all the pictures."

"My mama has a solid pink bathrobe," Emily Cruthers offered. "Maybe she'd let us dye it blue."

"She would never," her brother, Leroy, piped up. "She loves that thing. She said Daddy gave it to her on their wedding day. Anyway, it's see-through. Won't do."

"My mother can make the costumes for Mary and Joseph." Janice Richards spoke loud and clear, prim and proper. "She's got plenty of new fabric stashed away. I saw a piece of pale blue with silver threads running through it. I'm pretty sure there'd be enough for a robe. That would catch the candle glow and really sparkle. She also has brown corduroy and burlap — everything she'd need to make Joseph's. And my aunt Jane is coming to visit with her new baby, a month old — perfect for the baby Jesus."

A long moment of silence followed. I guessed that Celia was as shocked by Janice's offer as I was.

"You think she'd let her baby do it? A real, live baby?"

"Sure. If I ask her. If I'm the one holding the baby."

Oh, dear. Does Celia understand what Janice is saying?

"And you're sure your mother will make both costumes?" Celia asked, clearly skeptical.

"I said it . . . as long as I'm Mary and Coltrane is Joseph."

I knew Celia had her heart set on playing Mary. If Janice was Mary, that left no major female role, unless Celia took the angel of the Lord, which I was pretty sure Celia saw as a lesser role than Mary.

"Well, that can't be decided until the auditions." Celia kept her director's voice.

"It can if you want my mother to make the costumes. You don't think she'll do all that work or donate all that new fabric for somebody else to be Mary and Joseph, do you? You don't think Aunt Jane would let anybody but me hold her baby! Get serious, Celia Percy." Janice nearly spat Celia's name.

"Anybody got a donkey they can bring in?" Chester asked, breaking the tension. I loved him for it.

"Got no donkey, but my uncle's got a jackass he'd likely bring. Lives just beyond the ridge and down a way. I'll ask him . . . if you want," Hayford Bell offered.

"Our granddaddy runs the zoo in Charlotte." Janice's voice came again, smooth as butter. "It has a real live camel."

"Janice!" Coltrane sounded like he'd choked on his tongue.

"I'm just saying, Coltrane. It's better than a donkey — or a jackass."

"So what?" Hayford countered. "A jackass here is better than a camel there!"

"The thing is, I'm sure, if I ask him, that

he'll ship that camel here by train for the program. The zoo has special railcars for animals, you know — like they do for the circus. They send animals out on exhibition all the time. How do you think they get elephants from town to town?"

I had no idea, so I doubted any of the children did either. There was a long silence. I wanted in the worst way to caution Celia. This all sounded too good to be true.

"I reckon a real camel would be a sight better than a jackass." Hayford's voice fell.

"Would he give us camel rides?" a voice I didn't recognize piped up, hope thrilling through the room.

"Well, maybe," Janice considered.

"Janice —" Coltrane broke in.

"Shut up, Coltrane! I said maybe; I didn't say yes. I'll have to write and ask him. Then I can confirm it with you, Celia."

"But —" Coltrane broke in again.

"I said, shut up! Maybe I can write him tonight and get the letter in the mail right away. There's not much time."

"That'll be swell, Janice. Thanks." Celia's conflicted enthusiasm waned. "Okay, let's audition for roles. Shepherds? Angels? Kings?"

"I'll show you how to do Mary." Janice Richards again. I was tempted to peek but made myself stay put in the next room. There was a long pause, and I could imagine Janice's portrayal — serene and smug smile, arms cradling an invisible baby, eyes daring anyone to challenge her. I pitied Celia.

"Okay, anybody else want to audition for Mary?" Celia offered, quieter now.

"Not if you care about costumes, they don't," Janice countered boldly. "Coltrane, I think it's time we went home. This is all over anyhow. Let's get our coats."

"It's not over, Janice," Celia nearly whined. "We still have to finish auditions, and Mama made cookies."

"Auditions for the minor roles. We don't need to stay for that. Besides, we have cake at our house. Just be sure to give us plenty of lines. I don't want to be one of those Marys that never says anything — and lines for Coltrane, too."

"What about rehearsals?" Chester asked, seconds before the bell jingled over the front door, signaling the departure of Janice and Coltrane.

"I'll post the schedule at the general store. We'll rehearse Thursday afternoons — after school at the church — once Thanksgiving's past." Celia's words might have reached Janice's ears before the door closed, but I wondered. Clearly Celia tried to maintain order after that inauspicious departure, but the wind had been stolen from her sails. The rest, all but the cookies, was an uphill climb.

CHAPTER FORTY-EIGHT

Celia confessed to Miss Lill Thanksgiving morning that she'd hoped to have a whole choir of baby angels singing carols around Mary and Joseph and baby Jesus. "But there's no white robes to be had. And I was hopin' somebody'd build a stable backdrop out of wood they had laying around. But nobody wants to give up two-by-fours, and everybody's broke and busier than bugs, even Olney Tate. I don't know what I was thinking, Miss Lill. I don't even have a costume for the angel of the Lord."

"What about an old sheet or tablecloth? I'm sure we can find something in the linen closet. We can cut something out of one of those. I'm fairly handy with a needle and thread."

"I already asked Mama. She looked and said there wasn't anything but Miz Hyacinth's lace and damask tablecloths, and she'd defy the whole Union army before she'd let anybody cut those up."

"The whole Union army?" Miss Lill chuckled.

"Her very words." Celia sighed but didn't dare say she'd already given the extra old linens her mama had remembered to the couple in the church shed, along with one of the pies baked yesterday for Thanksgiving. Her mama hadn't checked the outdoor pantry yet. Celia wasn't looking forward to that.

"I sort of hoped some dads would give up their Klan robes, but Mama said I can't ask. It might bring on trouble. It sure seems like 'peace on earth' would turn those to a good use."

Miss Lill's breath caught and she straightened. Her eyes, full of sympathy before, flashed fear, the very reaction Celia's mother had warned her about.

Something about that reminded Celia of the letter she was supposed to give Miss Lill — the one Ida Mae had given her. Before her mother gave her another job, she'd best run upstairs and find it, make sure she hadn't lost it.

Thankfully, it was still there, tucked inside her schoolbook, not creased or mussed in any way. She'd withheld the letter out of love for Miss Lill, but her conscience pricked just the same. Still, she struggled. *It would be awful to give her something from her rotten husband on*

Thanksgiving Day. Maybe this should just dis-appear.

"Celia! Are you up there with your nose in a book? Get down here and help your brother set the table!" Celia's mama brooked no argument.

Celia couldn't decide what to do with the letter. Ruining the whole of Thanksgiving seemed cruel. *Later. Tomorrow or Saturday. Not today.*

"Celia Percy! Did you hear me?" her mother's call came again.

"Right away, Mama!" Celia stuffed the letter beneath her mattress. *Out of sight, out of mind.*

Joe and Joleen Earl arrived half an hour before dinner. Reverend Willard arrived right on time. Celia had never seen a table laden with so many good things. It pushed every worry about the letter from her mind. Her mama had baked for hours yesterday, glazed the ham Ida Mae sent, and plucked the turkey Joe Earl shot. That morning she'd stuffed and roasted it in a hot oven, filling all of Garden's Gate with fragrances of clove, wild thyme, sage, onion, and turkey.

Miss Lill had spent the morning peeling and chopping root vegetables for Celia's mama. Celia and Chester set the table over Miz Hyacinth's ivory lace tablecloth. The reverend brought bouquets of sweet-smelling cedar and juniper berries. Miss Lill twined them through groups of tiny gourds and pumpkins, then set beeswax candles aflame down the center of the table.

Never had Celia seen a prettier picture — sparkling glassware and silver, white china that gleamed in the candlelight, and the faces of people who loved one another — like something out of a magazine.

When Reverend Willard asked the blessing, it was one of true thanksgiving. Celia felt she approached a burning bush . . . holy ground. The wonder of the day and the peace and joy of the makeshift family gathered there filled her like no meal ever had, ever could.

It wasn't until time for dessert that the fat hit the fire.

"Lilliana," Celia's mother called, "could you help me in the kitchen? Celia, you and Chester clear the plates."

"Yes, ma'am." Celia didn't need to be asked twice. And she didn't need to strain her ears to hear her mother.

"I just don't understand it! I baked three pies — apple, sweet potato, and pecan — and put them in the pantry on the porch. The apple is gone — simply gone."

"You don't imagine somebody just came up on the porch and took it, do you?" Miss Lill looked at Celia, who busied herself scraping plates into the compost bucket without being asked.

"Who would know where to look?" her mother worried. "Olney made that door so you'd never see it if you didn't know it was there. And that's another thing. Marshall came up to split wood yesterday, and here it was already split while I'd been down at the store. What's goin' on? Am I losin' my mind?"

"Well, I don't know anything about the wood, but don't worry now. Two pies is plenty. The dinner was lovely, Gladys. Please don't fret. I'll get the coffee." Miss Lill patted Celia's mama on the back to reassure her.

Celia finished scraping the plates, then lifted the bowls and platters from the table, eager to help. It also gave her an opportunity to pile a cookie tin with leftover turkey and stuffing and all the fixings, cover it with a tea towel, and set it in the pantry on the porch, praying there'd be a moment when her mama and Miss Lill were distracted so she could slip it over to the church shed. She just didn't expect that moment to come in the form it did.

CHAPTER FORTY-NINE

The Earls had just left and Reverend Willard was saying his goodbyes, standing long at the front door, turning the brim of his fedora in his hands, as if loath to leave.

"Thank you for inviting me, Lilliana. It means everything to me to be included in your family here."

The pupils in his eyes grew, and I knew his words were not spoken lightly, but I also knew it was more than my family he longed for. As much as I wanted to, I could not reach out to him, dared not respond. The moment grew awkward, just before Ruby Lynne crept from the shadows.

"Miss Lilliana?"

Reverend Willard stepped back as if caught stealing cookies.

"Ruby Lynne! It's so good to see you. Happy Thanksgiving!"

"It's not." She shook her head. "Can I come in?"

"Ruby Lynne —" Reverend Willard reached

for her hand — "can I help you?"

"No, Reverend. You can't. I need Miss Lilliana. Please."

The girl looked so frightened and pitiable that I nodded to Reverend Willard, trusting he'd understand my message to go, that we'd be all right. He tipped his hat to both of us. "Good night, ladies." Then he added to me, "Call me if you need anything." That warmed my heart. *Galahad at the ready.* I couldn't help my thoughts.

"Come, Ruby Lynne. You're always welcome." I reached my hand out to her and she ran up the steps into my arms. "Ruby Lynne! What is it?" I thought I saw something move in the trees beyond. "Come inside."

I peered into the gathering gloom and demanded as fiercely as I could muster, "Who's there?" Images of Rhoan Wishon and even Gerald sped through my brain. But no one answered, and Ruby Lynne fell to weeping. "Come in. Come right in." I pulled her into the parlor, where we'd already built a fire. Celia and Chester stood wide-eyed in the hallway.

"I'm in trouble — so much trouble, Miss Lilliana." The girl was trembling, frozen clear through in a coat that barely covered her.

"Ruby Lynne, what's happened? Are you hurt? Did your fa — did someone hurt you?"

She cried harder.

"Celia, Chester, go ask your mother to

bring us a pot of tea — and the sugar bowl. Then you two get upstairs and stay there."

"Yes, ma'am." The two ran off.

"Now tell me what's happened. Should I call Dr. Vishnevsky?"

"No! Please don't do that!"

I was at a loss. I saw no signs of bruising, no cuts. But I of all people knew that such marks were easily hidden by winter clothing. "Tell me what I can do."

Listen. It came as clear to my mind as an audible voice.

I guided Ruby Lynne to the settee nearest the fire and pulled an afghan around her shoulders. She clung to it, still shivering.

"You're frozen through. Let me take off your boots." I knelt to pull them off, but she cringed backward.

"I can't stay. I just . . ." But she couldn't finish.

I sat next to her, waiting. Ruby Lynne alternately stared into the fire and searched the room. I saw longing in her eyes, then worry bordering fear.

"We can wait until you're ready, Ruby Lynne. There's no hurry. You're safe here and welcome — always."

Gladys must have already had hot water on the stove because it was no time at all before she carried in a tray of hot tea and slim slices of sweet potato pie dolloped with whipped cream.

"Just tea, please," Ruby Lynne said, her fingers still shaking as she cradled the warm cup in her hands.

"That's not like you, Ruby Lynne Wishon. You've never turned down one of my pies." Gladys's concern matched my own.

Twin tears trickled down Ruby Lynne's cheeks. "I can't eat. I just can't."

"You look mighty peaked, child." Gladys pressed the back of her hand to Ruby Lynne's forehead, then her palm to her cheek. "You don't feel feverish."

"I missed my monthly. Twice. Maybe three times now." Ruby Lynne blurted the words, surely before she lost courage.

Gladys sat down on the rocker with a thump. "Lord, help us now."

"You've been through horrendous things, Ruby Lynne. It could just be the stress of all that's gone on. That's happened to me before."

Momentarily, Ruby Lynne looked hopeful, then shook her head and stared into the fire. "My breasts are swollen. The sight of food makes me sick. Most anything I eat comes back up. I heard Ida Mae tell her daughter once those are signs." She turned to Gladys and me. "I'm scared. If my daddy finds out, he'll kill me. I know he will."

Not if he's the father! But then, he just might — if he's the father. I looked at Gladys. I was out of my territory.

Gladys breathed deeply and rose to the occasion with the sense we needed. "We need to get Granny Chree or Dr. Vishnevsky to examine you. Pregnancy is one thing. But it could be something else."

"Daddy'd never let Granny Chree touch me."

"But she's a woman, and that might be easier —"

"Don't matter what's easier for me. It matters what he'll say, what he'll do if he finds out. I know from last time she helped me. I can't risk it. I just can't."

Gladys and I looked at one another.

"You're willing for Dr. Vishnevsky to examine you?" I asked, thinking how brave and frightened this young girl was.

Ruby Lynne bit her lip till I saw a spot of blood, then nodded, swiping away tears that insisted on falling. "But you can't tell — not Daddy. Not anybody. Promise me."

I had no intention of telling her father, but pregnancy was not something she'd be able to hide long — if that's what it was.

"There's nobody we want to tell, Ruby Lynne," Gladys answered for me. "But if you're pregnant, you'll need special care. You're far too young."

Ruby cried all the harder and I pulled her into my arms, glaring at Gladys. Why did she have to be so blunt — as if Ruby Lynne had any say in this? If Rhoan Wishon had raped his daughter, it was not her fault in any way. "Gladys, call Dr. Vishnevsky."

Before she could, the telephone rang. I gasped, fearing it might be Ruby Lynne's father, not sure I could keep the anger from my voice, determined though I was not to give her away.

"I'll get it," Gladys said.

But it wasn't her house or her battle. I drew a deep breath. "No. Let me. . . . Hello?"

"Did you have a happy Thanksgiving, Lilliana? A shame you missed your father's wedding this morning."

My heart jumped into my throat and every muscle in my neck and jaw tightened. There was no mistaking the voice at the other end of the line. "Gerald."

"Why haven't you returned the papers I sent?"

A million things swept through my brain the moment I recognized his voice, making it hard to concentrate on what he was saying, except that Father had remarried. It felt like he'd spit on Mama's grave. "Where are you?"

I heard the smirk in his voice. "In Philadelphia, at the moment. Do you want me to come down there?"

"No." That was one thing I was certain of.

"Then sign the papers and send them back."

"What papers?"

"Don't play games, Lilliana. You're not

400

good at them. I'm holding a signed card from your postmistress that tells me my attorney's letter was received at the No Creek post office well over a week ago. You should have signed the papers and sent them by return mail. Are you telling me your Ida Mae didn't give it to you?"

"Ida Mae's gone to her sister's in New York. I don't know when she'll be back, and she didn't give me anything before she left. What are you talking about?"

"An easy way out for you, if you want it, if you're smart enough to take it."

"Gerald, I have no idea what you're talking about."

"I'm tired of this, Lilliana. Stop playing games. Either you come back to Philadelphia and we go the medical route, or you sign those papers saying you deserted me. Your choice — I plead that you're insane and guilty of adultery, or I plead that you've deserted me and committed adultery. Either way, you don't get a penny. Do you understand me?"

"I don't want anything of yours."

"I suppose you're living off your aunt's estate."

"I haven't inherited anything — just as I told you I wouldn't. I'm living here thanks to my aunt's blessing through a trust, but I don't own Garden's Gate, and neither can you, no matter what you do or how long you wait. I imagine your lawyers already know that. Contact Rudolph Bellmont, my family's lawyer in North Wilkesboro, if you don't believe me. I know he'll explain everything."

"A pity that. But that does mean there's no reason to prolong this."

I didn't know what to say, and I knew anything I said would be used against me.

"Don't push me, and don't sleep too soundly, Lilliana." The phone clicked into its cradle.

There was no chance of that.

CHAPTER FIFTY

Celia and Chester had gone upstairs as Miss Lill ordered. They'd even brushed their teeth and gotten ready for bed. Celia heard Miss Lill talking on the phone but figured it was Doc Vishy. After she heard the telephone click, Celia cracked her door into the hallway to listen, and she heard plenty.

"You all right, Lilliana?" Celia heard her mother ask.

Miss Lill didn't answer right away. When she did, Celia didn't know who she meant.

"He's intent on ruining me. I just don't understand —" But she stopped talking then. "I can't think about this now. We've got to help Ruby Lynne."

Celia wondered if she meant Rhoan, Ruby Lynne's daddy, but couldn't figure how. Celia didn't know a lot about courting, but she knew about dogs in heat and that's how they came to have pups. Humans couldn't be much different. She also knew there would be yelling and screaming and crying when

Rhoan Wishon found out. Even Celia knew a girl was supposed to keep her legs together until marriage. And who was the father, anyway? Celia prayed it wasn't Marshall. They'd kill him for that, she was certain.

Celia stuffed her pillow and dirty clothes into a long sausage roll and pulled her quilt over the mound, shaping it to look like a body on her bed. If her mama peeked in, Celia hoped she'd quietly shut the door, believing she was sound asleep for the night.

Celia pulled her shoes off and her coat on, waiting until she heard her mother and Miss Lill usher Ruby Lynne into Miz Hyacinth's old room before slipping down the stairs in her socks and out the back door. They were saying things her mama didn't want Celia or Chester to hear, and that meant all the grown-ups would likely be busy for another half hour or more, once Doc Vishy came.

Celia tied her shoes on the back porch in the light that shone from the kitchen window and pulled the cookie tin of food from the outdoor pantry. It felt ice-cold, but she figured cold food was better than no food. Her breath fogged in front of her face. She shivered in the frigid air that swept down from the mountain but ran, as fast as her feet would carry her, over the familiar dirt road to the church, circled wide through the graveyard, and crept quietly toward the shed.

A light burned through the church window

and Celia saw Reverend Willard walking up and down the aisle, surely practicing his sermon. He did that often, once it was too cold to preach to the tombstones outdoors.

Silently Celia lifted the latch on the shed door. "It's me, Celia," she whispered and slipped through the door, closing it just as softly.

"Welcome!" The woman's voice came through the dark. "We didn't expect to see you today, Celia."

"We sure enjoyed that pie. Ate every last morsel." Celia heard the smile in the man's voice.

"Clay all but licked the plate!"

"Happy Thanksgiving!" Celia felt her tinned offering small. "I brought you some turkey and fixings. Sorry they're near frozen."

"Turkey? I can't believe it!" The woman's voice sounded like awe to Celia, like she expected Moses did on Mount Sinai, and her heart warmed.

"Mama's a real good cook. I wish I could have invited you to our table."

"You've done more for us than any other human being, Celia Percy. Please don't fret about a thing. Even the baby leapt inside me when she heard you coming."

"She? How do you know she's a girl?" Celia had always wondered if there was a way to tell.

The man laughed. "She don't. She's hoping."

"I'd love a girl-child — to plait her hair and tell her stories, teach her to cook and sew and keep a home." The woman's voice faltered. "If we get us a home."

"*When.* We will, Charlene. We will. I promise it. When we get to Tennessee. You'll see. When we find your people, we'll get a fresh start."

Celia's eyes had become accustomed to the moonlight that shone through the shed window. She saw the couple clasp hands, saw the man wrap his arm around the woman heavy with child. She wondered if it had been that way for her mama and daddy before the moonshine came between them. They'd been poor, too, and they'd needed a chance, a foot up, as her daddy used to say. He'd found it running 'shine for somebody. She didn't know who, but like Ida Mae, she had her suspicions. Guzzling the 'shine had raised a demon between her mama and daddy and they'd fought all the time, sinking deeper into debt, until he was arrested. Celia had hated her daddy's weakness.

She didn't want that for this couple. She had to be the foot up until they could find real help. And not for them only, but for their baby about to come into the world.

"I'll pay you and your family back for every

morsel once we get on our feet, Celia, I swear it."

"No need. But I reckon it was you split that wood yesterday."

"It's the least I can do. I made sure to wait till I knew nobody was home."

"Thing is, you got to stop. That's Marshall's job and he needs it. Just take what I bring for now. I want to help. You can work it off once you get on your feet." But she didn't see how that would happen anytime soon. Nobody'd give him a job, and without a job how could he earn money, buy food, pay rent?

"I'd best get back. I'll take the pie plate. Mama's missing it."

"Please, tell your mother thank you." The woman meant well, but Celia couldn't do that.

"Are y'all warm enough?" Celia could see her own breath in the shed.

"These quilts are wonderful. We're toasty — just fine."

"I stuffed those newspapers around the window and door, and that helped a lot. Thank you. I'd really like to do something for your family. If not splitting wood, there must be something." The man's brow wrinkled.

Celia nodded. "I know, and I appreciate that — I do. But it's best you let it be for now. Please. I'll come tomorrow, if I can."

"We're all right. We'll be all right, won't we,

407

Charlene?"

"We will. We have to." Celia heard determination in the woman's voice.

Without another word Celia took the pie plate and slipped through the shed door, silently closing it behind her. She steered wide behind the cemetery, noting that the light in the church had gone out and the light in the parsonage beyond burned softly through the curtains.

She walked home, more slowly than she meant to, taking in the stars — brilliant in their spheres — and the clear, cold night. She left the pie plate on the back porch, so it would look like whoever took it had returned it, and cracked open the back door. All was quiet. She took off her shoes, tiptoed through the kitchen, and crept up the stairs, slipping through her door moments before she heard Miz Hyacinth's bedroom door open and grown-ups whispering in the hallway.

Celia drew a deep breath and released it. It took less than a minute to change her clothes and crawl beneath the quilt on her bed. She shivered from head to toe, still nearly frozen from her late-night venture. But she wasn't sorry. She'd helped somebody, fed somebody.

It made her think of the stories Doc Vishy had told her and Chester of how people had helped him and others persecuted during the Great War. He'd crossed Europe on foot, half-starved, before finally reaching a port and working his way across the Atlantic to New York. If people hadn't helped him — and he said the few who did had risked their lives to do it — he'd never have survived, never have made his way to New York or from there to No Creek. If he hadn't come to No Creek, he couldn't have saved Chester's life the night of his appendix attack. And what would Celia's life be like without her brother? She scrunched her eyes at the horror of the thought.

Celia had been careful to think of them as "the man" and "the woman." Without names they'd not been quite real, and what she was doing was not real — not really stealing, not really lying. She could stop anytime — that's what she'd told herself.

Charlene. Clay. They used their names freely in front of her, and they called her by her given name. *No pretending. It's what friends do. Friends means helping one another.* She'd taken that step and could no longer go back, no longer imagine she could stop, and truth be told, she didn't want to.

CHAPTER FIFTY-ONE

Dr. Vishnevsky confirmed Ruby Lynne's pregnancy and predicted the baby due in early spring. I nearly cried to realize she'd been raped even before she came to us that first time. Evidently Ruby Lynne had already done the calculation, for while his confirmation seemed to carry the weight of a death sentence, she didn't seem surprised, only resigned.

Ruby Lynne refused to give the doctor the name of the father, which convinced me all the more that it was Rhoan Wishon. I wanted to call the sheriff.

"No!" Ruby Lynne cried. "Daddy'll kill me! He'll kill me! You don't understand. Promise me you won't tell him!"

"No one is calling the sheriff without your say-so, Ruby Lynne," Dr. Vishnevsky soothed. "But you must realize that you can't keep a pregnancy hidden. You're already beginning to show."

Ruby Lynne didn't answer. Dr. Vishnevsky

continued, "Besides that, you need extra care, good food and rest, and to be excused from some of your heavier chores. You're young to be having a baby. Some precautions are needed."

But she couldn't seem to hear him. She was terrified, and in order to calm her, to help her sleep, he finally gave her a mild sedative. Gladys and I stepped out into the hallway but kept the door open. We heard him talking softly, reassuring her as best he could that he would be available anytime she needed help or to talk, and that if she wanted, he would deliver her baby or arrange for her to go away to a hospital in Winston-Salem or Asheville — both far from No Creek. He didn't speak of her father but said she wouldn't be alone. Finally she fell asleep.

Dr. Vishnevsky packed his medical bag and we all tiptoed downstairs into the parlor.

"I still think we should alert the sheriff. Ruby Lynne cannot go back into that situation." My head pounded. I felt like tearing my hair out.

"I agree that it's not safe." The doctor nodded. "I found signs of further abuse — tears, cuts, bruising — that were not there when I examined her before."

"Who knows how many times she's been through this?" My stomach roiled.

His eyebrows rose and he passed a weary hand across his furrowed forehead.

"We must call the sheriff!" Why couldn't they understand?

"If you do that, you're as good as signing Ruby Lynne's death warrant." Gladys was firm. "And the sheriff and Rhoan are drinking buddies — good ole boys in a holler of no account. You can't depend on justice for Ruby Lynne, any more than we could with the Klan attack."

"Rape is a grave accusation. Unless you have witnesses or proof, or unless Ruby Lynne admits it . . ." Dr. Vishnevsky shook his head, agreeing with Gladys. "Is her father actually the perpetrator? I don't know. If so, why is she so afraid of telling him?"

"Because that would expose him to others. He may well have threatened her if she tells." I should know. I knew about men who beat, then threatened a woman into silence. I pushed my shaking hands behind me. Still, I had no proof, and Ruby Lynne refused to name the father. But it was clear that the abuser wasn't going to stop. "We can't do nothing! We can't possibly send her back there!"

"We can keep her here." Gladys spoke quietly. "Until Rhoan comes for her."

I closed my eyes, and memories of Gerald coming after me and dragging me from my father's house rose before me. I couldn't let that happen to Ruby Lynne.

"Call me if there are any changes. Other-

412

wise, I expect her body will heal in time. She needs rest and nourishment. She's not been eating enough or properly." Dr. Vishnevsky turned to Gladys. "A balanced diet, greens, if you can get them, and red meat. I suspect some anemia."

"Yes, Doctor."

"Thank you for coming, Dr. Vishnevsky. I'm sorry we called you out on Thanksgiving. I didn't know what else to do."

Dr. Vishnevsky smiled and placed his hand on my arm. "Never hesitate to call me. I wasn't feasting anyway."

While he put his coat on, Gladys ran to the kitchen and wrapped a large slice of pecan pie. He was nearly out the door when she slipped it in his hand. "For later, with something hot to drink."

"Thank you, Mrs. Percy. Thank you." He tipped his hat in his old-world way and was gone.

The clock in the parlor ticked so loud my head hurt. *What more can we do?*

"Lilliana, there's something you should consider."

I pulled my hand away from my brow. "What?"

"What if it isn't Rhoan's?"

"What do you mean?" I wasn't in the mood for riddles, from Gladys or anyone else.

"What if she wasn't raped? What if she let . . . let somebody get to her and things got rough? What if she's sorry now but wasn't sorry to start?"

I thought I might throw up. "How can you say that? You saw what she looked like when she came here, what she'd been through — apparently not for the first time! And it's happened again. Again!" I struggled to keep my voice down.

Gladys sighed heavily and sat down on the settee, her head in her hands.

I was sorry in an instant that I'd yelled at her. I wasn't angry at Gladys. She was my ally. I was yelling for Ruby Lynne, for me, and for all the women who'd ever said no to a man who didn't stop, who insisted on having his own way, "rightfully by marriage" or not.

Gladys looked up, moistened her lips, and whispered, "What if it's Marshall's?"

CHAPTER FIFTY-TWO

Rhoan Wishon wasn't in church on Sunday, which made Celia think that either he was out looking for Ruby Lynne or he was off on one of his many trips to nobody knew where. All anybody ever knew for sure was that Rhoan Wishon was a "businessman" and had "business dealings" all across the state and even west, into Tennessee.

Nobody else knew that Ruby Lynne was staying at Garden's Gate, as far as Celia knew, and as her mama had told her, that was safest for everybody.

Ruby Lynne's being there took the focus off of Celia and Chester, which was just fine in Celia's mind. It gave her more freedom to come and go, made it easier to collect and deliver her food wages from the general store to the shed behind the church.

She just hadn't figured on bumping into Marshall and his rake when she came out of the shed late that Monday afternoon.

"What you doin' in there, Celia?"

"Marshall! You like to scared me to death! What are you doin' here?"

"I'm sweepin' up the last of the fall leaves, although, I have to say, looks like somebody got here ahead of me. Didn't leave me much to do."

"That's mighty good of you."

"It's my job — mine and Uncle Olney's."

Celia took his arm and steered him away from the shed. "How was your Thanksgiving? I bet your aunt filled you all to the brim. She makes the best sweet potato pie I ever ate, and if I had to guess, Olney shot a turkey up off the ridge that —"

"Celia Percy — turn me loose! What you jabberin' on about and what you up to?"

"Up to? Nothin'. Can't a body be friendly?"

Marshall harrumphed. "Who do you think you're talkin' to? Do you know when you lie, or are about to, your ears turn pink? Do you know that?"

Celia didn't. But betrayal by her own ears made her mad. They'd made it halfway through the tombstones when Marshall stopped in his tracks. That wasn't far enough. "Why'd you stop?"

"Because you're workin' hard to get me away from that shed. What you hidin' in there?"

"Hiding? What am I hiding? Why would I be hiding anything in some dumb old shed? I got to get home. Mama will have supper on

416

the table, and if I'm not there, I'll miss and get in big trouble."

"Then I guess you won't mind if I take a look." Marshall started back toward the shed.

"No! Don't do it!" Celia's heart nearly burst from her chest.

"You gonna tell me why I shouldn't open that door?"

"I'm gettin' ready for the Christmas play. I'm keepin' my props in there and I don't want anybody to see — before Christmas Eve." It was a wonder how telling one lie made telling the next one easier.

"It's not likely I'll be seein' your Christmas program, Celia — me goin' to Saints Delight and you directin' your program right here at Shady Grove."

"Well, I thought you and Olney and the family might like to come. I want it to be a surprise." Celia's palms were sweating, even though it couldn't be above freezing.

Marshall heaved a sigh of exasperation and waited.

Celia's head pounded. She hadn't wanted to tell anyone, to trust anyone, or to get anyone else involved. Already Olney knew, but he hadn't interfered once and might have even figured the squatters had gone on by now. If Marshall opened that door, he'd be bound to tell Olney and maybe Reverend Willard. Olney couldn't be part of it beyond the help he'd given or he'd lose his job. Reverend

Willard would be in a fix what to do and might have to turn them out, being subject to the church and all.

"Celia? This got anything to do with that sack of food Uncle Olney had me leave behind the Belvidere stone?"

Celia swallowed. "Can you keep a secret?"

"If it's a secret should be kept."

"You ever wrung a chicken's neck?"

"What?"

"You ever wrung a chicken's neck? I found one and I need to wring its neck. I don't exactly know how and I don't want to ask Mama."

"Is it one of Miz Hyacinth's chickens?"

Miz Hyacinth was dead, so to be perfectly accurate, it was not, but to continue stretching the truth to Marshall was as bad as lying outright to Olney. "Sort of."

"What do you mean, 'sort of'?"

"Well, she's not much of a layer anymore, and she's one of the strays roosted in the trees till Miz Hyacinth bought more after Miss Lill came, so she's set for roasting sometime."

"Then why don't you ask your mama?"

Celia licked her lips. She needed help. Charlene and Clay needed help, but bringing anybody else in was dangerous. And yet she needed someone who could do things she couldn't, things she wasn't sure how. "I'm gonna trust you, Marshall."

"You know you can."

"There's a man and his wife hiding in that shed what's starving, and the woman's about to bust a baby. The man wants to work but nobody'll give him a job. Ida Mae run him out of the store because he's a Yankee and a drifter. I've got to get them some food. I've been working for potatoes and such at the store, but they need meat. The woman's poorly. The man does what he can to pay back — cutting firewood up to the house when nobody's home and sweeping up the leaves here in the churchyard at night when Reverend Willard's over to the next town and I don't know what all. He's not a mooch."

"Celia Percy. You do beat all. Does Reverend Willard know about this?"

"No."

"Your mama?"

Celia shook her head. "Mama said not to bring home strangers or strays. She put her foot down, but I know she wouldn't want them to starve. She just won't listen, and I fear she feels so beholden to Miss Lill that she wouldn't ask her to give more. I can't let them starve, Marshall. Jesus wouldn't want that."

"So you're taken to lying and stealing. You reckon Jesus wants that?"

"Everything I borrow from anybody, I keep a record. Clay says he'll pay back every penny, and he's already doing every odd job he can by night. Even if he doesn't pay it

419

back, I'll sweep Ida Mae's store clean till I'm twenty. I look after the chickens at Garden's Gate ever since we came to live there. Miz Hyacinth bought them special for me to mind, said I'm their caretaker — so it's not exactly stealing. Sometimes you got to cull the flock for poor layers, you know. I just never wrung necks. I need someone to cook it, too."

"I can't get Aunt Mercy involved in that."

The weight of impossibility lay heavy on Celia. She turned to walk away.

"Hold on. Didn't say I wouldn't help. I know what it is to be hungry. Besides, it appears this fella's been doin' some of my work while I get paid."

Hope sprang in Celia's heart.

"I'll wring its neck and we can both pluck. I reckon Granny Chree might be up for handling the stewpot if we bring it clean. Least we can ask her."

Celia's smile swelled from the center of her being. "Thank you, Marshall."

Chapter Fifty-Three

"I've come for my girl! I know she's here." Rhoan Wishon's words carried his menace straight to my heart, but I stood my ground and blocked the front door. I'd protect Ruby Lynne with my dying breath.

"Ruby Lynne's not well, Mr. Wishon. She needs rest and nourishment. I don't believe it's safe for her to stay with you. She's welcome here."

"She's not sick, just clumsy, fallin' into walls and such. Says so herself. You layin' that at my door?" Fury built in his eyes.

"Only you can answer that." But I knew. In my heart, I knew it was him.

He stepped closer, so close I could smell his cigarette-stained breath, foul but sober. "It's you brought that buck into your home — you and that Percy girl. Don't imagine you all won't answer. Now let me see my Ruby Lynne, before I force my way in."

Gladys's words flew through my mind again, a raven chased by a hawk. But I couldn't believe it. I'd trust Marshall twice over Rhoan Wishon. "The fact remains that Ruby Lynne needs care and you're not there to give it. Let her stay here long enough —"

He cut me off, shoving past me.

"Pa! Don't hurt her. Please! I'm coming. I'm coming, Pa. Miss Lilliana just took me in for the night. I got lonesome being home by myself. That's all."

I hadn't heard Ruby Lynne come down the stairs. Her face was white as a sheet, except for the bruise under her eye — so white her few freckles stood out like soot on snow. "Ruby Lynne, you need help. You need to tell —"

"I'm goin' home with Pa now, Miss Lilliana. Thank you for taking me in."

"Ruby Lynne —"

"I'll be all right. Don't fret. Pa'll take care of me, won't you, Pa?"

She looked up at him, so helpless and small. For a moment he looked at her with the concern I might imagine of a father, but then spoke gruffly. "Ida Mae told me she saw that nephew of Olney's slinkin' around the house before she left. He been out there while I been gone? Tell me the truth now!"

"No, Pa. Not once. I swear it."

He raised his hand as if to strike her. "Don't you lie to me, girl!"

"I'm not, Pa! I swear! I haven't seen Marshall."

"Mr. Wishon!" All the horror I felt came out in my voice.

Rhoan glared at his daughter but paused. "Get on out to the truck. I don't want you hangin' around here. You understand me? I said, do you understand me?"

"Yes, Pa." I barely heard Ruby Lynne's reply.

"Mr. Wishon —"

"Stay out of my business, woman!" he shouted as he followed Ruby Lynne down the steps and to the road. "I won't tell you again!"

He barely allowed Ruby Lynne time to close the door to the truck before gunning the motor and roaring off.

I was relieved to see him go but greatly feared for Ruby Lynne.

CHAPTER FIFTY-FOUR

Dusk swarmed over the hillsides and shadowed the glen surrounding Granny Chree's cabin in the woods. She stirred the pot of chicken stew meant for Clay and Charlene. She'd always understood things before Celia explained. That meant the world to Celia now.

"Mmm-mmm. Smell that, chile. That's goodness and health — in the meat and in the broth. You tell your friends to eat every bite and drink every drop. It's healing in their bones."

"Yes, ma'am. Thank you, Granny Chree. I wish I could pay you somehow for all you're doing."

"Pay me? The good Lord don't charge me for the gift of heaven. Why would I charge you for cookin' a chicken? You're a good girl, Celia. But you got to be careful, and you got to be careful involvin' Marshall. What folks might forgive you for they never gonna forgive him. You know that."

"Yes, ma'am." Celia did know it. Sometimes she wanted to pretend that the people of No Creek were better than that, but she knew in her head that they were just people, fearful people. They'd share with others they saw as like them, but Charlene and Clay, from a different state — outlanders — and Marshall, whose skin wore a different color . . . never. As long as folks stared at the differences and not the sameness, Celia knew they'd never bridge the gap.

It was the same, Doc Vishy had told her, with the Jews in Germany. People were getting all stirred up and stepped off into factions. Only now, Adolf Hitler, the bully in charge, was throwing Jewish people into camps, separating them from their families, taking their homes and all their belongings. Lots of Jews were beaten with no law coming to their defense according to news and the rare letter Doc Vishy had received smuggled out of Europe. Doc said that Jews were forced to wear Stars of David — yellow six-pointed stars cut from cloth they were to sew to their jackets, making them clear targets for the bullies.

He'd read part of a letter to Celia on her last visit, though neither of them talked about it in town. It sounded like the Klan gone wild to Celia. Doc Vishy had only lived in No Creek four years, so he qualified as an outlander, too — a different religion and, according to the Klan, a different race. Even Celia couldn't trust that the town wouldn't turn against him at some point, no matter that he'd doctored more than half and saved the lives of some.

What would they do to the Tates and Marshall and Reverend Pierce and the people of Saints Delight and even Miss Lill if Rhoan Wishon got them all stirred up about Ruby Lynne and if Ida Mae kept on about seeing Marshall over her way? It didn't bear thinking on.

"How be Ruby Lynne?" Granny asked as she stirred the pot.

Celia didn't know what to say.

"She in the family way." Granny made the statement as if fact, though how she knew, Celia didn't know. "Three, four months along, maybe more, I'd figure."

"She came by Thanksgiving night. Scared near to death. I think somebody'd beat her again." In Celia's mind that was much more worrisome than expecting a baby.

"Mmm-mmm." Granny shook her head, her brow furrowed. "I was afraid of that."

"Her daddy came to get her."

"He know?"

"I don't think Ruby Lynne's told him. He yelled at Miss Lill somethin' fierce. Blames her for bringing Marshall into Garden's Gate. Thinks she started something up between him and Ruby Lynne with those readin' lessons. He called it a courtin' school a while back and — and worse." Celia swallowed. "I'm afraid for Ruby Lynne and for Marshall when her daddy learns she's gonna have a baby."

"Marshall know this? Olney?"

"I don't think so. I heard Mama and Miss Lill talking. They're scared what Rhoan might do, but Miss Lill says she knows Marshall didn't hurt Ruby Lynne."

"You mean she wants it that way."

"She thinks Rhoan Wishon did wrong by his daughter." The thought made Celia sick. She wondered again if all fathers were wicked deep down or if it was the drink that made them so. She couldn't say much about her own.

Celia had long ago given up the notion of waving down the railway owner and asking him to help get her daddy out of prison. She wasn't even sure she wanted him to come home. His release would come too soon as it was.

He'd seemed sincere and sorry when she and Chester and their mother had visited him in prison, like he wanted things to go right when he got out, like he wanted to be a better man. But Celia thought of Ruby Lynne and Rhoan. *Wishing comes easy. Change don't.*

Christmas play rehearsals started on the first

Thursday of December. Janice and her brother, Coltrane, showed up on time for the first one and did a good job, even though it galled Celia how Janice had manipulated the part away from her. Still, she considered it the director's job to see that the show ran smoothly. If letting Janice play Mary and have lines was what it took for professional-looking costumes and the greater good, so be it.

"I wrote a letter to my grandpa, asking about the camel. We just have to wait for an answer. He's pretty busy, so it might take a while." Janice smiled.

Celia didn't know whether to be excited or wary. Coltrane just shook his head. That didn't feed Celia's confidence about getting the camel.

It was a relief knowing that Mrs. Richards was making the costumes for Mary and Joseph. Mrs. Richards was well-known and admired for her sewing skills and creativity, so Celia had no doubt they'd be spectacular, since her own kids performed the roles.

That night, over dinner, Celia filled her grown-ups in on the play. "Other kids mostly have their costumes already. Near every boy or their brother's been shepherds or kings — and every girl's been in the angel choir, or their sisters were, or their moms can trade costumes and props around, so we'll have at least some baby angels in white. The thing that always seems to go missing is halos. But

Pearl Mae said she'd cut pieces of the baling wire behind the store for me to bend and make halos. They might be kind of crooked and a little bit rusted, but that might still be good, don't you think?" Celia could hardly catch her breath for the excitement of it all.

"Would you like to paint them gold — or silver? Maybe I can order some glitter to sprinkle on the wet paint. I wonder if the Sears and Roebuck catalog sells glitter?" Miss Lill seemed more than willing, even eager to participate.

"Wow! So the candlelight catches it and makes them twinkle and shine." Celia said that over and over to herself, thrilled with the pleasure of anticipation. "Won't you come to church with us, Miss Lill? You can't miss the Christmas play, and coming now builds up to it — all December. It's the best ever. I'll sit with you."

Celia saw that Miss Lill wanted to come, that for some reason she struggled with saying yes and she struggled with saying no. Why she'd refused for so long was still a mystery to Celia.

"I don't know. Maybe. I'll see."

That would have to do. Maybe if Celia built excitement about the play, that would help Miss Lill slip in to join them. Celia knew that "slipping in" was sometimes easier than jumping two feet forward. "Joe Earl was in the store earlier today and promised to

429

practice 'Silent Night' and 'Hark! the Herald Angels Sing' and 'What Child Is This?' on his fiddle. You'll sing 'Silent Night,' won't you, Mama? You've got the sweetest voice in all of No Creek!"

"I'll start the singing and motion for the congregation to join in," her mama agreed.

"It's going to be wonderful!" Celia was sure and certain. "The thing we don't have is a white robe or some kind of gown big enough and long enough to reach the floor so I can rightly perform the angel of the Lord. That worries me most of all."

"I'm sure we could fashion something out of one of the bedsheets here," Miss Lill offered.

"Cut up Miz Hyacinth's pristine white sheets when we've only enough for the beds in use?" Celia's mama retorted. "You walk over my grave first!"

Celia appealed to Miss Lill with the eyes of a puppy. "I reckon they're yours now, aren't they, Miss Lill?"

"Celia Percy!" Her mama pounded her fist on the table, a sure sign that the conversation was closed.

Celia sighed. "Well, what am I gonna do?" No answer was forthcoming, so she reverted to old inspiration. "I still wish we could get ahold of one of those old Klan robes. That'd do in a pinch — minus the hood."

Miss Lill's eyes shifted and she straightened

just a little. Celia smiled weakly, figuring Miss Lill believed, as her mother did, that the very idea of angel attire being made from Klan robes was sacrilegious. Celia considered that might be true, but she was desperate.

CHAPTER FIFTY-FIVE

Since Jesse'd read letters from Biddy Chambers and written to her on Miz Hyacinth's
behalf all the years she'd been blind, it was
natural that after Miz Hyacinth passed, he
continued to write across the pond — natural
and a joy for him. He considered it providential that he was sitting in the parlor at
Garden's Gate reading aloud his most recent
letter from Biddy Chambers when Rhoan
Wishon all but hammered down the front
door, hollering for Lilliana.

Lilliana and Gladys both jumped nearly out
of their skins.

"Perhaps you'd like me to answer that,"
Jesse offered, clearing his throat.

Lilliana paled but stood and straightened
her skirt. "I — I should. It's Rhoan Wishon."

That went without saying since he'd not
stopped spouting off at the mouth. "Woman,
get out here!"

"I must insist, Lilliana." Jesse walked
toward the door. He couldn't let a woman

432

face the likes of an angry Wishon, drunk or sober, and he couldn't yet tell which Rhoan was. Lilliana didn't fight him on it, and for that he was grateful. Who did Rhoan Wishon think he was, behaving like a lunatic on a lady's doorstep?

Jesse hadn't quite made it to the door when Rhoan pushed it open and thundered in.

"Rhoan? Is that how you enter a lady's home?" Jesse pretended to be shocked, hoping to settle the man down.

"Reverend Willard. Day to you. I didn't expect to see you here."

"Nor I you. Certainly not in such a state."

"You would be, too, if it was your girl."

"My girl?"

"Ruby Lynne. She's gone and got knocked up, and it's that Marshall boy — Tate's nephew — what done it. Black as the ace of spades, and on to my Ruby Lynne." Rhoan had turned redder and redder with every word till his face went from a Christmas cactus to a flaming beet.

"What?" It took Jesse a moment to get his bearings. "I'm very sorry to hear about Ruby Lynne, but, Rhoan, those are strong allegations. Did Ruby Lynne tell you that Marshall's the father?"

"Didn't have to. Ida Mae told me she saw him slinking round my place the day I drove her to the train over in Asheville. Now he's run off."

"That's a far cry from —"

"You say. No offense intended, Preacher, but this ain't your business! This is mine!"

Lilliana apparently refused to listen to any more because she stepped to the center of the room. "That's like saying you bedded Ida Mae because you drove her to Asheville."

"If you were a man, I'd punch you in the face. Did you hear that, Preacher? That woman's got a devil in her and she's spreading her filth up and down the street. Ruby Lynne'd never met that buck before she came here."

"You're jumping to a lot of conclusions, Rhoan. You need to calm down and think this through, not run wild with accusations that have no ground." Jesse stepped into the space between Lilliana and Rhoan. He didn't trust that Rhoan wouldn't hit her, woman or not.

"I've got ground enough. You're besotted and blinded by this woman, Reverend Willard. You need to rip those scales off your eyes before you go telling the rest of us what to do. She's brought shame on this house, and now on mine! Old Mr. Belvidere would sit up in his grave if he knew. He'd set you all straight. He knew where folks belonged." Rhoan stepped closer to Jesse but his eyes bored into Lilliana's. "And since he's not here to do it, I will. Mark my word!" He slammed his fist against the doorjamb and turned on his heel.

"Rhoan!" Jesse called after him. "Rhoan!" But the man was off the porch and out to his truck, gunning the engine, never looking back.

"What will he do?" Lilliana's limbs shook despite her brave stance.

"No telling." Gladys pressed trembling hands to her face. "Somebody better warn Marshall. And Olney. I hope Marshall has run off, but he's probably just out working for somebody."

"Rhoan Wishon is crazy! He's guilty, and he's barking up the wrong tree, making a show so nobody suspects him!" Lilliana all but cried.

"You can't be sure it was him," Gladys whispered.

Sure or not, Jesse had no doubt what Rhoan and his "friends" would do to Marshall once they got ahold of him and, because he lived with them, the Tates.

CHAPTER FIFTY-SIX

Two things happened the week of December 7 that changed every home in No Creek, the world, and Celia's life forever.

The first came during Sunday morning service, which had stretched into the afternoon, what with a church business meeting, then a coffee-and-fellowship hour before the preaching ever began. Reverend Willard was just finishing a long-winded sermon on repentance and forgiveness, which needed, in Celia's mind, to be heard most by folks who weren't there. He finished with the Oswald Chambers reading for the day — one he said he was partial to.

" 'For godly sorrow worketh repentance to salvation.' " — 2 Corinthians 7:10 . . .

"Conviction of sin is one of the rarest things that ever strikes a man. . . . Jesus Christ said that when the Holy Spirit came He would convict of sin, and when the Holy Spirit rouses a man's conscience and brings him into the presence of God, it is not his relationship with men that bothers him, but his relationship with God — 'against Thee, Thee only, have I sinned, and done this evil in Thy sight.' . . . The surest sign that God is at work is when a man says that and means it. Anything less than this is a remorse for having made blunders, the reflex action of disgust with himself. . . . Examine yourself and see if you have forgotten how to be sorry."

Celia rubbernecked to find Rhoan Wishon and see how he took the reverend's words, but Rhoan wasn't there. Only Troy took up space in the Wishon pew, and he seemed mighty pleased with himself, as if none of the sermon applied to him, which Celia considered nothing more than a Wishon trait.

It was a shame the ladies of Garden's Gate held such worry for Ruby Lynne, because today was the first time Miss Lill had accompanied them to church since Miz Hyacinth passed. If not for the Wishons' trouble, Celia believed the day would have been just about perfect, until the last hymn.

The news came from Joe Earl, who'd missed the entire service sleeping off his Saturday night binge at the Whistle Stop Bar & Grill. Everybody was singing the final stanza when Joe, still wearing his rumpled boozing clothes, black hair sticking up straight from the night before, rushed into the church, down the center aisle, and up to whisper loudly in the preacher's ear. "The Japs are bombing Pearl Harbor! Fifty planes or more — thousands of our boys dead! War, for sure!"

Reverend Willard paused, and Celia could tell he struggled with whether or not to take Joe Earl's word. But who, drunk or sober, would make up such a thing? For her part, she'd never heard of Pearl Harbor and had no idea where in the world it was. But Joe was truthful enough when sober, and at least a dozen people sitting near the front of the church heard, so the hymn faded as gasps and murmurs raced through the pews.

Reverend Willard closed with a prayer, which was his normal practice. "Dear Lord and Father of us all, we've heard disturbing news today — news of the bombing of one of our naval bases by the Japanese."

Intakes of breath and even a little whimpering came from those who hadn't heard Joe clearly.

"Such news could strike fear in all our hearts did we not know that You are in charge of this world and our lives, that nothing happens without Your knowledge, and that You alone can bring good out of the horrors man perpetrates for evil. Protect the men and women in our armed services. Give President Roosevelt and our government and military leaders wisdom and discernment. Keep us from jumping to wrong conclusions and remind us daily that we are all in desperate need of forgiveness and of Your grace and mercy. Help us to reach out to friends and neighbors, especially those who have loved ones serving in the military, and make us a comfort and blessing to those in need. Let us be Your hands and feet to those we live among. Through Jesus Christ our Lord, amen.

"Let's all go home now. Those of us who have radios can listen to the news firsthand and open our doors to neighbors without radios. Most of all, friends and brethren, pray."

Not another word of encouragement was needed.

At home, Miss Lill fiddled with the radio dial. The first station she came to was already telling the story. Regular broadcasts were interrupted to tell the story again and again, with few updates, throughout the afternoon. Pearl Harbor had indeed been bombed by the Japanese that morning, laying waste to an entire naval base, sinking ships, killing thousands. Throughout the evening they kept near the radio, hearing of more devastation, waiting for President Roosevelt to speak.

But it wasn't until the next day that the president broadcast, sober and grim, as he addressed a full session of Congress, the American people, and the world.

"Mr. Vice President, and Mr. Speaker, and members of the Senate and House of Representatives: Yesterday, December 7, 1941 — a date which will live in infamy — the United States of America was suddenly and deliberately attacked by naval and air forces of the Empire of Japan.

"The United States was at peace with that nation and, at the solicitation of Japan, was still in conversation with its government and its emperor looking toward the maintenance of peace in the Pacific."

That sounded like slick dealing on the part of Japan to Celia.

"The attack yesterday on the Hawaiian Islands has caused severe damage to American naval and military forces. I regret to tell you that very many American lives have been lost. . . ."

The president went on to list a whole string of places the Japanese had attacked just since yesterday. Celia had no idea where any of those places were — Malaya or Hong Kong or Guam or the others — or what the people were like who lived there. Miss Lill had shown her Pearl Harbor in one of the atlases in the library, but it was so far away Celia couldn't grasp it. Still, it felt like the world had gone mad. *Is this the end? Does it mean Judgment Day?*

The president concluded, "With confidence in our armed forces, with the unbounding determination of our people, we will gain the inevitable triumph — so help us God."

Three days later, the United States declared war on Germany. Other countries followed. It seemed the entire world exploded in war. Folks in No Creek could hardly think on it, could hardly speak for the horror of it all.

The second great announcement of the week came in the form of a letter to Celia's mama from the state penitentiary. Owing to good behavior and a reduced staff over the Christmas holidays, Fillmore Percy was going to be released from prison on December 20. Somebody needed to go fetch him. Celia knew that didn't affect the state of the Union, but it would change Celia and Chester's world overnight, not to mention their mama's.

Secretly, Celia's heart thrilled that her father would be home in time to see the Christmas play she directed, that he would see Chester walk toward the manger so lordly but humble and read the Christmas story straight from the Bible at the preacher's pulpit, and her in a dazzling white robe — if she could only find one — and a glittered halo as the angel of the Lord. He'd hear their mother sing. *But does this mean returning to our cabin? Does it mean leaving Miss Lill and Garden's Gate and all these rooms full of wonderful books?*

And when Daddy comes home, will he take to drinking again? Will he run 'shine and risk his life and ours all over again? Will he land back in jail? Will he turn mean like Rhoan Wishon? He never was that kind of mean, but what about now?

Celia knew there was a curse in the misery of moonshine and those who made it, those who ran it, those who bought and sold it, and those who drank their coin and families away. She'd seen it firsthand and wanted no part of it — never again. Even more, she wanted no part of the tension it raised between her parents.

If Daddy can be the friendly, smiling man he was when we visited him in jail, if he can live like he talked then — full of promises to not drink and to work hard and pay our way — well, that's one thing. It might be worth giving family life a try. But if it means more of the same as before, I'd just as soon he stay in jail and rot.

CHAPTER FIFTY-SEVEN

The day the letter came from the state should have been a joyous occasion for Gladys and a time of wonder for Celia and Chester — a family reunited. But they each responded differently, and I realized that they'd each weathered a different storm with their husband and father. Not one of the little family felt strong, and every one conflicted.

In all the time they'd lived at Garden's Gate, none of them had spoken longingly of him except Gladys. She longed for the man she once knew — the man she'd married, the man who'd fathered her children — not the man who'd broken them all through drink and shame and incarceration. And yet I saw her struggling to accept the inevitable, to make the most of it for the sake of their children. I watched in awe of her.

"After all," Gladys said to me over tea one night after the children were tucked into bed, "he is their father — the only one they've got. He paid a dear price for our protection.

I know he did. That's got to count for something, doesn't it?"

How can I answer that? How can I know? I've never met the man, but based on the likes of Rhoan and Troy Wishon, and the drinking habits of Joe Earl, what I see is that moonshine leads to ruin — for good men, if Fillmore Percy is one, and bad. It's like rain falling on the just and the unjust. They might all benefit, but they all get wet. "You know you're welcome to stay as long as you wish, Gladys. Forever, if that's what you want."

She looked at me, a mixture of sadness and relief and resignation. "I appreciate that. More than you'll ever know. You've been real good to me, Lilliana — you and Miz Hyacinth. I could never ask for or imagine better friends."

I sighed. "You've been that friend to me, Gladys. I hope I can stay here — forever. As long as I have a home at Garden's Gate, you and the children do, too." But I wondered. *What is Fillmore Percy like? Who is he, really — when not mixed up with moonshine and such? Could he live here with us? Might he turn mean like Gerald? It might be good to have a man in the house, in case Gerald returns — in case the Klan returns.* "Even if you don't ultimately stay, you don't have to go right away, you know. You can bring Fillmore here for a time, let him acclimate, get used to things."

"You mean get a job."

"Well, that, too, at least until they call him up. I suppose he's young enough that will happen."

Gladys shook her head. "Fillmore will hate that I've told anyone, but he'll not enlist and he won't be drafted. He's got bad eyes and flatfeet to boot." She sighed. "I'm ashamed to say I once thought that military pay would come in handy, but he'd never pass the physical. So, a job . . . I don't where or how he'll do that. Who has work here, and even if they did, who would offer it to an ex-convict?" Worry lines furrowed her forehead. "He'd have to go away someplace nobody'd know him . . . but so soon after coming home. I just don't know. I'd be beholden if you'd let me work on here — cooking, cleaning."

"Of course. Only you're not beholden — I am. I don't know how I'd get on without you, Gladys, and I'll be so entirely lonesome when you go. What will I do, rattling around alone in this big house?"

"I don't like the idea of you living here all alone, especially not with Rhoan Wishon angry and on the loose. Not with that husband of yours out there."

"Neither do I. It would be a great gift to me if you and Fillmore felt up to staying, at least for a while. I know you'll want to be in your own home, and he may not wish to live here —"

"Fillmore's a proud man, but he's been humbled, so I can't say. He needs a job — for the money — but also to show him that he can do something besides running 'shine."

"Stay, at least while you all settle in. We can't take away Olney's work — Aunt Hyacinth would turn over in her grave. But there are things he could do to help here, things that might make him feel staying on is a fair trade. The barn hasn't seen a coat of paint in years. Aunt Hyacinth's trust provides for those improvements. And who knows? Maybe things with Rhoan will settle down by then, too."

"Don't fool yourself. Ruby Lynne's going to have that baby, and nothing will ever be the same."

"But when she has it and he sees that it can't possibly be Marshall's —"

"You can't count on that. You can't be sure, even if the baby's white as the driven snow."

"I know Marshall, and I know Ruby Lynne. I lay my bets on Rhoan Wishon."

Gladys was quiet.

"You can't believe Marshall beat and raped her. It's not in his nature." I knew the nature of such men and Marshall didn't fit that bill.

"No, I don't. At least I don't want to. I hardly know what to think. But I don't believe Rhoan, as bad as he is, would do that

446

to his own daughter."

"Not even when he's drunk?"

"When Ruby Lynne came to us this last time, he'd been out of town for days, remember?"

I did remember, and that made no sense — not unless Ruby Lynne waited long after he left to come for help. But that didn't seem likely. As much as I hated to admit it, Gladys was right. It didn't add up.

CHAPTER FIFTY-EIGHT

"Mama's going to be fit to be tied when she gets back," Pearl Mae lamented over the general store ledger and her inventory list.

Celia hummed louder as she dusted twice over the picture frames Pearl had set in the front window, containing photos of every No Creek man already in uniform and names of those who'd just enlisted. Every mother or sweetheart in No Creek was proud to donate pictures so all could see.

Celia kept on as if Pearl's worrying aloud over such details had nothing to do with her. Despite her humming, Celia feared it had everything to do with the food and blanket she'd "borrowed" for Clay and Charlene.

"I just don't understand it," Pearl mumbled. "Mama did inventory just before she left and —"

"How is Ida Mae? Has the baby come yet?" Celia knew to keep on the good side of Pearl. Her job at the store was all that stood between the couple in the shed and starvation.

"Not as of last night. Mama called long-distance when Ophelia was on the switch-board. We have a code. Mama asks for the call to be directed to Ida Mae. That way I know to reject the call. Soon as the baby comes, she'll call for Ida Mae and when I reject the call, I'll hear her tell the operator, 'Oh, I'd hoped to tell her that my niece birthed a baby boy — or girl.' Saves a bundle in toll charges."

Celia stopped sweeping and leaned on her broom. "Isn't that cheating? Like stealing money from the telephone company?"

"All depends on how you look at, I guess. Mama says they can afford it and our code serves the greater good."

Celia went back to her sweeping. She didn't know about long-distance calls or how their code served the greater good, but that's how she felt about "borrowing" food and such to keep the McHones in body and soul. *Ida Mae can afford to give up a little food and a blanket or two to keep the McHones from starving and freezing, and hopefully, one day soon, they'll bring a baby into the world. Babies are worth everything. Folks will surely see that, especially during this season of Christmas, what with the birth of the baby Jesus just around the corner, and charity and goodwill on folks' minds. What if that old innkeeper hadn't given Mary and*

Joseph a spot in the stable? Where'd we be then?

Celia thought happily of the baby belonging to Janice's aunt and how exciting and wonderful it would be to have a real live newborn in the manger at church. *Everybody'll be surprised at that! Wonder if the McHone baby will be born by then?* She stopped sweeping. *If it is, I sure hope they'll be able to keep the baby quiet during the play.*

"I guess I'll have to report it to the sheriff." Pearl had been mumbling on while Celia mused, so Celia had missed a good part of those mumblings. But now she perked her ears.

"Say what?"

"Guess I'll have to call Sheriff Wilkins. I hate to do it, make a fuss and bring the law out here so close to Christmas, but somebody's getting in somehow. You haven't seen anybody suspicious lurking around here after hours, have you?"

"Nobody at all." Celia felt her armpits sweat.

"I had that Marshall, Olney Tate's nephew, lined up to do a little work out back for me the other day . . . unloading crates and such."

"Marshall'd never steal."

Pearl shrugged. "Somebody is. He unloaded that truck and was gone directly, before I could pay him — before I even saw him. I

450

was working on the front window. Wonder if he just took his pay in store goods. Mighty fresh if he did."

Celia waited, her chest tight. Did Pearl consider that fair? Celia and Clay could make her borrowing right later, but she couldn't let Marshall be blamed for what she'd done, not if Pearl meant to call the sheriff. For all Celia knew, Clay might have come and unloaded the crates thinking he was giving back somehow. She had mentioned the job to him in passing but told him not to take on chores nobody knew about. He'd said that helping out was only right and he couldn't take charity without showing he was willing to work, if only folks would let him. "Marshall wouldn't do that."

"Not twice he won't. Not if those night riders get ahold of him."

"You mean the Klan? What have they got to do with anything?"

Pearl shrugged again. Celia hated that shrug. "All it takes is a word from Mama. Mama says sometimes it's better to let nature run its course than to bring in all the formalities. Just delays and muddies things, you know."

Celia hadn't known — hadn't even suspected that Ida Mae or her husband, Ray, might be members of the Klan, although everybody knew it only cost ten dollars to join. "I'm sure Marshall didn't take anything.

I was here that day you were working on the window. Remember? I saw him leave and he didn't have a thing — just the clothes on his back." That Celia had seen him was a lie, but she was sure he wouldn't take a thing.

"You can fit a mighty lot underneath a coat." Pearl raised her eyebrows significantly. "Just sayin'."

Details from the bombing at Pearl Harbor broadcast over the radio all that first week. Jesse kept busy calming fears — rational and irrational — and praying with those in need.

The *Journal-Patriot* reported that several county men were stationed at the scenes of Japan's attacks in the Pacific. Nobody from No Creek had been stationed at Pearl Harbor or any of the other bombed sites, but Joe Earl had a second cousin whose brother-in-law was on the *Arizona* — now trapped in a watery grave beneath the harbor in that sunken ship. The very idea made Jesse sweat bullets.

Joe Earl took to drink to steady his nerves racked in grief over his second cousin's brother-in-law, whom he never knew or even heard of until that week. But it didn't take much to set Joe off on a binge, and beyond that he was terrified and certain he'd be drafted and sent to fight the Japanese, whose language he couldn't make head nor tail of. "How will I know what they want? How will

I know how to reason with 'em?" Joe was brought to tears all over again and reached for his liquid comfort.

Jesse whisked the bottle out of his hand. "That's not going to help you or the nation, Joe. You've got to get hold of yourself. You're digging your grave with every guzzle."

"That's a harsh thing to say, Reverend, to a man in the throes of grief."

Jesse didn't think it wise to point out that Joe didn't even know the name of the deceased. "You've got to take hold, Joe, so we can all pull together. We may each be called to serve in this war. There's no shirking duty when it calls."

"I don't own a telephone. I don't expect nobody to call me. I don't want nobody to call me."

"That's not how they do it."

"How, then?"

"They'll send you a letter."

"I'll tell Ida Mae I want my box closed soon as she gets back in town. Oh, I wish she'd hurry up. How long does it take for babies to get born, anyhow?"

Jesse knew from experience that it wasn't worth answering every one of Joe's questions when he was drunk. They came in rapid-fire succession and then repeated, like a stuck Victrola recording. The best practice was to walk Joe around the perimeter of his house and up and down his lane in the cold, fresh

453

air, then bring him in for steaming cups of coffee. By the time he'd repeated that three times, Joe was relatively sober — as sober as he ever was — with a powerful headache.

Tedious though this practice was, Jesse often learned things about his flock during Joe's drunken bouts that he would not have otherwise heard.

"You know I like Olney Tate, don't you, Preacher? I never done him no harm nor talked against him like some. And he never bothered me — no, he didn't. He's a good man. Was always good to Miz Hyacinth and I thought the world of her."

"I appreciate that about you, Joe. You're a fair man, by and large."

"Yes, sir. I mean to be. But poor old Olney's in for it, what with the night riders, don't you know?"

Jesse's heart constricted. "What have you heard?"

That set Joe on his guard. "Oh, I don't know that I've heard nothing about Olney. But I might have heard something shady about that nephew of his — that Marshall fella." He shook his head as Jesse kept him from stumbling down the plank step outside his house.

"Marshall's a good worker, an honest young man. There should be no talk against him."

"Well, I'm not saying there is, and I'm not

saying there ain't. All I know is that Ruby Lynne Wishon is knocked up and Ida Mae seen Marshall sniffin' round her house. And Ida Mae's daughter Pearl — you know Pearl?"

"Yes, I know Pearl." Jesse's dander was rising. Ida Mae's gossiping tongue was running loose and wild once again and she wasn't even here. He couldn't count the number of fires he'd been forced to douse over the years from that undisciplined organ.

"Well, Pearl told me things have been disappearing from the store while Ida Mae's been gone, and the only one she rightly suspects had motive and opportunity is Marshall. Now, ain't that some piece of news, Preacher?"

It was news to Jesse. He was sick about Ruby Lynne's pregnancy, and he could imagine any number of people in these times stealing a thing or two from Ida Mae's store, but he couldn't imagine Marshall being responsible for either.

"Preacher? Did you hear me?"

"Yes, Joe, I heard you. But I can vouch for Marshall's character. He wouldn't have done those things."

"Don't much matter. He's colored."

"Of course it matters! How can you say such a thing? That kind of gossip can get a body killed and you know it, Joe."

"It weren't me that said it, Reverend Willard, honest. It was Troy Wishon. Said he figured Marshall's guilt is good as gospel. Who else'd it be, sniffin' after Ruby Lynne after she took a shine to him, teachin' him to read and such? And he was over to the store helpin' Pearl with some work just before she discovered goods gone. Must have been a whole lot for her to notice. Fool boy."

Jesse felt like punching Joe Earl. "You're jumping to conclusions. You're all jumping to unfounded conclusions!"

"Not me, Reverend. But folks is stirred up. Even Gladys Percy said one of her Thanksgiving pies went missing. You remember? How do you reckon that? That Marshall must be stealing just to steal — that's how they do, you know. His aunt Mercy would've cooked up a dinner just as good. He's not gone hungry. Now I reckon he'll go hungry and more. They'll see to it."

"Who'll see to it?" But Jesse knew.

"The night riders," Joe whispered as Jesse walked the man to his chair, then closed his eyes to pray.

Jesse determined to put a quick end to such talk. He'd no sooner gotten Joe settled than he made time double-quick up the road to Rhoan Wishon's house.

Rhoan usually attended services on Sundays when he was in town, but Jesse didn't consider him a regular and he'd missed last

Sunday. Rhoan's business, whatever it was, took him west to Asheville and east to Winston-Salem on a regular basis.

Jesse had a pretty good idea of what kept Rhoan in the money — more money than anybody in town except the estate of Miz Hyacinth — and Rhoan's wasn't an industry he'd approve. But it was the industry that more men in the county depended on than not. Rhoan also, Jesse was fairly certain, ran the enterprise that had led to Fillmore Percy's incarceration and the threat his family lived under.

Rhoan was just slamming the trunk of his oversize car when Jesse entered the drive.

"Rhoan! Good morning to you." Jesse intended to keep the conversation positive as long as he could.

"More like afternoon, Reverend."

"That it is."

"What brings you out this way?" Rhoan hefted his chin and the belt at his waist, and Jesse wondered how a man who drank as much hooch as Rhoan was reported to down kept so trim.

"I'm worried about something, Rhoan, and hoping you can help me."

Rhoan's face softened, the guarded heft to his chin relaxing. "Do what I can."

"Yes, I know you will." Jesse wished the man would offer him a seat in the house and a cup of coffee to ease into the conversation, but that wasn't Rhoan's way. "I've heard talk that Troy is accusing Marshall of —"

"Of raping my girl. I told you. Knocked her up, Reverend. I didn't want that word to get out, but you can't keep something like that hid here."

"No, you can't keep a baby hidden, but I don't believe Marshall is responsible. Has Ruby Lynne accused him?"

"She don't say who, but she don't deny it. That's good enough for me. There's nothing you need concern yourself with here, Reverend. It's a matter will be taken care of."

"That's exactly what I am concerned about, Rhoan. Sentencing a man without proof or trial and taking the law into your own hands — or what the night riders consider the law."

Rhoan's jaw hardened. It wasn't common to speak in broad daylight of the "night riders." Talking of the Klan in hushed and respected — or feared — tones was enough.

"I know you're concerned for Ruby Lynne. Any father would feel protective of his daughter and angry that someone had taken indecent and violent advantage of her. I don't blame you in the least. I'm concerned for Ruby Lynne's sake — for her health and well-being and that of her baby. I missed seeing her in church on Sunday. I hope she'll come back, know that she's welcome and no one at church is going to feel any differently toward her." Jesse said the words, but he knew they

458

weren't entirely true. No Creek was no different from anywhere else in its desire to gossip and finger point, especially if it meant bringing a wealthier citizen or his family down to size.

"You believe that, Reverend?"

"It's what ought to be. I'll do all in my power to make certain it happens. Just as a man should not be accused without proof — just because his skin's a different color. I'll do all in my power to protect and stand for him, too. Marshall's a fine young man, and you and your family have known Olney Tate all your life. There's not a better man around. You're barking up the wrong tree." Reverend Willard hoped Rhoan felt some level of shame for what his father had done to Olney's father.

Rhoan removed his cap and kneaded the back of his neck with strong fingers. "Ida Mae saw the boy round here. She told me."

Jesse nearly swore.

"Who else could it be? You tell me that."

Jesse could hardly believe Rhoan asked that question. Wasn't it likely Rhoan himself — forgetful and mean as he could be when drunk?

"It wasn't me, if you're wonderin' that. I don't remember all I do when I been in the drink, but I swear I'd never do that."

"I'm not accusing you, Rhoan, though there

are some who might. You need to think on that."

"I won't. I say it's that Marshall. He's not from around here. You can't be sure about him."

"If it was Marshall, the baby's color will be an indicator. You know that."

Rhoan straightened but paused, considered. "Reckon so."

"If that baby's white, you need to look elsewhere. You need to wait before making such an accusation, and you need to get Troy to stop stirring up trouble."

"Ha! I ain't controlled Troy since he was nine years old."

"You have influence over him. Accusing the wrong man will make it worse for everyone, including Ruby Lynne . . . and it could turn deadly. I count you an honorable man, Rhoan, and trust you to do the right thing by your daughter."

Rhoan turned away so that Jesse could not see his face. After a few moments he said, "I swear, Reverend, sometimes it's hard to know what that is."

Jesse pressed his hand onto Rhoan's shoulder. "For all of us."

Rhoan swiped his arm across his eyes. Jesse wondered, with mild surprise, if Rhoan Wishon had ever shed a tear. If he was shedding one for his daughter now, that was a good and hopeful sign.

CHAPTER FIFTY-NINE

News of the mounting death toll from the attacks in the Pacific and determination to help the county raise $4,000 for the Red Cross created a fervor in the No Creek General Store and Post Office like it hadn't seen in years. The *Journal-Patriot* called for every American to contribute.

Celia listened to the store radio and to folks coming and going as she swept each afternoon, gaining little by little an understanding of where each family stood in terms of what their contribution to the war effort might be.

News of enlistments — in droves across the state — came by newspaper and radio. Mixtures of war excitement and fury at the Japanese and Germans and Italians lit the faces of every male casting their bravado across the store planks, all the while mothers and sweethearts pasted smiles beneath red-rimmed eyes and worry-wrinkled brows. Mixtures of fear and pride for their sons and husbands and sweethearts fueled talk of "sacrifices that must be made for our boys."

To enlist now or wait for the draft was the debate in every household, some of them heated to the point of not speaking. Everybody Celia heard talk stood in favor of whupping Germany and Japan, but there was more to going off to war for family men. Each penny was counted twice, a whispered knowing among women in the community that a man going off to war couldn't be counted on to spring plant or bring in the crop or pay the mortgage, no matter how noble his intentions or how he vowed to send home every penny he made. All the talk sparked memories and reminiscences of the last war — the Great War, the war meant to end all wars — and what that had meant for the women and children left at home.

The women of No Creek had lived with the specter of moonshine too long. Some feared what their men, far from home, might do with regular paychecks. When their families were out of sight, would they be out of mind, too?

"I never thought when President Roosevelt signed that Selective Training and Service Act last year that it would mean much — all our men and boys made to register for a draft." Pearl Mae shook her head. "Who could take war here seriously? I surely didn't — not till Pearl Harbor. Now it's not about Europe so far away — it's about us — every body and soul right here in the county."

"It's all people talk about. It's nearly Christmas, but seems like everybody's forgot this year," Celia lamented.

"Well, that's something I wish they wouldn't forget. Between the pilfering and people so afraid to spend a dime for not knowing what'll happen next, sales have dropped off. Mama's not going to like this. No, she'll not like it one bit."

Celia knew her pilfering had best stop. Nothing had happened yet, but she worried sick over what might happen to Marshall if Pearl called in the Klan, even though they had no proof he was the thief. All the while she feared for the McHones, especially Charlene. She wondered if Clay might be drafted, and if he was, what would happen to Charlene and their baby? She also knew that Pearl Harbor and the draft were not the only things pressing the heart of one No Creek citizen — Doc Vishy.

Celia watched as Doc Vishy's fingers fairly trembled when he withdrew the rolled-up newspaper and a scuffed-up envelope that looked like it'd traveled round the world and back from his post office box that afternoon. For all the years he'd lived in No Creek, Doc Vishy had written to folks in foreign countries and they'd written him back, but it had been a long while since he'd received a letter. He ordered his newspaper straight from New

York City, where he used to live, no matter that it arrived days late.

If Celia wanted to know anything of the world beyond Asheville or what the radio told her, she asked Doc Vishy. Whenever he picked up his mail and paper, Celia made it a point to sweep the porch outside the store, hoping to catch a few words with her friend. This time, he stood on the porch beside her and tore the letter open straightaway. His breath caught and his eyes filled.

"Ghettos for Jews," he whispered, pushing his fedora farther back on his head. "They're all over Poland. Concentration camps in Germany take in more Jews and political prisoners every day. Pogroms crossing border after border. This madman, this Hitler, won't rest until he's eliminated every Jew from Europe. Then he'll tackle the world. What is an ocean to him?" He didn't seem to realize he'd not said goodbye, not ruffled Celia's hair in greeting or parting as he'd done since they'd first become fast friends.

Celia watched him limp down the post office steps and up the hill toward his house. He looked older, more tired than she'd seen him since he'd moved to No Creek. For two years, ever since he'd saved Chester's life, his steps had lightened through helping to relieve the suffering of locals, glad of their acceptance. Even if sometimes they begrudged the "foreigner" and "that Jew man," they

464

called for him when someone was sick beyond home remedies or in case of a bad accident. But lately, what with news of the war and the Klan all stirred up, it was as if the clock had been turned back on Doc Vishy — closer to the suspicion he'd endured when he'd first come to No Creek. Folks appeared more standoffish, less eager to have him treat them.

Celia didn't know what ghettos were, or concentration camps, but she knew from the doc himself about the pogroms that had killed his wife and children in Europe years before he'd come to No Creek. He'd told her that he'd not been able to do a thing to save them, and that had grieved him to the point of despair and refusal to use his gifts and knowledge of healing until the night Chester's life hung in the balance.

Now she knew he worried for longtime friends and distant relatives in Europe that he'd mentioned from time to time.

As terrified as he was for Jewish friends abroad, Celia's fear for her friend crept closer to home as anti-Jewish sentiment raised its ugly head and crept through the hills around them — all the while local KKK members sharpened their talons against coloreds and Catholics — folks said they were mostly Italian anyway, weren't they? — and Jews.

Doc Vishy dared not share his worries in the general store, but Celia knew he would spread the New York newspaper across his table the moment he returned home and devour every word, finding more information than columns of the local *Patriot* provided.

Celia had nearly finished sweeping the porch when Troy Wishon sauntered up the steps, ignoring her. She followed the door's bell jingle into the store.

"What can I do for you, Troy?" Pearl smiled, her eyes bright as Christmas tree bulbs. Celia knew Pearl nurtured a yearning for Troy, no matter that he was five years younger and never cast glances at any one of the Mae girls.

"Need me a length of rope."

"Rope? Got some in the back. Want to help me get it?" She smiled all the brighter. "Those coils are mighty heavy."

"Don't reckon I'll need a full length for this job. Twenty, thirty feet'll do. Just cut me off a piece. I'll wait right here, take advantage of your nice warm stove."

The light left Pearl's eyes. She lifted her chin as if the likes of Troy Wishon never mattered a whit and walked briskly to the back storeroom. Celia swept dust from the corners into the far aisle.

Pearl returned with the rope wound and bound into one tight coil. "Don't know what you can do with that. Rhoan always buys the full length."

"Don't need so much for a tree."

"A tree?" Pearl frowned. "You got a

466

lightning-struck tree you're tying up?"

Troy laughed. "That's a good one. Got some fellas comin' over from the next county. We'll be stringing something up, all right, but a tree's not what we got in mind." He winked and plunked his money down, then snickered his way out of the store.

Pearl's eyes went wide. Celia swallowed, forgetting her pile of dirt.

"You best go on home now, Celia. It'll be dark soon and your mama'll be worried."

"I'm not done."

"Done enough. I'm afraid there might be trouble."

"What did Troy mean — what's he gonna string up, and what fellas?"

"I don't know a thing, and neither do you, but I don't like the sounds of it. You go on home now. I'm closing up early. I don't want any part of whatever's comin' down the pike."

"Should we call Sheriff Wilkins?"

"He'll be knee-deep in it for all I guess." Pearl crossed the floor in three long strides and grabbed the broom from Celia. "Tell your mama to lock the doors and windows. Go on now. Don't make me swat you out the door with this."

Dusk had gathered by the time Celia, breathless from running, swung open the back door at Garden's Gate. Miss Lill was bent over the kitchen table, spreading something across it.

Celia's mother stood with her palm on her cheek. "I swan. The whole town wondered what became of that. Old Mr. Belvidere vowed somebody stole it. Wherever did you find it?"

Celia crept in between the two. She dropped her schoolbooks to the floor as her heart slammed against her chest. Spread across the kitchen table was a white robe and hood — full Klan regalia.

"Celia, you're home." Miss Lill looked like she'd been caught at something, but she turned back to Celia's mother, her face flushed and eyes uncertain. "I have an idea, but before I say more, I need to ask you something. I found this in Aunt Hyacinth's chest — the one at the foot of her bed. There was a false bottom. I figured she'd hidden it. Do you have any idea why she'd have such a thing? Did she have any connection?"

"Miz Hyacinth?" Celia's mama looked as if she might fall over dead right there. "Of course not! She hated the Klan."

"That's what I thought — she said as much. Then how — ? Why — ?"

"Her daddy was the headman in the Klan around here — for years and years. They held meetings right there in the front parlor, where you let colored children in today. That legacy with the Klan's the only thing gave Miz Hyacinth any grace after you and my Celia invited the Saints Delight Church folks into the house. Don't you know that?"

"I don't know anything. How could I?"

Celia's mother sighed. "Sometimes I forget you weren't born and raised here, Lilliana. I'm sorry. Miz Hyacinth hated the Klan and everything they did. That's why she changed the name of this house to Garden's Gate soon as her daddy died. It used to be Belvidere Hall. She hoped to erase the past. I guess you never can, not entirely.

"My, my. This robe disappeared the night they set to lynch Olney Tate's daddy. Rhoan's daddy had old Mr. Belvidere so stirred up he was going to lead the lynching. They were thick as thieves in those days. Mama was up here cooking dinner for the family at the time. She said Miz Hyacinth begged her daddy not to have any part of it — to stop it, that the Tates were good folks. But he wouldn't listen. And yet, when the time came to dress, nobody could find his Klan robe or his gun. They all — Mama said even Miz Hyacinth — tore this house up one side and down the other. Never found either. Now you've gone and found both."

"Did he go? Did he take part?"

Celia's mama shook her head. "Took that missing robe and gun as a sign from God that maybe he wasn't to go — least Miz Hyacinth convinced him of that. But he was terrified the Klan would think he was a coward and had no idea what that might bring. That night the old man suffered a final stroke. Never spoke another word, though Mama said his eyes said plenty. Miz Hyacinth nursed him till the day he died."

"Aunt Hyacinth must have been the one to hide them — that gun in the box Celia found . . ."

"She must have. To keep him from going, from doing the wicked. Imagine that. And now, after all these years . . ." Gladys's voice held the wonder Celia felt. "She couldn't have been much more than your age. What a strong, brave woman."

"Braver than I've been."

"What you gonna do with it?" Celia asked, too fearful to touch the robe, too curious to resist.

"I was thinking," Miss Lill said, "that it should serve a good purpose."

"A Klan robe? What good purpose could that ugly thing serve? More likely burn it." Celia's mother huffed but still fingered the cloth.

"What about . . . ?" Celia whispered but couldn't bring herself to say it.

"Do you think the angel of the Lord could redeem this wicked garment?" Miss Lill smiled at Celia.

Celia grinned. "I reckon the angel of the Lord could do about anything."

"The thing's twelve sizes too big for her!" Gladys protested, slipping her hands over

470

Celia's shoulders. "I won't have my daughter parading through No Creek in a Klan robe!"

"It's all that you say, that you see, now. But we could cut it down. I'm handy with a pattern and a needle and thread. Do you think anybody'd recognize it for what it is? We could make the skirt full and even cut some wings."

"It's a great idea!" Celia couldn't believe such good fortune. "Pearl said that if I really came up with a costume, she'd donate some tulle for wings. Wouldn't that look grand?"

"I don't know. The idea of traipsing up and down the aisle of the church in Klan regalia, even if it doesn't look like it . . ." Her mama worried the tea towel at her waist. "I'm not superstitious, not more than the next person, but it just doesn't seem right."

"Nobody'll ever know, Mama. Like Miss Lill says, it'll redeem this filthy garment for a good purpose . . . kind of like the Lord washes us, don't you think?"

Celia's mama looked from one to the other of the woman and woman-child before her. Celia knew she was taking their measure, judging how steep the stack of votes against her was. Finally her mother dropped her hands to her sides. "All right. All right. But neither of you are to ever tell a living soul about this, do you hear me? If they catch word that we cut up the Klan robe of old Mr. Belvidere, we'll all be swinging from the rafters. Do you understand, Celia Percy? Not a word to a living, breathing soul — ever!"

"Yes, ma'am." Celia bit her lip. Now was not the time she wanted to bring up Troy Wishon and his rope or his sniggering or Pearl Mae's fears. But waiting smacked of too little too late. "There's something I need to tell you."

CHAPTER SIXTY

Celia's story from the store gripped each of us to our toes. After my experience with the Klan, I dared not take Troy's words or Pearl's worries lightly. The fact that he did not acknowledge Celia's presence but spoke in front of her and that Pearl thought it important to send Celia directly home gave me a turn worse than any since that awful night.

"We can't be sure that's what he's got in mind," Gladys cautioned. "You know what a sensationalist Pearl is. She'd see ghosts in her own shadow."

"Be that as it may, I think we'd best all stay inside tonight and bolt the doors and windows, like Pearl said. I'll take the front rooms. Celia, take the upstairs, and, Gladys, the back door, please."

"Where's Chester?" Celia's voice wobbled.

"Upstairs, doing his homework, where you should be." Her mother sent her off with a gentle swat on the behind.

Once Celia was out of the room, I whispered to Gladys, "Those Wishons terrify me, especially Ruby Lynne's father."

"He's arrogant and gets crazy drunk sometimes, I'll grant you. But Troy worries me more."

"He's never given me trouble, not like his older brother."

Gladys raised her eyebrows. "None that you know of. You don't know who was behind that hood in the window . . . so you said."

"I didn't — I don't. I thought it might have been Ruby Lynne's father, but he was evidently in Asheville at the time."

"Evidently," Gladys snorted.

"And he's not too happy with you, Miss Lill." Celia offered little comfort, standing in the kitchen doorway. "I think — I think maybe we ought to warn Olney — and Marshall — just in case."

"I thought I told you to get upstairs, young lady!" Gladys dug both fists into her hips.

"She's right, Gladys. They burned crosses in the yards of the Saints Delight members already. We should get word to them."

Gladys threw her hands up. "How? Not one of them owns a telephone, and no one is stepping outside this door tonight." She turned back to Celia. "Did you do as you were told?"

"I locked the windows like Miss Lill said. But I don't want to be up there alone, even with Chester. There's safety in numbers, remember, Mama?"

Gladys relaxed her arms. "Come here, darlin'. Safety in numbers. That's right. I think we'd best keep the outside lights burning tonight."

"I've never heard of them hanging a white woman," Celia considered in the hours after supper. "I don't reckon they'd do it."

"You don't know what they'd do," Chester affirmed, "so you best stand clear. We best all stand clear."

"Wiser words were never spoken." Gladys stood and stacked the plates. "I want you children to get upstairs and get ready for bed. It's past time. We're scaring ourselves silly and there's no need."

"Don't you think we'd best stay dressed, Mama, in case we have to run out of the house real quick?"

I looked up at Gladys. How real did she think this scare was? I could guess from the false bravado in the lift of her chin.

"I think we've had enough of this foolish talk. The two of you get upstairs now. I'll come say prayers with you once I get the table laid for breakfast. May as well keep the inside lights off." Gladys said that last as if it were an afterthought of no account, but I knew better. Lights on outside, lights off inside. We'd be better able to see anyone approach before they saw us.

Chester appeared in the doorway with a

baseball bat nearly as big as he. "Don't worry, Mama. I won't let anybody come near you or Miss Lill. I'll sleep with this beside me."

My heart slipped at such gallantry and Gladys turned away, barely keeping her chin from quivering. "Thank you, Chester."

Once the children climbed the stairs, I placed a hand on my friend's back. "I'm so sorry, Gladys. I've brought this on all of you with my helping Marshall and then Ruby Lynne."

Gladys shook her head, swiping at tears with her apron's hem. "No more than Celia did, no more than my husband did by getting himself mixed up with no-goods and going off to jail. You and Celia and Miz Hyacinth did the right thing. I'm just so scared."

By the time prayers with the children were said, the dishes done, and all the lights turned out, it was nearly nine thirty. Gladys's door closed. I stood alone in the darkened kitchen, my forehead pressed against the cabinet. Not since Aunt Hyacinth died had I felt so weary, so frightened or hopeless. *Please, God, show us the way forward — for us, for Ruby Lynne, for Marshall, and all here.*

I kept praying as I climbed the stairs. I prayed that Celia and Chester slept, that they'd sleep through the night, dreaming uneventful dreams, and that nothing would harm them or Gladys. I prayed for Fillmore's return home, that it would be a joyful homecoming for their family and the start of something good. I prayed that my past would stay past, and I prayed for peace in my heart, my soul.

"Fire!" Chester called from the top of the stairs, his baseball bat silhouetted by the moon and a light brighter still streaming through the hallway window. "The barn's on fire!"

Aunt Hyacinth's barn! I raced down the stairs, stumbling through the dark kitchen, and out the back door. Lurid flames leapt twenty, thirty feet into the blackened sky. "Fire! Fire!" I screamed as I might do in the city, expecting someone to telephone the fire department, expecting people to run out of their houses to help. But no one came.

Night riders in flowing white robes and hoods with cut eyeholes strode from the back of the barn. Horses neighed, some rearing back on hind legs, as frightened by the shouting and flames as I. Gradually, no matter where I stumbled, the riders stalked closer, surrounding me. Their pointed hoods, garish and demonic against the flames, made them loom ten feet tall. Two on foot bearing torches came closer.

"Stop! Stop!" But I knew my screaming was in vain. The kitchen door opened and I saw three figures emerge from the dark. "Go back inside!" I cried. "Please," I begged the approaching giants, "don't hurt them."

Not a man answered me, but one grabbed my arms and wrenched them behind my back, roughly binding my wrists. Another wrapped a gag around my mouth, nearly choking me. If God meant to punish me for my sins, then this was it. I knew they meant to hang me. I saw the rope looped over the saddle horn of one of the riders. *God, save Gladys and the children! Save them, Father! I'm sorry for what and who I am, but save them!*

"Get the other one!" That and Gladys's screams were the only voices I heard before a smack to the back of my head knocked me senseless.

CHAPTER SIXTY-ONE

Celia pulled Chester through the shadows, around the house, and to the edge of the road.

"We can't leave Mama! We can't leave her!" Chester cried. "Let me go. I'll beat 'em off!"

"We can't stop them by ourselves, Chester. We got to get help. You go for the preacher. Tell him to bring anybody he can trust. I'll go for Doc Vishy. Now, run — fast as you can — and if you hear horses behind you, dive into the ditch. Keep your face down. Don't let them see you."

Chester's face looked as bloodless and frightened as Celia felt. The trembling in his body mirrored her own. Sending him to Reverend Willard was best. He was closest, and Chester would be safe there. Reverend Willard would know what to do, who to call, and he had a telephone. Whatever else happened, their mama and Miss Lill would need Doc Vishy, and Celia knew every shortcut through the woods and town, places even horses and riders couldn't go.

She hated leaving her mama but made certain Chester was on his way before slipping around the back of the barn to head through the woods. Quiet as she was, a pine branch snapped and a horse and rider emerged from the woods, not ten feet from her. Celia crouched backward, her face down and pale hands tucked inside her armpits, hoping to merge with the surrounding dark brush and leaves.

"That barn's tinder. Leave it. We got one more stop to make, boys." The rider patted the rope slung over his saddle horn. The responding laughter of the men made Celia sick.

Marshall. There was no way she could outrun horses to reach the Tates and warn them, and she had to save her mama and Miss Lill first. *Doc Vishy.* He could phone Reverend Willard and — and do what? Who in No Creek wasn't part of the Klan? She didn't know, but maybe they did. She tore through the woods, no longer mindful of the noise she made.

The roaring of the fire behind her and the raucous laughter of the men drowned out every other noise. She could no longer hear her mama's screams, hadn't been able to see her or Miss Lill since her mama had forced Chester and her around the side of the house. *Please, God. Let them be all right. Let there be somebody — anybody — to help. Don't let them hurt Mama or Miss Lill. Don't let them do to them what somebody did to Ruby Lynne. Give me feet like the wind. Make Doc Vishy brave. Make Reverend Willard brave. Stop those men in their tracks. Please, God! Please!*

Celia pounded on Doc Vishy's door, the life of her mother depending on it. "Doc Vishy! Doc Vishy! Help! Help me!" Heart in her throat, Celia's words came without the strength she'd intended. But the door opened just the same and she fell into her friend's arms. "They've got Mama and Miss Lill! I don't know what they're doing to them, but please — please come!"

"Who has them?" But he didn't wait for an answer. "Did you call the sheriff?" Doc Vishy was pulling on boots and stuffing his night-shirt into his pants.

"Night riders — Klan — they're burning the barn and got hold of Miss Lill. Mama rushed to save her, but she sent me and Chester away. Pearl Mae thinks the sheriff is one of them. Chester's gone for Reverend Willard."

"Good. He'll know what to do." Doc Vishy pulled his coat and hat from the hook beside the door and grabbed his medical bag. "My car. We'll take my car."

Celia fell into the front seat as Doc Vishy gunned his motor and it roared to life. Celia had not ridden in many cars and she gasped as he sped through the inky night, round twists and turns on back roads to Garden's Gate.

By the time they reached the church, flames climbed above the trees beyond the cemetery. Celia saw Doc Vishy's knuckles clutch the steering wheel in a death grip, his entire body straining forward as if urging the car faster uphill. The house came into view — still standing, not burning, at least not where they could see.

Doc Vishy plowed into the yard, unmindful of the picket fence or the garden, and shone his headlights on the house. Reverend Willard was bent over someone on the porch. Celia could only see a woman's legs sticking out. She couldn't tell if it was her mama or Miss Lill, but she threw open the car door before Doc Vishy had screeched to a stop and rushed up the steps. "Mama!"

It was Miss Lill on the porch floor. She didn't move and Celia couldn't bear to think what that meant. "Where's Mama? Mama! Where are you?" she cried, the tears she'd held in so long now streaming down her face.

"Your mother's all right, Celia. She's okay." Reverend Willard embraced her but turned right away back to Miss Lill.

"Mama's inside, getting some cold water for Miss Lill's head." Chester spoke from the shadows. Celia hadn't seen him before, but now she grabbed him in a bear hug and the two clung fast.

"There's folks on their way to help, but the barn's gone. We've got to contain it, keep the house from catching fire. That's the main thing now." Reverend Willard looked up at Celia as Doc Vishy pushed past her, kneeling beside Miss Lill.

"Is Miss Lill dead?" Celia whispered.

"Hold this flashlight, Celia. Hold it steady."

Celia did her best, but the light wobbled wildly.

"Nyet," Doc Vishnevsky whispered, taking Miss Lill's pulse, listening to her heartbeat through his stethoscope. "She is very much alive." He pulled back her eyelids. "Unconscious, but very much alive. She's going to have a terrible headache."

"There's more." Reverend Willard's voice quavered now. "Gladys heard them say they were not done this night."

"Marshall." Celia couldn't stop the tremors in her hands or her voice. "They're going after Marshall — and they still have the rope. I saw it."

Celia's mama opened the front door and stepped out with a bowl and towel. "That's what I think, too. Somebody's got to go help. Somebody's got to stop them!"

"I've got my bat!" Chester pulled himself to his full height, and her heart broke for love of her brother.

"You're staying right here, Chester Percy. I don't want you or Celia out of my sight." Their mother's word was law.

"Your mother is right. She needs you here to help with Miss Lill. Get a pillow for her head and a blanket. Wrap it around her. She may still go into shock, but do not move her into the house until the fire is contained," Doc Vishy ordered. "No more can I do here now. We must go to the Tates', Reverend Willard. Pray that we are not too late."

"Doc Vishy," Celia's mama began, "it's the Klan. You —"

"If not me, then who?" Doc Vishy slammed his medical bag closed. "Reverend Willard, we take my car. Fastest that way." He stood. "Keep cold compresses against her forehead and that knot on the back of her head. Keep her warm, but mind you watch that fire. Pull her off the porch if the house catches."

Celia stepped back, slid off the porch, and slipped through the garden as men pulled up in trucks and wagons loaded with hoes and rakes and fire-slapping rugs and five-gallon jugs ready to take on water. She glimpsed Clay McHone appear from the dark, grab a rug, and run toward the barn, beating flames. Celia slipped through the cars and trucks as the men raced toward the barn and began dousing water on the back of the house. In the commotion of doors opening and slamming, she pulled open the back door of Doc

484

Vishy's car and slipped through to the floor, curling herself as small as possible into the darkened space.

Doc Vishy's car raced over time and space, stumbling through ruts and swooping over hills that slammed Celia's stomach into the floorboards and up into her throat. If she grunted aloud, the two men in the front seats didn't hear.

"You are praying to your Jesus, yes?" Doc Vishy didn't ask but ordered. "And I pray to Adonai that we are not too late, that we will be able to stop this madness."

"They didn't rape or kill the women. I'm praying they're just out to scare."

"Reverend Willard, you know better than that. They might not kill white women, but Marshall is vermin in their eyes — as Jews are to Germans. They will not hesitate. They will torture in their cruelty, and they have no consequences."

"Well, there should be con—"

"But there are none! Go in, but go in with eyes open!"

Celia had never heard Doc Vishy so angry, so full of fight.

The car lurched to a stop and both front doors flew open. Celia pushed her head up from the floor and peered over the seat backs. Doc Vishy had left the headlamps burning, just as he'd done at Garden's Gate. The lights shone onto the Tates' porch, where Mercy Tate was kneeling over Olney, his head bashed so that blood oozed out onto the porch floorboards. Their children cowered in the doorway, but Marshall was nowhere in sight.

"Reverend Willard! Dr. Vishnevsky! Thank God you've come! They've taken Marshall and liked to kill my Olney. Oh, dear God, save him — please save him, Dr. Vishnevsky!"

"Which way?" Reverend Willard left Doc Vishnevsky to tend Olney and headed into the woods, the direction Mrs. Tate pointed.

Celia crept from the car and followed Reverend Willard through the snakelike shadows cast by leafless trees and spindly pines, careful not to step on branches, careful to keep a distance. It wasn't hard to find the night riders' trail. Smoking torchlight flickered through the trees. Clawing fingers of flame licked the sky. The sickly-sweet stink of gasoline came on windless air and Celia's stomach roiled.

One man alone, what can he do? Will they even care that he's the preacher?

The clearing came up too soon. Torches had been thrust into the ground and a wooden cross burned in the center. Horses were tethered nearby — all but one that stood beneath a big old oak tree. A rope had been slung over the sturdy branch of that ancient oak, and Marshall, his face badly beaten and

486

his clothes doused in gasoline, was being hoisted onto the saddle of the horse. One end of the rope was noosed around his neck.

Dear God, what can we do? How can we stop it? Celia's heart raced.

In the moment that Reverend Willard stepped into the clearing, Celia wondered if he'd made his peace with God, if he was ready to go with Marshall into the beyond of what happened when a person's heart stopped beating.

Will they really kill Marshall? The preacher? Would they kill a girl? Could she dare them, shame them out of their meanness? She had to try.

Celia, sweating and trembling from head to foot, was about to step into the fray when Doc Vishy bounded into their midst. "What do you think you're doing? Have you all lost your minds?"

"Stay out of this, Doc. You got no call —"

"No call to what? To help a man? To save a man's life? To keep you from doing the unthinkable? No more 'call' than I had to save your son, Hiram Lester!" Doc Vishy pointed to the man who'd spoken. "Oh yes! I recognize your voices — all of you!"

"Keep talking, Jew man, and what's to keep us from swingin' you next?"

Celia recognized something in that man's voice, but she couldn't place it, muffled as it was through his hood.

"It's your kind brought us into this blamed war with Germany and —"

"Doc — don't —" Marshall's cry could barely be heard.

"What kind of talk is that?" Reverend Willard stepped forward. "Dr. Vishnevsky's treated the families of No Creek for two years. If your wife had had to go to Asheville or Elkin or Winston-Salem to the hospital, Ned Jefferson, she and your son would have died in childbirth. Now you pay him back by threatening his life?"

The man recoiled as if slapped by the preacher's recognition. A couple more men stepped back, not so ready, Celia thought, to be called out from their hidey hoods.

"We're a community in need of one another," Reverend Willard geared up. "No Creek is too small, too isolated to turn on our own. If you want to fight somebody, go fight the Japanese or the Germans where you're needed! We're at war, men. Your homes and families are at stake not from the Tates but from real enemies. We can't spare one man to a noose!"

Celia circled a copse of pines, keeping low to the ground and out of the light cast by the torches.

"We're not leaving our women for the likes of him. He's not one of us. We mean to protect our own, Reverend. We got no quarrel with you. You go on home now and take the doc with you."

"I will not leave him." Doc Vishy's voice quavered in anger. He dropped his medical bag to the ground and stood tall. "Take this man down."

"You can cut him down all right — when we're done." The man hoisting Marshall set him steady in the saddle. Celia didn't recognize his voice and figured he must be one of the men from the next county Troy'd talked about.

Doc Vishy walked toward the horse. A man shot at the toe of the doc's boot. The doc stopped short and Celia nearly jumped out of her skin. The horse beneath Marshall reared as the man on the ground caught his bridle to steady him. Marshall barely stayed seated.

"Not another step."

"If you believe this man is guilty of a crime, charge him legally, but don't take this vigilante law into your hands. You'll all be guilty of first-degree murder!" Reverend Willard pleaded. "You'll hang — each and every one of you. Then where will your families be without you?"

"Ha! I don't reckon we'll hang for making the court's job easier, will we, Sheriff?"

"Shut up, you drunken fool!" Celia recognized Sheriff Wilkins's voice.

"How will you look your wives and children in the face tomorrow when they ask you how

Marshall and Dr. Vishnevsky and your preacher died — and where you were when it happened?" Reverend Willard rolled on. "Because that's what this will come to, you know . . . unless you cut Marshall down and let him go."

"He raped a white woman, Preacher, filled her with his seed. You don't think that's cause — an eye for an eye and a tooth for a tooth?"

"And he's been stealing food — and chickens — from near every farm and a long list of goods from the store." Celia knew that was an exaggeration, for she was the thief, not Marshall, and she'd kept a list beneath her mattress of each and every item owed.

"You have proof of neither, and yet you're willing to kill a man on account of gossip — kill three men?" Reverend Willard's challenge thrilled Celia's heart, but his gamble that the men were better than that terrified her. She couldn't let those good men take it alone, especially not when she was the thief.

Celia stood to step out and say, *"Four! Three men and a girl!"* But a horse stepped forward, blocking her view before the words left her mouth.

"What you reckon?" A man on the far side of the horse spoke. "I'm not gonna have killin' the preacher and the doc on my hands. That's not what I come out for. What he says is right. We got no proof. The girl won't say."

"My word's proof enough!" the man on the

horse, the one blocking Celia's view, hissed. It could have been one of the Wishons or even a half-dozen other men Celia could imagine.

"No, it ain't — not for all this. You come talk to me when that baby's born black as coal."

The man on the horse swore aloud, then beneath his breath where others couldn't hear said, "I'll make half a dozen babies with that girl. Not a one will see the light of day." But Celia heard.

The other man had already stalked off through the woods, back toward the Tate cabin, hollering, "Boys, come with me!" Celia recognized the limping gait of Farmer Drew. Her breath caught with the realization that there were more ways than voices to identify a man. Two more men backed from the group, leaving quietly.

The man on the horse swore again, louder this time. "Cowards! Fools!" He cocked his gun.

Celia grabbed a stone from the ground and threw it hard against the horse's haunches. The horse whinnied, reared, and kicked, causing its rider to slip in the saddle as he grasped his gun in one hand and fumbled for the reins with the other. The gun shot wild and the knees of the Klansman danced before Celia's face. She fell backward to the ground, catching sight of the contrasting dark-and-light toe of the rider's shoe in the torchlight.

Klansmen dove to the ground with the gunfire. The horse Marshall sat on reared again, unseating him. Doc Vishy rushed forward, lifting Marshall to his shoulders. Reverend Willard grabbed the horse and climbed up, loosening the noose from Marshall's neck. Doc Vishy released him and pulled him to the ground.

"Now go!" Reverend Willard shouted in waves of rolling thunder Celia didn't know he possessed. "Get out of here! Go home! And may God forgive you!"

Chapter Sixty-Two

The knot on my head Sunday morning was nothing compared to the pain in my heart.

Reverend Willard said that Olney Tate lay in a stupor from the Klan's beating. Marshall's skin burned in open wounds from the beating and lacerations he'd received before being doused, head to toe, in gasoline. Mercy Tate was frantic with good cause, she and their children terrified the Klan would return to finish the job on both men.

Reverend Willard and Dr. Vishnevsky had carried Marshall back to the doctor's car, where they found Celia hiding on the floor of the backseat. *What could that child have been thinking?* At least she was all right, but what she must have seen and heard! Last night she wouldn't talk about it, but nightmares would surely haunt her for months.

The barn was gone — nothing but ashes. *Thank You, Lord, that the house wasn't touched — nothing but a few burned shingles that can be replaced.* It appeared our cow had been turned loose, but we'd no idea where she was now. At least those arsonists had the decency not to let her burn alive.

Over breakfast Gladys tried to explain to me how most of the men in the county saw joining the Klan as a civic duty. "They say it supports family life and values and keeps outsiders from taking over."

"Outsiders? Like poor, young Marshall or his faithful, hardworking uncle, or Dr. Vishnevsky, the only doctor this county has? I'm not feeling charitable toward those views."

"I'm not asking you to be charitable, Lilliana. I'm trying to help you understand that snubbing your nose at an entire community of men will not change them. They believe in what they're doing — at their core. And that's what's so dangerous."

"Not all of them, Mama." Celia stood in the kitchen doorway, still in her pajamas. "Mr. Drew walked out — him and his sons. Said he wouldn't be part of killing Doc Vishy or the preacher. Said the only proof he'd take is seeing if Ruby Lynne's baby comes out black as coal."

I closed my eyes and buried my forehead in my hands. *And then they'll lynch Marshall — even if the baby is just a shade dark, no matter whose it is.* "That only means they're not done."

"How do you know it was Mr. Drew walked out? Did they take off their hoods?" Gladys

494

wanted to know. I wanted to know, too.

"No, ma'am. I saw his limp — the one he's had ever since Joe Earl's mule kicked him last fall." Celia swallowed and stepped forward. "I recognized somebody else, too — or at least I know how I will."

"What's that supposed to mean?" Gladys challenged. "No — don't tell me. I don't want to know. You understand this, and you understand it well: I don't want you stepping in more trouble, Celia Percy. You stay out of it — all of it."

"But, Mama —"

"Not another word! Now I'm going to get Chester up and you're both going to eat breakfast and dress for church. We'll go on as if this was any other day." She jerked off her apron and dumped it in the dry sink. "Can't have them thinking they've scared us into oblivion. Can't have that."

"No, ma'am," Celia whispered, slipping into her chair.

I wouldn't go against Gladys, but I needed to know. The moment she left the room, I asked Celia, "What did you mean, you'd know how to recognize somebody?"

Celia whispered, "I heard one of the men good as say he fathered Ruby Lynne's baby — and that he'd make more — and that not one would 'see the light of day.' "

My stomach fell through my feet. "Who was it? Did you see his face? Recognize his voice?"

"No, ma'am."

I looked away. The threat remained but hope was lost.

"But I can tell him by his shoes. Nobody around here wears such fancy shoes — nobody I ever seen. They were new — anyways, looked new in the near dark. But if I was to see them again, I'd recognize them sure."

"Could it have been Ruby Lynne's father?"

"I couldn't tell, Miss Lill. Might have been, but talking through those hoods makes things sound different — at least the way this one was talking. Mad, clean through, when Mr. Drew walked out and took his sons along, swearing like anything. That part's not so unusual, but those shoes — they were uncommon. I saw some like them in Pearl Mae's catalog at the store. I forget what they're called, but I could find the picture again — I'm sure of it."

"You're positive he didn't see you?"

"Not a chance. Too much going on, and I was careful."

"Ruby Lynne's got to tell who the father is. Reverend Willard doesn't believe Marshall can sustain another beating."

"Unless I can prove who it is I overheard."

"Oh, Celia. That won't be enough. They'll never take your word for it unless Ruby Lynne backs you up."

"Then you'd best talk to her again, Miss

Lill. Make her see they'll kill Marshall if she don't tell."

Celia was right. I'd already tried to convince Ruby Lynne to speak out, but that was before Marshall was nearly hanged. "I'll speak to her this morning, before church if she's there. If I can't get her alone at church, I'll go out to their house this afternoon."

"Don't go alone." Celia's eyes looked so much older than her years.

"No. No, I won't go there alone."

Chapter Sixty-Three

Celia didn't need to be told twice to brush her teeth or dress for church. She even volunteered to take the Christmas cactus down to the church early — "to decorate the Communion table, it being near Christmas and all."

Celia knew her mama was too tired and worried to be suspicious, but she also seemed glad, tempted to believe that Celia was onto a new project, especially when Miss Lill offered to walk along with her.

"Chester and I will be down directly. Mind you stay clean before church, Celia, and don't give Lilliana trouble."

Celia rolled her eyes, as every near twelve-year-old worth her salt would at such a reminder. "Mama."

"I'm just saying." Her mama hesitated, then stroked Celia's chin. "You're growing up, you know. You look real pretty."

"Thank you, Mama." She wouldn't call her mama a liar, just "mother-blind."

Celia believed in Providence, evidenced by the fact that Ruby Lynne met them on the road, as nervous and eager to find out what had happened the night before as Celia was to tell her. But Miss Lill halted the graphic details with a stern warning. "Ruby Lynne, you've got to say who the father of your baby is. They all believe it's Marshall and they won't stop just because last night didn't go as planned."

Ruby Lynne turned away. "They won't believe me. They'll say I'm lying. Daddy'll beat me raw — and then what about the baby? What if he kills it — and me?"

"It's not Marshall's, is it?" Celia asked, determined to cut to the chase.

Ruby Lynne looked at Celia, unable to look Miss Lill in the eye, and shook her head.

"But if you don't say whose, they'll kill Marshall."

Miss Lill took Ruby Lynne by the shoulders to face her. "Celia's right, Ruby Lynne. They'll kill him. Do you understand? They'll kill him!"

"Daddy'll kill me!"

"We can protect you from him — take you away —"

Ruby Lynne pulled away.

"You've got to be brave, Ruby Lynne, and trust —"

But Ruby Lynne fled into the church, away

from Miss Lill and Celia and all their demands.

Folks started coming into the church, whispers of last night's doings on every furrowed brow and gossiping lip.

"Celia, you need to get that flowerpot to the altar."

"Would you take it, Miss Lill? I need to see to something — about the play."

Miss Lill gave Celia the stern look Celia knew was meant for Ruby Lynne. "Don't be late to the service. I'm here because of you, you know."

"Yes, ma'am." Celia waited until Miss Lill had gone in; then she slipped in the back and up the outside aisle to the pew the Wishons frequented. She plunked down beside Ruby Lynne, who still sat alone, but Ruby Lynne turned frosty and looked straight ahead. "Ruby Lynne," Celia whispered, keeping her own eyes forward, "I overheard something last night — a man brag what he'd done to you. It wasn't Marshall, and he wasn't sorry. He said he'll do it again and again." Celia left off the part about the baby's life, knowing that might be more than Ruby Lynne could bear.

As it was, Ruby Lynne began to tremble.

"Ruby Lynne, I can find that man. I saw his shoes — different from everybody else's and new. I know I can spot him. I'll back you up — every word — I swear. You won't be alone. Miss Lill and me, we'll take on your daddy or whoever we need to."

Tears filled Ruby Lynne's eyes and Celia knew she'd made her point. She pressed Ruby Lynne's arm and slipped from the pew, keeping her eyes on every man's shoes till she reached the pew up front where Miss Lill and her mama and Chester already sat.

"Where you been?" Chester asked.

"Nowhere, that's all."

It was a mercy Pearl Mae began singing "Hark! the Herald Angels Sing."

The church was packed. Celia was fairly certain that wasn't just because it was almost Christmas. *More like they want to see what Reverend Willard preaches on and to show they're God-fearing and couldn't possibly have been traipsing through the woods in bedsheets, burning down barns, tying up women and caught red-handed stringing folks up.*

Each time folks stood up to sing and brought their feet from beneath the pews, Celia strained to see what they wore. She saw nothing but brown work boots for the boys and most men and black leather for the fancier men. *Maybe it was somebody from the next county. But how would they get over here to bother Ruby Lynne? Unless her daddy led them to her.*

That idea sickened Celia all the more, but she held a low enough opinion of the Wishons

501

to know it wasn't far-fetched. *My daddy's bad for bootlegging and getting caught and living the life of a jailbird, but he's not that low. Compared to that, he's not low at all.* It was a new thought to Celia, and she pushed it away, not quite willing to forgive her daddy — not yet — and intent on the worries at hand.

Jesse set his prepared sermon aside, fairly certain that preparation for the baby born in Bethlehem wasn't on the mind of his congregation. Yet nothing short of the peace that baby brought could heal the hate he'd seen in the woods last night.

He could still smell on his hands the stench of the gasoline he'd washed from Marshall's body as Dr. Vishnevsky treated the bloody lacerations. Anger and grief had warred inside him through the night. What they needed, to a man, was the man Christ Jesus. Jesse knew he needed Him most of all.

He understood that the men of No Creek were bred and nurtured with the foundation of an eye for an eye and a tooth for a tooth. Those were words they understood, took to heart and lived by.

He could think of nothing more to the point of their need than a message by Oswald Chambers that he'd encountered in his seminary days and again in *My Utmost for His Highest.*

"Lord," he prayed as he stood at the podium, "fill me with Your Spirit, and give me the words You want me to speak. Let Your Spirit find willing hearts and open minds in this room to receive those words. Through Jesus Christ our Lord, amen."

"Amen" resounded through the church as the congregation sat.

"The text for this morning's sermon is meant as much for me as it is for each of you. These are not my words but our Lord's words from the first of the Gospels, Matthew 7:1. 'Judge not, that ye be not judged.' "

Feet shuffled beneath the pews. Backs straightened, and mouths turned grim but eyebrows rose in curiosity.

Jesse ignored the lifted chins. "This morning I'm going to read words written long years ago by another pastor, words that speak directly of this Scripture." He opened his well-worn copy and read directly from Chambers's writing, infusing his first line with thunder, giving long and pregnant pauses where they were due.

"Jesus says regarding judging — *Don't.* The average Christian is the most penetratingly critical individual. Criticism is a part of the ordinary faculty of man; but in the spiritual domain nothing is accomplished by criticism. The effect of criticism is a dividing up of the powers of the one criticized; the Holy

Ghost is the only One in the true position to criticize, He alone is able to show what is wrong without hurting and wounding. It is impossible to enter into communion with God when you are in a critical temper; it makes you hard and vindictive and cruel, and leaves you with the flattering unction that you are a superior person. Jesus says, as a disciple cultivate the uncritical temper. It is not done once and for all. Beware of anything that puts you in the superior person's place.

"There is no getting away from the penetration of Jesus. If I see the mote in your eye, it means I have a beam in my own. Every wrong thing that I see in you, God locates in me. Every time I judge, I condemn myself."

He stopped now and took a long breath. "Oswald Chambers, the writer of these words, inserts a Scripture here. Romans 2:17-20. Would someone like to stand and read that for us?" He waited, his head down and intent on his own Bible, but no one stood. No one spoke. The creak of a pew sounded loud in the church.

"Sister Pearl, you bring your Bible to church. Will you read for us?"

Pearl Mae gasped. It was not a normal thing to ask a woman to read Scripture when men were present, but this was not a normal

504

day and Jesse was determined to shake them from their sleepy forms.

When no one spoke, Pearl stood, face flaming, and fumbled through her Bible for the page. She lifted her voice, stood ramrod straight, but stumbled over the first line. " 'Behold, thou art called a Jew . . .' " She glanced around, but still no one spoke. Pearl drew a deep breath, then read clearly, though her shoulders hunched. " '. . . and restest in the law, and makest thy boast of God, and knowest his will, and approvest the things that are more excellent, being instructed out of the law; and art confident that thou thyself art a guide of the blind, a light of them which are in darkness, an instructor of the foolish, a teacher of babes, which hast the form of knowledge and of the truth in the law.' "Tears pooled in Pearl's eyes as she looked at the preacher. Jesse nodded, and she sat down.

He took up his book again and continued to read Chambers's words, more quietly now, so people leaned slightly forward to hear.

"Stop having a measuring rod for other people. There is always one fact more in every man's case about which we know nothing. The first thing God does is to give us a spiritual spring-cleaning; there is no possibility of pride left in a man after that. I have never met the man I could despair of after discerning what lies in me apart from the grace of God."

When he'd finished, heads were bowed. You could hear people breathing — not moving, but breathing, barely.

At last Gladys Percy stood to sing. " 'O holy night! the stars are brightly shining . . .' " After the first verse a few more people stood, brought out of their stupor, and then a few more and a few more.

Before the last verse finished, Jesse noticed Celia Percy slip from her pew, tiptoe down the outside aisle, and slide through the back door. Celia had become very good at slipping around unseen, as she'd done last night. He needed to have a talk with the girl or her mother. Things could have gone so differently last night. He'd not be able to forgive himself if anything had happened to Celia. What she'd seen was beyond anything a child should ever see or know. Celia Percy might not like to hear it, but even at nearly twelve, he still counted her a child.

Celia took her post outside the church door, freezing though it was. She hoped the preacher wouldn't start another sermon in the midst of his goodbye prayer. Her nose might form icicles if he ran on and on.

But it wasn't long before the doors opened and the congregation poured out — a little quieter than usual, a little slower and more thoughtful, as if they feared to break the preacher's spell or maybe find fingers pointed their way. Celia stood with her back pressed against the church to get a good view of each and every person's feet as they stepped down the outside stairs.

The church had nearly emptied and the line of those leaving had dwindled to a trickle when Ruby Lynne stepped outside, followed by her father in his brown leather lace-up shoes. "Not him," Celia whispered, turning away when Rhoan and Ruby Lynne Wishon looked her way.

Confused and nearly disappointed, Celia felt herself blush and leaned down to retie her saddle shoes. Rhoan and Ruby Lynne walked on toward the parking lot. Nobody else came out the door. Celia sighed, uncertain, wondering how she'd ever get to the next county to look at the shoes on men's feet and where she'd do it, or who'd believe her enough to get her there.

Just inside the church door she glimpsed the pant leg of a tan suit. Beneath that suit leg peeked the front toe of a tan-and brown-tipped shoe. Celia's breath caught. She gulped, cold caught in her throat. The foot stepped back inside the church. Celia thought she might faint — or lunge after the shoes.

A few moments later the shoes emerged again — this time both of them. A woman —

Pearl Mae — stepped between Celia and the man just before Celia's eyes reached his face. Pearl took the man's arm, leaning into him as they walked down the stairs, blocking Celia's view. It was all Celia could do not to push Pearl out of the way. When the two reached the bottom step, the man pulled away, Pearl still chattering. Celia saw the man lift his fedora above the crown of Pearl's perky, feathered hat, but Pearl and her Christmas bonnet stood between Celia and the man.

Celia nearly tripped down the stairs, past Pearl, in time to see the man walk away — nothing but his back and fedora visible to her through the stark branches of the elm outside the church until he reached the parking lot. His swagger looked familiar, but she had to be sure. There were only five vehicles there: Farmer Drew's wagon, two faded pickups, Rhoan Wishon's black sedan, and a two-tone brown and wood grain sedan with a roaring engine — the same two-tone color as the shoes. Celia knew that car — everybody did. Just before the driver pulled open his front door, he turned, looking back at the church with a grim mouth and deep freeze in his eyes. When he caught Celia staring, open-mouthed, he blinked, climbed into his fancy car, and started the engine.

"Ruby Lynne!" Celia called, running toward the Wishons' car.

Ruby Lynne turned, flushed, and glanced worriedly toward her daddy, making Celia stop in her tracks.

Celia mouthed, *I saw!* She pointed toward the two-toned car.

Ruby Lynne didn't answer but nodded once, her eyes on Celia as they drove away.

Celia didn't even try to talk to her mother. She went straight to Miss Lill, catching her hand before the family group reached Garden's Gate.

CHAPTER SIXTY-FOUR

"You're absolutely certain? And you promise you've not exaggerated anything — not one word?" I grasped both of Celia's arms and locked eyes with her.

"Every word I said is the gospel truth, Miss Lill. Every single word. And it was his shoes — the only shoes like that in the whole church, in the whole of No Creek. They match the colors on that car of his. I don't know why I didn't think of that before."

"Still, we must get Ruby Lynne to say."

"She nodded when I called to her, but she's afraid. She's right — her daddy won't believe her, and he'll beat the tar right out of her till she lies, till she says it was Marshall."

"Not if we take Dr. Vishnevsky and Reverend Willard. He won't touch her in their presence."

"They can't stay with her forever."

"They won't need to. Safety in numbers, remember? If Rhoan threatens her, we'll bring her here."

"He'll never allow it, don't you see?" Celia pleaded.

"We have to make him."

Celia was scared, and so was I — with good reason. But it meant life or death, sooner or later, for Marshall and probably Olney and maybe even his family. I knew the fire in the barn had been a warning to me of what would come next. If they'd burn me out, they would surely burn out the Tates, and they'd proven they could do worse. We couldn't wait. "We'll go now. Reverend Willard's probably still at the church."

"Sometimes he takes Sunday dinner with one or another of the congregation."

"We have to try."

"I'll go for Doc Vishy."

"No, Celia. I'm not letting you out of my sight." It might have been the better part of judgment to send Celia home and do this alone, but I knew her account of what she'd seen last night would validate everything I said, the cause of Reverend Willard, and the influence of Dr. Vishnevsky. Celia's presence might also help persuade Ruby Lynne to tell the truth. If the younger girl could be so brave, perhaps Ruby Lynne could, too.

Chapter Sixty-Five

Celia counted it a good thing that Miss Lill was the one who took the word to Reverend Willard. He'd believe her quicker than he'd believe Celia. And he loved Miss Lill in his way. Even Celia could see that.

"This is quite an accusation, Celia. You're certain you can identify him? It was dark out there in the woods." Reverend Willard held Celia's eyes.

"There was torchlight enough and that burning cross made it bright. I saw his shoes when the horse reared. Why a fellow'd wear fancy shoes to do such a thing, I don't know, but he did."

"Arrogance, because he believes he can get away with it," Miss Lill said as if she knew.

"The quicker we get him behind bars, the better for everyone." Reverend Willard pushed long fingers through his hair. "But I'm not sure about pressing charges. Ruby Lynne's still a minor. So much depends on Rhoan."

"I was wrong about Rhoan Wishon — at least about that. But he's her father; he's got to step up, for his daughter's sake. We can't let this go on longer. Ruby Lynne's vulnerable every minute. That wicked man will just hurt her again and again, don't you see that?"

Miss Lill's combination of anger and fear overwhelmed and perplexed Celia. She half feared she'd set them all on a wild wagon ride down a steep and rutted mountain trail that they'd never get off. *What will Ruby Lynne's daddy do to keep us all quiet? What won't he do?*

Celia worried about that from the moment Reverend Willard telephoned Doc Vishy, asking him to bring his car and medical bag to the parsonage, but not saying why. She knew he didn't trust their "tele-Mae" operator to keep quiet, and quiet was of the essence if anything good was to be accomplished. It was clear they couldn't count on the sheriff. How they'd stop things with no authority — and Rhoan Wishon the most powerful man in No Creek — Celia had no idea.

By the time Doc Vishy drove Reverend Willard, Miss Lill, and Celia into the lane at the Wishon farm, it was well past one. Apparently the Wishons had already enjoyed their Sunday dinner, as Rhoan and Troy were leaning against the front porch steps smoking Camels.

"What brings you all out here, Reverend?"

513

Rhoan's voice took a sharp edge.

"We need to talk, Rhoan. I'm glad you're both here."

Troy straightened up. Rhoan tossed his cigarette into the shrubbery.

"Might we come in?" Doc Vishy asked as politely as if he'd come to make a house call. "The ladies ought not to stand in the cold."

Rhoan glanced at Miss Lill, took in the bandage on her head and the way the reverend guided her up the stairs. He looked as if he was about to object but saw no way clear of letting a bandaged woman escorted by the preacher inside his house.

Celia scooted close after Miss Lill.

Ruby Lynne came out of the kitchen, her eyes wide, drying a skillet and wrapped in an apron that pulled too tight across her growing middle.

"You go on, Ruby Lynne," her father said. "This won't concern you."

"As a matter of fact," Doc Vishy said, "it most concerns Ruby Lynne."

"I believe you'll want Ruby Lynne to stay, Rhoan." Reverend Willard spoke as if they were friends.

"Don't you reckon you've all done enough damage?" Troy stood unwavering by the door. "Buttin' into things not your business —"

"The welfare of members of the church is my primary business," Reverend Willard cut him off. "And I believe Ruby Lynne's condition requires the attendance of Dr. Vishnevsky."

"Why'd you bring this woman to my home?" Rhoan lit another cigarette and blew smoke right at Miss Lill. "You know what I said about her."

Celia could feel Miss Lill tense for a fight. Every word from Miss Lill — even her presence — rubbed Rhoan Wishon the wrong way. Celia slipped her hand into Miss Lill's palm and squeezed, hoping to settle her down, persuade her to let Reverend Willard do the talking. They needed Ruby Lynne's daddy to listen.

"We've learned the father of Ruby Lynne's child, Rhoan, and we're here —"

"We all know the father!" Troy shouted. "And it would have been taken care of if you and your Jew friend didn't butt into things not your business."

"Marshall is not the father." Reverend Willard held firm.

"Says you," Troy snorted.

"You say you've learned who the father is," Rhoan challenged. "Ruby Lynne tell you?"

Ruby Lynne cowered by the door.

"No," Reverend Willard continued, "but I'm hoping she'll verify the truth we all know."

Everyone stared at Ruby Lynne, who stepped back, looking like she might puke. "Don't ask me. I won't say. I've told y'all

515

that. I won't say."

"Because it's that thievin' n— !"

"He's not a thief!" Celia shouted. She wouldn't let Marshall be accused one more time because of her cowardice. But this time Miss Lill squeezed her hand.

"Because you're sweet on him, ain't you, girl?" Troy ignored Celia and pushed, mocking.

Ruby Lynne shook her head — not so much to deny it, Celia thought, as to refuse to answer.

"The father was overheard last night, a confession clear as any a courtroom might require." Reverend Willard looked steadily at Rhoan.

Rhoan straightened. Everybody knew he could be a mean drunk, and Celia wondered if he feared what he'd done in a stupor.

"Nobody's accusing you, Rhoan, of anything but jumping to the wrong conclusion — and of not being here to protect your daughter." Reverend Willard did not back down. "Isn't that right, Troy?"

Troy shifted, his eyes caught in disbelief. But he recovered quickly and feigned bravado. "I never accused Rhoan of nothing. All along I've said it was —"

"It was you!" Miss Lill nearly spat. "You raped your niece when your brother wasn't here — and you did it more than once!" Then she glared at Rhoan. "While you were off running moonshine, no doubt."

Rhoan flinched. "Now, look here, woman —"

"Yes, see here!" Miss Lill all but shouted. "Your own daughter's been too afraid to tell you that your brother —"

"Lies!" Troy shouted. "Pack of lies! Rhoan, you know you can't believe this slut! She ran off from her own husband."

"You better have proof, Preacher," Rhoan threatened. "Comin' into my home, accusin' my own brother —"

"I heard him." Celia's words came out hollow. Everybody turned to her and she turned to Troy. "I heard you last night, at the hanging."

"Goes to show she's lying — there was no hanging!" Troy laughed too loud.

"Because Reverend Willard and Doc Vishy stopped it when your gun went off!" Celia was mad now.

Rhoan blinked. "How do you — ?"

"I was there. I hid in the back of Doc Vishy's car and followed Reverend Willard into the woods. They didn't even know I was there till afterward."

"Little brat's makin' things up." Troy stubbed his cigarette on the floor.

"I heard you say you'd make half a dozen babies with that girl — and not one would see the light of day."

Ruby Lynne's face flushed bright and her

517

red-rimmed eyes flared in fear, then anger. She looked from Troy to her father, everything in her turned to pleading.

Miss Lill groaned.

Rhoan looked as if he'd been slapped awake, the air sucked right out of him. "Troy?"

"Lies! You know I'd never —"

"Ask her!" Doc Vishy ordered. "Ruby Lynne, you must tell the truth. Now is the time."

"Ruby Lynne, you've got to say!" Celia pleaded. "Tell him. Your daddy won't hurt you — he's askin' you. Tellin' the truth is the only way to stop Troy from doin' it again."

But Ruby Lynne didn't look convinced. She looked terrified and most of all like she wanted to seep into the floorboards.

Rhoan took his daughter's arm. "Ruby Lynne. Is what this girl says true? Answer me."

Troy stepped forward. "Now, Rhoan —"

"Shut up!"

The room grew quiet.

"Ruby Lynne," Troy started, "you don't want to be turning on family just because you're sweet on some —"

"I'm not sweet on anybody!" Ruby Lynne near exploded. "I never was." Now she spoke to her daddy but stared full at Troy. "He came when you were gone — always when you'd gone up to Asheville or wherever you go for

—" She stopped.

"The girl lured me, Rhoan. You know what a vixen she can —"

"You raped me!" Ruby Lynne whispered, whimpered, but her tears were lost when Rhoan pushed her aside and rushed his brother, shoving him to the floor. He pummeled Troy's face with his fists.

"Rhoan! Rhoan!" Reverend Willard grabbed Rhoan's right fist in midair and Dr. Vishy grabbed the other, pulling him off Troy before he beat him to death.

Miss Lill swept Ruby Lynne, weeping uncontrollably, into her arms. Celia was left standing on the sidelines, not knowing what to do or where to look.

"Let the law handle this, Rhoan." Reverend Willard kept hold of the man.

"He won't live to see the law!" Rhoan wiped his mouth on his sleeve while Troy pulled himself to a sitting position on the floor. "Don't even think of running out that door. I'll shoot you dead before you cross the yard!"

"We need to calm down." Reverend Willard stood between Rhoan and Troy.

"I'll kill you," Rhoan threatened Troy.

"And go to jail for murder!" Miss Lill's voice surprised everybody. "That won't help Ruby Lynne. You being gone is the worst thing in the world for her. That's what gave your brother the opportunity in the first place! She needs your protection, Rhoan Wishon, not your anger."

"Then you best call for the sheriff before I do him in. I'll see you put away for the rest of your natural life, Troy. Ruby Lynne will —"

"There's got to be a better way than dragging Ruby Lynne through a court of law and all over the front page of the newspaper." Reverend Willard relaxed his hold on Rhoan.

Rhoan turned on him. "Then you tell me what that is, Preacher. He ain't goin' free."

Doc Vishy loosened his tie. "May I make a suggestion?"

"Please!" Miss Lill spoke despite Rhoan's glare.

"Reverend Willard made a good point last night. Young men are needed to fight Germany and Japan." Doc Vishy turned to Troy. "Enlisting would get Troy away from No Creek for however long this war lasts — at least. Longer, if he promises never to return to the county."

"You can't do that! You can't make me!" Troy attempted to rise from the floor, wiping blood from his nose, but only got as far as his knees.

"How old are you, young man?" Doc Vishy asked.

"He's twenty-one," Rhoan answered for him.

"I'm not going!" Troy's eyes widened. "You

520

can't make me. We agreed to pay —"

Rhoan pushed Reverend Willard aside and grabbed his brother by the shirt collar, jerking him to his feet. "You'll enlist tomorrow morning first thing or you'll leave here today with a bullet between your shoulders."

"If you stay, Troy, you'll go to jail for rape," Doc Vishy said. "I will testify to the beatings and violation I've treated Ruby Lynne for over the last months."

Troy fumed.

Rhoan winced at the doctor's words. He wiped his jaw, considering. "You'll enlist, and no matter what, you'll never set foot in this house again — not anywhere in No Creek. You hear me?"

"Rhoan," Troy pleaded, "you got to understand —"

Rhoan jerked Troy's collar upward until Troy stood on tiptoe to keep from choking. "You hear me?"

"Yeah, I heard you." Troy was strong and muscled, but he was no match for his work-hardened older brother. "I got it."

"Until then, Rhoan, perhaps you can ask Sheriff Wilkins to give your brother a room in his jail tonight." Doc Vishy's solution surprised them all. "For everyone's safekeeping."

Reverend Willard placed a hand on Rhoan's shoulder. Rhoan dropped Troy to the ground.

"I'll telephone the sheriff," Doc Vishy spoke quietly and stepped into the kitchen for the phone.

CHAPTER SIXTY-SIX

When the sheriff arrived, I watched as the ropes binding Troy's wrists behind his back were exchanged for handcuffs. No one mentioned that Celia had recognized the sheriff in the woods the night before. Having Rhoan Wishon appeal to the sheriff made all the difference.

When they'd left, Rhoan sat down on the couch, propped his elbows on his knees, and ran his hands through his hair and across his jaw.

"I didn't think you'd do it. I didn't think you'd stand for me against Uncle Troy," Ruby Lynne spoke softly, still from the kitchen doorway.

Rhoan looked up at his pregnant daughter. "I had no idea. None."

Ruby Lynne looked away, relief and sorrow weighing down her shoulders.

"Why didn't you tell me? Why didn't you tell me what he was doin' to you all this time?"

"I never thought you'd believe me. I feared you'd believe him. You always believe him — your baby brother. You protect him — all the time."

"But I didn't protect you."

"You never did. Not even from you, when you're drunk."

"I'm sorry, baby. I'm sorry." Rhoan shook his head, too sorrowful to look full in Ruby Lynne's face, but reached his arms toward her, waiting for her to come to him. She didn't. "What can I do? How can I make this right?"

I couldn't hold back. "You can't. But you can stop accusing an innocent boy to begin with!" I wanted to dig my nails into Rhoan Wishon's arm and make him see, make him feel.

"And stop drinking," Ruby Lynne spoke, still quietly. "When you get drunk, you don't know what you're doing, Daddy. And when you're sober, you don't remember."

The lump in Rhoan's throat went up and down. "Did I — did I ever — ?"

"No." Ruby Lynne crossed the room then and sat beside him. "Only Uncle Troy ever did that. I couldn't stop him. I wasn't strong enough. But you slapped me around — left bruises a couple of times on my arms, my face. You can't do that anymore. I'm gonna have a baby. I'm gonna be a mother."

Rhoan buried his face in his hands. "I

didn't know what I was doing. I never should've done it. I never will again, I swear it."

"Does that mean you'll stop drinking?" I wanted to know.

"Miss Lill!" Celia urged, and I knew she was cautioning against demanding the impossible.

"Yes," Rhoan said. "Not another drop. I swear it."

By the time we left an hour later, Ruby Lynne and Rhoan sat across the table from each other with hot coffee and a fragile peace. I felt Ruby Lynne would be all right for now, that Rhoan was so horrified by what his brother had done that he now meant to protect her.

But I didn't believe Rhoan would give up hard liquor and said so to Reverend Willard and Dr. Vishnevsky. "Leopards don't change their spots."

"No, I'm not sure I believe they do," Reverend Willard replied, resigned as near as I could tell. "But I hope for more and better from him. He's going to be a grandfather one day soon. Surely that changes a man for the better, doesn't it?"

CHAPTER SIXTY-SEVEN

Celia's twelfth birthday came on the fifteenth, but even that momentous event seemed lost to her — an anticlimax to all that had gone on.

She heard the phone ring and her mama take the call Monday morning before school. *Why is it every time that telephone rings it's bad news?* She couldn't tell what was going on at the far end of the line, but she saw the squaring of her mama's shoulders. Celia heard the click as her mama replaced the receiver in its cradle, and she waited long moments till her mama turned, a smile pasted across her pale face.

"Your daddy's being released a few days early — this afternoon. I'll go up to fetch him. We ought to be home on the last train."

Celia felt like the earth had just opened up and swallowed her whole. Turning twelve was not all it was cracked up to be.

CHAPTER SIXTY-EIGHT

We heard over the radio that the train was delayed for ice on the tracks. We celebrated Celia's birthday quietly, cutting the applesauce cake Gladys had baked that morning — a recipe Celia loved and one that had been passed down through their family for generations. But Celia barely ate.

I tucked Celia and Chester into bed around eight and said prayers with them. Neither asked to stay up and wait for their family's reunion. Both prayed for their parents' safe return that night, but neither looked excited, not about Celia's birthday, not about their daddy coming, not even about Christmas.

My heart ached for the uncertainty in their faces, for the nervous twitch in Celia's eye and Chester's need for extra hugs. I understood how they felt — what it meant to not know whether to trust someone and wonder, even fear how they were going to treat you, no matter how many times they said sorry.

I went to my room after that but heard the

door open and close about 9:15. I turned off my light and pretended to sleep. I knew the children pretended the same. Best to give Gladys and Fillmore some time to settle in. It was their first night together in nearly two years. About ten I heard footsteps on the stairs — two sets — and a little giggle from Gladys. I turned over, breathed easier, and went to sleep.

Granny Chree hadn't been to my kitchen since Thanksgiving — far longer than our usual stretches between tea and conversation — so on Wednesday, the week before Christmas, I decided to pay her a visit. It was a good time to be out of the house while Gladys and Fillmore spent time together — only a few days left before school let out for the holidays.

I'd met Fillmore the day before. He seemed to be settling in with this family pretty well, though Celia kept her distance from her father. It had to be hard for him with no real privacy with Gladys and the children. My being away for a few hours might help.

The week before, I'd made up packets of the herbs Granny loved that grew in Aunt Hyacinth's garden beds. I'd dried them at the end of summer and tied some with red ribbons. Monday morning, early — even before Gladys had left to get Fillmore, the morning Gladys had baked Celia's cake —

I'd baked several loaves of pumpkin-cranberry bread, intending them as gifts. We'd already heard talk about the likelihood of sugar rationing but were determined to make this a sweet Christmas — one to remember, what with Fillmore coming home and all we'd been through.

My basket was heavy, laden with all the good things I thought Granny Chree might accept from me. Along with the herbs, I'd slipped in a loaf of pumpkin bread, a tin of loose tea, and a pound of coffee.

Frost crunched beneath my feet as I walked through the fields and up the mountain, the earthy scent of damp ground and molding leaves strong in pine-sheltered places. Clouds hung dark and heavy, pregnant with the coming snow. I was glad to make the trek now. By evening we might be battling a winter storm.

The first sign of trouble was that there was nothing but cold on the winter air — no scent of woodsmoke from Granny's cabin chimney, no fragrance of soup bubbling or fatback frying from her outdoor kitchen.

"Granny!" I called from the edge of her cabin's clearing, wanting her to know a friend was near. "It's me — Lilliana Grace!" But there was no answer. "Granny?" I'd reached the door. I knocked, something I'd never had to do to reach Granny's welcoming arms — arms that reminded me of dear Sarah. Still no answer. I pushed against the cabin door, but the bar on the other side must have stood in place.

I walked around to the side of the cabin and peered on tiptoe through the window glass. No fire burned in the grate. No lamp lit the darkness. If the bar had not been set, I would have thought Granny was out. Now fear swelled in my throat. I knocked on the window — Granny's only window — tentatively at first, then frantically. I couldn't quite see her bed, but the foot of the cot looked as if a quilt was bunched there — not neatly made as Granny would leave it.

I couldn't get in the door, but if I could climb on something, I could crawl through the window if it wasn't locked — or break it if necessary. I dragged a thick log from her woodpile by the front door, standing it on end. Steadying myself against the cabin wall, I climbed and pushed up the window.

"Granny? Granny Chree?" Still no answer. Grasping the window's ledge, I pulled myself up and through and into her dry sink — bone-dry. I scrambled over the side and felt my way through the dark to Granny's little bed near the fire.

There was something beneath the covers, but I couldn't quite see or bring myself to touch it. I felt for the table, then for the kerosene lamp and box of matches that I knew stood there. It took a moment for my eyes to adjust to the flare of the lamp and courage to turn and see what I might find. The cabin wasn't freezing, and that gave my trembling heart hope. The fire or the stove couldn't have been out for long.

"Granny?" I whispered, lifting the lamp and turning toward the bed.

She lay peaceful, a woolen blanket pulled up to her chin. I felt for a pulse, as I'd seen Dr. Vishnevsky do, but knew, even before I touched her, that I wouldn't find one. "Oh, Granny!" I sank to the floor beside her bed, clasping her hand — cold as the stones in our garden.

Instantly, there were a thousand things I wished I'd said, questions I wished I'd asked, love I wished I'd found more ways to pour into this dear woman, this precious friend to my aunt, to me. The weight of this hard land with its hardened souls and its unspoken codes, added to the loss of Mama and Aunt Hyacinth and now Granny Chree, pressed my heart to the ground.

I lost track of how long I sat on that cabin floor, my hot head pressed against Granny Chree's cold hand. Tears came, washing my face and her fingers — an anointing for burial. I cried so hard that eventually against all sense, I slept, then woke, having dreamt of the fierce little lady who met me first among the herb beds at Garden's Gate, digging plants I'd known nothing about then. How much I'd learned from her — about plants and flowers and herbs and the ways of nature, about other people, about the love of the Almighty, about me.

At last I dried my tears and sat back, looking full in Granny's face. I wanted to remember that the lines of care and age were gone, how relaxed and near lovely she looked. I noticed for the first time there was something clasped in her other hand . . . paper.

I pulled the lamp closer. It was a note, and beside her hand, on the bed, was a man's sock, stuffed with something that crinkled, like paper. I saw the word *Testament* at the top of the page and gently pulled it free from Granny's grasp.

My Last Will and Testament
I don't know if this is what you call legal and binding, but it's my will and I want it done.
My name is Alma Tatum Chree, and my money sock goes to Marshall, the nephew of Olney Tate. Marshall, you are one of the finest young men it has been my pleasure to know in this life. Use this money to get away from here and begin a good life. Don't look back. You are made for more than you will find in No Creek. If my son had lived, I would have wanted him to grow like you and your uncle, Olney Tate.
This cabin and all the rest of its contents

go to my young friend Lilliana Grace. Your aunt Hyacinth Belvidere owned the land and now I guess you do, so it's rightfully yours anyway, and don't nobody interfere with my wishes. Lilliana, use my cabin as a place to get away and meet your God, dream the dreams you have not allowed yourself to dream. Don't let nobody keep you from it.

Tell that preacher over to Saints Delight to bury me beside my Shadrach on the mountain and say words over me. Never mind that I wouldn't attend his church. I found God on His own mountain. No church building could hold me after that. Let there be singing when they remember me, come spring, but no crying. I won't have it. I have lived a good life. Now I go to a better one.

Granny Chree

I breathed deeply, not knowing whether to laugh or to cry. *It better be laughing, as you've given us all orders not to cry. But how can I help it? How can we?* The vessel that lay empty in that bed had housed a treasure beyond knowing, beyond realizing until it was taken from us — from me.

I straightened the covers over Granny's feet, kissed her cheek, and blew out the lamp. Closing the window, I took her will and the money sock and left by the door, leaving it unbarred, as Granny had always done. I made it home just before the snow began to fly.

CHAPTER SIXTY-NINE

Jesse sorrowed for the loss of Granny Chree but was glad to help Lilliana with her necessary errands — first to visit Reverend Pierce, who promised to see to Granny's wishes, though he couldn't guarantee no crying come her service in the spring. Granny had been a longtime fixture in No Creek, beloved and needed at one time or another by nearly every family, whether or not they owned up to her doctoring.

"She was a force to reckon with, that woman was. Lived through slavery days, Reconstruction, and now Jim Crow, never once bending to an earthly soul, far as I know. Must have been over a hundred," Reverend Pierce guessed.

"A hundred and three this spring." Lilliana spoke quietly. "And the wisest woman after Aunt Hyacinth that I've ever known. I will sorely miss her."

Jesse nodded, his heart too full to add a thing. "I'm sorry to rush this in any way, Lilliana, Reverend Pierce, but we'd best make our other stops before the snow gets too deep."

"That's right. You all go on now. My Marion and I'll see to Granny Chree as soon as the snow stops. We'll see that she's buried right where she says. I know the spot. And we'll plan a service come the spring thaw."

"When the lilacs bloom." Lilliana looked him in the eye. "She loved lilacs."

"Yes, ma'am." Reverend Pierce grinned. "She told me once that God must have known we humans couldn't abide such divine beauty for long — that's why their growing season's so short."

"Mama!" Lilliana whispered.

Jesse saw Lilliana's hand go to her throat as if capturing a sob — something more than the beauty in the thought the reverend had repeated. He hoped someday she'd share whatever it was with him.

He helped her down the reverend's snow-covered path and into the car he'd borrowed from Dr. Vishnevsky the day before. "I'd best drop you off at Garden's Gate before going on to Dr. Vishnevsky's and returning his car. The snow's getting too deep."

"No. I want to place this into Marshall's hands myself. I don't mind walking back."

Jesse pressed the clutch and put the car in gear. He knew better than to argue with such a woman, but he had no intention of letting

Lilliana Grace Swope walk a mile on slippery roads in the snow. He was sure the good doctor would agree.

They reached Dr. Vishnevsky's just as dusk gathered. Jesse turned to Lilliana. "You've got to be bone weary."

"I must do this. I won't rest until I do."

He smiled. "You grow more like Miz Hyacinth every day."

Lilliana's smile lit her face and Jesse's heart. With renewed energy he set the parking brake and ran to her side of the car, pulling a blanket from the backseat to cover her head and shoulders as best he could as they fought their way toward the doctor's house. Boxes of old newspapers and scrap metal — coat hangers and aluminum pots — stood in rows beneath the overhang on the doctor's porch, ready for Tuesday's collection of scrap metal to be used in the manufacture of war materials. No one could question Dr. Vishnevsky's support of the war effort.

Even before they knocked on the door, they heard laughter from the front room. Dr. Vishnevsky opened the door, his face wreathed in smiles Jesse had seldom seen. "Come in! Come in! You must be frozen through. Take off your shoes and stockings and set them by the fire to dry. I have the teakettle boiling."

In the front room lay Marshall on a camelbacked settee, smiling just as big as the doctor. Both men surprised Jesse and did his heart good. "You two look in far better form than I expected."

"Marshall is good medicine for me," Dr. Vishnevsky chuckled. "I did not realize how long it's been since good company sat at my table."

"Or how you will miss him," Lilliana offered.

"Miss him? Oh no, my dear. Marshall and I have decided he will be the perfect boarder here — my assistant — as soon as he's done being my patient! He has an eye and heart for healing and for helping others." Dr. Vishnevsky beamed. "Sit, sit. I'll bring the tea."

Jesse waited until the doctor left the room to look at Lilliana. He didn't want to usurp her news or the gift of Granny Chree, nor did he want to destroy the spark of happiness before him. Lilliana looked taken off guard, too.

"What is it?" Marshall caught their reservation first. "Uncle Olney? Aunt Mercy? They all right? Did they — ?"

"I saw the family yesterday. Olney's going to be fine. He's resting well. Says he'll be nearly right as rain by the New Year, as long as that leg heals straight."

"That's good. That's good," Marshall said, but the joy had left his face. "Do you think they'll come back, Reverend? Doc thinks not — at least that what he say, but I don't know."

Jesse sighed. "I hope not. Troy was the biggest instigator, near as I can tell, and Rhoan and the sheriff personally drove him to Winston-Salem's recruitment office. They waited till they saw him enlist and arranged for him to stay with a friend of the sheriff's until he's taken in by the Army, so at least he's gone. You can thank the good doctor for that."

"I do," Marshall vowed. "He told me what Troy done to Ruby Lynne."

"It was terrible — wicked of him. But it's out in the open now. There's still the thefts to contend with. Troy adamantly denied having anything to do with those."

"I didn't steal a thing, Reverend Willard. I swear it."

"I believe you, Marshall. I'm not sure they do. It helps that Troy's gone, but the truth is, I just don't know what to expect from them, especially once they get drinking." Jesse hated saying that. It was as if he'd pushed the warmth from the room.

"Marshall, there's something we came to tell you," Lilliana began. "Granny Chree thought the world of you, you know."

"And I think the world of her. She's a fine woman." Marshall hesitated, then looked as if he feared what was coming. "What you mean, 'thought'?"

"I found Granny Chree in her cabin earlier today." Lilliana swallowed. Jesse saw that she was unable to continue.

"Don't be sayin' that." Marshall shook his head as if she could take back words, turn back time.

"She left a will." Lilliana pulled the folded paper from her pocket. "I want you to read it — read it for yourself." She handed Marshall the paper.

Marshall stumbled through the words and Granny Chree's chicken scratch handwriting. His eyes filled and he swiped his sleeve at the moisture. Lilliana handed him the money sock, stuffed to the gills with coins and bills.

"Why she do that? Why she do that for me?"

"She loved you," Lilliana spoke quietly. "She saw good in you that we all see. Why wouldn't she?"

Dr. Vishnevsky walked in at that moment with a tray of cups and saucers, a pot of tea, and some kind of sweet bread. He stopped in the middle of the room, sensing the change.

"Granny Chree passed this morning." It was all Jesse needed to say.

Dr. Vishnevsky set the tray down heavily.

Marshall handed Granny's will to the doctor. Dr. Vishnevsky read it and smiled again. He took his glasses from his face, his smile fading to wistfulness. "She's right, you know. Granny Chree was always right. As much as I want you to stay, this is no place for you, my friend. You deserve better than this town is ready to offer you."

"Nowhere could I find better friends than

I've found here." Marshall's words were choked. "You and Ruby Lynne taught me to read, Miss Lilliana. And, Doc, you give me a home and hope for new work."

"Those are only beginnings of the good things ahead," Lilliana insisted. "But I think Granny's right. It could be safer for you — somewhere else."

"I'll think on it." Marshall turned away, unwilling, Jesse knew, to let Lilliana see the wrinkle in his chin.

CHAPTER SEVENTY

News of Granny's passing hit Garden's Gate hard.

"I can hardly believe she's gone," Celia's mama declared over supper. "Seemed like she'd be with us forever."

Miss Lill nodded. Celia's heart lay heavy, and Chester looked like he couldn't take one more piece of bad news.

"She lived a good long life. I reckon it was her time. The good Lord knows what He's doin'," her daddy tried to comfort them. Celia shrugged him off. What did he know of Granny Chree and all she'd done to help at Garden's Gate, for Miss Lill and Ruby Lynne and for Celia and the McHones, for the whole of No Creek, what she'd meant to them? He hadn't even been around for two years.

Celia had done her best to avoid being alone with her daddy since his return from prison. She didn't know what to say to him, and she'd grown beyond the games of hide-

and-seek they'd played before he went away. Chester kept a wary eye, but she could tell her brother was glad, with a feeble hope, to have a man in the house, his daddy to look up to. Secretly Celia dared him to break her brother's heart and swore what she'd do if he did.

She was thankful for her job at the store, especially with school letting out till the New Year. If she took her time and dawdled on her way home, stopped by the church shed with a thing or two for the McHones, she could get home just as the family sat down to supper and excuse herself to read in her room right after the dishes were done. Nobody stopped her. Nobody questioned. Everybody was trying to find their own space in the newness of it all.

Celia had just dumped the contents of her dustpan into the store's rubbish bin and stashed her broom when she glimpsed her daddy out the window. She hadn't known him to venture outside Garden's Gate since he'd returned, though that morning he'd talked on replacing the singed shingles on the house roof. Maybe he was really going to do it. Maybe he'd come to the store to buy them. If he was trying to help, be part of the family, then she could meet him partway — she wanted to meet him partway. Maybe she'd walk home with him after all.

Celia took her time pulling on her coat,

finding the buttons, expecting her daddy to walk through the door any moment. Three or four minutes passed and he didn't come. Finally she peered out the window again. Dusk was settling in, but she saw him down by the street talking to a man. They seemed to be friendly, but Celia couldn't tell who it was, couldn't see their faces clearly, just their backs and coat collars pulled high to caps. She saw her daddy knead the back of his neck — a thing he did when considering something. After a time, her daddy turned toward the man and shook hands. The tall one handed over a brown paper sack, which her daddy tucked beneath his coat.

Knots formed in Celia's stomach. She'd heard her mama talk to her daddy about getting a job, even if he had to go away to do it. They needed the money if they were ever going to make it on their own again. But this didn't look like talk about a job her mama would approve.

Celia turned away from the window. She could march out there and take her daddy's hand. She could tell him to stay clear of men handing out brown paper sacks that fit inside a man's coat. But did she want to? If he was running hooch again, he'd surely be caught, maybe go away for an even longer time. Then Celia and Chester and their mama could stay at Garden's Gate, stay with Miss Lill in her house of books and music and peace, for good. Maybe she should just let things play out.

While Celia was considering, the bell jingled over the opening door. Rhoan Wishon walked in. She no longer needed to guess who her daddy'd been talking to or what he wanted.

Celia lit out for home, forgetting about the packet of bologna and crackers she'd planned to take to the McHones. Every step of the way her heart beat flickers of anger and spite, disappointment mingled with determination for revenge.

By the time she reached Garden's Gate's back door, it was dark. She could see her mama and Miss Lill through the kitchen window putting supper together, her daddy standing in the hall doorway, smiling and chatting with a confidence he'd not shown since coming back. Celia hated him for the deceit of it, and she hated that her heart brimmed over with anger and frustration.

She turned away, wished she could run away. She found a spot on the woodpile, a place around the corner of the porch sheltered from the wind whipping down the mountain but with a full view of the night sky. Stars in their trillions danced with clarity. Too many to wish upon, and Celia knew that wishing did no good.

God, I know You're out there. I know You see. What do I do, Lord? How can I stop him? He's gonna break Mama's heart all over again. He's gonna shame Chester and me in school — again. He's gonna take to drinking and runnin' 'shine and get caught. It'll go on forever. I don't want him to go down, God. I want my daddy to be a daddy . . . even if it means we leave Garden's Gate. I just want a home, with real parents who love me and Chester, and no hooch. No Wishons. No Klan. Please, God, show me what to do. I know You see me sittin' here. I know You saw what went on down at the store. And please, God, help Clay and Charlene. They've got a baby on the way and I can't take care of them much longer, but You can. Amen.

That night, after everyone had gone to bed, Celia heard her parents whispering on the other side of the wall — intense and angry, her mama pleading and getting louder by the minute, then low swearing by her daddy and quiet threats by her mama. Celia had no doubt what their argument was over. She rolled over to face the wall and pulled her pillow over her ears. *Please, God,* she prayed, *time's runnin' low. Please.*

Celia spent Saturday morning early dusting the library shelves in the children's room. She'd just made it to the *W*s on the fiction shelf when her daddy walked in.

"Celia." He said it like somebody'd say,

"Good morning."

"Daddy." It was hard for Celia to call him that with the hardness in her heart.

He seemed to be waiting for her to say more, but she didn't fill the space, had no desire to and didn't know what to say to a man she'd held secret hopes for, a man who'd made her mother cry after she'd held everything together for them all for two long years.

"Your mama told me what you did, identifyin' Troy Wishon and helpin' Ruby Lynne."

Celia kept dusting.

"I'm proud of you, Celia. That was a brave thing to do, a good thing."

"It needed to be done." Celia warmed but felt the swelling of her own heart at his praise was a betrayal.

"Yes, it did. Not many girls your age would do all you did. I heard you're directing the Christmas pageant, too. I'm lookin' forward to seein' it."

She wanted to tell him that she didn't care what he thought about the Christmas play, that he should have been there to protect them from the fire and the Klan and the likes of Troy Wishon, but she didn't. She just kept dusting places she'd already dusted.

"Well, that's all. I just wanted to say."

Celia glanced up at him but quickly looked away. She heard him hesitate, then walk down the hallway toward the kitchen. Celia closed

546

her eyes, willing away tears of frustration. She clamped her lips and steeled her will.

CHAPTER SEVENTY-ONE

Miss Lill and Celia's mama cut old Mr. Belvidere's Klan robe down to size that morning and planned to create flowing skirts from the voluminous white fabric. Joe Earl had promised to shape frames to hold the tulle wings for the angel of the Lord. It might not be ready in time for the last rehearsal, but that was okay with Celia. She was willing to make a stunning debut on Christmas Eve — as Janice promised she and Coltrane, as Mary and Joseph, would do, along with her aunt's baby, who'd be arriving by train just in time to play the baby Jesus. Still no word about the camel.

Celia had just left the two women upstairs discussing their sewing project and come down to begin preparing lunch when she saw her daddy in the adult section of the library, replacing a book on the top shelf. Celia ducked behind the corner of the wall and took her place at the library desk, ready to sign out whatever book he wanted. *It's a hope-*

ful sign, him reading. She thought the words like a prayer of gratitude and waited. But his footsteps went the other way. The back door opened and closed.

Disappointed, Celia left the desk and wandered toward the kitchen, stopping at the bookcase she'd seen her daddy near. She looked up at the top shelf where she'd seen him reach, curious as to what might have caught his interest. It was a section on geology — rocks — something she couldn't imagine her daddy thinking about. Even she, curious about most everything, wasn't too curious about rocks. A book had been pulled just a couple of inches forward, like he wanted to remember where it was. She dragged the library stool over to stand on and pushed the book into place, but it didn't go all the way back on the shelf. Something kept it from sliding full in. Celia swallowed. She stepped up to the next step on the stool and then to the top so she could see what was back there.

A bottle. A bottle of liquid clear as rainwater.

Only, Celia knew it wasn't rainwater. She shoved the book back into place as far as it would go and climbed down, roughly pushed the stool to the corner, and stood, thinking. Finding a man's stash was one thing — near criminal as far as the unwritten code went. Touching it was enough to get some men killed. But moonshine was killing her family,

549

bottle by bottle, run by run, day by day.

Celia stood until she heard the clock chime the three-quarter hour. Everybody'd be coming in for lunch at noon, and she hadn't even started the tomato soup. But now she was alone. The grandfather clock in the hallway ticked louder than usual or maybe just seemed to. Undecided, Celia pulled an apron off the kitchen hook and pulled bowls from the cupboard. She opened the jar of tomatoes her mama and Miss Lill had put up in summer and started to mix the roux, just as her mama had taught her. She lifted a loaf of bread from the bread box and a crock of butter from the counter. Holding her breath, mind whirring, Celia stood for a full minute with a knife in hand, ready to slice bread. The clock in the hallway continued to tick. Funny how she'd never much noticed it.

Decided, Celia lifted the soup pot off the burner, set the knife on the table, glanced out the window to see if anyone was near, and raced back to the library shelf. She jerked the stool into place and climbed to the top, pulling the rocks book from the top shelf, not caring that it slammed to the floor with a crash. She grabbed the bottle and, heart pounding, ran it to the kitchen. She stood over the sink, yanked the cork, and poured every drop down the drain, her chin quivering and teeth gritted together.

"Celia?" Miss Lill stood in the hall doorway,

the rocks book in her hand. "I heard this fall." She stared at the bottle in Celia's hand. "Is everything all right?"

"No, ma'am. But maybe now things will get better." Celia breathed hard, stood straight, and replaced the cork.

She walked the bottle outside and slammed it into the trash bin on the back porch so hard it broke. When she looked up, her daddy stood ten feet away, staring at her with an open mouth.

Celia gulped but stared back, eyes flaming, then turned and walked into the house.

CHAPTER SEVENTY-TWO

I didn't know what happened — why the book fell from the top shelf or what affected Celia so or what started Fillmore bawling as if the world had come to an end, right there on the back porch.

Over and over he cried to Gladys that he'd turned his daughter against him, that he couldn't live with that, that he was no good and should never have come home.

Had he and Celia argued? Fought? I knew Celia was struggling with his presence and the fear of whether or not to trust him. But he was her father, and I knew in some conflicted way she both loved and hated him. I understood that inner war, that love and hate, that desperate need for love and yet distrust of a parent who'd hurt you. Fillmore had been selfish and irresponsible in the past, but he wasn't intentionally cruel, and he seemed to have changed or was in the process of changing. For all I could tell he wasn't physically or verbally abusive to Gladys or the children. He really seemed to love them.

I'd never seen him drunk and I'd come to understand since living in No Creek what too much drink could do to a man. At least I'd seen it with Rhoan Wishon and Joe Earl — one mean, one out-of-his-head silly. As far as I was aware, Fillmore hadn't taken so much as a drop since coming to Garden's Gate, had never come in drunk or even smelling of liquor. That was no excuse for past behavior, but if he was truly trying to reform, shouldn't that count for something? A second chance?

Celia had retreated to her room, and I took the steps to my own, hoping to give the couple some semblance of privacy. Second chances were what Gerald had begged for, then demanded, and guilted me into giving time and again. But with him there was no change, no reform. Rather than my forgiveness and second chances helping him, his hitting had become more frequent, more cruel, as if the forgiveness gave him license to do it again. Each time it grew harder for him to restrain himself until he seemed to take it for granted that he had the right, as long as he begged forgiveness and reminded me of Jesus' command to forgive seventy times seven.

Was it that way with Fillmore? Who was I to judge the life of another, to encourage amends if there was danger or to discourage amends based on my own experience?

And yet I knew what it was to be without love, without a father to protect me or a husband to cherish me. My heart bled for Ruby Lynne. It seemed like Gladys and Fillmore had the potential for a flourishing marriage in a way that I didn't. It seemed that Celia and Chester had the potential of having their hopes fulfilled for a father, a family, in ways that neither Ruby Lynne nor I had.

I sat in my room for an hour, not really understanding all I knew, until I heard a knock on the door at the end of the hallway.

"Celia?" Fillmore's voice called softly, sadly, tinged with hope. No answer. He knocked again. "Celia, I'm not mad, honey. I want to talk with you. Please open the door."

Answer, Celia. Whatever it is, talk to him. He's come to you. I held my breath. Moments passed and I heard Fillmore's footsteps back away. Then I heard the door open.

"Daddy?" I nearly cried for the little girl I heard in Celia's voice.

"Baby, I'm sorry."

"Are you gonna run 'shine for Rhoan Wishon?"

Fillmore gasped. "No — well, I thought about it. I'll say true. There's just no work for me here. How did — ?"

"I saw you down by the store, talking to him, taking the bottle." Celia's voice was older now, accusing.

He didn't say anything for a time, and when he did, it sounded like he was trying to get hold of his emotions. "He offered me a job. I said I'd think about it. But now I know. I won't do it — never again. I can't bear to lose your love or your respect. I'm sorry for all I put you and Chester and your mama through."

"Then what'll you do? You can't sit around here. Everybody here works." Now I heard both the child and the grown-up in Celia's words, the hope and the fear to hope.

He sighed loud enough to breathe life into the walls. "I don't know yet. Your mama and I are talking about it. What with the war on now, I could join up if they'll take me. Even if they won't, there's factory work for ship-building over in Norfolk. Maybe I can get on there after Christmas. I'm handy with a wrench."

"You are, Daddy. You are."

"It might mean living apart for a time, till I can save enough to send for you all. But I could get back here, maybe once a month or every two. Your mama thinks Miss Lilliana would let you all stay here till I can get things settled for us."

"You mean we'd leave No Creek?"

"Well, not right away. But maybe, in time. We got nothin' here, darlin'."

"We got friends."

"That we do." He paused. "Reckon we'll just have to take it a day at a time. Can we do that, Celia? You and me?"

"Yes, Daddy. Yes, we can."

There was no more talk, and I imagined a father-daughter hug just then, at least that's what I wanted to imagine. And for just a moment, I wanted to imagine it was my father and me.

A tentative peace settled over the little family. By nightfall I noticed that Gladys and Fillmore touched each other more — just a shoulder squeeze in passing or a hand on her back as they stood by the kitchen sink, sipping coffee, looking out into the dark together as if they could see a future the rest of us couldn't.

Across the table at supper, Fillmore had watched Celia and Chester with solicitous eyes, as if looking for signs of hope, determined to make any inroad count. Celia met him with brief, shy smiles of her own. Chester pretended to be oblivious to the emotions and nuances swelling around him, but from the continual jiggling of his leg and the shoe that sometimes found its way to my foot beneath the table, I knew he was not.

What I saw was hope. Hope that things might mend. Fragile, but real. It was possible, I knew, but not guaranteed. In watching the Percys, I realized that in order for a marriage to succeed, in order for a family to survive and thrive after hard times, each member needed to commit, to work at it, to give it all they had, even when afraid.

More than anything I wanted with my own father what I'd overheard and now saw between Celia and her daddy. But my father had never apologized, had never asked forgiveness no matter how many times his hand or belt had been raised against me, no matter how many times he'd stepped out with women other than Mama.

Gerald knew where I was, had been to No Creek, so surely my father knew. Not once in these months had he contacted me; not once had he tried to help or defend me from Gerald. According to Gerald, Father had gone on with his life, remarried, for all I knew taken in stepchildren. Imagining that things would change between us, that he would want me as his daughter, be willing to work to forge a relationship, was just that — an imagination, a fantasy I had always nurtured. I knew, deep in my heart, that no matter if he lived another fifty years, nothing would change because he would not — perhaps because he could not.

It was that knowing, the realization that I needed to move forward in truth and the reality of life, which prompted my letter.

Dear Father,

By now you know from Gerald that I am living in No Creek, that I came to Aunt Hyacinth for refuge after Mama's funeral. You will know by now, too, that Aunt Hyacinth has passed.

I could not tell you where I'd gone. I overheard your conversation with Gerald in the church after Mama's funeral and learned, though I'm sorry to say I'd suspected already, that I cannot trust you. That conversation told me so much, truths I hadn't wanted to face before.

I realize now that no matter how much I want or might try to make you love and care for me as your daughter — something I longed for all my childhood and adulthood — desires for your own happiness and concern for your reputation are greater than any love you might hold for me. It is a truth and freedom to say that, to stop pretending, stop hoping otherwise. I should have realized it sooner. It would have saved so many years of pain.

I knew, even before that day in the church, that you'd long been unfaithful to Mama. You did not cherish her for the wonderful woman she was — the faithful wife and loving mother, no matter how ill you used her. I never understood why you didn't love her — or me. There are so many things I've never understood.

Gerald told me you have remarried. Please be kind to her, whoever she is, and to any children you may yet have. Love them, be true to them. Give them a chance to love you in return.

I won't try to contact you again, Father, and ask that you do not contact me unless you find in your heart that you truly love me, that you repent of all the hurt you've caused in my life and Mama's, and that you want to start afresh. I will never expect that, but I would not turn you away. I needed to say goodbye. You have moved on in your life. Now I must move on in mine.

Your daughter,
Lilliana

CHAPTER SEVENTY-THREE

Once I'd mailed the letter, a new freedom entered my soul. A lightness born of truth that had needed to be faced. There would still be Gerald to deal with — Gerald and whatever he planned next to secure the divorce he wanted on the terms he wanted — but I'd laid one ghost to rest, and I was thankful.

Snow from earlier in the week covered the ground, and we were all more than grateful for the fire Olney's son had started in the church stove Sunday morning. Reverend Willard was nearly through his sermon and about to call for the final hymn when the church door opened and a rush of frigid air blew through the pews. I was sitting midway in the church, beside Chester, but could sense heads behind me turn and saw those before me look back, craning necks. Even then I might not have turned if Reverend Willard hadn't stopped his sermon midsentence. He looked as if he'd seen a ghost.

From behind me a clapping began, a jarring, solitary set of hands slapping loudly together, breaking the peace and our concentration, combined with feet sauntering up the center aisle a step at a time.

Before I turned, before he spoke, I knew the rhythmic steps of that swagger. My heart all but stopped beating, then pounded like mad.

"Please come in and join us for our final hymn." Reverend Willard, pale, spoke calmly.

"Final hymn indeed, Reverend. And a round of applause for your final sermon."

"Final sermon?" Whispers ran through the church. "What does he mean? Who is that?"

"What do I mean?" Gerald took up the question as if he'd been asked directly.

"Please, Mr. Swope, kindly take a seat."

"You'd like that, wouldn't you, Reverend Willard? You'd like me to sit down and say nothing about your luring my wife to your home in the dead of night."

Gasps and whispers rushed through the pews.

"You'd like that better than being named in scandal, than having your church called into question, than being cited as the culprit in my divorce case."

"Divorce?" The ugly word spread like miasma through the congregation.

I closed my eyes, willing the nightmare to go away. Knowing it wouldn't, I stood up and turned. "Gerald. Stop it."

"What?" He acted surprised, as if I'd pulled a rug from under his feet. "I shouldn't come to defend my wife? Or is it you I should be questioning? Are you saying it was you who chased after the good reverend and not the other way around?"

"Mr. Swope, this is not the time or the place," Reverend Willard began.

"On the contrary, it's the perfect time and the perfect place to reach those willing to speak out." He shrugged. "I had no choice. My *wife* deserted me and refused to sign the papers I sent her, forcing me to come. Perhaps that's what you wanted, Lilliana?"

"Gerald, please!" I begged.

"I understand the Belvidere family has lorded it over this community for generations. Well, it stops here. Today. My lawyer is waiting outside to take affidavits testifying to the character or lack of character in Lilliana Swope — *Mrs. Gerald Swope,* in case any of you have not heard that she's married — and in your Reverend Willard, a womanizer unfit to lead your congregation. At the very least, your board of elders will want to hear the facts, perhaps consider disfellowshipping them both? Your own postmistress, Mrs. Mae, was an eyewitness to their encounter. Mrs. Mae, perhaps you would like to lead the way. My attorney is waiting in my car, where he'll keep the heater running."

All eyes turned to Ida Mae, who'd returned from her niece's the night before.

"Mr. Swope —" Reverend Willard tried again but Gerald cut him off.

"Don't try to silence an eyewitness, Reverend. Remember, I was there. I saw you with my wife!" He turned again to Ida Mae. "Mrs. Mae, your voice will be heard at last. Tell them what we saw. Tell them all." It was not a request but an order, and Ida Mae stood as I would have done at his command just eight months before.

"I — I can't say what they were doing, Mr. Swope. They — they were just talking — like anybody who'd go to the preacher to talk over worries. I know you said what it was, what you believed, but . . . I can't swear to something I didn't see."

"Thank you, Ida Mae," I said, still standing, still breathing.

Rhoan Wishon stood and my heart sank. If anyone in No Creek held a grudge against me, it would be Rhoan. If anyone held sway with the men of No Creek in a perverse way, it was he. With Rhoan leading the congregation against me, others would follow, just as the Klan had followed the Wishon brothers to burn my barn to ashes, to beat Olney, to lynch Marshall. Troy wasn't the only Wishon who'd stirred the community against me. No wonder Mama'd left No Creek the first chance she got. There was no standing against a town ruled by such ideologies, no room to grow.

Gerald's condemnation wouldn't hurt my body, but it could alienate me, make me the outcast here that he and the elders of our church in Philadelphia had threatened. I couldn't stay if that happened. It would kill my spirit, rip the community apart. I sat down, my knees too weak for more.

"Mr. Swope, my name's Rhoan Wishon. I don't know you, and you don't know me, but everyone here does. I don't know what your problem is, but I will tell you now that Reverend Willard is a man of the highest character and the rock of our community. He's helped us all out from time to time, kept us from making bigger sinners and bigger fools of ourselves than we had in mind.

"As far as your wife goes, I guess you don't know her as well as the rest of us do. I grant she's something of a know-it-all and stubborn to boot — like my dog when it gets ahold of a bone. But she's a good woman and an upstanding one. She's done a lot for our community and for the . . . the church down the road. Not a man or woman here will speak against her. You have my word on that."

"And mine." Fillmore Percy stood. Celia jumped up to join them, then Gladys and Chester and Pearl Mae. One by one, by twos and threes and families, they stood. They

564

stood for Reverend Willard and turned to face Gerald with grim mouths. Gladys pulled me to my feet again, and I saw, I couldn't deny, they were standing for me, too.

I turned toward my husband, the man who'd believed he owned me as men own cars or cattle. His face turned crimson, his eyes uncertain, then disbelieving. Finally, smoldering, he turned and walked out of the church, leaving the door wide-open behind him.

Reverend Willard called the church to order and we sang the last hymn, "Amazing Grace."

"Amazing grace! how sweet the sound — that saved a wretch like me! I once was lost but now am found, was blind but now I see" — in that moment the words spoke to my inner being, were written for me in ways I'd never understood before. I could barely choke back the gratitude that threatened to overflow.

We'd just sung the "amen" when Celia tugged on my arm and beckoned me to lean down to listen. "It was me — my fault. I forgot. I meant to tell you, but I didn't want to bring it out and make you sad. There was so much going on — and then I just forgot. I'm real sorry."

"What are you talking about?" I was swiping away tears, trying to get hold of my emotions, of the swirling in my brain.

"A letter came for you, from an attorney-at-law in Philadelphia. I reckon that's the papers he was talking about."

Celia's eyes widened as if she was afraid I'd be mad. But I wasn't. I wasn't anything, and that was a wonder. I hugged her tight. "It's all right. Whatever it is, it's all right. It will be all right."

There wasn't time to think of what that meant, of what not seeing or signing Gerald's papers meant for the future. Gladys and Celia flanked me, each taking an arm, and walked me out of the church, Fillmore walking before me and Chester behind as my rearguard, armor for my body and spirit, and a force to reckon with.

We walked past Gerald and his attorney, waiting in Gerald's heated car. They appeared to be arguing. I saw the anger and mounting threat in my husband's face, the man who'd once vowed to love and cherish me but who I'd nearly allowed to destroy me. People walked past him, either turning away or pointing as they would point to a caged animal in a zoo.

I realized he no longer held sway over my spirit. Neither Gerald nor my father claimed hold over me now. I didn't feel dirty or guilty or afraid. I felt nothing at all, except the swell of my heart for the family and community that had claimed me as their own, and the joy that perhaps God loved me after all, that perhaps I, Lilliana Grace, was worthy to be loved.

CHAPTER SEVENTY-FOUR

Celia saw that life at Garden's Gate took on new joy after Sunday's drama. The excitement of Christmas coming and hopes of the worst being behind lifted each heart. Finally it was the afternoon of Christmas Eve, the day Celia had called for a dress rehearsal in the church.

During the solemn procession of the kings, Rob Taylor dropped his box of marbles that he'd brought for the baby Jesus and everybody chased them on all fours up and down the aisles and between the pews. Tommy Tuttle didn't want to give back the cat's-eye shooter he'd found, but Rob yelled that it was handed down from his pa and Tommy'd better give it back or there'd be war worse than Pearl Harbor.

The fight was in full swing when Reverend Willard walked in and broke it up. He gave Celia a withering look. "I don't know what will happen here tonight, Celia, but I'm holding you responsible. You said you could handle this. You told Ida Mae you have it covered, and I backed you up."

Celia sighed. She'd already decided that directing plays wasn't the glory she'd imagined. But it was Christmas Eve, and the show must go on. That was before Janice's mother showed up to collect her children and dropped the bomb that changed everything.

"No, my sister is not coming and will not be donating her baby to play baby Jesus or anybody else! The idea!" she huffed. "Janice, Coltrane, come on — we're already running late. I don't know why you insisted on coming here when you know —"

Janice near pushed her mother out the door but whispered to Celia, "Don't worry about a thing. I'll just bring a doll."

Everybody went home to eat supper and change into their costumes. They promised to meet back at the church fifteen minutes before the Christmas Eve service began.

Celia stayed behind to spread straw for the manger scene. When everything was in place, she pressed her nose against the cold windowpane of the church and sighed. It had been a trying December, what with the barn burning and Olney's beating and Marshall's near hanging and Troy Wishon going to war and her slipping food over to Clay and Charlene and all the bickering of the cast, not to mention Granny Chree's passing and that Gerald man showing up and her daddy and the hooch.

At least there was still some snow on the ground from the week before. A real Christmas Eve snowfall would give the pageant just the right touch, but there was not a cloud in the sky and dusk was falling fast.

She'd just turned out the church light when she glimpsed somebody through the window, a form slipping out the back door of the parsonage with a jug wrapped in tea towels. She knew the preacher was sitting down to supper at Garden's Gate before the service. It was common enough for ladies to drop food off in the kitchen of the parsonage, but nobody took it out. And this was no lady.

Celia peered out the church door, following the form back through the cemetery. "Clay," she whispered. With all that was going on the last few days, she'd all but forgotten them, except to slip little bits of food over now and again — not enough by half.

"Charlene must be like to bust any minute. They must be near starving." Celia grabbed her coat and ran for the church shed.

A crack of light peeked round the frame of the partially open door. She pressed her ear against it. Low moans rose from inside. Human moans. Gently Celia pulled open the door. "Jiminy!" She whistled. For there, on a pile of dirty blankets and clothes, lay Charlene, in full labor. Clay crouched beside her, with what appeared to be a jug of water.

At the sound of Celia's voice, both faces shot toward her, Charlene's eyes wild with fear.

"Is it time?" Celia saw that it was, but what could she say?

"We need a midwife or a doctor," Clay pleaded, "or anybody who knows about birthing babies."

"Jiminy!" Celia repeated. "Granny Chree up and died and Doc Vishy's tending Marshall. Ida Mae's the only other one that busts babies, but she ran you out of the store."

"The baby's coming now!" Charlene cried, groaning in pain.

"Then it's got to be Doc Vishy. I'll get him!"

Clay grabbed Celia's wrist, his eyes pleading. "He won't run us out, will he? We can't leave now. My wife needs help. I saw what they did to your barn."

Celia shook her head. "Not Doc Vishy. He wasn't part of that. He don't even come to this church, but he's friends with the preacher. He'd never run a soul out, and he'll make sure the preacher knows you need to stay."

Clay released her wrist. "I'm trusting you, Celia Percy."

Celia straightened. "You can." She slipped from the shed and ran on winged feet to bang on Doc Vishy's door. Breathless, she explained as best she could while Marshall helped gather blankets and basins and sheets. Celia and the doctor rushed through the dark to his car and drove as fast as they could toward the church. The thin layer of gravel crunched as they pulled into the parking lot and jerked to a stop.

"You're sure to find the surprises, Celia Percy!" Doc Vishy panted as he hurried along beside her.

By the time they reached the church shed, the woman's pains came unbroken. Doc Vishy greeted the couple solemnly, hung a lantern on a nail above them, rolled up his sleeves, and set to work.

The baby's head crowned before Celia realized the time. She clapped a hand to her forehead. "I've got to go! I'm the angel of the Lord!"

Doc Vishy chuckled without looking up. "I expect you are."

Warmth spread from Celia's head to her toes as she reached for the shed latch. At last she'd done something right, something good. But she knew she couldn't claim the timing. That was something more.

She fled, her heart too full for words, and raced home, the lusty cries of a newborn baby ringing in her ears.

"Celia Percy!" her mother exclaimed. "Where have you been? It's time to leave for the church and you haven't even eaten your supper!"

Celia didn't answer but wolfed down corn bread and pinto beans while her daddy helped pull the redeemed Klan robe over her head and stick her arms through. Miss Lill straightened the tulle wings Joe Earl had made from Pearl Mae's never-used wedding veil, and Celia jammed a crooked baling wire halo on top of her head. All four Percys and Miss Lill raced down the hill to the church, catching up with Reverend Willard at the steps.

There was still no camel, but Farmer Hanson and Mr. Brenner, true to their reluctant word, had tied their sheep and Jersey cow outside the church along with the jackass belonging to Hayford Bell's uncle. The town's few motorcars and pickups sat in the church-yard, and harnessed horses nibbled hay near the shed. Celia wondered if they had any idea what was going on just beyond their heads.

The strains of Joe Earl's fiddle cried, "O Come, All Ye Faithful" through the door and out into the starry night. Shivers ran up Celia's spine as she tripped up the stairs in her costume. Her parents and Miss Lill slipped into a pew near the front, next to Ida Mae and her husband.

Everybody was there in full costume except Janice and Coltrane Richards. "Where are they?" Celia hissed, not wanting to break the mood of Joe Earl's fiddling.

Ralph Brenner spoke up. "Janice said to tell

you they left tonight for their grandmother's house in Asheville."

"Asheville!" Celia shrieked.

"Yeah. She said to tell you they've been planning it since Thanksgiving. Said you'll just have to make do and wanted you to know that your play will be ruined without Mary and Joseph. She said you shouldn't have given them so many lines. Said she took her doll with her."

Celia was too mad to cry.

Ralph nodded. "What ya gonna do?"

Celia had no idea. The church was nearly full. Joe Earl played "Away in a Manger" and everybody sang. He played "Hark! the Herald Angels Sing" and everybody sang. Celia started sweating beneath her redeemed Klan robe. Reverend Willard began to speak.

Chester said, "I got to use the john."

"You're just nervous, Chester. Sit still," Celia ordered, wondering if she could hide in the outhouse till everybody went home.

And then it was time. Reverend Willard motioned to Celia to begin the children's pageant. Celia panicked. None of the angels were big enough to say the lines she'd written for Mary. All the bigger boys were already wise men and head shepherds.

She pushed Chester, more solemn and nervous than lordly and humble, to the front of the church. In the high, sweet tones of childhood he began to read, " 'And it came

573

to pass in those days that there went out a decree from Caesar Augustus, that all the world should be taxed.' "

The manger at the front of the church remained empty. Celia pushed forward the shepherds with their crooks. A troop of tiny angels made their way to the front and stood in a crooked line behind the empty manger. The wise men strode up to the front with their presents of marbles in a box, red currant jelly in a jar, and a cut-glass bottle of clover leaf honey, all of which had seemed far more practical and pleasing to Celia than gold, frankincense, or myrrh, which they didn't have anyway.

Folks began to whisper. "Where's Mary and Joseph? Where's the baby Jesus?"

Celia felt like crying.

Then, from beyond the church door, she did hear a cry — a baby's cry. It dawned on Celia that she didn't need Janice Richards or her cousin's baby or her doll or her annoying little brother after all. She had the real thing right out there in the church garden shed!

Celia swiped hot tears from her eyes, took a deep breath, and rushed to the front of the church. "Fear not, ye citizens of No Creek! For behold, I bring you good tidings of great joy which shall be to everybody! For unto you is born this day a Savior, which is Christ the Lord. You're gonna find Him wrapped in swaddling clothes, lying in a manger. Come on! Follow me, and see this thing which has come to pass!"

"Hey!" Rob Brenner yelled. "That's my line!"

Celia ignored him.

"Come on, ye citizens!" Celia poked and prodded until she'd led the puzzled congregation out the door, down the church steps, past the cow and three sheep and jackass, past the smattering of motorcars and trucks, and to the shed, where the horses stood sentinel, chewing hay.

"Well, I never," huffed Ida Mae.

"Celia," Reverend Willard whispered a little too loud, "this is going too far!"

But Celia ignored him, too, and threw open the shed door. There, through the steamy breath of tethered horses, lay a startled young Mary, a protective Joseph, and a screaming baby Jesus wrapped in an old coat. The glow from the lantern light above their heads cast a warm halo about the new family. Kneeling before them with his open medical bag of gifts and sleeves rolled high was Doc Vishy, the wisest man Celia knew.

A chorus of "Well, I'll be!" echoed through the crowd. "A baby! They've got a real baby in there!"

Ida Mae broke the spell. "It's that thievin' Yankee I told you about! Look there — isn't that your missing quilt, Gladys?"

Farmer Brown stepped up to examine the

pile of goods beside the young father, but Celia rushed forward. "It was me took those things — everything y'all are missing. Clay and Charlene McHone needed help, but there was nobody here to give it, nobody willing."

Clay stood. "I'll pay back every penny. I swear it. Soon as I can earn the money. I'll do any work you need . . . for as long as you need."

"Celia Percy — you mean you stole right under my nose?" Pearl sounded mixed — incensed and in awe.

"Celia!" Her mother shook her head, but her daddy laid a hand on her shoulder.

"Everything I took from you, I earned, Pearl, and it was Clay unloaded those crates for you. It was Clay swept up the leaves outside the store and in the churchyard by night. He's been choppin' wood for us when nobody was home. Clay helped put out the fire at Garden's Gate — the fire that could have killed us all — the one the Klan set." The fire in Celia left her as she stared into the faces looming around her. Her voice came quieter now. "Anything you think different you can deduct from my pay to come."

But Pearl looked again at the young couple and backed down. "Reckon I'll leave that to Mama."

Doc Vishy stood on stiff knees and stepped between the new family and the church members, rolling down his sleeves and raising his voice over the baby's wailing. "I imagine it was something like this that cold night in Bethlehem, don't you, Reverend Willard? Two young and lonely travelers far from home, looking for a place to stay the night, looking for something to eat, a helping hand — forced to a place outside because there was no room in the homes of citizens?"

Reverend Willard nodded in wonder and answered from the crowd, loud enough that everybody heard, "Mary brought forth her firstborn son, wrapped Him in swaddling clothes, and laid Him in a manger. He, too, was surrounded by gentle beasts while all the hosts of heaven sang. Yes, Doctor, I expect it was very much like this." The reverend laid his hand on the head of one of the tiny angels. "Like tonight, His birth brought out the wisest of men. His life and death and resurrection brought people of all nations together — to reconcile, to heal, to save."

Everybody, it seemed to Celia, held their breath, starstruck. Only the snorting of the horses could be heard — that and the screams of the McHones' new miracle. Every eye stuck on that baby.

Softly, like a mist rising, Gladys Percy, Celia's own mama of whom she was so proud, began to sing until her rich alto voice filled the night around them. " 'Silent night, holy night, all is calm, all is bright.' "

Celia realized it was calm, even with the baby's wails. She saw her daddy's chest expand as he watched her mama sing.

Hats slipped reverently from heads. Stars shone brightly, almost close enough to touch.

She heard Farmer Brown say, "I reckon I could use some help on my upper forty. Need plowin' come spring. Nothin' till then, but I could send over a bushel of apples and a smoked ham — for the baby."

Reverend Willard laid an appreciative hand on Mr. Brown's shoulder. "Thank you, brother."

" 'Round yon virgin mother and Child. Holy Infant so tender and mild.' "

The new mother looked so young, so fragile and frightened and weary. Celia glanced at Ruby Lynne and couldn't help but wonder what she was thinking in that moment.

The baby wriggled, all wrinkled and red, its tiny fists groping the air, but didn't scream so loudly. It seemed her mama's singing calmed even the newborn. Celia puzzled if it was a boy or a girl and was amazed that her own wonder of a baby had overshadowed even that.

Mrs. Brenner said, "I have some baby clothes our Myra has outgrown and more diapers than two babies need. I'll send Rob over with some in the morning."

" 'Sleep in heavenly peace.' "

Ida Mae offered "a whole bushel of sweet

taters, a jar of jelly, and just a little candy to perk up the new mother." And an admonition: "Why on earth didn't you tell me your wife was about to birth?"

"You called him names and swung a broom at him. What was he gonna say?" Celia couldn't keep quiet.

Ida Mae clamped her lips together, embarrassed, but still worried and tender-eyed over the baby.

Celia's daddy stepped up behind her and, bending her angel wing just enough to get close, whispered in her ear, "I'm proud of my girl."

Through her own tears Celia heard offers for help and promises of a little of this and a little of that fly thick and fast through the last lines of her mother's hymn.

" 'Sleep in heavenly peace.' "

Gifts for the baby. Gifts for the family. Gifts of love poured over strangers and friends alike this Christmas Eve — another suture, Celia figured, in No Creek's deep wounds.

Chester nudged Celia's side and the two grinned. She caught her brother's hand and held tight.

EPILOGUE

When April's jonquils and wild violets gave way to May's budding lilacs, we prepared for Granny Chree's memorial service. The night before the service I cut bouquets of lilac buds from Aunt Hyacinth's garden and brought them into the house to force their bloom into a heady perfume.

Nearly half the town planned to meet beyond the church and walk up the mountain together. It would be a solemn farewell and a joyous celebration of Granny Chree's life.

I woke while it was still dark and heard the first whip-poor-will of spring call, Mama's signal for comfort in the night, Aunt Hyacinth's signal for joy, and mine for hope and new beginnings. It was fitting. It was a year since we'd laid Mama to rest.

I slipped to the front porch and watched as dawn drew its rose-and-golden fingers through the sky. It would be a beautiful day, a glorious day, just the day Granny Chree had ordered.

Before the rest of the family rose, I dressed and stole away to the Shady Grove church cemetery and Aunt Hyacinth's grave. It had been too long since I'd stopped by. The inscription had finally been chiseled into the stone hewn in Asheville and shipped by rail. It had been set at the head of Aunt Hyacinth's grave the month before, thanks to an early spring thaw. All things considered, it seemed fitting that Aunt Hyacinth had a separate plot and stone from the Belvidere family space. I laid the first bouquet of lilac blossoms across its top.

"I knew you'd want to be part of this day, Aunt Hyacinth. Granny would have had it no other way." I pulled the few stray leaves away from the base of her stone. "We've all come so far, haven't we?" I whispered. "Further than I could have ever imagined."

I gave her the latest news about Ruby Lynne and the baby boy she'd birthed, her plans for college and becoming a teacher, and the home she'd found with an aunt in Tennessee. "I think Rhoan's still running moonshine, but he tells Jesse from time to time when he's had a letter from Ruby Lynne. I think it makes him proud that she stays in touch.

"Dr. Vishnevsky received a letter from Marshall. You'd think he and Olney were the proudest of fathers. He said Marshall's doing well in school, that he intends to become a doctor one day, as soon as his service in the military is done, though we all hope this war will be over before it's his time to go. Granny's gift more than paid for his first year of schooling, and Marshall is earning the money for the second himself."

I told her all the news about the Tates and how Clay McHone was going to rebuild our barn next month — with the help of a number of men from town. "The McHones moved in to make up Dr. Vishnevsky's new family right after the baby came. You should see the doctor. He's so happy, Aunt Hyacinth, like a grandfather with baby Cecilly — they named her after Celia.

"You'd be so proud of that girl. She's taught me so much about being brave and stepping out to help others, all the while becoming and remaining true to myself.

"Chester's helping me plant a victory garden. He combs No Creek every week from one end to the other, as far as his new red wagon can go collecting scrap metal and rubber and paper — everything imaginable for the war effort.

"Fillmore has a good job at the shipyard in Norfolk. Gladys and the children will be moving there this summer, once school's out. I don't know what I'll do without them, especially Gladys.

"And Gerald — well, you know about him. You always seemed to know that he wouldn't rule my life forever. You imagined that God has a hope and a future for me that I couldn't conceive. Thank you for believing in that future, for believing in me when I couldn't. I think, though I can't see the road ahead clearly just yet, that you were right."

A rustle in the maple near the church caught my eye. A red-winged blackbird burst from its nest, spreading its beautiful wings in flight. My breath caught, and a song of gratitude filled my heart. I turned back to Aunt Hyacinth's stone. I wanted to tell her everything.

"Celia gave me the divorce papers she'd been hiding beneath her mattress, hoping to spare me. In the end, Gerald is claiming desertion and suing me for divorce. It's not the sensation of insanity or adultery that he'd hoped to claim to gain the church's sympathy, but he'll be legally free to remarry . . . perhaps without the church's blessing, unless he can convince them I've done things he can't prove or that my running away from him is abandonment. Maybe he'll convince them, but I no longer care. I'm not ashamed, just so thankful to be away from him, to not live another day afraid.

"I wake up each morning now and the day is fresh and clean, full of hope, not laden with worries or guilt, and I sing, 'Great is Thy faithfulness! Great is Thy faithfulness! Morning by morning new mercies I see.' A year ago I couldn't have imagined that.

"Our library's doing well — busy. There was a drive to collect books for the armed forces, especially more recent fiction. So I've donated a box and inserted a card in each book assuring the reader that the librarians of Garden's Gate are praying for him. Your books are going far and wide, Aunt Hyacinth, blessing our men in this awful war."

I reached down to touch her stone, so wishing it was her frail hand I could touch again, feel her warmth and see the joy in her face that I knew sharing her books — the ones she'd preserved and collected over her lifetime — could bring.

"I'm teaching a class for adult readers over at Saints Delight Church on Friday evenings, and I love that. I especially love the children who come to the library. We still have our battles and cruel lines of segregation here. It seems it's easier for us to condemn the Germans for hating Jews than to own in the mirror what we do to each other. I guess it's one step at a time, one foot in front of the other.

"Your friend Biddy is getting on but still writes when she can get letters through. The war's terribly hard on Britain. Jesse and I share her letters and we pray for Biddy and her family every day. He misses you so." A sigh escaped my lips, but I gritted my teeth, determined not to cry this day. "You know I do.

"I'm sorry for the secrets we kept so long — yours, mine, Mama's, our family's. They're never worth keeping, are they? Secrets hurt. They shame, sometimes even where there is no real shame.

"It's taken me all this time, but I know now that shame doesn't come from God. I've wasted so many years believing God couldn't love me, that He was ashamed of me and didn't want me, that I wasn't enough as I am for Him to look at . . . and that I deserved all the punishment from my father and Gerald because I was bad — so bad at my core and so dirty inside. I thought He was standing over me, ready with a sledgehammer, waiting for me to trip up. I know now that God's not like that. He's not like sinful man. I've learned that believing in the everlasting love of God is a choice I can make — a choice to believe — each day, if I need to." I could not stop the tears. "I won't waste one more day, Aunt Hyacinth. I promise. You taught me so many good lessons."

"She's still teaching us, isn't she?" Jesse stood beside me.

I jumped, startled. "I didn't hear you come."

"Don't worry." His eyes twinkled. "Just arrived. Your 'secrets' are safe with me."

"Now I know what you heard. I suppose I

should feel embarrassed." I smiled. "But I don't. You're coming up the mountain? For Granny Chree?"

"Wouldn't miss it." He hesitated. "But there's something I want to tell you first, before you hear it elsewhere."

"That sounds ominous."

"Not ominous, but it could be lengthy. Possibly lengthy." He seemed nervous, anxious.

"Jesse? What is it?" I laid my hand on his arm.

He pulled an envelope from his coat pocket — an official-looking return address stamped in the top left corner. "My chaplain's orders have come through. It's time I walked in the footsteps of our old friend Oswald Chambers. Do more than talk the talk." He smiled.

I tried to smile in return.

"I'll go for training, but eventually I'll be stationed overseas, at least I hope so. I don't know where yet, and I don't know if I'll be allowed to say. But I know it's the right thing. I know the Lord is leading me for the sake of our men and boys who know Him and especially for those who don't." His eyes searched mine.

The lump in my throat swelled and wouldn't go down. I turned back to Aunt Hyacinth's stone. I'd known he would volunteer. Somehow, I'd just known. What would No Creek do without him? *What will I do without you?*

I nodded, doing my best to get hold of my emotions. "When do you go?"

"Five days."

"So soon?"

"I've known for a couple of weeks but didn't want to say anything until arrangements were finalized for another pastor, and well, because goodbyes are hard. Reverend Peoples will arrive on Monday so I can introduce him to the congregation Wednesday night, before I go. He's a good man, an older man with much pastoral experience."

I looked away. "That's good. We'll need someone who . . ." But I couldn't finish. I drew a ragged breath, staring at Aunt Hyacinth's stone, willing it to give me strength. "I'll carry on writing to Biddy and save her letters for you — every one."

"Lilliana." He turned me to him, but I couldn't meet his gaze. "Lilliana, look at me, please."

I tried so very hard to keep my face composed.

"I know it will be another year before you're legally free. I'll be gone during that time and for who knows how long this wretched war will last. But I'm hoping we can — I —"

I pressed my fingers against his lips. "Don't. Not now."

He closed his eyes, drew a breath, and nodded, releasing me and stepping back. "No. You're right." He breathed again and opened his eyes. "May I write to you? Will you write to me?"

"Yes." I smiled, genuinely glad for that. "Yes, I will write as often as you write me."

It seemed in that moment that the sun came out in full.

"Good." He took my hand and pressed it between both of his own. "That's good."

We turned back to Aunt Hyacinth's stone. I traced the letters in her epitaph with my finger: *She Loved Well.* "That was her legacy to us all, wasn't it? I hope that can be said of us one day."

Jesse smiled, pressed my hand to his lips, to his heart, and released it. We turned as one and together walked up the mountain.

NOTE TO READERS

Years ago, my brother, Dan Lounsbury — wonderful writer, editor, and friend — took me for a drive in the foothills of North Carolina, not far from the farm where we were born. He showed me a street and a church he knew I'd appreciate because of the irony of their name: No Creek. Named because, you guessed it, there was no creek.

Now that might not seem too surprising until you realize that we were viewing a Baptist church, and nearly every older Baptist church throughout the foothills of North Carolina was built near water, most often a creek. Creeks, as Rosemary Belvidere said, "run like a widow's tears" through those foothills. Churches were built near water for the purpose and convenience of full-immersion baptisms and were often named for the creeks by which they reside: Grassy Creek Baptist Church, Mountain Creek Baptist Church, Big Ruin Creek Baptist Church, and so on.

My brother and I sat in the car, staring at that No Creek sign just because he knew I'd want to. In that moment the name of a community was born in my mind. Fully blown characters as real as the man who ran my small-town post office sprang to life and peppered the No Creek of my imagination. I knew those characters' names, their quirks, their faults and failings and their strengths beyond measure. I was privy to their back-stories, and I dearly loved them. So I wrote their stories — short stories.

Sometimes I read those short stories aloud in café open mic sessions. I saw that listeners responded to those colorful characters — loved them — nearly as much as I did. But my stories were vignettes, moments in each character's life. There was no overarching story to connect them, nothing to tempt a publisher of full-length novels.

So for years, those stories and the very real-to-me people that filled their pages sat in a drawer . . . until I realized that no story line from the people of No Creek could unite them. They needed characters drawn from the outside, people who didn't understand them but wanted to gain acceptance, who'd come from far away with issues of their own, to live and thrive — or die — among the locals in that time and place.

Questions of faith, concern for the oppressed, and stands against injustice claim the heart of my books. Exposing and fighting marital and domestic abuse and race violence have long been passions of mine. Readers may know that from the books I've written, might have guessed it based on my upbringing in the South through years of the civil rights movement. Jim Crow, following the failings of Reconstruction cut short, created a rough and ragged world of its own. Those remnants and attitudes sadly, tragically, have not altogether disappeared. We've come far, but there is still much work and healing to do and it can only be done when we reach out to others in compassion, respect, and appreciation.

What might not be so clear, because of my great love and respect for the church and the faithful of God, is that I'm also passionate about exposing the dangers of church leadership abuse and bringing healing to its victims. As Christians, we don't want to think such abuse exists. We hate the very idea. We want to believe that shepherds of our flocks are trustworthy, blameless as far as humanly possible, and embody the list of qualifications for elders and deacons found in 1 Timothy 3. But where there is power there is temptation to abuse that power, and reports in our daily news make it clear that in some places, in some churches, terrible abuse exists.

The horror of abuse — physical, emotional, mental, spiritual — reeks not only in those churches reported in the national and global news, but in churches, priesthoods, elderships, and pastorates not yet exposed. Dirty secrets are known to hide within the confines of cults, but they can also be hidden within the walls of legitimate churches. It is for the victims of abuse — those who've known intimidation, indoctrination, and physical, emotional, and spiritual trauma — that my heart bleeds. It is especially for them and for all who are willing to help in the healing process that *Night Bird Calling* is written and prayed over.

If a person has never experienced abuse, it is sometimes hard to understand why a victim tolerates it — why they don't report it, stand publicly against it, expose it, or simply leave the abuser or abusive community. Sometimes those abused are too intimidated, too afraid of what will follow for themselves or loved ones if they expose an abuser. Sometimes they know of nowhere and no one to run to, no one to trust — have even been taught not to trust outsiders or the police, or are so beaten down they don't believe in their own worth or that they deserve love or protection. They may even believe they deserve the abuse and become unable to stand for themselves. But sometimes even the severely downtrodden can be roused to help and protect others they deem in need of protection. That God-given desire to help and protect is where Lilliana of this story, abused herself, finds some of her strength to help Ruby Lynne.

It was pointed out to me, during a vulnerable time in my young life, that God hates abuse and that oppression is one of the reasons He severely warned and chastised His own people, Israel. Bottom line: God does not tolerate abuse. Never has. Never will.

It was a revelation to me at the time that allowing oppressors and abusers to go unchecked is not a sign of forgiveness or a freedom or gift to them — even if they stand in places of marital, administrative, political, or spiritual authority, no matter the moral lens of the time or place. I learned that for the sake of the abuser as well as the abused, abuse must be stopped and the horror exposed. We were not created to be doormats.

The Scripture pointed out to me that registered, that allowed me to say, "No more!" is found in Matthew 18:6 — "But whoso shall offend one of these little ones which believe in me, it were better for him that a millstone were hanged about his neck, and that he were drowned in the depth of the sea."

That is the message Lilliana discovers in this story. No matter how she feared and had suffered, she did not want that millstone to be the end for her abuser. She just needed the abuse to stop.

Night Bird Calling is a work of fiction. Its characters are fictitious, except for the off-stage characters of Oswald and Biddy Chambers. Theirs is a love and lifelong-ministry story worthy of books, despite the fact that Oswald's life was cut short. His wife, whom he affectionately called "Biddy," recorded his talks in shorthand and faithfully transcribed them. Those writings, particularly in the devotional book *My Utmost for His Highest* that Biddy published after Oswald's passing, have long been a great blessing and source of conviction for me. In that book you will find insights upon insights into life and following in the footsteps of Jesus, into building an intimate, full, and rich relationship with Him.

I hope, as you read *Night Bird Calling,* that you will consider those around you — family, friends, colleagues, students, even strangers. If someone you know is or was intimidated or abused in any way, please reach out to them and let them know that abuse, oppression, attitudes of control or lording over a person or over a congregation do not come from God, do not come from the lover and Creator of life. Lovingly point those abused and those who abuse to our Savior, who forgives the repentant, who loves and heals each of us, cruelly broken though we may be. All we have to do is ask Him. Know that He holds accountable those who abuse authority and power, whether in relationships of marriage, family, community, or the church. Know that the pain of those abused is not forgotten and that the abuse is not their fault.

Show others that you love them — love them with the perfect, healing, unrestrained love of Christ.

Scripture tells us that we are so dearly loved and delighted in that we are rejoiced over with singing. With great loving-kindness has our Father drawn us. He never means us harm but offers each of us hope and a future.

God's great love and blessings for you,
Cathy Gohlke

If you or someone you know is in an abusive situation, the National Domestic Violence Hotline is there to help. Call 1-800-799-7233.

DISCUSSION QUESTIONS

1. Lilliana ran away after learning of her husband and father's plans to have her committed. Given the time and viewpoints of the police and church community, do you think she had other choices? What might those options have been?

2. Once she was safe in No Creek, Lilliana said she would rather die than go back to her abusive husband. Have you ever felt that hopeless or known anyone who felt that desperate? What did you do, or how would you counsel someone in that situation?

3. In the news we frequently hear of spousal abuse, workplace abuse, or abuse by people in political and spiritual authority. Sometimes it seems that abusers are all but excused. Sometimes they are exposed, sometimes they are prosecuted, and sometimes they are simply removed from their positions of authority. What public action

or punishment do you think is appropriate? What kind of consequences would you have liked to see for Lilliana's father and husband?

4. Celia often leapt into situations without realizing the full repercussions of her actions. List some of those situations. Did they ultimately lead to good changes or transformations? Did you find yourself cheering for her, admiring her innocence? Or growing frustrated with her lack of fear?

5. Lilliana unexpectedly found herself enmeshed in situations of abuse and racial injustice in No Creek. Why did she choose to take on these battles? Have you ever found yourself in a similar situation, where you felt convicted to get involved in a domestic, workplace, political, community, race, school, or church situation that appeared oppressive or off-kilter? If you're able to briefly share about the experience without betraying confidences, please do so.

6. In No Creek, making, selling, or running moonshine was a way of life, especially during the Depression. Addiction and the consequences of addiction often followed. Today, many depressed rural communities are riddled with issues of addiction to drugs

and alcohol. Are there remedies? What are they? How can we help?

7. Lilliana expressed doubt that Rhoan Wishon could change, saying, "Leopards don't change their spots." Do you believe change is possible for someone like Rhoan? Like Troy? Like Fillmore? Like Gerald? Why or why not?

8. Do you see parallels between the treatment of Jewish people in Europe during WWII and the treatment of African Americans in the US at that time and before? Do you think the people of No Creek or across America saw those similarities? Why or why not? Do similarities exist today?

9. Much has changed since the days of WWII and the world painted in *Night Bird Calling*. Legal rights, cultural expectations, and opportunities for women and minorities have come a long way in the last seventy-five years. So has our understanding of the proper treatment of other human beings, regardless of race or gender. Discuss what has changed, why, and what still needs to change for the good of all.

10. Citizens of No Creek, like much of America, wanted nothing to do with the war in Europe until Pearl Harbor was

bombed and the war came home in a very personal way. Once Congress declared war on Japan and Germany, the country mobilized, united in a way that it has not been since. What do you think inspired that unity? Do you see that spirit in our country today? Why or why not?

11. List some of your favorites characters or scenes from the novel. What made these so memorable for you?

12. What would you like the future to hold for Lilliana, for Jesse, for Ruby, for Marshall, for Gladys and Fillmore, for Celia and Chester?

ABOUT THE AUTHOR

Three-time Christy and two-time Carol and INSPY Award–winning and bestselling author **Cathy Gohlke** writes novels steeped with inspirational lessons, speaking of world and life events through the lens of history. She champions the battle against oppression, celebrating the freedom found only in Christ. Cathy has worked as a school librarian, drama director, and director of children's and education ministries. When not traveling to historic sites for research, she and her husband, Dan, divide their time between northern Virginia and the Jersey Shore, enjoying time with their grown children and grandchildren. Visit her website at cathygohlke.com and find her on Facebook at CathyGohlke Books and Bookbub (@CathyGohlke).